PALE MOON
RISING

BY
SCOTT PERDUE

PublishAmerica
Baltimore

ISBN: 1-4137-3656-4

PUBLISHED BY PUBLISHAMERICA, LLLP

www.publishamerica.com

Baltimore

Printed in the United States of America

To the all men and women of the US Armed Forces: It takes courage to stand in the door—Thanks!

ACKNOWLEDGMENTS

Most importantly, I would like to thank you, the reader for taking the chance and picking up my book. I hope you like it! Writing is a solitary endeavor, the biggest kick is when people read it and like it—the feedback is not immediate like flying, but it is fun! Without the support of others writing would be impossible. My wife, Dana, has put up with a lot during the creation process as well as the numerous moves and countless days and nights worrying about me while I was deployed in the US Air Force. Courage, integrity, honor, persistence, unconditional caring and the best advice around—without you I wouldn't be here and I am forever grateful. But I do love you better! My three girls—they all make me very happy, I love them more than life itself. Without friends like: Bob Ellis, Dwight Hill, Buc Johnson and Lyn Freeman this work would likely not have made it to print. They read my scribbling, critiqued my story lines, suggested changes—with the greatest of patience. My editor, Susan Johnson did a fantastic job going through the manuscript word by word—maybe someday I'll learn how to spell. Finally, I would like to thank all my friends from the Army and the Air Force—none of my characters spring from you, as far as you know. Any mistakes are my own and if you find one or just want to chat, visit me at www.scottperdue.com.

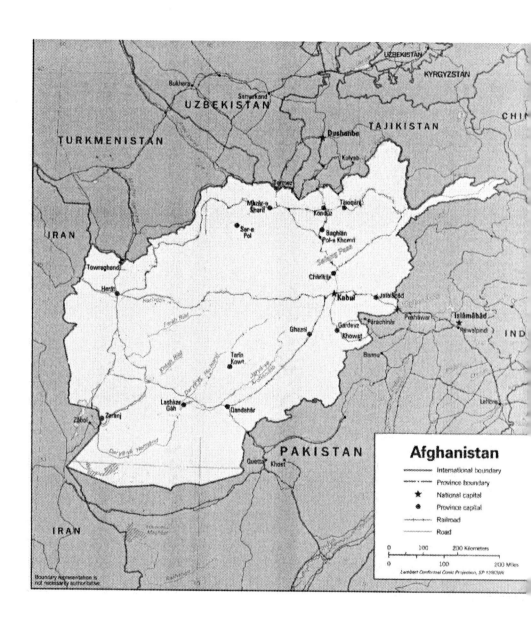

PROLOGUE

11 September 2001
New York, USA

"United Two Five Two, turn right heading 310, proceed direct Lanna when able and then own nav. Contact New York center 122.375."

"Right heading 310, to Lanna, then own nav. Center on 122.375, Good day. United 252." Mike Eldridge, First Officer of the United Airlines Boeing 767, replied as he dialed the new heading into the flight mode panel.

"Good morning New York Center, United 252 with you climbing to FL 280, direct Lanna."

"Roger, United Two Five Two, New York Center. Climb and maintain FL 350." Eldridge set 350 in the altitude display of the Flight Mode panel and repeated, "350" to Captain Gary Eller.

"350," Captain Eller repeated as he pointed at the altitude display with his finger, and then punched the AP1 button to turn on the autopilot. He said, "Autopilot's on." Glancing at Eldridge he asked conversationally, "What do you think about the bid lines for this month? They're looking kinda shy on hours."

"Yeah, they are. I've been looking through open time and there isn't enough there to fill up the month. It's rough, I don't know what I'm going to do, but that don't stop any of the bills." Eldridge smiled in reply.

"I know, I know, the lines are getting a little thin these days," Eller commented and looked out the windshield for traffic. Climbing out of the New York area it was very busy with other flights all over the sky. After a moment, he heard a coded knock on the door. Looking at Eldridge again a smile lit up his face, "There's the knock. Our number one must have breakfast; she's a little early today. I'll buzz her in."

Captain Eller reached back with his right hand to the rear of the center pedestal and pressed the door release button. The door violently flew open and slammed against the wall behind his head. Surprised, Eller looked over his shoulder to see what the commotion was. He saw three swarthy men rush through the door. Before he could shout or say a word, the first one threw his left arm around the Captain's neck and violently pulled his head back. With a grim, determined look on his face, he produced a razor knife in his right hand and slashed it across the Captain's throat. The next two men through the door attacked the First Officer, one behind the other, trying to cut him as well. Mike Eldridge responded, instinctually grabbing his approach plate book; he swung it up between himself and the onrushing attackers. With his other hand, he reached for the autopilot disconnect button and thumbed it off. The autopilot disconnected and the airplane began to enter a gentle right turn with the nose dropping.

Unattended, the plane began to descend and accelerate. Eldridge, fighting for his life, continued to fend off the two men. Bleeding profusely from several cuts on his arms, Eldridge managed a hard, savage punch to the head of the one closest to him. Driven by fury he cocked his arm and hit him again. The attacker fell unconscious and the man behind him pushed him on top of Eldridge, pinning him underneath the unconscious man. The third intruder reached around the unconscious attacker, punching Eldridge repeatedly in the head. With his body and his arms pinned, Eldridge could do nothing to fight him off.

In the sudden chaos that had enveloped the cockpit, a fourth man appeared in the doorway. Shouting in Arabic to the man holding Eller's limp body he said, "Ahmed, release the Captain and remove him from the seat. Do it quickly."

Ahmed reached around the Captain, feeling for the seatbelt buckle, finding it slippery in blood he twisted it and released the seat belt. Wiping the blood soaking his hands on the Captains sleeve, bright red contrasting with the white of the shirt, Ahmed then put both arms under Eller and pulled him slowly out of his seat.

"Put him in the galley and help Mahmoud dispose of the First Officer. Quickly, the plane is going out of control!" The newcomer directed. He was Mohammed El Baridi, an Egyptian, and the leader of the hi-jackers. After Ahmed removed the Captain from the cockpit, El Baridi reached around the seat, pulled the track lock, slid the seat aft and to the left and then moved around it to sit down in the seat.

As El Baridi sat down, Eldridge managed to throw his attacker off him and pushed the man towards the Egyptian. Eldridge grabbed at the throttles, clicked off the auto throttles, and pushed them forward to the stops. Standing, he lunged toward El Baridi and threw a roundhouse punch as hard as he could. Connecting to the side of his face, he knocked him sideways into the left window, temporarily stunning him. Eldridge prepared to throw another punch; he did not see Ahmed sprang back through the door with a knife in his hand. Ahmed held his left arm up to deflect any blows, reaching Eldridge he shoved the knife under his left arm and in between his ribs as hard as he could. Eldridge grunted and collapsed across the center pedestal, his eyes open and staring blankly.

El Baridi shook his head groggily. The big airliner had begun to roll into a steeper bank, accelerating during the scuffle, the wind rushed by the windshield at over 400 knots. He grabbed the controls and abruptly rolled the airplane out of the bank. Beads of perspiration were breaking out on his forehead as he fought to control the airplane. Grasping the throttles he pulled them to idle and shouted angrily at the man, Eldridge had knocked to the floor: "Mahmoud quit lying there. Get rid of him and get the GPS setup. Now!"

Mahmoud and Ahmed pulled Eldridge off the center pedestal and dragged him out of the cockpit into the galley. Leaving a trail of blood smeared across the floor, they dumped him unceremoniously on the galley floor. On his way back through the cockpit door Ahmed reached down and picked up a backpack from the galley. He closed the door firmly behind him. Inside he sat down on the jump seat behind the center pedestal and opened the backpack. He pulled a small handheld GPS unit out, connected a remote antenna, and stuck it to the window next to the Captain's seat. He turned it on and set it on the pedestal behind the throttles. Looking at El Baridi, he said solemnly, "The GPS is on, it must awake."

El Baridi nodded gruffly, "Turn off the ATC transponder and when the GPS comes alive, dial in our point. Hurry, there is little time."

Mahmoud climbed into the First Officer's seat and settled in.

Leaving the throttles near idle El Baridi turned on a northerly heading and continued the descent. Baridi looked at Mahmoud, "We must fly below 3,000 feet to avoid radar. We will turn back when the GPS says it is time."

"I think we should turn back now. It is Allah's will we should be first," Mahmoud replied loudly.

El Baridi shot him a dirty look, with a furtive glance at the third hi-jacker sitting on the jump seat, he looked back out the front, "Ahmed, take Abu and go back into the cabin and see how the others are doing. Make sure and control the passengers, keep them in their seats. I will call if there are any changes."

"Yes, I will. When will you call and make our demands? I want to hear them

9

tremble!" Ahmed said excitedly.

"Go now! I will call you when I need you. Close the door." El Baridi exploded.

As Ahmed and the other hijacker closed the cockpit door behind them, El Baridi barked at Mahmoud "Keep your mouth shut, you know they do not know what we are about to do!"

"I will be careful. But we should turn back soon, we do not want to be late!" Mahmoud replied.

In the Galley Ahmed began searching the cabinets. The first two cabinets held soda and ice, finding one with food he took out several trays. Tearing the foil covering off the trays, he began eating the food.

Abu stood nervously in the hallway. "Ahmed, what did Mahmoud say? What did he mean by being first?"

Leveling the plane about 3,000 above the ground El Baridi glanced at the GPS time-to-waypoint window. "It will be time soon to turn. Where are we?" El Baridi asked.

"The GPS does not say. I think that big valley in front of us is the Hudson River. We must be north of New York City." Mahmoud said. "Keep on this heading of around 230 degrees and keep the city on the left."

"I will do that. Look out for other airplanes; watch for others that might try to intercept us. I do not think the Americans will be able to send the Military so quickly; but we must be prepared," El Baridi said.

The big Boeing airliner skirted Newburgh, New York and flew between the ridgelines running in a southwesterly direction on the west side of the Hudson River, generally towards Philadelphia. This September Tuesday was spectacular, a turquoise blue clear day all over the east coast and the visibility was better than 10 miles.

Somewhere west of Somerville, New Jersey, El Baridi glanced at the GPS on the glare shield, rolling the aircraft into a 15 degree bank left he said, "It is time we must turn back."

As he rolled out on the bearing to the target he asked, "Mahmoud, what time does the GPS give us now?"

Mahmoud, could not believe his eyes, the handheld GPS device had been showing them right on time, but after they had completed their turn, it suddenly showed them getting there late. With fear in his eyes, he looked at El Baridi, "Mohammed, I do not know what happened, but the time is now 15 minutes late."

"You are a fool or cannot read! How can that be? We were on time when we turned around!" El Baridi screamed. Angry, he did not look at his fellow hijacker; he pushed the throttles to the stop and leaned forward to squint out of the windscreen.

In a few minutes he saw the Lower New York Bay and knew he was off course, he turned the big aircraft 15 degrees to the left.

Mahmoud, trying to be helpful, said, "There is Sandy Hook on the right. There is the Verrazano Narrows Bridge. You are on course. Soon we will see the Trade Center."

As the huge 767 airliner flew over Staten Island, El Baridi descended to less than 1,000 feet above the ground. He knew he could find the towers; it was easy to see their general location because of the smoke from the first aircraft that had struck 15 minutes ago. The smoke obscured the south tower a little bit, but he was not worried, they had discussed this part of the plan a thousand times. He descended closer to the ground, going as fast as the airliner would go. All he had to do was look for the capitalist symbol at Liberty Island, his next navigation point, he would use it to turn and line up with the south tower. Suddenly, he was surprised to see three or four tall cranes jutting into the sky 200 to 300 feet in the air in Bayonne, New Jersey. As quickly, as he could he turned sharply to the left of the Marine Terminal. Flying over Ellis Island at 500 knots he turned sharply to the right and flew towards the World Trade Center Towers, the cranes had put him slightly off course, but he knew he could find the towers easily.

Seeing Battery Park slide by on his right Mahmoud said excitedly, "Mohammed, you are going very fast. You must line up on the South Tower. Remember how long it takes to turn this aircraft."

"Do not bother me, I am flying the aircraft. I know what I am doing. We are pointed at the corner, but I want to hit the face that is on the south side. We will make it." El Baridi replied.

"You must turn, you are going so fast you will miss it. You must turn now!" Mahmoud shouted. "You must turn!"

The 390,000 pound jetliner was moving over nine miles a minute skimming the rooftops over southern Manhattan and its flight path was going to overshoot the tower. "I have the airplane in bank, but it is not turning! Help me!" shouted El Baridi.

Passing over Rector Street, Mahmoud reached down, grasped the First Officers control yoke, and began pulling back towards his lap. At the last minute, the aircraft finally began turning and seconds later struck the south tower of the World Trade Center at 9:03 a.m.

6 October 2001
White House Situation Room, Washington DC- 26 days later

At the morning meeting of the war cabinet, twenty-six days after the terrorist attack on the World Trade Center, the President grimly welcomed everyone to the meeting of his Security Council. After a few words, he nodded at the Director of Central Intelligence. The DCI cleared his throat and stood up, looking briefly around the room he turned back to the President and began speaking, "Mr. President, as you know we have had a Special Activities Team on the ground for ten days preparing the way for our guys to put boots on the ground in Northern Afghanistan.

"Three days ago Uzbekistan granted basing rights, which means we can start to match up Army SOF units with my teams on the ground. The first SOF A Team met with my guys on the ground yesterday and will begin working with the Northern Alliance in a matter of days. They are currently working their way to the front lines in country in the northern pocket. A second team already linked with Special Forces will enter from Uzbekistan and join the Northern Alliance south of Mazar-e Sharif in less than a week. The Northern Alliance factions are prepared for them.

"Per your orders I instructed the SA Team yesterday to work with their Northern Alliance tribal contacts to stand down Military operations and hold in place. I have taken the liberty and instructed them to concentrate on sabotage operations against Al-Qaeda and Taliban installations. I expect things to ramp up as we, and the Army, can get more folks on the ground. According to plan, after we have started the bombing campaign we will release the Alliance troops to go after the Taliban."

The DCI looked towards the Secretary of Defense, nodded, and abruptly sat down.

"Sir," the Secretary of Defense, staying seated began, "We have Combat Search and Rescue assets located in Pakistan, ready to pick up any downed airman in the southern part of Afghanistan today. We expect to have a CSAR network up and running for the north in a few days to a week's time. They will be operating primarily out of Tashkent with a Forward Operating Location in Dushanbe and near the border.

"I expect that the initial target set that we nominated for our strikes will be exhausted very quickly. Even if we have to hit the same target more than once we will probably be out of clear targets within two days, five at the most, of the start of the bombing campaign."

The SecDef, to this point had held his hands folded calmly on the table in front of him, opened his hands wide in an expansive gesture, "If I may say so, sir. I don't think that our initial target set will have a large impact on the Taliban. Their center-of-gravity is not their infrastructure, more than anything else; it is their people, their fighters, and their heavy weapons. It is a fact that we will achieve air superiority very quickly, but beyond that we need to define the next step of the war."

"Yes, I agree." the DCI interrupted. "I think we need to make the Taliban cease to exist as a Military force. It is my view that the Taliban and Al-Qaeda are inextricably linked; you can't have one without the other."

The President interjected flatly, "We will give them a chance to do the right thing. If we go to war, we do not do so against the Muslims or the Afghani people. If the Taliban will not turnover Usama Bin Laden and his underlings, the Taliban itself will be targeted. There is time yet to determine the next step in the war."

The President did not usually interrupt a speaker before he was finished, after a short silence, the DCI continued, "From a strategic point of view we need the Northern Alliance factions to close the gap at Salang Pass in Baghlan Province, and trap the Taliban in the North. It is imperative we do this before winter sets in. I've gotten reports that lead me to believe that the Taliban is likely to fold very quickly if we can bring sufficient assets to bear. There are a lot of factions involved here and we feel that money can induce a lot of Taliban supporters to switch sides without fighting."

The Chairman of the Joint Chiefs of Staff, silently observing the exchange, interrupted emphatically, slapping the table with an open palm, "To do that, Mr. President, we need to rely heavily on SOF and CIA teams on the ground to direct our air assets directly on Taliban and Al-Qaeda forces in the north. The Tribals haven't been able to win an open battle with the Taliban in quite sometime and no matter how much money we spread around we still need to show results on the ground; results the Tribals will see. I agree that closing the Pass is a good strategic goal, but it is probably not sufficient to motivate them."

Everyone at the table grew silent, some turned slightly towards the Chairman, surprised by his outburst. Everyone eyed him expectantly, the room utterly silent.

Holding their attention, the Chairman went on, "Our allies, of the moment, are interested in two things, money and prestige. The CIA has the money and since our Military has a good reputation, we have an initial advantage. But this will not last long. We need to show results, and quickly.

"It is my opinion that the SOF/CIA teams need to do more than coordinate with the Northern Alliance. They also need to focus on frontline Taliban. We need to use the teams to nominate and validate targets for our tactical air assets. It will be a very dynamic situation on the front and this is the only manner in which to degrade the effectiveness of the Taliban. There is no one else that can reliably direct bombs on those targets, targets that will do the most good for those on the ground. By doing that we will embolden our allies and drive a wedge of fear between the Taliban and their supporters.

"If the immediate objective of this war is to destroy Al-Qaeda and the Taliban, then we must have our guys on the ground direct the fight. The teams on the ground are very vulnerable and by having them participate in the action we put them at risk. On the other hand if we do not integrate their participation, we stand to lose our momentum quickly; both in Afghanistan and throughout the war on terror." Finished, the Chairman dramatically looked around the room into each eye, as if he was speaking to each one individually.

The President, leaning forward on the table, glanced significantly at the Secretary of Defense, "What do you think?"

With a hint of an impish grin on his face the Secretary of Defense looked back at the President through his thick glasses, "I think the Chairman is right. Politically, you are making an ultimatum to the Taliban by asking them to give up al-Qaeda. If that does not succeed, and I do not believe that it will, then we must focus on a strategic response. On that level, we stand a real chance of looking impotent, as we have in past responses to terror, if we do not use every means to focus our power on the Taliban center of gravity. The infrastructure of Afghanistan is not a center of gravity, this is a country not far removed from the middle ages. In fact, the Taliban has made almost every effort to turn the clock back 1,000 years. The Taliban and Al-Qaeda fighters in the field are the real strength and we need to destroy them as soon as we can." The Secretary of Defense replied.

The President breathed deeply, in the expectant silence he looked down at his hands, "Gentlemen, you present me with few choices. When can we begin to use our air assets against Taliban troops at the front?"

"Sir, as a prerequisite we need CSAR coverage and our SOF troops on the ground with the Northern Alliance." The Defense secretary replied matter-of-factly.

Sensing that everyone was waiting for him, the Secretary of Defense went on, "Mr. President, we are prepared to begin operations against southern targets tomorrow and should be able to use our air against targets in the north on or after the 13th of October. I expect to have at least one A team in country by then, possibly two, with more on the way. We will have to build slowly."

The CIA Director broke in, "Our only specialty teams on the ground right now are in the north. We have no reliable contacts in the south and it will take a little time to build this. I recommend our initial focus be in the north. I understand that the air assets cannot initially focus on the north, but that is where our ground forces are."

"Okay, if the Taliban do not turn over UBL and his men by tonight's deadline then we will begin the first phase of the campaign. The first phase will be infrastructure targets in the south. As soon as our assets are in place we will focus on the second phase, Taliban and al-Qaeda in the north." The President deliberately made eye contact with each person at the table in turn, "Ladies and Gentlemen the country needs results. Let us be clear on this, we do not want to be hasty, but we must act decisively, and quickly, or we stand the real chance of losing a war we cannot afford to lose."

Everyone at the table nodded silently; concern, and worry painting their faces.

Just before noon the next day the President walked into the White House Briefing Room, thronged with reporters as he stepped up to the podium. In the harsh lights of the TV cameras, he stopped and peered into the audience. Clearing his throat, he began his prepared speech.

"Good afternoon," he began, "On my orders the United States Military has begun strikes against al-Qaeda terrorist training camps and Military installations of the Taliban regime in Afghanistan. Our Military action is designed to clear the way for sustained, comprehensive, and relentless operations to drive them out and bring them to justice. We will do everything in our power to provide food and medicine to displaced Afghanistan citizens; our action is not directed at them. It is the Taliban regime that did not meet our demand to turn over al-Qaeda in their midst. It is the Taliban regime that is a partner in terror. And now the Taliban will pay a price."

CHAPTER 1

5 October 2001
Dushanbe, Tajikistan

Deep in the Gissar Valley, the morning sun was just shining over the tops of the Karacegin mountain range. The valley formed a narrow slash between two mountain ranges whose peaks reached from eight to 13,000 feet. Barely perceptible in the pre-dawn, they loomed darkly in the gloom and haze. To the southwest a shelf of clouds blocked out the remaining stars. Here and there, bright pinpoints of light shone in the darkness, strung together by the dim gray roads of the 13-mile wide valley.

The early morning quiet was split by a distant deep throated thrum growing louder by the second. Soon an accompanying high pitch whine from the jet engines of an American C-17 cargo plane flying slowly down the valley from the east could be heard. It lumbered south of the town of Dushanbe, Tajikistan roughly following the Dushanbinka River towards the town of Hisor. Shortly after passing Hisor, position lights blinking at regular intervals to mark its progress, the big airplane turned to the southwest. Holding the new heading for a minute, the aircraft then made a left turn to reverse course, heading northeast. Over Hisor, it turned once again to a heading of 100 degrees and began a slow descent for the airport south of Dushanbe.

Aboard the C-17 Globemaster the cargo of 30 US Army Special Forces troopers, from A Company 2nd Battalion 5th Group (A 2/5) of Fort Campbell, Kentucky, were busy checking their personal equipment for the fourteenth time. Twelve of the men were from ODA 225, or A Team 225, ready for action in the field and the rest were B Team members who would prepare the support base of operations for the Special Forces while they were in country. They were the lead element of TASK FORCE SCIMITAR, the spearhead of America's war on the terrorist rulers of Afghanistan.

16

As far as they were concerned, they were landing in Russia. For most of them Russia had been their chief enemy as long as they could remember, but now they were to be friends.

Captain Mark Goode was in the jump seat in the cockpit. He was the new commander of 225, he had been put in command for what was, potentially, a very sensitive operation, the first Green Beret Team in the war. At the moment, Mark was fascinated by the view from the front of the huge airplane. He watched the aircraft let down slowly into the murk made darker by the sunrise over the mountains, he wondered what would go through his sister's mind if she was making this approach. After all, his sister was flying in the Air Force and she might be coming this way before too long. To him this was very different from his normal job; it was fun to see it from another side.

The co-pilot was wearing NOGs, night vision goggles, carefully scanning for obstacles and calling out the position and distance of the ridgelines as they flew the double NDB approach in the hazardous terrain.

All of a sudden, the runway lights popped on just ahead, revealing them high and fast on their approach. The pilot pulled the throttles to idle and began a rapid, rather steep descent. The crewman next to Mark began calling altitudes at 100 feet and the pilot aggressively flared the big airplane about thirty feet above the ground. The airplane shuddered as it touched down and the pilot called for reverse thrust. Braking the airplane as hard as he dared, he danced the rudders madly trying to keep it aligned between the dim runway lights. Slowing to a brisk walk, they turned off the runway onto a taxiway and followed a truck with a flashing light to a dark parking apron, devoid of anything else.

The co-pilot, taking off his night vision goggles, looked up at Mark with a sardonic grin and said, "Welcome to Russia, err, I guess it's Tajikistan now. Home of friendly, newly converted capitalists. Oh, by the way did you know that Dushanbe translates roughly into English as Monday? This place started as a market and Monday was the day of the week it was open."

The flight, calm and controlled until the furry of the landing was suddenly everyday again. Mark was taken aback, he couldn't change gears that quickly and all he could offer was a lame, "Thanks for the travel guide notes, what do they sell here?"

"I believe this is THE place for Bukhara carpets. If you're a rug kicker you can get one cheap here!" answered the co-pilot as he folded up his checklist and stowed his equipment.

Mark silently nodded and turned to join his men. With a wave he said, "Thanks for the ride. See you guys next time."

Making his way aft he noticed all the men had already begun taking apart the tunnage holding their equipment to the floor of the airplane. Brushing past him the Loadmaster said loudly to no one in particular, "Hey, let's not get excited. Let's not get hasty. I still gotta drop the door, none of ya can drive out until I do that."

Mark walked up to his vehicle parked alongside the left side of the fuselage. It was an M1028 armored hummer painted a light tan. SFC Wilkerson, the team sergeant for 225, poked his head out of the gunner's cupola on the roof with the gun mount in his hands, and said, "Hey, sir. Do you think this'll be like the Gulf War for us? Maybe we'll be running around in hummers just like that old TV show *Rat Patrol*. Ha! Better'n walkin'!"

"You were there, I wasn't. I've no idea how this is going to go down, Gary. I'd be prepared for anything. This is all in a hurry, honestly, I think we'll be making it up as we go along," Captain Goode replied with a shrug.

Reaching the tail of the airplane, the Loadmaster unlocked the ramp and with the flip of a few switches began the opening sequence. As the ramp reached level, he paused the extension of the cargo floor. The Load walked out to the end of the ramp to look for obstructions before it reached the ground. Finding none, he let the ramp continue down until the proximity switch shut the motor off when the ramp reached the ground. He stepped off the ramp and made sure the wheel ramps touched the ground. Standing up he motioned to the Army troops to begin unloading.

Out drove three tan Hummers, two of which were towing small trailers carrying dark green ATVs. Two M923 5-ton trucks followed with trailers attached and finally the three hummers of CPT Goode's A Team.

Pausing on the ramp with their engines idling, Special Forces troopers in each of the Hummers popped out of the gunner's cupolas and mounted their weapons. Within five minutes, the convoy was armed and ready to roll. Two M2 50 caliber machine guns and an MK-19 automatic grenade launcher were mounted on the Hummers at the front and back of the convoy. As the troopers finished their work, the Loadmaster was already raising the cargo ramp on the C-17. The shrill whine of the jet engines starting filled the air and once they were spooled up, the big aircraft began taxiing out for takeoff. Everything had gone smoothly so far and they had spent less than 15 minutes on the ground dropping off the Special Forces troops and their equipment.

Mark laughed to himself wondering if the co-pilot was going to be disappointed at not getting to kick some rugs with the local merchants. Somehow, he felt that these new capitalists would not give easily on their prices.

Mark made his way to the Company Commander's vehicle. As he got there a raggedy looking car resembling a Land Rover pulled up to the front of the convoy. Out of the car emerged two Tajikistani Army Officers in dress uniforms; pistols at their belts. Mark scanned the aircraft ramp around them noting that all his troopers were either out of sight or lounging with their weapons, some of them with their night vision goggles on. Appearing like there was no particular order, they actually had both sides of the convoy covered with clear fields of fire. This was supposed to be a friendly area and these officers were supposed to be friends. But they were new friends.

Mark's company commander walked up to the two Tajiki officers and held out his hand in greeting. He greeted them in Russian. Shaking hands all around, the Tajiki officers looked a little startled, but heartily replied in Russian. It became apparent to Mark that as soon as the smiling and backslapping was over they would be moving off the ramp. He turned towards the rear of the convoy, seeing his team sergeant he signaled to mount up. Abruptly, the two Tajiki officers returned to their car and Mark jumped in the next to last Hummer as the convoy followed them off the ramp.

Driving between two large dilapidated hangars they turned right off the ramp and stopped at a large building adjacent to the control tower. One of the Tajiki officers got out of the car and walked up to a big garage type door. Pulling out an over-sized key ring, he began searching for the key to open the padlock that held the door shut. After several moments of flipping through the large collection of keys, he found the one he was looking for, opened the door and gestured them inside.

Two of the troopers in the lead Hummer dismounted and joined the small group of Americans and Tajikis at the door. They all walked into the building and began to methodically check it out. Inside the warehouse was completely empty, with the exception of small heaps of trash and a thick layer of dust. The side they entered had regular garage type doors; the other side of the warehouse had recessed truck docks. Along both walls were small offices or storage rooms. There was even an ancient bathroom of sorts; at least it smelled like it.

The Company Commander motioned Mark over to him and instructed him to get all the vehicles inside and unload what they could. This warehouse was to be their new home. Mark went back to the convoy and conferred briefly with the drivers. Before the gray dawn had turned light enough to see, all the SF vehicles and personnel were inside and out of sight.

Inside, the troopers dismounted from the vehicles and without comment or orders began preparing the building for occupation. Leaving the ATVs in their trailers, the rest of the vehicles were unloaded and in the wide expanse of the warehouse the troops established an operations/command area, a barracks area for the B Team and another one for the A Team, a motor pool of sorts and an armory. In a few minutes, several of the Commo troopers had a satellite link setup with voice and data back to the group forward command post, established at a base in Europe. Within an hour most of the men were beginning to relax and break open MREs for breakfast, one or two taking some to the guards posted outside of the building.

Satisfied that things were well in hand and the troops were taken care of, Mark went to look for the commander. He found him setting up a laptop computer in the commo area, "Sir, I'd like to send some guys out to patrol the area around us and get a feel for the lay of the land."

Distractedly, the CO glanced quickly at Mark and then back at his work, "The Tajikis want us to hold tight in the building. I'm as uncomfortable as you not knowing what is around us, but I think we have to honor their request. Do the guards have clear fields of fire outside?"

"Yes, sir. I've got guys watching each side of the building and two on the roof. It appears this place was used as an old shipping and receiving area when this was a Russian base."

Gesturing with his arm back toward the docks, Mark went on, "If you look out the window on the truck dock side there is a stretch of railroad tracks. As far as we can tell none of the buildings we can see around us have seen much use lately. We'll setup for a recon of the local area when darkness falls," Mark answered.

"Great. Are all the guards up on short range Fox Mike? I'm trying to get this CP up and running as soon as I can, we need to have radio connectivity with everyone as soon as possible." The CO replied, "Oh, and Mark, I expect we'll get further tasking pretty soon, so stand by."

"Yes, sir. The local radios are up and all the men have checked in. Is that all for now?" asked Mark.

The CO gestured towards the sleeping area, "Sure, get something to eat yourself, and some sack time. We'll be out with the night crawlers before long."

Mark realized that he had fallen asleep, when he became aware of the staccato rattle of a diesel truck idling outside of the warehouse. Unsure of the time, he got up and headed for the CP area. He found the commander busily composing his email report. "I've been sacked out, what's up?"

Without looking up the commander kept typing, "That's your transport outside. We just got a message from group. I'm sending you and eight guys to meet with a CIA guy from Jawbone, their SA Team in-country. Group wants a team in-country, and that means you. Plan on a stay of at least two weeks without resupply."

"Why aren't we going to do a Helo insertion?"

"The weather has turned pretty sloppy and the weather guessers think it'll be that way for another week or two. Our helicopters aren't here yet and the OGA's choppers won't fly in this shit," the Major replied.

"Then why the civvie trucks? We've got wheels of our own. Sir, you know we'd be better off driving ourselves. These guys don't know how to drive, we shouldn't trust our lives to them."

"Well for one reason or another, the Tajikis don't want our presence known at the moment." The commander said, "And apparently, the CIA doesn't want to advertise that we're here either. You're going in country with a minimum of stuff. Take your basic load, commo gear, and dump everything else. The CIA says they already have transport setup when you get to the border."

"I see, does that mean you want us to leave the heavy weapons here? If we take 'em we'd be loaded down if we have to go on foot." Warming to the new mission, Mark asked one more thing, "What are we going to do liaise, train or fight?"

The Company Commander paused a moment considering the risks of sending out a partial team on an undefined mission with little intelligence. Realizing that this was just the nature of this war, he cleared his throat and said, "Mark, I'd say keep out of any fire fight you can avoid. Train where you can make a positive impact; realize that we don't have a very good history with these folks. Overall, you'll be our eyes and ears on the ground so get as close as you can, but be prepared to shoot and scoot if you need to. It remains to be seen what your end game mission will be. I'm not going to hamstring you with specific orders at this point, use your judgment, and keep in touch. I don't think you'll see any other US Army on the ground, though. It'll be just you doing your thing and the Air Force doing its thing. Have any of your guys done any CAS control before?"

"I went through AGOS School with the Air Force a few years ago on a Forward Observer familiarization deal. I believe one or two of my guys worked with the Air Force and did some CAS in the Gulf War. But other than that no," Mark replied. "We'll do our best and make it up as we go along." With a big grin he finished, "My favorite kind of orders."

"Fine, saddle up, the truck will take you as far as the little town of Farchor. I checked on the map, it's on the Afghani border south of Dushanbe on the A385 road. There you'll meet up with Dave the CIA guy, I don't know anything more about him. He'll take you in country. For this mission I expect we'll be working with those guys pretty closely. Once you get in-country check in every twelve hours, and let me know if you can't make the next commo."

"Thanks, I'll see ya when I see ya. Have fun here in the rear." Mark grinned turning to leave.

"I suppose I have to say 'Be careful out there,' don't I?" the CO jested.

"Yeah, that goes without saying. High Speed, low drag; that's us." Mark waved as he went to roust his guys up from their naps.

"Sergeant Wilkerson," Mark called as he approached the A Team area, "We're gonna saddle up. Only eight are going on this trip."

Gary Wilkerson sat up and swung his feet to the floor. "Great, I didn't like these drafty old buildings anyway. We're all switched on, what's the scoop?"

"Well, you know the situation and the Intel as well as I do. We're going on a basic Poop and Snoop mission. Avoid if we can, fight and run if we have to. We'll make up the rest as we go. That civvie truck outside is waiting to take us to meet a CIA guy at the border near the town of Farchor. We leave as soon as we can get our shit together. After that I'm not sure how the transpo situation will develop so let's plan on being on foot."

"What alternatives for transpo do we have?" Wilkerson asked.

"Not sure. We've got to leave our Hummers here. If we can buy some old Soviet trucks we can stay on wheels. Worst case, I expect we can requisition some packhorses. I really don't want to go in stripped down for a force march so early in the game.

"Anyway, let's have everyone carry their personnel weapons, make sure they have sound cans for the M4s. I'm bringing my H&K Mk 23 pistol with sights and a KAC sound can; the guys can bring their M9s. I'd like four M203 grenade launchers and two M249 SAWs. We'll need some range and accuracy, so tell Luke to bring his M24 Sniper Rifle," Mark directed.

"What about demolition stuff?"

"Yeah, I don't see us doing a lot of demo, but we could always use some C4, say, maybe four pounds? Oh, and let's bring a few Claymore mines as well. And the SOFLAM laser marker with several extra batteries."

"Yes, sir. Sounds good. Is a basic load of ammo with two reloads and six boxes each for the SAWs, okay? I figure we'll take a shit pot full of batteries."

"Great, the current words are Toucan Sam and we'd better check out at least two weeks of crypto. Let's get 'em rolling," Mark finished.

SFC Wilkerson stood up and began rounding up the team. It was time to get everyone on the same sheet of music as fast as he could.

The team was busy preparing to move out when Luke approached the Captain, a pensive look on his face. He stood by quietly a few minutes. Finally, Mark turned to him and asked, "What's up, Luke? You got something on your mind?"

"Yes, sir. It's like this. I'd much rather take the Barret, than the M24."

"It's pretty heavy. What if you have to hump it?"

"Yes, sir, it's 28 pounds, but I really think we need the firepower. M4s are cool and all, but they have no range, and the M82 will beat the M24 any day of the week. I really like it better."

"Okay, Luke. You're the shooter. Go ahead and bring it. You'll probably need around 250 rounds, that's pretty heavy, spread it amongst to the guys."

Although it was less than 100 road miles from the Dushanbe airport to the border town of Farchor it took nearly four hours of jostling in the back of the canvas covered civilian truck before they finally got there. Roads in the former Russian states were barely more than the dirt tracks they had been for centuries. Finally, the truck stopped outside of town on the side of what had, decades ago, been a paved road. The team, waiting inside, held their weapons nervously. Suddenly, the rear canvas flap was pulled aside, a grinning American face in its place. Behind the face stood Mark, their commander.

Framed by a backdrop of a broad brownish-green country side ending in a picturesque mountain range abruptly rising 8500 feet from the valley floor, the grinning face said, "Hey, guys I'm Dave and I'm going to be your tour guide from here on out. Come on out and we'll get started."

Dave was the CIA Special Activities Team operative and their contact. As the SF men clambered down from the truck, Dave stood happily next to a gaggle of 16 wiry Afghan horses. Gesturing with his arm over the horses and towards the Afghani border, "Gentlemen, your magic carpet awaits. Indian country is just over the river."

Frankfurt, Germany

The cold wind whipped stinging rain into Abu Fakhim's face as he hurried across the Eiserner-steg Bridge spanning the Main River in Frankfurt. He pulled his coat tighter around his neck and walked quicker; even in weather like this it was shorter to walk than to take the U-bahn to the Fussganger shopping center on Zeil Street. Driving and parking was even more trouble. His apartment was in Sachsenhausen on Drei-Konig Strasse and his store was across the river in downtown Frankfurt.

He was a fifty something Pakistani rug merchant, specializing in wool-on-wool, wool-on-silk Persian type rugs, primarily Bukharas, Tabriz or other handmade rugs from the Hindu Kush, Turkey, Tajikistan and Iran. For years, he had been comfortable shipping small quantities of bulky goods all over the world; sometimes the merchandise he handled was not officially sanctioned by the national governments of the countries his shipments passed through. He had good customers in Germany, but his best buyers were in other Western nations like the United States. Germany was a convenient transshipment point, customs inspections were lax and their banks were strictly mainline. It was also a very comfortable place to live. The plumbing worked, the food was great and he had built a very comfortable life here. He did not intend to ever go home to Pakistan; it was safe here in Germany.

He had grown up in the Bazaars of Islamabad and found the hustle and bustle of trade the European way to be very easy. His services were much in demand as a bridge between those of his old world and the modern nations of the Western world. Today, however, he was worried. Today he was preoccupied, he had a shipment due out for an irritable customer and money was an issue. If he did not get the money, it would be hard to send the shipment. The shipment must go out; there was no backup plan, no other way to get it to its destination in time. He did not want to keep it; it simply had to go out tonight. He had control over quite a few bank accounts, some were his, most of them belonged to others; but it was not a good thing to mix accounts together. No, it was best to keep unpleasant things separate.

Unlocking the front door to his shop, he went quickly to his office in the back of the store. Ignoring the answering machine blinking at him on his desk, he shook off the rain as he took off his coat. Hanging it up he rubbed his hands together and turned up the heat on the radiator attached to the wall.

Sitting down at his desk, he pulled an address book out of the top drawer and began flipping through it. After a little searching he found what he wanted and reached for the phone. Dialing the number, he brushed a shock of greasy black hair from his face and sat back in his chair.

When the ringing stopped, he hunched over his desk and said in Arabic,

"Hello, Hello."

"Hello," a male voice intoned.

"Who is this?"

"Who is this? You called me," the man says, with sarcasm.

"It is Abu Fakhim. God is great." Skipping the niceties of conversation Fakhim continued quickly, "Tomorrow we shall meet Allah's promise, but I need a number today."

The man on the other end of the line answered flatly, "Inshallah, the number is 2215227." Abruptly the line went dead.

Fakhim scribbled it down on a pad; they used a simple code using number substitution to access the contact phone that changed every day. He added the base number they always used to the number given then put down his pen and started re-dialing the phone.

When the phone line clicked, he blurted, "Hello, Hello. It is Abu Fakhim."

"Hello, Hello. Fakhim is that you?"

"Yes, it is Abu Fakhim. How is your health?" Fakhim asked.

"My health is good. Praise Allah. What is it you need today?"

Holding the phone closer to his ear and cupping the mouthpiece with his free hand, Fakhim spoke stridently into the handset. "You know that the evil Americans have shut off money to several of my customers. It puts a bind on many of them. It is a problem and I need help, today!"

"Yes, I have heard of this charade. It is of no meaning. Do not bother me with it. We have other problems."

"Yes, I agree it is a small thing in God's scheme. Unfortunately, it is a thing that will get in the way of our commitments. Money is what makes the wheels turn." Abu breathed into the phone nervously.

"If you have not made the last shipment yet, it is your fault. You have been paid. Do not come running to me for more money."

"I am so sorry, but it is not a small matter. It is a large matter. You do not have enough money here and I don't keep it for you. We have the last shipment due tonight. You know how we have done this each time. One transaction would have been too big and would have attracted attention." Fakhim pleaded. "Please, this is by your direction. I need your help. What do I do?"

"I have spoken. We will not continue this conversation. You will solve the problem. Or, perhaps you would prefer to come home. You have become soft from living with the infidel. Perhaps you need some help in remembering where your loyalties lay."

This evening, he thought. He had until the evening to solve the problem. He went back to the front door to open his shop for the day, his hand shaking slightly.

Greeting his first customer, a German that had called for an appointment yesterday, Fakhim called for his helper to unroll the nice 10x14 Tabriz the customer had requested. There were ten other carpets prepared for this customer, one always needed to have a selection, and time to talk.

Distracted, Fakhim tried to focus on his customer, "Perhaps you would like this wool-on-wool with silk inlay? It is beautiful. It took over a year to make this by hand. This is over 100 years old. Perhaps you would like some tea, some *chai?*" He asked. Turning to his helper he said, "Mahel, show him the rest of our stock, in particular the special ones we have recovered from Iran."

Brooding on his financial problems, he barely listened to the customer's comments, relying on his helper to kick carpets for him.

To his surprise, the customer bought the first Tabriz he had looked at and paid cash for it. With 24,000 Deutsch Marks in hand it occurred to Fakhim that he would be below the bank's cash alert level for daily transactions. He decided that the man on the phone would have to pay dearly for a loan. He did not loan money, there was no future in it. He did not want to go back to Pakistan or anywhere else, but he would not work for free. There was no way out of this situation easily. He would scale down his participation. This time he would loan them 80,000 DM, but it would cost them double the next time, or more. After lunch he stopped at the bank to get enough money to cover the shipment tonight. Putting the money into his coat pocket, he went back out into the weather.

Locking up his shop at six p.m. he made his way to the parking garage two blocks away where he kept his car. Turning northwest on Bockenhiemer Landstrasse, he drove carefully to his warehouse in Rodelhiem. Thinking of the irony he chuckled to himself that his warehouse was in an old US Army storage area. He could find no cheaper large storage area, nor one more private than the old V Corps heavy equipment maintenance and storage complex.

He needed a private area for his bulky carpets. Sometimes he made and received large shipments and the railhead at the complex was very convenient for that. Best of all, no one would notice the comings and goings of freight and trucks; after all he was in the shipping business. Tonight was just another shipment; two narrow boxes five feet long and weighing about 30 pounds. Packaged and labeled as car parts he was sure they would make it through any inspection, especially since they will be included in a sealed Conex box of real car parts that was headed to the United States.

Driving through the narrow gate he waved at the guard lounging at the old Military police guard shack. He was a tenant and a regular visitor. Turning left as he drove through the gate, he passed along the front of the complex with the long maintenance buildings stretching away from him on the right. He came to what had been the offices of an Air Force unit assigned to support V Corps during the Cold War days. He parked in front of the office door and went inside. Turning on the lights, he walked down the hall skirting around piles of carpets to what had been a maintenance bay for small vehicles. He stopped to turn on the light in the bay and picked up a box of mothballs from the table next to the door. Two slender boxes with stenciled markings identifying them as exhaust parts for Mercedes automobiles were on saw horses in the middle of the room. He opened the first one and spread a handful of mothballs alongside the missile body to mask the scent of solid propellant. Working quickly he did the same to the second box, closed and sealed the lids.

Looking at his watch he realized that he had little time. The container truck should be here in a few minutes. He opened the door beside the bay's garage door and looked out into the night. He was thinking that 50,000 dollars was a lot of money for two small boxes. Maybe he was in the wrong end of this trade.

A German tractor-trailer truck carrying a rusted shipping container drove into his small lot and backed up to the maintenance bay. He opened the garage door and wheeled his cargo to the back of the Conex. The driver had swung open the door and crawled inside. Abu picked up the first box and passed it to the driver, who had crawled some ways inside the container. Carefully placing the new boxes amongst the old, the driver stowed the boxes, not too conspicuous, but not to hidden. After finishing with both boxes the driver closed the doors and took a new seal from his pocket. After installing the new seal on the door handles, complete with the customs inspector's impression, he turned, grinned at Abu and said, "You have something for me, yes?"

Abu passed him a thick manila envelope. He turned quickly, went back inside the bay and closed the doors. The driver left Frankfurt headed north on Autobahn 5. He was due in Bremen in less than 12 hours. The container would be on a ship bound for the United States by noon tomorrow.

Kabul, Afghanistan

Driving into Kabul from the south, a faded tan Toyota Land Cruiser rolled quickly down the A1 Highway. Slowing as it neared the center of town, it dodged heavy foot traffic as it made its way along the crumbling road. At the National Zoo, it turned left onto Asamayi Wat moving slowly, finally coming to a halt at Zarnegar Park. The vehicle traffic was light, but in the Bazaar district the foot traffic was heavy, men and clumps of women dressed in traditional Abayas covering them from head to foot walked in groups all over the roads. Finally making its way through the throng, the Land Cruiser turned right and then left on Bibimahro passing the Silver Bazaar. After a few blocks it turned left again into the parking lot in front of what had been the Afghan Air Authority building.

The driver, Malik Zwahari and the passenger on the left side of the car got out. The passenger was carrying an AK-47 and he scanned the street left and right looking for anyone that did not belong. Malik went around to the passenger side and opened the door for the third passenger. Stepping out of the car, Ahmed Youseff, squinted in the sun.

"It is funny. We live here now and the American Embassy, crumbling to dust, down the street is a symbol of America's future. It is ironic." Malik observed to Youseff.

"There is no room for irony or humor. The fall of the Americans is foreseen. Their Embassy is in ruins, soon they will be. Let us go inside," Youseff replied.

The two men walked to the door, opened it and went inside; the bodyguard scanning the activity around the building followed and stopped just inside the door.

Walking into a large office on the first floor, Youseff said, "Salam a likum."

"Likum Salam," replied Ahmed Mustapha, one of Usama bin Laden's chief lieutenants.

"How is your health? Did you have a safe drive from Kandahar?" asked Mustapha solicitously.

"I am well. God willing. The drive was long and dusty, but there was not much traffic. We need to get the helicopters operational, it would make travel easier," Youseff said as he sat down in one of the office chairs.

"It is true. The Taliban and the Mullahs are concerned with their teachings and their pogroms. They do not see the needs or the opportunities of power. Most of the old Soviet equipment does not work; we must see what we can do. Helicopters would be valuable now that we are spread out." Mustapha smiled.

"Would you like some *Chai*, perhaps you are hungry. I received a call today from our rug merchant in Germany. He is worried about the feeble American charade to cut off our funds. He must make the last shipment of Strelas tonight and feels he is too poor to do so," Mustapha continued.

Youseff waving away the tea, asked, "What will he do?"

"I am not worried. The Pakistani weasel will do as he is told. He has done very well for himself, living off of our table. He will make the shipment. Although, he will probably try to make me pay for it next time. Soon we will not need him." Mustapha observed with disdain.

"Inshallah. It has been almost a month since our glorious blow against the infidel. Are they preparing a strike, what will be their response?" Youseff asked

"I have gotten reports that the CIA has sent spies to spread money around the Northern Alliance. It will buy them little. Time and righteousness are on our side," Mustapha said.

Leaning forward Youseff asked, "Perhaps we should capture these spies. Where are they operating? How many are they? What are the Americans trying to do?"

"I am not worried about Fahim or Dostum. They are weak and are driven by greed. Money will not buy them success and their followers will slip away in the night when the money is gone. Thanks be to our great one Usama, with Massoud gone the Northern Alliance has no leaders. Fahim will not move if God himself whispered in his ear. If Badakhshan province and Fahim fail, the middle of the country will not support Dostum. Huq in the south will be ours in a matter of days, he will tell us what he knows and pay for his sins. The Northern Alliance is falling apart. They cannot live in the mountains forever; they will die or join the Taliban. It is only a matter of time!" Mustapha declared.

"This is as it should be. I have no sympathy for the argumentative, unwashed tribes of the north. What will the Americans do? Surely, they will respond. Surely, they are preparing now to strike us. What of their President's call for the Taliban to give up Usama?" Youseff asked.

"Usama is not worried. The Taliban will not comply with the bleating of the American president. Without us the Taliban could not rule this country. They are not the power here. We provide the backbone that makes this country strong; as I said the Taliban are only interested in teaching the Koran to women and children. We spread its word across the world!

"The Americans cannot decide what to do? Perhaps they will send more cruise missiles, but all of our camps are empty. We have spread our most important operations to the caves. Perhaps they will send bombers to strike the Taliban, but what will they destroy? Every bomb they send will be a hollow bark in the night. They will not hurt us in the caves. Hussein was generous in his teachings about underground fortifications. Our program has yielded much success; the Hindu Kush has many of our new command areas. The CIA's own complex at Tora Bora is filled with our men. We have learned from their cowardly response in Somalia, Bosnia, Kosovo and everywhere around the world. The sunset of American power has come. They cannot hurt us here," Mustapha preached.

"We will bring the Americans to their knees!" Mustapha said, finishing in a flourish.

"Yes, already they are weak and fearful, it is plain that Americans will not travel. In less than two weeks we will strike another blow and their economy will come crashing down, like a house of cards. Their greed will consume them, one after another. It will be our joy to watch." Youseff added.

"You are right. Their president will not have time to deal with us; he will have his hands full trying to save his own skin. This is our time; we will wash the face of the earth clean of the infidel. God has willed it. Allah, Arhkbar!" Mustapha said.

"What if our warriors fail? It is always possible that they will be caught?" Youseff asked.

"Mumpkin. All our warriors have been in place for years. The Americans will not suspect them. They will turn their heads to this new weakness—diversity; they will ignore the truth. They are afraid and no longer can face death; they run from it like children. When they do that they will fail. Our weapons are almost in place. Everything went smoothly during our glorious day in September, we were happy with four successes. More were planned, but we succeeded beyond our imagination. And if this new strike fails we have another," Mustapha concluded.

CHAPTER 2

Cold, wet and dark, Jenn thought as she backed out of the narrow driveway of her house in Mildenhall. *Summer is long gone I miss the sun already.*

She was on her way to the squadron, at O-dark thirty, to make sure she had all her ducks in a row before brief time. *Preparation Prevents Piss Poor Performance* she recalled one of her dad's homilies as she turned left onto A1101 on her way north. This was going to be one of the biggest days of her life.

Jennifer Emily Goode was a First Lieutenant in the United States Air Force. Five foot eight inches tall, blonde, blue eyed she was assigned to the 492d Fighter Squadron where she flew the F-15E Strike Eagle. She had dreamed of flying the big McDonnell Douglas fighter ever since she was in high school in Chinquapin, North Carolina. Like most of her crewmates, she refused to call the jet a Boeing, even thought they had bought McDonnell Douglass before she joined the Air Force. McD built fighters; Boeing built targets. She had desperately wanted to be a fighter pilot and now she just as desperately wanted to be a Flight Lead. Today was her 2-ship Flight Lead check ride and she was scheduled to fly with the Squadron Commander.

Stay next to the curb, she told herself as she guided her American left-hand drive Honda Civic onto the left side of the road. Turning left again onto the Flight Line gate from A1065 she stopped at the gate and showed the guard her ID card.

The Security Police at the gate were on full alert, dressed in utilities/MOPP Two, Kevlar Helmets, web gear, gas masks in pouches on their hips and loaded M-16s. There were three guards working inbound traffic, each with a radio attached to the top ring of their web gear. One stepped up to the car and looked her ID over. He scanned her face and the inside of her car, while another guard circled it, looking under it with a mirror on a pole. Yet another watched the whole scene with his M-16 in his hands the muzzle pointed towards the ground. While he looked somewhat casual, she realized that the observer had the weapon pointed at her, it may be pointing to the ground but it was just below her face and the guard with her ID card was standing to the side leaving a clear field of fire.

"Ma'am, here's your ID back. We're still on Threatcon Bravo. Good Morning, ma'am," the guard said as he handed her ID back through the window, saluting her with his right hand as she took the card back.

"Thank you, have a great one," she said nervously, as she took her ID, returned his salute and drove through the gate.

Going through the roundabout she glanced at the mounted F-100 painted in a colorful 48th Fighter Wing Statue of Liberty design from the early 60s, thinking how the times had changed. It was almost a month after the terrorist attack on the Twin Towers on September 11th. Everyone seemed jumpy and pissed off at the same time. Told to vary their way to work each day, beware of strangers around their houses and cars; the threat of potential terrorists was ever present these days. She was constantly looking behind her, checking six for terrorists. On base, the Security Police, expanded by augmentees from every unit on base, were constantly patrolling in HMMWVs with World War Two fifty caliber M2 machine guns on top. She had seen the preparation for Kosovo even if she did not get to go and two NATO Tactical Evaluation war games, but this was far more intense than anything she had ever seen. This was no game.

"Morning, ma'am, can I see your Line Badge?" said the airman guarding the entry to the 492d Fighter Squadron, the Mad Hatters.

"Good morning, Airman Frist. How are you this morning? Have you been on duty long?"

"Not really, ma'am. We're doing six on, six off right now. I've been here since two. It's kinda early, are you flying today?" Airman Frist asked brightly.

"Yes, I am. I've got a 2-ship check ride with Lieutenant Colonel Randleman. Brief is at 0735," Jenn replied.

Offering a salute Airman Frist said, "I thought I saw the commander earlier this morning. Oh, well, good luck, ma'am."

Returning her salute, Jenn opened the door and noticed that all the lights were on in the squadron soft side. The squadron buildings were made up of unprotected administration offices built alongside a reinforced concrete bombproof bunker capable of withstanding a direct hit from a 2,000 pound bomb and equipped with a pressurization system to survive a chemical warfare attack. Wondering who beat her into work she turned left into the shelter, also known as Hard Ops, where all aircrew flight planning and operations, in peace or war, takes place.

Pausing at the first heavy metal pressurized door that sealed the building as part of the chemical warfare system she turned on the entry light so she could make her way to the duty desk. Feeling along the wall for the light switch under the chest high desk she first turned on the overhead lights and then the back lighting that illuminated the two huge grease boards that showed the squadron schedule for the day. She quickly scanned for her name to check her sortie for any changes since she left last night.

Finding no notes on her flight or in the remarks area, she signed the flight release form on the clipboard on the duty desk. Continuing down the hall into the flight planning room, she turned on the fluorescent lights revealing a large square room with low ceilings and bare concrete walls painted in what could best be described as faded blue or maybe green. There were six large waist high flat-topped tables. Underneath each table were drawers containing enough maps and charts to plan a flight anywhere in Europe. Under the glass tops on each table were large-scale maps of various parts of England and the European Continent. Along one wall, was a large file cabinet that held thousands of small-scale maps covering all of England. Another wall held a board where Teletype messages covering the weather and notices for various bases and low level areas were posted. Yet another wall had a four-foot square metal door that could be used as an escape to the outside if the main entrance was blocked or damaged. The last wall held three large computer systems, AFMSS II, used for flight planning and preparing data modules to transfer the planning information electronically to each airplane. Each of these systems was housed in large green crush proof deployment boxes. Four rooms branched off from the main Flight Planning room. Each one of these was a Briefing room containing a large table, eight chairs and large white dry erase boards on each wall.

Jenn headed for the C Flight Briefing room she had set up last night and flipped on the lights there as well. Quickly scanning the dry erase boards she had put up for her briefing, she picked up her Line-up card from the table and went to the message boards to check the Low Level notices and the weather for the day.

"No purple airspace, weather 3100' broken here and 2,000' scattered at the range and the low level," she mused. "Should be no problems. VFR to the low level and the range, then get vectors for the initial back here. Great!" She walked back to the duty desk to update her line-up card and see if the Top three had assigned any jets yet.

"Hey Trash, you got a line up for today yet?" Jenn said to the Major John "Trash" Cannon, the squadron supervisor for the morning.

"Mornin' Jiggy. No jets yet, but I don't see any problems and I've even got two spares. But I do have a change for ya, Stroker had to come in last night to go to the command post, so he's not in crew rest this morning. I'm going to keep your check ride up, but Grumpy Westin will be your number two," Trash replied with a smile on his face.

"Thaaat's juuust grrreeeaatt. He's the USAFE IG guy isn't he?" Jenn asked with a worried tone in her voice.

"Yep, I don't have anyone else that can be your SEFE this morning and I really want to get your ride off. Don't worry, I know Grumpy, he's a good shit. You'll do fine. He'll be here at show time."

Making her way back to the briefing room she ran into her crewmate, Captain Nesbit, the WSO she would fly with for the check ride. "Hey, Hustler how ya doin'? Did you hear Stroker got called in last night and won't be flying with us this morning?" Jenn asked.

"Morning, Jiggy. Yeah, I heard Grumpy was gonna take his place," Hustler commented. Nesbit was an experienced Weapon System Officer who had over 1700 hours in the Strike Eagle, and had seen combat in three different countries. Of medium height, with short brown hair and a broad face, he had the appearance of being heavy set. In fact he could bench press 280 pounds and did so as often as he could.

"I came in early to make sure I had my shit together and just found out. Do you think Grumpy's gonna change the profile?" Jenn asked despondently.

"Well, if I was a betting man I'd say you better check the weather around the island. We never did get Intel involved in our plan did we? Humm. Yeah, I know Grumpy and he likes to do things...shall we say, short notice. You know, "Flexibility is the key to airpower,'" Hustler said lightly.

"Yeah, right...flexibility...Is Pinto in yet?" Jenn asked. "We'd probably better get organized." Captain James "Pinto" Williams was the WSO who would be flying in the number two airplane in today's flight.

Walking in to her briefing room she found Pinto and Lieutenant Colonel Grumpy Westin sitting at the table talking. As she walked in Grumpy stood up and shoved his hand out to shake. Jenn saw a man in his mid-forties about six feet tall, with very short brown hair, graying slightly at the temples and dressed in the standard USAF flight suit with Velcro patches, also known as a green bag.

Jenn grasped his hand, and before he could speak, said, "Good morning Colonel, I'm Jiggy Goode."

"Morning, I'm Grumpy Westin. I'm glad to see everyone is here bright and early. Thanks for letting me stand in for Stroker this morning," Grumpy replied.

Jenn began feeling a little like she was starting that slide down the steep slope to losing control. She swallowed, trying to push the butterflies down her throat, and jumped in to brief Grumpy on the overall plan for the day. "Yes, sir. I checked the weather, NOTAMS and there aren't any British Royals flying today, so no purple airspace. We've got the priority for jets and there shouldn't be any admin problems today. Lieutenant Colonel Randleman gave me an industrial target in Land's End on the west coast. I've planned a low level ingress/egress with a pop for one and a loft for two."

"Yeah, I saw your plan. It looks like a good one. I like the Pop/Loft combination, it's one of my favorites for deconfliction, surprise and standoff. Trouble is, that's not the Frag. Here's your fragged target for the day."

Pulling out a 1:500k scale map of central England Westin pointed to some Red and Blue squiggly lines drawn on the map and said, "Here's the forward edge of our lines. On the dark side they have SA-9/13s and ZSUs at the front. There is an SA-2 here at Shobdon Glider port, an SA-5 at the second Glider port to the southwest, and a Mig-29 CAP at RAF Valley. You have to ingress at Brize Norton and egress north of Birmingham. The target is the Power Generation Station at the Lyn Clywedog Dam. Your weapons load for the day is four each Mk-84s. Need I remind you that the ROE prevents you from dropping short rounds on the Dam itself? Do you have any questions?"

"Ahhh, yes, sir. We've got one hour and five minutes to the brief," Jenn said slowly, disappointed that her planning was wasted, thinking about all the things that needed to be done in a very short time. This day sure wasn't going to go smoothly now.

"Jiggy," Grumpy interrupted her, "Listen, I'm a player today. You are the Flight Lead, do what you gotta do. Don't forget to give me a job. And please call me Grumpy, we're flying together, okay?"

"Okay, sir, Ummm, Grumpy."

"Let's do it this way. Hustler, you do the route in and out and the air-to-air game plan, I'll help you with the charts," Jenn started shakily.

Gathering steam she went on, "Pinto, you've got AFMSS. Get the DTM load together and let's set the TOT based on the Wainfleet range time. Setup training PACS for two Aim-9s, two AMRAAMs and Mk-84s on one and three left and right, no wing tanks."

"Grumpy, you've got the Pop plan and brief, I'll help you with the overall flow."

"Sure, Jiggy. Do you want me to make copies as well?" Hustler interjected as he picked up Grumpy's map.

"You bet. I'll get the Lineup card," Jenn replied.

"Come on Pinto," Hustler said. "Let's go pick the points. By the way Jiggy, what do you think about a 10/20 high Pop?"

After a short pause she replied, "Yeah, that sounds good. We can have both sets of bombs in the air before the first one impacts and two can avoid lead's bomb frag pattern by staying high." As Hustler left she tried to say thanks with her glance as he walked out the door.

Jenn went to the map bank to pull a 1:50k map of the target area to begin detailed planning of the attack. The power generation station was located on the southwest side of the narrow valley occupied by the Clywedog dam. Visual target acquisition would be limited by the narrow deep valley as well as limiting the run-in and the weapons delivery.

Joining her at the planning table Grumpy noted that "The highest terrain in the area is this 500 meter mountain southeast of the target area, maybe we could use that as an initial point."

"No, I think it's a great lead-in feature, but the road intersection just beyond that peak would be better as the IP. We could use that east-west road running out of the intersection as our hack point and by splitting the peak in tactical formation, with two on the right, we should be in good position with the valley as the reference for the run-in to the action point," Jenn replied.

"Yeah; you're right. Lead could follow the general run of this river valley and use the bigger road on the left as a pull-up reference," Grumpy noted.

"The power station hugs the east side of a very steep rise and the valley itself is very narrow. I think the roll-in will have to go up that river valley, but avoid the village of Llanidloes." Taking a pop attack-planning template, Jenn lined up the roll-in line down the river valley. "The pull down point will actually be over the village and for a 10 degree pop the pull-up point will be abeam the junction of A470 and the river. If we run-in tactical formation then Two will have to action left a bit before popping. That will put you in trail by a few seconds making it easy to keep track of me during your pop."

"Yeah, that looks good. Your bomb fall line will be south and west of the dam and mine will be parallel to it," Grumpy observed with satisfaction.

"I also think you should plan a split after the target for flight path deconfliction and SA. Two comes off north and One comes off south, we can get back together going east," Jenn asserted.

"Okay, I think I can put it together. Do you want me to run the numbers?" Grumpy asked.

"No, we don't really have time and the squadron standards for a 10/20 High are made for planning situations just like this. They are based on AGL, so the only thing you'll have to do is convert them to MSL for us to use. Oh, and make sure to note the timing throughout the pop flow so we can build SA where each jet should be. I think the run-in is probably at 540 knots," Jenn directed.

Hurlburt AFB, Florida

His turn to fly, Captain Jason Gorman released the brakes on the AC-130U and slowly advanced the power on the Herc's four turbo-prop engines.

"Set takeoff power," he said as he glanced at the airspeed indicator and then out at the runway. Seeing the windsock out of the corner of his left eye he noticed there was a slight right crosswind, he fed in a little right aileron and left rudder as the big airplane accelerated down the runway.

Jason Gorman, a little less than six feet tall and wiry, was an Air Force Academy graduate on his first operational tour. He was a New Yorker who had never been out of the city until he left for the Academy. His father, a Port Authority big wig, had been an Air Force B-52 bomb Nav during the Viet Nam War and had made sure that he was going to the Academy. A mission ready co-pilot for nearly 21 months he was feeling very comfortable with the big rattletrap they called the Spooky. *I'm more than ready to check out as AC*, he thought to himself as he rotated the nose after passing though refusal velocity, feeling the airplane gather speed and fly itself off the ground.

"Gear up," he called.

Trimming quickly, to keep the nose from rising, he smoothly accelerated to climb speed and as he passed though 1,000 feet called for climb power. Turning left on the outbound heading he was met by a fiery red sunset in the west, framed by a broken cloud cover; the sky above was dark, almost black, and the ground was sliding from gray into night. In between, what was left of the sky and the bottom of the clouds were brightly lit in a riot of autumn shades of reds and yellows. The Spooky was taking off into that spectacular southern Florida evening for a training mission over the Eglin ranges. Tonight was a live fire night; they would exercise the 105mm main gun and the Bofor's 40mm. Their objectives for this sortie were to test some new software for the IR sensor for

SCOTT PERDUE

the FCO as well as train two crews of gunners. His job would be to monitor the airplane, its systems and attitude, watch for traffic, talk on the radio and monitor what was going on in the back. He would be busy, but not as busy as the shooters.

The AC worked the radios as Jason flew Spooky 21 through the darkening sky. Once the Range Controller had cleared them onto the range he told Jason to take the radios. Leaning down the AC picked up his night vision goggles, he adjusted them and snapped them into the track on his helmet just above his forehead. Turning on the goggles, he began tweaking his sight system that looked out his left window, prepared for the first order of business—to sight in the guns, and coordinate them with the Fire Control computers, the FCO's IR system and his sight. A complex task, they would spend the better part of the next hour fine tuning the system. Jason mused to himself that since they would not be working with a ground controller tonight, he would be talking to the ranger by himself and it might get a tad lonely.

Jason could make out the run-in line to the target on the ground and he turned to line up the aircraft so that it was flying directly at the target. "We're lined up," he said over the intercom.

As Spooky 21 entered the range airspace the AC took the yoke and giving it an almost imperceptible wiggle he said, "I've got it."

After passing the target just out his left window the AC began a slow turn to the left and began a wide orbit around the target about 2,000 feet above the ground. The live fire target for tonight was a Conex box; in a former life it had been a shipping container plying the ocean between the United States and Europe. Beat up by the dockworkers for the shipping company, its last career was to be a target for Spooky 21. After tonight it would be a twisted pile of tortured metal.

The AC established the turn and called for Jason to engage the autopilot in attitude hold. If the AC needed to override the autopilot he could add pressure to the yoke to shallow or steepen the bank in order to maintain the target in his window.

As he listened to the chatter between the FCO and the AC, with the occasional "gun ready" calls of the gunners in the background, Jason mused about his predicament. He was almost 100 percent sure that their unit would be deployed somewhere in the world—real soon now. President Bush's speech after 9/11 had made it clear that the US would go after the terrorists which meant that virtually every Spooky Gunship would be deploying somewhere. His dilemma was that he had a slot for the Aircraft Commander's course in

November. The trouble is that all C-130 upgrades took place in the schoolhouse in Arkansas and slots were hard to come by. If he went to the upgrade course he could be an aircraft commander, but he was sure he would miss out on the war. He could not decide if an early upgrade to AC was better than a ticket to the big game for his career.

A big 'THuuuuMMP' from the 105mm cannon, a significant change from the staccato knocking of the 40mm, brought him out of his reverie. He glanced guiltily around the cockpit checking the altitude, airspeed, and bank angle. As he scanned the engine instruments he wondered how long he had been daydreaming. He did not remember hearing the switch to the 105 call. Finding everything normal he resolved to do a quick check every two minutes.

After scanning the instruments and checking the location of the aircraft for the third time Jason began thinking of Jenny. It seemed as if his thoughts turned to Jenny a lot these days.

Jenny was a high energy blond, with an easy laugh and a smile that would light a dark night. He had spent almost every day of the most intense year of his life with her. He knew what the score was. It was easy for him to figure out when people were working a scam from a mile away and not one of them had ever taken advantage of him. Jenny was different. Jenny was chasing a star he had never seen and he just could not get her out of his mind. He had seen her in class on the first day of pilot training. The class commander had gotten up in front of everybody that day and had spent what seemed like an hour on a welcoming speech and through it all he had not heard a word. He could not take his eyes off of this blond, one of twelve women in the class, in the row next to his just a few seats over. Her hair, cut short, fell straight down to her jaw with a slight curl at the bottom. Her nose was thin and her face had a softly chiseled look that seemed like it came from delicate, fragile marble.

He had been trying to figure out how to talk with her when he heard the commander say, "…and if any of you need to wear glasses, bring 'em in tomorrow. You're already in pilot training don't worry about it. We want you to see!" He resolved to bring his glasses in the next day.

During the next several classes he had mused over all the pick-up lines he knew, trying to come up with one that he could try out on Jenny Goode. Already, he could see that beguiling smile in his mind and he just had to figure out a way to meet her. During the last class of the day the commander got up on the stage again and announced how the class was to be split into two groups, or flights, and how each of these flights would proceed through training more or less separately. He was beginning to get worried when the commander announced that the flights would be filled in order. He grinned to himself when he realized that in the inexorable way of the Military, they were going to be together; it was meant to be, their last names were next to each other in alphabetical order.

The rest of pilot training was a blur to him. Time, day and night, flying and studying all merged together until there was little room to do anything but what the Air Force wanted you to do. Academics came easily to him while Jenn studied very hard. Since they were tablemates, they naturally spent a lot of their time studying together. Jenn was a natural in the air and he had to work at it, which he thought was unfair because he was a very good athlete. But in baseball and tennis, you did not have to think at six to seven miles a minute.

Their friends in UPT called them JJ, because they were always together. They were very good friends. They each seemed to know what the other was thinking and what the other was worried about. They seemed to compliment each other's faults; one was always there to help the other over a bad spot. She had swept him along with her enthusiasm, her zest for life and for flying. By the end of that intense year of pilot training they had grown closer together, shared more successes and failures and had more in common with each other than he had with anyone in his life before. They had grown beyond friendship, but instead of making things easier, things just got more complicated. They both knew they would be going their separate ways. He was going to C-130s and she was going to fly the Strike Eagle; something she had been talking about since day one. He tried to formalize their relationship, but in retrospect, their careers had gotten in the way. He could still hear her words just before graduation. They had a fight and she told him "that you just don't believe in anything bigger than yourself." Those words haunted him every day.

Shooting the ILS back at Hurlburt, Jason noted that he was going a little high on glide slope, he lowered the nose and then pulled off some power to keep the speed nailed. When the landing lights illuminated the runway, he checked his aim point just beyond the 500' markers on the runway and shifted his gaze to the end of the runway so that he could judge his height above the ground using the runway lights. At 30', he pulled the outboard engines to idle and checked the descent. At 10', he pulled the inboards to idle and began a slow flare touching down gently on the aft trucks.

Kabul, Afghanistan

In a long, rather dark room of the former Afghan Air Authority, with only a colorful carpet for decoration, at least a dozen men gathered. Dressed in colored robes, each man had a long beard and a turbine covering most of his head, more than a few had beards tinged with white. The men sat along the walls talking in twos and threes. Some sat cross-legged, some with their legs tucked under them, everyone of them made an effort to hide the soles of their feet.

One tall Arab, at the end of the room, sat under the only open window wore an American Military camouflaged fatigue jacket. Next to him, a short and swarthy man dressed mostly in white, with a long red faded cloth draped around his neck sat quietly watching all the attendees. The tall man with the gaunt eyes leaned next to his neighbor and asked, "And your son? He is fourteen now is he not? A fine young man. I hear that he is not in the Madrasa, when will you bring him to our cause. We need more faithful recruits like him."

A nervous look flashed across the shorter man's face, turning his eyes away from his questioner's eyes, he replied haltingly, "Soon enough, I imagine. He is keen, but I insist that he finish his studies. The base also needs educated men. Soon he will go to the Madrasa."

"Which Madrasa will he attend? Will it be here or in Pakistan?"

Trying to hide his worry, Ahmed Mustapha stood up to welcome his fellow area managers to a high level conference. He began talking in a very loud voice. "Allah Arkbhar. We have reached a great day. You are here today to report on our movement from the training camps. Our new cave system should be running. The Americans favorite weapon, the cruise missile, will threaten us no longer."

Barely audible, the man in the camouflaged jacket said, "God is great! Our cause shall not fail. Attend to Mustapha, and God willing we will sweep the infidel from their sins in life. A new day is dawning, it is our day in the sun."

Pausing, Mustapha looked at the tall man on his left and after a moment continued, "First I will tell you of where our sword shall fall next. In two weeks time we have another glorious strike against the overly proud Americans. By evil measures, they were able to keep their society from crashing after the god given strikes last month; thanks be to Atta. This time, with a second strike, the impotence of their government and their absence of will, will be their destruction. They still cower in fear from our power in their own country. In two weeks we will incinerate them in a ball of fire!"

"We will spread fear around the world with strikes in Southeast Asia and Europe. No one can ignore our power, or our reach. We will cleanse the world of the infidel and purify it with a righteous fire!" Mustapha said with a grand gesture.

"Now that you know the details of our plans, we will hear what has been done with the caves. Ahmed Youseff will tell of the preparations in the Kafar Jar Ghar Mountains," Mustapha said as he gestured to Youseff and sat down again.

"We have built more than 50 caves in the Zabol and Ghazni Provinces. The smallest observation outpost will care for 20 men; the largest training center will house 300 of our faithful. Allowances have been made for food, sleeping, and storage for our weapons; we have enough weapons to last 100 years. There is enough food in each cave for the long winter." Youseff began.

During Youseff's pause to breathe, a man along the opposite wall asked, "This is well and good. You are very prepared to live. I wonder how you will talk to each other in those caves if we are attacked," Hamid Mohideen leaned forward and asked.

"We have radios and cell phones," Youseff answered.

"You have no land telephones? Are the radios VHF or HF?" pressed Mohideen.

"A few caves have land telephones, the rest are cell phones. The receiving towers are on all the big ridges. There is never any trouble. As for the radios, we have both kinds. They are new ones from France. But come, we are not threatened here in our home. Afghanistan is our strength and no Army can reach us over the mountains," Youseff offered.

"Yes, Yes. Youseff continue. What of the training camps?" Mustapha interrupted.

Feeling more confident, Youseff continued, "We have places to train 3,000 or more new recruits. If needs be we can train many more than that. We have camps and villages and places were we could train them in firing rifles and other weapons, we can run them through rugged mountains and teach them how to use explosives. We have lost nothing by moving into the mountains. We have gained, because local Afghanis no longer interrupt us."

"Very good. Since last month, we have received 200 new people to our cause a day. They come across the Pakistan frontier in large groups. All clamoring with hope and new faith and wanting to join our cause and become God's fighters," Mustapha said.

"We must train these new people how to fight and work with a commander. We will have need of more fighters soon, even here in Afghanistan," Mustapha said as he nodded and looked around the room. "The Taliban have not succeeded in destroying the Northern Alliance."

"What of Tora Bora?" Mustapha asked, looking directly at the man who had questioned Youseff.

"The mountains are not tall, but they are rugged. The British left watch houses all over the Khyber Pass, and pushed the natives into caves for hundreds of years. The Pathans are savage warriors and when they live in towns, all their houses have gun ports. We have had witless teachers, better than the British. The American CIA built our biggest caves themselves. We have one complex that has more floors than the largest building in Kabul and it has its own power and air handling system such that you would not know you are underground. This place alone can house thousands and not notice thieves knocking on the door.

"We too have weapons and food. We also have tanks inside guarding the entry of some of our largest caves. They cannot be breached. We can talk amongst separate caves by using land telephone lines buried in the ground between caves. We can talk with you here in Kabul by radio or cell phones. We can also reach the European communications satellites to talk with our followers in the rest of the world. It is a simple matter to do this thanks be to our French friends," Hamid Mohideen replied.

"We have places for 10 to 15,000 fighters to live. We have many caves and many ways between each cave. The locals do not bother us in this area. We deal with them harshly if they stray and they learn their lessons. We also have developed paths over the border with Pakistan should we need to travel without being seen by outsiders."

"You have done well, Hamid. Tora Bora is our best complex. Our caves there are hundreds of feet inside the rock of the mountains. They can never be breached by those bombs the Americans used on Saddam and cruise missiles are nothing but a knock of the door," Mustapha commented.

Looking slowly around the room Mustapha went on, "Fuad Saleh is here to tell us of the Salang Pass caves, north of Kabul. It is here that is the only place the Northern Alliance threatens us.

Leaning over his crossed knees Mustapha continued, "Fahim controls Golbahar and it is very near the Baghlan road in this area. We must keep this road open if we are to prevent the Northern Alliance from threatening Mazar-e Shariff and Kunduz. This area is important to the Taliban and us although they put little faith in roads. Fuad tell us, what have you done."

Fuad Saleh, a short man without a flowing beard, but with a chin adorned by a few scraggly hairs began speaking hurriedly, "We have caves on both sides of the valley of Chahar Dar. From the southern caves, we can move easily to defend the Salang Pass. We have Russian Artillery placed to cover the road and the Taliban has promised to provide tanks from around Baghlan for our use here if we need them. We also overlook the western side of the road from the ridges with five caves, each with Russian ZU 23mm anti-aircraft weapons. Each of these Russian guns can easily cover the road. If the Northern Alliance try to use the pass we can make sure they cannot."

Sitting along the wall, another man interjected, "Yes, the Russian weapons work very well against the Tribal cavalry. The horses cannot stand the noise and carnage. Without horses, they are cowards; they are not fighters on their feet. With fast firing weapons like that there will not be many left if they try anything."

"We have long range HF radios and satellite phones setup to talk with our soldiers around the world, as well as here in Afghanistan. The area is very quiet and Afghani locals do not bother us, preferring to stay near their villages. We are sure there is nothing to see from the air, no American spy knows we are there. We can protect the pass," Saleh finished and leaned back against the wall.

CHAPTER 3

5 October 2001
RAF Lakenheath, Suffolk England

Jiggy walked up to the duty desk one minute before step time, her lineup card in her hand. Hustler and Pinto already at the desk were leaning against the counter chatting with the Top three. She tucked a stray hair back into her bun and said, "Hey Trash, are our jets crew ready yet?" she asked.

Sitting in his office chair, Trash looked at her and asked, "Yeah, is your flight all here?"

Jiggy looked around, counting noses, she did not see Grumpy Westin. Without all the members of the flight, they could not step to the airplanes. It was not cool to be late at step time. One of the basic rules of flying fighters is that you are on time, maybe not early, but never late. "Has anybody seen Grumpy?" she asked, frustrated.

Hustler shrugged without comment. Pinto glanced down at the counter sheepishly. "Last I saw he was in the DO's office on the phone."

Jiggy felt the back of her neck getting hot, flushed with anger, embarrassment, and trepidation she spun on her heel. Turning left, she went to the Director of Operations office, located behind the duty desk. Curiously, it was right next to the entrance to the restrooms, which served double duty as part of the shelter's chemical decontamination facility. Poking her head in the door, she saw Grumpy on the phone writing on his lineup card. She knocked on the open door.

"Yeah, we'll be there at 1015," Grumpy said looking up at the knock, almost dropping the phone pinched to his ear by his shoulder. "Gotta go, see ya," he blurted and hung up the phone.

Grumpy smiled sheepishly, "Sorry, I was just finishing a phone call. Hope I'm not late." He got up and walked quickly around the desk. "I'm good to go!"

Jiggy forced a smile, she was running out of patience flying with this stand-in, "That's okay, I won't hold it against you till the debrief. Let's get our step brief."

Calm down, she thought to herself, *I must get through this, regardless of what happens. Today should be like clockwork, I sure put enough planning into it, but so far, it has been like pushing a wet noodle.*

"Trash, we're all here or accounted for," she said, putting her lineup card down on the duty desk. She took out her pen out to fill in the tail numbers of their jets and the parking locations.

Trash Cannon quickly made a head count, when he had everyone's attention he looked back at the grease board, "Jiggy and Hustler have 305 in Tab Vee 11, Grumpy and Pinto have aircraft 312 in 23. The weather has scattered out here and the overhead pattern is open. Right now, we're on runway 24 and all the Nav aids and cables are up. You guys are my priority, so I've got spares in case your jet's crump. Before you go hot footing it for the spare, give me a call on the radio. Have you guys checked purple airspace and booked the low level time?"

"Low level is booked and we called the ranger, no purple today," chimed in Hustler.

"Okay, this is our only go today, so your jets won't turn. Don't take too long, I don't need the hours, and we've got First Friday tonight. Any questions?" Cannon finished. Each squadron would usually fly the same jets in two banks of training flights called goes, each day. Today the Mad Hatter's had only one go scheduled, with any luck the maintenance crews would be able to make it home for the weekend.

Everyone in Jiggy's flight left the Hard Side together and went down the hall to the Life Support Room in the Soft Side. There they put on their jackets, zipped their G-suits, slung on parachute harnesses, gathered their helmets and charts together and stepped out for the van. Jiggy's flight piled into the Life Support van, with another flight; ready to get dropped off at each Tab Vee. The driver, looking forward to the weekend was in a good mood, asked happily, "Mornin' gentleman and ladies. Where to?"

"Deray is in 11 and 23," Jiggy blurted.

"17 and 34 for Fazer," Dweeb, the other flight lead added. With a crooked smile he looked at Jiggy and asked, "Hey Jiggy, you using standard Mode one and two?"

"Yeah, I'm using 11 and 12 for Mode one and squadron standard for Mode two. Why?"

The van driver turned left after leaving the squadron area. Entering the aircraft movement area, he crossed the taxiway, headed for the closest TabVee, number 17, first. The next one would be 11 and then he would backtrack to go to the others at the far end of the squadron area.

Once it was obvious that the driver was headed for his jet first, Dweeb looked at Jiggy with his characteristic lopsided grin, "Oh Jiggy, I'm just on Wainfleet before you and wanted to check up on you, that's all. Hey, I guess I'm the winner of the drop off derby. Bet I'll beat you to the end of the runway, what do you say?"

"You're on. First flight to EOR wins. Five bucks to the Blue Tail Fund," Jiggy shot back. Still new as a crew dog in the squadron, she was the squadron snacko in charge of snacks, sodas and t-shirts and coins and stuff. The snacko was always short of money.

"Hell no. The loser buys the first round and I like Guinness," Dweeb shot back, his grin wider.

"Yeah right. Check is in the mail, just don't cash it yet," Jiggy rejoined, nervously.

"Whatever, here's my stop. See ya, bye," Dweeb said as he and his crewmate got out of the van in front of their TabVee. Shutting the door firmly, he slapped the side of the van.

The van pulled up to her TabVee, Jiggy picked up her helmet bag and climbed out of the back of the van. Before she closed the door on Grumpy and Pinto she said without a smile, "See you on the radio."

Turning to walk to the jet, Jiggy paused when she saw the F-15E Strike Eagle, sitting outside the hardened aircraft shelter in the morning sun. It glinted with promise and took her breath away. She scanned the airplane as she walked up to it; she never got tired of looking at it. Sitting tall on its gear, the jet was painted a dark battleship gray. It's twin tails climbed powerfully into the blue sky flecked with white puffy clouds. Happy, she thought to herself, she controlled this power. She was lucky to be here.

The crew chief had left the canopy down and she thought that it looked like a large clear blister, smoothly faired into the fuselage. It struck her that it looked almost like a forehead. With the larger canopy, it seemed that the top of the airplane was more balanced and prettier than the light gray F-15C. The nose holding the APG-70 radar jutted forward and to her it really did look like a beak. It is an Eagle and it's waiting for me!

The Crew Chief opened the canopy and slid the boarding ladder onto the canopy rail. Finished, he wiped his hands on a rag and stuffed it into a pocket of his uniform. Leaning down he picked up the forms, lodged on the nose tire, and walked out to meet her. Snapping a salute, he said, "Good Morning, ma'am. How are you today? The jet is crew ready and code one this morning. Any chance of bringing it back that way?"

"Morning Sergeant Graves, I'll sure try. It looks beautiful this morning," Jiggy replied with a wide smile, as she returned his salute. Taking the forms from his hand, she began flipping through the pages to check the entries. She took a pen out of her left sleeve pocket, signed the release, and handed the book back to the Crew Chief. Heading for the front left of the plane she began her pre-flight walk around.

While she had been looking at the forms, Hustler had pre-flighted the SUU-20 munition dispensers attached to the wings. They held the BDU-33 training bombs they planned to drop on the range. He knew Jiggy would look at the bombs as well, but he felt more comfortable eyeballing them himself. Satisfied that each of the twelve 25 pound blue bombs was ready to fly, he went back to the cockpit. Pausing at the bottom of the ten-foot ladder, he bent over at the waist, threaded the leg straps between his legs, and snapped them onto his harness. Straightening he pulled on his gloves, climbed the ladder and settled into his seat.

Emerging from under the left wing Jiggy bent over to snap the leg straps of her harness around her legs as well. After snapping the first one she began briefing the Crew Chief, "Sergeant Graves, we're going to Brize Norton, just west of London, and let down for a low level route in Wales. We've planned to do 450 knots at around 500'. I'll be leading tail number 312 to a target near a dam in the middle of the country. Then we'll head for Wainfleet range on the east coast and drop some of these BDUs."

Finished, she straightened up. "We'll be back before you know it."

"Sounds like fun." Pleased that she was so friendly this early in the morning, Sergeant Graves suddenly asked, "Can I go?"

Following Jiggy up the ladder the Crew Chief watched her buckle in and helped her attach the Koch fittings from the ejection seat parachute into her torso harness. Standing on the ladder, he held out his hand to shake hers, "Have a good flight, Lieutenant. I'll be here when you when you get back."

Jiggy went through the start sequence smoothly and closed the canopy. With the Crew Chief waiting patiently outside, she looked at her watch for the exact briefed check-in time. Jiggy pulled the radio button on the throttle with her left thumb, precisely on the hack. "Deray 11, check aux."

"Two!" Grumpy replied on the back radio, radio two. The Strike Eagle was equipped with two UHF radios, the back radio, used for intra-flight comm, and the front radio for talking to everyone else.

Jiggy paused for a second and then pushed her thumb forward to check the flight in on the front radio. "Deray 11, check."

"Two!" Grumpy replied, on the front radio.

"Lakenheath ground, Deray 11, taxi two Bolar's with Bravo from 11 and 23. Wales South," Jiggy said on the front radio.

The Lakenheath ground controller responded immediately, "Roger Deray, Lakenheath ground, Taxi north to Runway 24. Squawk 2201."

"2201, Deray," Jiggy replied.

She looked at the Crew Chief, standing just left of the nose in an easy parade rest. When he saw her looking at him she touched her pointed thumbs together, her fingers curled into fists. Rapidly she rotated her wrists back towards her face, opening her hands. The Crew Chief nodded and relayed the signal to another crewman underneath the jet who pulled the chocks from the wheels. With the chocks pulled, the Crew Chief motioned her to roll forward, snapped her a salute and pointed to the taxiway.

Looking left and right to make sure no one was on the taxiway, Jiggy pushed up the throttles just a little to get moving. Rolling onto the taxiway she snapped the throttles to idle and pulled out of the TabVee area. She shot a quick glance back at the Crew Chief, seeing him watching her, she quickly flipped him a 'hang loose' signal as a way of saying goodbye.

The last check crews at the end of the runway were just finishing Deray when Fazer rolled into the blister at the end of Runway 24.

Hustler laughed and shot Dweeb the biggest grin he could muster. Pulling his mask closer to his face, he said over the intercom, "Hey, Jiggy, check out Dweeb just pulling into EOR."

Jiggy turned her head slightly to look at the two Strike Eagles pulling into the parking area, "Fazer buys Deray," Jiggy transmitted calmly on the Aux radio. Two quick clicks, a zipper, was her only reply.

Grinning in her mask, *things just might go my way today,* she thought. Over the Aux radio she said, "Deray push 11 Aux, Three main." After checking the flight in on the new radio frequencies she called the tower. "Tower, Deray 11 number one with two, rolling."

Without a pause, the tower controller transmitted, "Deray 11, Lakenheath Tower. Cleared for takeoff, turn right 060, climb, and maintain one one thousand."

"Deray 11 cleared for takeoff, 060, eleven thousand," Jiggy replied.

She clicked the bayonet connectors of her mask onto her helmet, looked at Grumpy, and nodded her head. Rolling slowly, she pulled out of the parking area and lined up on the centerline of the runway. Without stopping she pushed the power up to 80 percent rpm and did a quick check of the engines.

The aircraft slowly began accelerating. Jiggy quickly pushed the throttles through the Military power gate into afterburner and the jet leapt forward. Looking forward through the Heads' up Display she watched her speed quickly build. Jiggy eased the stick full aft as the aircraft passed 1500'. With the nose rising, she eased forward on the stick slightly and the big Strike Eagle climbed smoothly into the air. Less than 2300' had gone by and the 62,000 pound jet fighter was airborne, quickly accelerating to 300 knots.

Twenty seconds behind her Grumpy was airborne. A few seconds after that Pinto locked his radar onto Jiggy's aircraft. Over the back radio he said, "Two's tied."

Twenty-two minutes later Deray flight had switched off London Mil's air traffic control frequency. Descending over RAF Brize Norton, Jiggy was ready for the low level portion of her check ride. She turned slightly to avoid a small buildup of clouds.

"Deray, set Wessex altimeter," Jiggy transmitted on the aux radio.

"Twenty-five miles past Brize, we can descend to low level. Remember that low jet traffic is up the mouth of the Severn River to the northeast, that means they are coming towards us," Hustler said over the intercom.

"Thanks, I remember," said Jiggy. "How's our time looking?"

"Good, when are we going to push it up?" Hustler asked.

"I'm doing that now," Jiggy replied. Cycling the stick, she proposed the aircraft's nose up and down, signaling Grumpy to move out into tactical formation two miles out on her left wing. Once he had stabilized, she began a steeper descent and accelerated to 450 knots. Since Wales is a very mountainous country, she kept a watch on Grumpy's progress as he weaved through valleys and tried to keep up with her lead.

Approaching the turn point just southwest of Brecon, Jiggy glanced once more at Grumpy. Seeing Grumpy in position, she rapidly rocked her wings once to the right and settled back into level flight. Grumpy started a tight tactical turn. In seconds, his nose was pointing at her, and then even faster he was falling behind her flight path. As he continued his turn Jiggy waited until his nose passed her six o'clock and then she began her hard turn to the right. They rolled out in line abreast formation headed north towards the next turn point.

"We're getting close to the IP, any threats out there?" Jiggy asked Hustler.

"We're clear out to 80 miles. I'll give you an update at the IP," Hustler replied.

Checking Grumpy's position off the right wing, Jiggy glanced at the TSD, the moving map display above her right knee. She liked the monochrome screen because it was bigger and easier to see. Looking out the front windscreen, she checked her attitude relative to the ground. Satisfied that the airplane was not going to hit the ground, she looked at the target attack card. She had clipped the card to the left handhold on the canopy so she could quickly review the attack parameters for the upcoming popup.

Flying with her right hand, she reached across with her left and punched the Air-to-Ground button on the mode panel below the Up Front Controller. At the same time, she said, "I'm going air-to-ground."

"System's updated. You've got a good designation for the target," Hustler replied, "I'm going back to air-to-air radar."

"Okay," Jiggy said. With her left thumb, she transmitted on the aux radio. "Deray, push it up."

Seeing her 500-meter hill, the run-in feature she had picked just prior to the IP, she gently moved the aircraft a few degrees to the left; lining up with the road she knew was just beyond it. Crossing the IP, she hacked her stopwatch and turned to a heading of 347 degrees for the run-in to the pull-up point. Out of the corner of her eye, she saw the target designation diamond and the Azimuth Steering Line drift to the left.

Glancing at Grumpy, she saw that he was just a few degrees aft of the wing, in position. Seconds away from the pop, she looked to the front, scanning for her pull-up reference. She clicked the auto-acq switch on the stick aft once, switching to a manual CDIP pipper for the pop.

"One's up," she said over the aux radio thirty seconds after passing the IP. She sharply pulled four g and abruptly stopping the climb when the velocity vector touched 15 degrees nose up.

"Two's up," she heard Grumpy say six seconds later.

When she saw 2900 feet on the Heads Up Display she transmitted "One's in." Looking left to pick out the dam, she rolled about 120 degrees and quickly put five g on the aircraft, turning towards the target. She immediately saw the power station and told Hustler, "Target's in sight."

The Power Generation Station contained two small buildings next to a larger rectangular building. They clustered together on a flat spot just to the left of the

Dam. Jiggy noticed that the buildings were right next to a very steep rock cliff. Any long bombs would bring down rock and debris on top of the target. She set the velocity vector at ten degrees nose low. Thinking about the jet's tendency to trim out to level flight, causing a 1g climb, a classic banana pass, she pushed slightly on the stick to keep the dive at ten degrees. She concentrated on the pipper rising to the target, in the background she heard Grumpy say "Two's in."

The pipper approached the target when she heard Hustler say, "Ready, Ready, pickle." With the pipper at the bottom of the target, she pressed the pickle button. In the back of her mind she thought that the Pop delivery was on profile, just as planned. She began her safe escape maneuver, pulling up the ASL at 5g. Reaching the horizon she relaxed the backpressure on the stick, rolled into 80 degrees of bank and quickly laid on 5g again. When the jet had turned 60 degrees she relaxed the back pressure on the stick again, finally rolling out on a reverse course to her attack heading. With her left hand on the throttle, she pulled the Weapon mode switch aft to take command of the radar. In Auto Guns, she slewed the radar slightly in the direction of their egress heading.

Looking to her left she saw Grumpy about three miles away doing his safe escape maneuver, avoiding simulated bomb fragments. Checking left, Jiggy turned the airplane to get her formation back in a wide tactical formation. *So far, so good*, she thought. She could get back into standard two mile tactical as they egressed; things were going well.

Rolling out and breathing heavily, Grumpy physically turned his shoulders to make it easier to look for Jiggy. After a looking for a few seconds he did not see her and called out, "Deray Two, blind."

"Deray, continue, visual is at your right three o'clock, four miles," Jiggy replied easily.

Out of the corner of her eye a sudden change in the HUD symbology caught her attention. Jiggy quickly looked out the front, and noticed that the radar had snagged an air-to-air target.

"Deray One, snap lock, 060, eighteen miles," Jiggy called excitedly over the radio.

"Bandit, Bandit," Hustler added quickly.

"Deray Two, no joy," Grumpy responded.

Pinto, inside Deray Two, knew that was not true. He saw Deray One just fine and he had the bandits on the radar as well. "Hey, Grumpy, I've got those guys on radar. Give me a second and I'll get you a sort. He's probably got the near man."

"Bullshit, we're fat, dumb and unhappy. Don't say anything. Stay in search," Grumpy barked.

When Pinto did not reply, he added in a softer tone, "We're a training aid today. Let's see how she does."

"Damn, the threat is closer to Two, Hustler. Grumpy is gonna get shot, plus he doesn't see us. Hustler, what should we do?" Jiggy asked Hustler, the alternatives racing through her mind. The opposing jets were closing at over seven miles a minute. In just over a minute they would be a furball. She needed to do something, and RIGHT NOW!

Hustler made no reply, "No ideas, huh, Hustler?" she asked.

"Sorry, Jiggy. I've been briefed, you're on your own," Hustler said despondently.

Feeling reckless she blurted, "Fuck you then, you'd better keep the tape running." There was only one choice, she had to get her wingman out of immediate danger and then take on these Bandits by herself. To late to run, and no time left for anything else.

"Deray Two. Check 90 right and call the visual. NOW!" Jiggy commanded on the radio. At the same time she thumbed the Weapons Mode switch forward to radar missile.

"Hustler, you've got the radar. Go to TWS. Keep the lock I've got and see if you can sort out this formation," she commanded.

"Will do," Hustler replied.

"Deray Two visual," she heard Grumpy say over the radio. Seeing that the Deray's would not hit each other, and Grumpy was out of immediate danger, she turned to put the bandits on her nose and concentrated on trying to find them visually.

"Deray Two, pitch back in trail, and look for spitters," She commanded Grumpy on the radio.

"Deray Two," Grumpy replied.

Hustler quickly sorted out the oncoming formation, "Bandit is in wedge a mile and a half, we've got the near man, the leader. Trailer is on the right. I can't get a lock on the trailer. You'll have to pick him up visually and go heat. You've got the radar back, I'm outside."

In a split second, Jiggy checked for an in-parameters shot and pressed the pickle button to fire a simulated AMRAAM missile at the lead bandit. "Fox Three, leader, nose nine miles," she announced over the radio.

She pushed the throttles up to Mil and began desperately scanning the sky to the right of the first bandit for his wingman. She could feel the hair beginning to stand up on the back of her neck. If she did not find him soon, she might get shot. Pulling the Weapon Mode switch back to heat she smiled when she heard the familiar growl of the infrared seeker on the AIM-9 missile. *Now we are in the hunt*, she thought.

Jiggy saw the leader when they were three miles apart by looking through the TD box in the HUD. Knowing the trailer was to the right and about two miles back, she started scanning there.

"Tally trailer!" She yelled into the intercom. Pushing down the coolie switch on the throttle, Jiggy bore sighted the AIM-9 seeker, and turned hard to put the second Bandit on the nose. Once she had the Bandit within the steering circle on the HUD, she uncaged the seeker and released the coolie switch. She immediately heard a good sharp growl and pressed the pickle button to fire an AIM-9 heat-seeking missile.

"Fox two, trail bandit. Nose four miles," she said triumphantly on the radio.

"Fox One, lead F-15, Wales, northeast bound," a clipped British accent intoned over Radio One.

"Fox Three Kill, Lead F-3 southwest bound Wales, Fox Two Kill trailer," Jiggy transmitted over Radio One.

"Very good, Deray. We thought we had the jump on you today. See you next time," the Brit replied, rocking his wings as they merged.

Whew, she thought to herself, *that took a bunch of brain bytes, after this the range will be a piece of cake.*

The whole engagement, from the pop to the fight with the Tornados had taken less than three minutes.

When Deray flight had returned to the squadron building, Jiggy debriefed the entire sortie from flight planning to landing for over two hours, longer than the flight itself. She covered all her mistakes and noted the mistakes of each crewmember, noting techniques to use to avoid those mistakes in the future. The only dirt she left out was Hustler's betrayal coming off target, when the RAF Tornados had jumped them. She silently let the tape speak for her feelings on the subject. Hustler had squirmed a bit in his chair while it had played, but did not say anything.

Even though Jiggy had covered every action, good and bad, when she finished Grumpy had gone over the whole sortie in detail again. In fact, she had felt pretty good about the flight on the way home. It had started roughly and the Tornados had been a heart stopping few minutes, but everything had worked and she had pulled it off. Somewhere in the second hour of Grumpy's rehashing she was beginning to convince herself that she had actually busted the flight. It seemed as if she had done nothing right and Grumpy noted every detail. How could she pass when she had made all those mistakes?

Feeling that slipping feeling again, she was a little shell-shocked when Grumpy finally said, "Any questions, comments?"

"No, that's all I have," she said glumly, thinking of the party scheduled to begin in about an hour. Now she did not want to go. It had been a very, very long day.

"Good, let's go find the Squadron Commander," Grumpy finished.

Jiggy got up in a haze, thinking that she might as well take her medicine now. She was still young, they would probably reschedule her check ride after some re-training. It was not the end of the world. Yet. Jiggy followed Grumpy out of the Briefing Room redoing her hair into the tight bun she wore at work.

Knocking on the squadron commander's office door Grumpy said, "Sir, you got a few minutes?"

"Sure, come on in," Lieutenant Colonel Brian "Stroker" Randleman said as he got up and came around his desk. "Sit down." He gestured at the couch and chairs on one side of his office.

"Thank you, sir, but I'll stand for a minute. First Lieutenant Jenny Goode had a Two Ship Flight Lead check ride today. The profile was combat mission planning on short notice, a rolling takeoff, trail departure, visual formation and low level ingress to the target area. The target attack was a 10 degree Pop for lead and a 20 degree high Pop for two, simulated conventional Mk-84 weapon delivery. Coming off target, the flight had planned air-to-air opposition from a flight of RAF Tornados, medium level egress to Wainfleet Range. The events there were two radar bomb deliveries, two visual deliveries and two 10-degree box patterns. The flight returned to the overhead pattern for the full stop." Grumpy Westin dispassionately briefed the commander on the profile of Jiggy's check ride.

Standing mutely during Grumpy's monologue, Jiggy looked down at the blue carpet on the floor. Blue was the squadron color and blue was absolutely everywhere, walls, carpet, stationary and even the t-shirts they wore on Friday. Becoming aware of the pause, she looked up; okay this is it she thought.

Grumpy continued, "We had a rocky start, with a few items that were debriefed, but the ride went well. Overall qualified. Exceptionally qualified in the areas of judgment and situational awareness."

Stroker reached for her hand, shaking it he said, "Congratulations, Lieutenant. Welcome to the club! We need another good Flight Lead."

After all the pain of waiting, plus the rendering she had received during the debrief, she was still in shock when Grumpy took her hand grinning. "Good on ya! Jiggy, I'll fly with you anytime, but next time I want a shot too."

"Thanks a lot," and after a slight pause, she shot back with a forced smile, "don't go blind next time." In the next moment she realized what he had said about the encounter with the Tornados being planned and it stunned her that Grumpy had set the whole thing up. "I figure you owe me the beer today."

"Okay, thanks for the debrief," Stroker said ushering them to the door, "I've got a little more work to clear up. See you guys at First Friday!"

Within an hour the halls and the Ready Room of the squadron were crowded with the families of the squadron crewmembers. Food piled along the bar, kids running around everywhere, and the music was more than a little loud. Knots of people were packed in the room engaged in earnest conversations. The spouses, in their brightly colored civilian clothes, stood out against the drab green bags of the aircrew. The First Friday of every month the squadron had an informal social get together of all the aircrew and their families, it was a great way to let off steam and keep everyone close as a squadron family.

Seeing Hustler and Pinto at the bar, Jiggy picked up her mug hanging from a peg on the wall. She poured a beer from the tap, and walked over to them.

"Hey Jiggy, sorry about the bounce in Wales today. I was specifically briefed by Grumpy not to assist," Hustler said when she got within earshot.

"Yeah, he told me to shut up before we merged with those guys," Pinto added.

"That's okay," Jiggy replied. "I know he set the whole thing up. What were you saying about flexibility before the brief?"

"Key to airpower!" chimed in Pinto on cue.

"But Jiggy, look at it this way. You did a great job on your own. You pulled it out today, and besides you passed," Hustler shrugged.

"Jiggy, I guess I owe you a beer don't I," Dweeb shouted at her as he squeezed through the crowd.

"Yeah, you do, loser boy," Jiggy replied with a nod, relief showing in her voice.

"Well, have one on me. My tap is right over there. In fact, have all you want. I feel generous tonight!" Dweeb waved as he made his way through the crowd on his way past the group.

"That's cheating, I pay for that beer too!" Jiggy yelled at his back.

"If you ain't cheatin, you ain't tryin!" Dweeb saluted her with his beer mug, and with a big grin, disappeared into the crowd.

In a couple of hours the food was all gone, the kids were eating ice cream and watching movies in the main briefing room. The noise in the Ready Room had quieted down somewhat and the time had come for the official words of the evening. Stroker got up on the small stage and cleared his throat loudly.

The background noise had dropped dramatically when a deep voice suddenly carried over the crowd. "Burn him, he's a witch" another heckler answered, "Stand up!"

Stroker raised his hands and waving them in front of his face said, "Okay, okay. It's good you comedians don't get paid to be funny, you'd starve!"

With a grin he launched into his speech.

"Ladies and gents, I'd like to thank ya'll for coming to the Mad-Hatters First Friday. We're a close family and I love seeing all of you and your kids! I know how trying the last few weeks have been and I understand the stress ya'll have been under. I just want you to know you've been doing a great job and I know that together we'll make it through these troubled times." Stroker paused, picked up the beer mug on the table behind him, took a sip, and put it carefully back down.

"I've got some announcements, but first I'd like to welcome a few special guests tonight. Please welcome Lieutenant Colonel Grumpy Westin, from USAFE/IG at Ramstien. He's attached to us now so you'll be seeing his face regularly. Not a pleasant thought." The room erupted in laughter at Grumpy's expense, Grumpy grinned, shifted his beer mug to his left hand, and waved to the crowd.

After the noise had died down, Stroker went on, "The other important person tonight is our newest Flight Lead Jiggy Goode. I hear she waxed a couple of tornados all by herself. Great start on the air-to-air Top Gun. Congratulations Jiggy!" Everyone in the crowd turned to look at her and began clapping. Jiggy immediately turned beat red, gave a small smile and a slight wave. With a sheepish grin she tried to blend into the crowd.

"I know ya'll are anxious to hear my announcements, so I'll make them quick. First, the good news, and then the bad. The good news is that our NATO Tactical Evaluation scheduled for next week is canceled," His next comments were drowned by a raucous cheer as all the green bags in the room raised their beers and shouted simultaneously.

"As I was saying, our deployment to Incirlik next month is also canceled." Again, another rousing cheer from the green bags drowned the room in noise.

"Finally on a more serious note. We will get a shot at defending our country," the crowd went suddenly silent, "and strike a blow deep into the lairs of the cowardly al-Qaeda terrorists. I'm sorry to say the bad news is for our families. I just received word a few hours ago that we will deploy the entire squadron Monday morning." By this time you could hear a pin drop in the room. Nearly eighty people in the room and the only sound was breathing, or the occasional clink as a glass was put on a table.

"I would like the senior leadership to stay behind for a few minutes. Everyone knows the drill. Please go home, pack your bags, get into crew rest, and wait for our call. Your most important job this weekend is to take care of your families." Suddenly he had a frog in his throat and concluded, "I'm sorry to break the news this way. Thank you all for coming tonight, and God Bless you."

6 October 2001
Farchor, Tajikistan

Taking charge, Captain Mark Goode said, "Sergeant Wilkerson, let's split up the men and cross load the equipment. Each man carries their basic load, plus a share of the team equipment."

Dave the CIA guy, interrupted. "Ummm, Captain. First off these are small mountain horses and they won't be able to carry those kinds of loads. In fact, each one of us is quite a load by itself. I brought enough horses so we can use a few as pack animals, it would be better to load the spare equipment on those animals. And please let's use first names, I'm Dave," he said, holding out his hand to shake Goode's. By this time the team had gathered around them in a tight clot by the side of the road.

"Okay, I'm fine with first names, but we're still in the Army. I'm Mark. This is Gary," pointing first to Sergeant First Class Wilkerson and then the rest of the team. "This is Mike, Tyrone, Ethan, our Dave, Luke and that's John-boy," Mark said, introducing his team.

"Good to know you guys. Like I said, I'll be your tour guide as we figure out what we're gonna do here. I'm also a speaker; the Afghani's speak Dari around here and Pashto in the southern region. Very few speak Arabic or Russian. So far we've been able to develop a pretty good relationship with the local Northern Alliance folks."

Waiving at the native with him he went on, "This is Johar, he's one of the NA dudes, he'll be our pathfinder. He speaks Russian. This part of Afghanistan is supposed to be under Northern Alliance control, but it is hostile country so we have to be careful all the time."

Scanning the small group he continued, "We have to use horses because the Taliban basically owns most of the roads. So we have to use the paths through the mountains. It'll take a few days to reach our AOR." Flashing a grin, his wire-rimmed glasses caught the sun. "I hope you guys like goat, because that's about all we have to eat."

Mollified, Mark said in a more cooperative tone, "Okay, Gary let's split the team gear for the four pack horses. Dave, we still need to carry our basic loads."

Dave paused by his horse, "Sure, I figured. You gotta do what you gotta do. Let's saddle up, I'd like to make a few miles before it gets dark."

Mark looked over his team, catching the eye of the communications man he said, "Our Dave make sure your sat radio is on top. We'll need to check in with mother when we stop. We'll miss the first commo, but I don't want to miss the second."

Mike spoke up, "Sir, I read the report the Ranchers put together, its FM 31-27. I've got a pretty good idea how to load these horses. Plus, they say it's not a good idea to wear your web gear, it'll tear the shit out of your back."

Mark nodded his head, "Good idea Mike, let's get it down."

The team immediately began organizing the equipment and loading it on the pack animals. Working as a team, they finished quickly. The horses were equipped with wooden saddles covered with bits of carpet. Each man, carrying his personal weapons, mounted their horses. Following Johar down the steep hillside towards the river, they soon found out the stirrups were to narrow for their combat boots. It was difficult to hold on.

Johar, an Afghani of medium height, was wrapped in a combination of western clothes, a dark colored turbine on his head, and what seemed like baggy pants made out of sheets. So many wrinkles lined his face that you could not easily see his eyes. Instead of a beard, he sported a scruffy, fuzzy face resembling an old porcupine, punctuated by a toothy grin missing more than a few teeth. Approaching the riverbank, he chose a shallow grade to make it easier for the horses as they descended to the river. With his horse in the water, he stopped and turned back to face the soldiers lined up behind him and grinned his toothy smile.

The soldiers slowed down and bunched up as the horses waited to ford the river. Squinting his eyes, Johar said in a barely audible, halting English, "Path smooth, water rough. Holes in bottom. If you are falling, get to side." His charges just looked at him without comment. They all followed silently when he started to wade through the Amu Darya River, separating Tajikistan and Afghanistan.

Sitting atop his horse at the back of the file, waiting his turn, Mark watched seven awkward Americans guide their horses through the ford. Some were holding both reigns out wide like they were driving a wagon, a few were holding the small pommel of the saddle, the reigns grasped tightly in their hands, others appeared almost frozen in place. All of them struggled to stay on their horses. He chuckled to himself, as they looked more like a comedy movie from Hollywood than a modern version of the US Cavalry. This will be a fun mission, he thought sardonically, as he spurred his horse forward into the water.

Twelve miles and four hours later they had crossed at least six stretches of the river and had finally reached the road leading out of the Northern Alliance town of Yangi Qal'efi in Badakhshan province. No one had fallen in and they didn't have any stragglers. He was no longer amused at the picture of the Three Stooges as Horse Cavalry. Mark's butt was sore and he was tired of the jostling and never ending pounding as his horse took each step.

He pulled out his map and measured nearly 40 miles to the front lines around Taloqan, and this would all be in the mountains. It would be night soon and fortunately they would have to stop soon. Looking back on their day, he realized that the team had been on the road for over 20 hours so far. Suddenly, he realized that he was extremely tired. They had rode on, or in, the full spectrum of conveyances. Starting in a twenty-first century airplane, they transferred to driving twentieth century trucks and now they were riding on nineteenth century four-footed transportation. At this rate, he thought, they would be on foot before long. Well, they were infantry and walking was what they did, but it was much slower than riding.

In less than an hour they came upon a clearing about halfway up the side of a 6,000 foot ridge. The ridge framed the southern side of the broad valley they had spent the last few hours crossing. Johar stopped and purposefully swung his body off the horse. He stood looking at the ragtag horsemen coming up the trail behind him. Without comment, he began preparing a line to hobble the horses alongside one edge of the clearing.

"No fire," he said as he took the reigns of the horse of the first man to ride in and tied it to the hobble rope.

"Gary, I guess we're staying here for the night." Mark pulled SFC Wilkerson aside and pointed up the hill, "Let's set an overwatch security up there on that rock outcropping. Have two men do a recon of the local area. We'll be stopping here for the night and we'll need to set a guard. I'd say two on hourly rotations, one in camp, the other on that rock would be enough. What do you think?"

"Yes, sir. I think two on would be fine. I'll have the man in the camp be the relief for the overwatch. What say we have the Rally Point be that large knob down the hill about two klicks?" Gary said. "I think if we get hit tonight it would probably be a small force. They'd be restricted to pretty much up and down the path or up hill. Anything bigger than a fire team would be hard to infiltrate without being noticed. It would be better to have a Rally Point that's close."

"Good idea. Post a man with a SAW to bivouac at both ends of the clearing. That way if we have to throw up a hasty defense we can have firepower at both ends of the trail and converging fires up and down slope," Mark agreed.

Two of the SF Troopers scouted out the surrounding terrain for a couple of klicks around the bivouac then climbed two klicks up the hill. They paused for a few minutes, scanning down slope with binoculars for movement, and tell tale dust trails. On the way back down, one of them, Mike, settled on the rock outcropping that Mark and Gary had noted when they arrived. He arranged his MP-4 weapon, checked the batteries in his PVS-7 night vision goggles and scanned the countryside with his BN-5 low light binoculars. The moon illumination would be low tonight, but the sky was crystal clear. The stars by themselves provided plenty of light; it was so bright up here in the mountains you could almost see with the naked eye. Crisp and clear, it would be a cold night. With his night vision binoculars it would be easy to pick up any movement. After satisfying himself that he could respond to any initial threat and surveillance the terrain around the team, he spoke into the boom microphone attached to his ear.

"All clear," Mike said.

"Copy, let us know if you see anything. Ethan will be on the radio down here and will relieve you in an hour," Gary answered back.

Mark went over to the area where the pack animals were unloaded and helped Dave, the SF Trooper setup the LST-5 satcom radio. After spreading the mesh dish antenna, he pulled his compass out and arranged the azimuth of the antenna so that it would point at the commo satellite they would be using tonight. Dave picked up the antenna coax cable and attached it to the connector on the front of the radio.

Mark chuckled to himself as he worked on the radio, "Hey Dave, since this CIA guy's name is Dave, just like you, what say we call you OD? Just to keep you guys straight."

"Yeah, thanks Cap'n. I can see we look alike and you might get confused. Do I have a choice? My signal strength is a little low, could you rotate the dish up a few degrees?" Dave answered dryly.

"Yeah, you guys even sound alike. Maybe you were brothers in a previous life," Mark joked as he adjusted the elevation of the antenna.

"Sure, sir. Have your fun. You know we just laugh at your jokes cause you're the officer," Dave shot back.

Mark called mother back in Dushanbe to check in, he made a note to himself about setting up a resupply scheme with Dave. They would be fine for a couple of weeks, but then they would start to run out of consumables like batteries and water tabs, and food. If MREs could be considered food.

Mark looked around and saw Johar, wrapped in a blanket, eating a dinner of bread he pulled from under his western suit coat. The others in his team were settling down with MREs and their sleeping bags.

He made a quick tour of the camp, checking to see if everyone was ready to react if they were hit, and if the equipment was secure for the night. He spread his Gore-Tex covered polypro sleeping bag, pulled off his Hi-Tec boots, and slid part way into his bag. Over a Ham MRE he looked around and the thought occurred to him that for all of the technology the Army fielded these days, all of the men had web gear, boots and sleeping bags from Brigade Quartermasters. Government issue lowest bidder stuff just did not hack it in the boonies. *Ain't capitalism great* he thought, tonight he was gonna be warm and dry courtesy of civilian technology. In a few minutes he heard several of the men snoring. Making sure his own NOGs and weapons were readily available he burrowed into his bag.

Over the Black Sea

"Ready, Ready, disconnect now," Captain Skip Arnold transmitted over the radio as he simultaneously pressed the air refuel disconnect switch with his thumb. Pulling power slightly on two engines, he started to drop aft of the KC-135R tanker. In the cloudless night sky 100 miles west of Butumi, Georgia the gray tanker slowly pulled away from the big, black shadow that was the B-2 '*Spirit of Atlanta.*'

"Thirty-two thousand," said the disembodied voice of the tanker co-pilot over the radio.

Skip dropped the nose slightly to descend to 1,000' below the tanker's altitude. Reaching his new altitude he turned to put the next waypoint on the nose and engaged the autopilot and auto-throttles. Tonight, the '*Sprit of Atlanta*' was called Tyro 32. Having just completed its pre-strike refueling it would soon be feet dry on its way to attack their assigned targets in Afghanistan.

"Your jet," he said to the Mission Commander, Major Slim Williams.

"No, you keep it. Here's the comm card. Handle the radio too would ya? I want to confirm the targets and programming," Slim replied.

He pulled the left bayonet of his oxygen mask, releasing the mask so he could feel the cool air of the cockpit against his face. Still nervous when he was watching someone else fly the airplane, especially close to another airplane, he wiped his face with the back of his glove. They had already been in the air, about fourteen hours now. It was all a bit of a blur to him. Shifting his weight around, he put his feet on the rudders and pushed hard until his legs were shaking from the strain of his muscles. It was not that he was sleepy or anything, just really tired of sitting for so long. Relaxing, he shifted in his ACES II ejection seat again. He understood that the seat had to be firm so he wouldn't hurt his back during an ejection, but sitting here for most of a whole day was, well, a pain in the butt.

Skip said, "We're good for our first TOT in Gardez."

"Yeah. I'll get a patch map when we go feet dry and check the system. Then I'll double check the release program."

Slim pulled up the Armament Control page on the avionics display in front of him and checked the release program for each of the 16 JDAM weapons they carried. Each one was a standard Mk-84 2,000 pound bomb. With a GPS guidance package on the back, it was technically a GBU-31, but everyone referred to it a JDAM. Almost as accurate as the Laser Guided versions of the Mk-84, the aircraft system was able to inject target coordinates into the bomb's guidance brain before bomb release. In Air-to-Ground mode, the bomb under the pickle button was updated with the target coordinates of the designated target and each successive bomb/target set would automatically update in turn.

Once a target was designated, the aircraft would present steering cues for the crew to follow to get the aircraft in position in space to drop the weapon. This should allow enough reserve energy for the guidance package to correct the flight path of the bomb on the way to the target. If Slim left the autopilot engaged, the aircraft would fly to the release point and then, if he was pressing the pickle button, the bomb would automatically release when the system decided it was in parameters. The real trick was making sure the aircraft navigation system was tight and had minimal errors.

Confirming that the program setting the parameters and release order of each bomb was correct he looked outside and said to Skip, "Good to go. Where are we?"

"We're getting close to Baku," Skip replied.

"Great, I'll get a patch map of the oil fields there and see if the system has drifted any," Slim said, suddenly tired after all. With two ring laser gyroscopes and integrated GPS position it was unlikely the inertial navigation system aboard the B-2 had drifted more than a few feet since takeoff.

"I think I'll have something out of one of the box lunches. You want something?" Slim asked.

"Yeah, I'll take a soda and a bagel if there are any left," Skip said

"You bet," Slim said as he got up and squeezed between his seat and the center pedestal to reach their stash of food and drink just aft of the forward crew station. The good thing was that they would not have to fly back to the States after their strike. All they had to do was fly south to Diego Garcia in the Indian Ocean. A piece of cake!

"Magic, Tyro 32." Skip intoned on the radio, hearing no response he said again, "Magic, Tyro 32, uniform."

"Tyro 32, theeese ess Magik. Authenticate Bravo X-ray." A deep European accent replied to his second radio call. Skip had never been in Europe and could not tell whether it was a German, a Dutchman, or a Belgique. He did know that NATO AWACS were supplying the E-3 radar surveillance for the northern part of the Afghani operation.

"Tyro 32 has Juliet," Skip answered, making sure to check the time, he read the authentication letter from the columns of the comm card. They had checked a lot of crypto before takeoff and he wanted to be sure he had the right time group.

"Rogair, Tyro. You are cleared. Zee airspace is green. Check out on zis frequency outbound. You may strangle your parrot," the controller aboard the NATO E-3 radioed to Tyro 32.

Approaching their turn point in eastern Turkmenistan the big aircraft slowly dropped its right wing, silently turning south. Their pre-initial point was the town of Gereshk about 60 miles west northwest of Kandahar. East of Kandahar was the IP, a dry lake known as Lake Moqor, at the southwest end of a valley with Gardez in the northeast end.

Passing the IP, Slim turned on the radar again. He wanted a quick patch map of the Y road intersection southeast of Ghanzi to check the system before the first leg of their target attack pattern. A few seconds later with a good map he switched off the radar transmitter.

They had a hard Time on Target for their first target at Gardez. For the rest of their targets they had planned a racetrack delivery hitting Kabul, Bagram Airbase, circling back to Ghanzi and then Gardez again. In all it would take about four laps to hit all the targets they had planned for the night.

Glancing at the Up Front Controller that displayed Zulu time, Skip said,

"We're on time over the IP. Tape is coming on." To avoid confusion, Air Force guys worldwide used the time at the Greenwich Observatory in England. He also wanted to film the entire attack.

Slim reached up to punch the mode button, without looking at Skip he said, "Master Arm on. System's pretty tight, drifting south about two feet. We're in Air-to-ground. Radar's off."

"Copy. Autopilot's on and we're in auto delivery mode. RWR is clean. I've got a good picture," Skip replied, looking at the IR image of the target through the aircraft sensors.

Verbalizing for the tape, Slim said, "Looks like we've got a good designation. One minute out."

"Thirty seconds."

"Ten seconds. Good Steering."

"Five seconds. I'm on the pickle button."

With a small jolt felt throughout the aircraft, the bomb bay doors flew open on the bottom of the aircraft. Less than a second later the bomb release charges fired, shaking the airplane with a larger jolt and shoving the JDAM down below the slipstream. Shortly thereafter the bomb bay doors slammed shut again.

"Bomb's gone. We're sequencing to the next target," Slim said.

CHAPTER 4

7 October 2001
Red Sea, between Egypt and Saudi Arabia

Eight bodies, wrapped in coats and blankets, huddled against the cold wind whipping through the un-pressurized AC-130H droning south through the night sky. Windy, noisy, and dark inside the Spooky, the Red Sea glittered serenely below. Some of the people were trying to sleep, others were just thinking about what lay ahead. The cockpit door at the front of the plane opened spilling light into the cabin; one man slipped through and closed it behind him. He stopped outside the closed door and pulled two yellow foam plugs out of the zippered pocket on his left arm. Looking absently around, he rolled one and then the other, inserting them in his ears. Pausing briefly at the Battle Management Station, he watched the only crewman awake play a new color game boy. After a moment went on, yawning, he passed the 105mm gun mount hulking in the semi-dark.

Picking his way over sprawled bodies, he stopped at an open spot. Stretching out his sleeping bag he sat down on it, pulled off his boots and crawled in. The back of the airplane was quiet again. They were on their last leg deploying to Qatar and would have to fly most of the way down the Red Sea before being able to cut across Saudi Arabia. It was still several hours before they could land at the smaller Arab country jutting into the Persian Gulf.

A long flight from Florida, empty MRE bags and drink cans littered the floor of the aircraft. They had not stopped for more than fuel anywhere along the way and the plane showed it.

In the cockpit of the gunship, Jason was in the co-pilots seat. He had pushed the seat all the way back and angled it as far back as it would go. His feet were propped up on little rails at the bottom of the instrument panel; he was relaxed and not just a little bored. Slowly, he looked around at the other crewmembers in the cockpit.

To his left, the Aircraft Commander was sprawled in his seat, pushed back like his. The pilot, Lieutenant Colonel Mickey Saloman, had his head flung back on the seat back, his mouth wide open and his eyes closed. Saloman was a crusty vet of the gunship mission, two inches short of six feet; he was skinny and a bit drawn. His nickname was Skeletor, and he had served in Spectres for nearly twenty years. Jason had flown with Skeletor for quite awhile and had heard Saloman's Panama story at least a hundred times over.

Behind him the Flight Engineer was slumped over his desk, his back rhythmically moving up and down. Obviously asleep, Jason was glad he could not hear him snoring.

Except for a spotlight on the navigator near the door, the rest of the cockpit was dark with only the multi-colored panel lights of the instruments for illumination. The navigator had his feet propped on his little desk, reading a novel in a pool of yellow light.

After scanning the cockpit he began wondering about Egypt, he looked out the right window at the coastline. Orienting himself, he saw a concentration of lights at the town of Al Qusayr and thought he could just make out the lights of Luxor. He loved history and somewhere out there, hidden by darkness, was the Temple of Luxor and a collection of ruins dating back 3400 years. The Temple was dedicated to the Egyptian King of the Gods. Others were built by dynasties, or conquerors down through the ages, from Rames II who fought in Syria to Alexander the Great who subjugated lands as Far East as Afghanistan.

The irony occurred to Jason, he was passing Egypt, the western shoulder of Alexander's campaign to conquer most of the known world, heading to fight in Afghanistan, the eastern shoulder of Alexander's conquests. Alexander had fought in Kabul and entered Tajikistan through Kunduz, where he married the daughter of one his vanquished foes. Almost seamlessly, he started thinking of Jenny Goode, again.

Wondering where Jenny was tonight, he figured she was probably on her way to Afghanistan herself. He wondered what she would say, even more than that, what he might say if their paths crossed again.

Things were different now, everything was different from the last time they had seen each other. Since September 11, everything had changed. Some of his friends were fire fighters in Manhattan, some worked in the financial district. Several people he knew hadn't made it out of the inferno. Those that did seemed haunted, they all walked around in a daze.

His dad was the worst of all. His father's office was in one of the towers. He had not been there that morning, and ever since, he had been, well, lost. His dad was the kind of guy that had always been in charge, always had an answer, and always knew what was going to happen next. Only now, he didn't.

Jason was a New Yorker; he had spent plenty of time on the streets of the Upper East Side. He knew people were always working some kind of fraud for themselves, which is just the way life was. But now, everything was different. It was like his vision had suddenly cleared, or at least he saw things differently. He used to see people and things as bumpers, like those ancient pinball games in arcades. Everything and everyone was an obstacle to overcome or chart a path around. His time in the Air Force and flying were governed by that philosophy. Only now that did not seem to work anymore. People were more earnest, more considerate, or something. He was not sure what it was. It was not like being mad; maybe it was more like being pissed off, mad and single-minded at the same time.

At a loss to figure out what he would say, he concluded that if saw Jenny in Qatar he would probably just say hey. It would not do to let her know how much he thought of her. It would be better to talk about everyday stuff. Follow her lead, maybe she had changed, maybe she thought about him too. Who knows, maybe it would not happen.

"Jiddah Center, Spooky 23," Jason called on the radio as the big turboprop passed the Ra's Banas peninsula. Rolling the airplane into a left turn, direct to the east coast of Saudi Arabia, he wanted to make sure they were in radio contact before going feet dry in Saudi.

"Roger, Spooky 23, Jiddah copies you. Turn now 095 degrees and cleared direct Riyadh," the Jiddah center controller replied.

"Direct Riyadh, Spooky 23," Jason typed in the identifier for Riyadh VORTAC in the handheld GPS on the dashboard and then twisted the heading knob of the HSI heading bug to the new ground track. They had two good INS systems on board, but neither of them had a database of standard navigational aids and waypoints. It was easier to use a commercial GPS than to type in the coordinates in the INS.

Feeling the movement, the pilot, Skeletor Saloman, stirred, sat up and wiped his face with his hands. Blinking and looking around for a minute, his eyes settled on Jason, "Hey, where are we? We should be in Saudi by now."

"Yep, we're direct Riyadh right now, about 50 miles out."

"Great, I'll take the radio. Who are we talking to?" Skeletor asked.

"Riyadh Center. You've got the airplane. I've got to take a piss, back in a minute."

"Sure, no worries. Hey, wake up the engineer on the way out would you?" Skeletor finished.

"Hey, Martin. Martin," Jason said as he shook Sergeant Erdmann's, shoulder. "Wake up, bud. We're getting close."

"Humph, thanks for nothing," Erdmann replied, sitting up and rubbing his eyes.

Stepping down the stairs from the cockpit level he opened the door to what would be the cargo bay in a normal C-130. Instead, what greeted him was a semi-dark tube with lumps of sleeping bags, luggage on the floor and the big 105mm gun sticking out of the left side of the fuselage into the air stream. It's loud out here, he thought, as he turned left for the head.

Back in the cockpit, a few minutes later, he adjusted the seat to his favorite flying position. Getting close, there was no more time to relax. "What's up?" he asked.

"Riyadh just switched us over to Dawhah control, we'll be landing soon. Pull out the approach plate and see if you can get ATIS," Skeletor replied.

"You bet," Jason replied.

"Altimeter 30.14, VFR, north flow," Jason said after listening to the radio for a few seconds. "Do you want the TACAN approach or do you want to do a visual?"

"It's getting pretty light. I'd be happy with the visual, but just in case let's load the approach points in the INS. Does this place have a VASI or any glide slope guidance?" Skeletor answered.

"No VASI or anything. Just runway lights," Jason replied as he began typing in the coordinates of each point on the approach plate into the INS system.

"Spooky 23, Dawhah Control. Airport is 12 o'clock 18 miles. You are cleared visual approach runway 33," the Qatar approach controller said.

"Roger, cleared the visual 33, Spooky 33," Jason replied.

"Those guys sure don't want to work too hard getting us lined up do they?" he said as an aside to Skeletor.

"Nope, I'd hate to rely on these guys in bad weather. Lazy ain't the word. You'd be better off making it up for yourself," Skeletor agreed.

"I'll steer you to the waypoint before the FAF so you can get lined up," Jason said.

"Okay, good. Hey, Jason. Keep me posted on glide path. If you see me going low, sing out. I don't want to drag it in."

"No worries. I'm with ya. I'll just call out the altitudes on the TACAN approach," Jason finished.

The Herc descended on short final and Jason called out, "MDA."

"Landing," replied Skeletor. He started pulling back the throttles and lifted the nose slightly to check the descent rate.

"One hundred feet. On speed, descent rate 600," Jason said.

Skeletor refrained from making another check in the descent rate and the result was a rather firm landing. *Well at least we will not have to wake anyone up*, he thought.

With the four-engine turbo-prop rapidly slowing down, Skeletor had the rollout out under control, Skeletor called, "Flaps up, After Landing Checklist."

Clearing the active runway Jason began running the checklist and called ground control, "Ground, Spooky 23 clear of 33 on Alpha."

"Spooky, turn left on the parallel taxiway. Follow the follow-me to parking," the ground controller replied.

"Spooky, tally the truck," Jason said as they saw the small white truck speeding toward them on the taxiway.

On the ground, the crewman in the back of the plane, open to the outside, were assaulted by an admixture of smells. The air had a tinge of salt air, leavened with the sickly sweet aroma of less than sanitary human occupation, but the dominant aroma was the overriding tang of raw oil, pumped from the ground. The smell drifting through the fuselage acted like a spur, suddenly all the dormant bodies sprang into activity. In a whirl, sleeping bags were packed, clothes put away, and piles of luggage rearranged. Trash bags for all the junk on the floor were passed around.

The Follow-Me vehicle, an old Toyota pickup truck with a flashing light bar on top, led the gunship on a circuitous route across the ramp. First they passed a very busy cargo area packed with a collection of C-141s, C-5s, and C-17s; K-Loaders and forklifts scurrying between them like curious ants. Next they trundled by a parking area for regular C-130s. Followed by a very large display of Blackhawk and MH-53 Helicopters. A long stretch of fighters, F-16s, another of A-10 Warthogs, and finally 40 plus F-15E Strike Eagles. Four AC-130H's of their squadron occupied the last bit of open ramp area at the far end.

Seeing the gunships that had departed earlier, Jason said aloud, to no one in particular. "Hey, our bud's are at the end of the ramp. I guess that's gonna be home for a while. Man it looks like an airshow here, I've never seen such a collection of hardware on any one ramp."

The Navigator replied, "Oh, yeah. It looks like Career Day back at Mather in the old days. What a party that was!"

Yeah, thought Jason, *a party. With all those Strike Eagles, maybe Jenny was here after all.* They all had a big "SJ" on the tail, except for a few with "MH." He was still trying to figure out what base they were from, as Skeletor taxied the airplane into the hardstand, grabbing the brakes roughly as he stopped.

The Flight Engineer said, "I hope they have our Temper Tent Hilton ready. I've got this strange buzzing my head and the floor still seems to be moving."

"Yeah, the Temper Hyatt, complete with room service!" shot back the Navigator. "As long as it has air conditioning, I'm happy."

"A regular resort hotel, nothing but the best for our troops," Skeletor added.

New York City, New York

Heavy afternoon traffic crowded Highway 169 barely allowing room for a large gray tractor trailer rig pulling a rusty shipping container trying to make its way north from the Ocean Terminal in Bayonne, New Jersey. The big truck signaled a left turn onto I-78 as it pushed its way through the unyielding clot of homebound cars crowding the New Jersey Turnpike Extension. Slowly accelerating, the truck blended into the traffic. Crossing the river bridge it changed lanes again, moving into the right lane to join the southbound traffic on I-95. Thirty minutes later, the truck exited I-95 in Milltown, New Jersey.

Slowly winding through an old industrial area, the engine clattering loudly at high rpm as the driver kept it in a low gear, the rig finally turned into a dilapidated abandoned parking lot.

The sun was long gone as a dirty white Ford Econoline van followed the tractor-trailer into the poorly lit lot. It stopped, cut its lights and the engine. Two men, dressed in dark clothes, got out and walked towards the rig. As they approached, the drivers door popped opened and a plump, slightly balding man in his mid-fifties climbed down from the cab. About three days from needing a shave, he was an indeterminate time away from a bar of soap. Heavyset, he stood grimly in front of the rig with his feet spread out, waiting for the two men; his right hand in his jacket pocket. As they walked closer he decided to speak first.

"Hey, yoose guys. Where you from? Wha'd d ya want?"

"Hey, yourself. You have a delivery for us. I'm sure you were expecting us, we're just here to pick it up," the taller one said. Both were dressed alike in jeans, one wore a blue Member's Only jacket and the other had on a dark brown leather jacket. They both wore short curly hair and close cropped beards.

"Yeah, maybe, I do and maybe I don't," the driver replied. "Thing is, I expect to be paid in front. Ya, don't get credit here," the driver said through a toothless grin.

Stepping forward into the dim light created by the distant street light, the smaller of the two spoke for the first time, "Hold on, man. We want to see our stuff first!"

"Bullshit, pal. Don't fuck with me. It's my way or the highway, asshole. You're just a couple of stinkin' ragheads," growled the driver, thrusting his pocketed hand forward and moving threateningly towards the two. "I don't want your stuff, but you don't pay, it's mine, kapiesch?"

Backing up slightly, his hands spread out in a non-threatening gesture, the taller man tried to be conciliatory, "Okay, okay. No trouble. Let's just do it and get it over with. But we are Pakistani, we are not Arabs." Tapping the smaller one on the arm he added, "Ali give him the envelope."

Ali pulled a bulging letter sized manila envelope from the left pocket of his jacket and handed it to the driver.

The driver stepped forward and snatched it from his hand, "Yeah, just the same, it better be all here. Yoose don't mind if I just check it do ya?"

"No, just get it over with."

"It looks okay, 25 bills. You boys are okay by me. Let's go to the back, you first." The driver followed them around to the rear. Keeping them at arm's length, he unlocked the latch. Lifting the bar and then rotating it, he opened the door. The interior of the shipping container was filled with boxes of different shapes and markings, as well as packing material to keep the boxes from shifting.

"Two five foot boxes. They're there on the right about two boxes back. Hurry up. I ain't got all night," the driver said. Stuffing the envelope in the inside of his jacket, he looked at the two men scrambling inside the shipping container. They both had a self-satisfied grin plastered across their faces. The driver watched the two, thinking in disgust, this is too easy, fuckin' rug merchants and rag heads, they don't pay enough for this shit.

"Ali, they are here. Move that big box and we can get them out of the trailer," the taller man said as he spotted his objective. "Driver, would you help pull these boxes out?"

"Wha'dya think I look like? A stevedore, I'm a driver, you knucklehead. It ain't in my contract," the driver sneered.

"Sorry, do not worry," the taller man said.

The two Pakistanis pulled the boxes to the rear of the container. Stepping down the taller man said, "Ali, I will go and open the rear door of the van. Stay here."

After opening both rear doors of the van, he trotted back to the trailer and grasped the end of one of the boxes.

"Ali, pick up that end and we shall move the box to the van."

After the Pakistanis had closed the doors on their cargo, the driver watched them drive away before he moved. He pulled a new customs seal out of his pocket and calmly clipped it on the container lock. Then with a stamp, he squeezed the lead seal, counterfeiting a new seal. Climbing back into his truck he muttered to himself, "Fuckin' worthless rag heads. Good riddance."

Pulling back onto I-95 the grubby white Ford van negotiated traffic headed north back towards New York. The taller man, Bakhtiar Yamin, drove the van along with traffic; he had no desire to attract attention to himself. In the back of the van, Ali Zablah used a can of white spray paint to cover the exhaust parts label and the addressee. Using a template, he used black paint to put another label on with a new address and shipping details.

Still on I-95, the van crossed the Hudson River, exited the freeway and turned north on Broadway. It was late evening and there was very little traffic headed into the city, Bakhtiar thought this was the best time to drive through Manhattan; virtually no cabs. Turning on 187th Street he stopped at the curb before a small shop with a hand lettered sign above the door, "Rugs to Riches." He honked the horn twice and then both he and Ali got out of the van; he carefully locked it behind him.

The lights in the interior of the shop came on, a short man dressed in dark slacks, and a dark red shirt came to the door. He stepped out of the door and squinted into the night. It was Naji Fakhim; the New York end of the Frankfurt based family rug import/export business. Seeing the white van at the curb, he stepped out onto the sidewalk.

"Naji, we have picked up new rugs. All of them are here. Come we need to unload them." Bakhtiar said as he unlocked the rear door and opened it. The coppery light of a street lamp revealed ten rolled carpets, five to ten feet long and two wood boxes.

Naji, a rather nervous man, asked him, "Yes, yes. You are late. Was the traffic bad? Did you make all the pickup stops?"

"I said there were no problems. We made all the stops. Now open the door, or help us carry these rugs," Bakhtiar replied brusquely.

"Yes, Yes. I will open the door. There should be some good rugs in this new shipment. Some Afghan, some Bukhara, and some magnificent Tabriz. Very good, very good. We will do well with this shipment. I shall get the door," Naji said as he turned and held the door open.

"Ali, first we will take the wood boxes," Bakhtiar said.

Waving his hands Naji said, "Yes, yes. Those should go to the very back. Those are special. Have a care Bakhtiar, and take them to the very back of the shop."

Ali and Bakhtiar carried the last rug into the shop with Naji following close behind. Naji said, "I shall make some tea. You have worked hard. I shall make some tea. Come and have some tea."

He sat down on his favorite rug and poured three small cups of tea for his protégés. Sitting down as well, Bakhtiar took two lumps of sugar from a bowl next to the teapot and put them in his glass. Picking up a spoon, he stirred the sugar into the tea, tapped the spoon on the side of the glass and took a tentative sip.

"Very good tea. I just got it from India. It is fresh, it is very good," Naji said.

"It is fine. We must deliver the new carpets, have you called the buyer? Does he know they are in town?" Bakhtiar asked.

"Yes, yes. The buyer knows and will pick them up tomorrow. I have already received half the money. The rest will be paid on delivery. They are happy, they will pay," Naji replied.

"That is well. What time will they come tomorrow?"

"First thing. They will be here at seven. Have you opened the boxes? Did you pay the agreed amount to the driver?" Naji asked.

"Yes, I paid him what we agreed. First thing. That is good." Bakhtiar nodded, "I have no interest of what is inside and neither should you."

The morning traffic on the streets of New York were already busy when, just before seven, a U-Haul GMC step van pulled up to the rug shop on 187th Street. A colorful picture of the Space Shuttle painted on the side, it blended in with local traffic. Waiting in front of the shop for a place next to the curb, the driver flashed the bird every time someone honked a horn. After 15 minutes, a man left the shop next door to the rug merchant, got in his parked car and left an open spot for the step van. After parking, two Arabic men dressed in jeans, running shoes and leather bomber jackets got out of the step van.

The front door bell jangled as the two men walked in the shop. Smiling the first one said, "You are Fakhim, the shop owner."

"Yes, Yes. I am Fakhim. I am known as Naji. I am Naji Fakhim. And I am the owner of this fine shop. We sell fine imported rugs from all over the world. Perhaps you are interested in a rug?" Naji said anxiously. He had been the US outlet for his brothers smuggling ring for years, dealing with all sorts of people.

But he had never gotten used to it. The more nervous he got the more he talked, the more he talked, the faster he talked as well.

"We are here for our carpets. I am sure you were expecting us. I believe our carpets are boxed and ready for shipment," One of the men said curtly.

"Yes, yes. I am expecting you. We have your carpets. They just arrived last night. They are in the back of the shop. They are boxed and all ready for you to pick up. We have just one little thing. You see the delivery charges for the rugs have not been paid. Plus, there was a tax on importation. Usually for special orders, this is already done, but this time, it was not. This wasn't taken care of, we paid this tax out of our own pocket." Naji dithered.

Abdul Saleem, the man who had spoken first, stepped closer to Fakihm and said coarsely, "I was told everything was taken care of. All has been paid. What is this about a tax?"

Naji spread both hands in front of him, in a slightly higher pitched voice he said, "It is nothing really. It is just that sometimes shipments come in from overseas and it costs more tax than anticipated to get through customs." He looked up at them slowly, "Such is the case with your carpets."

Abdul looked around the room, he saw Bakhtiar and Ali lounging in the back of the store, flicking his head abruptly towards Naji he spat, "I see, you want more money? How much?"

"I do not want to offend you, it is not that I want more money. It is simply that these things cost money, sometimes more than planned. You have bought carpets before, yes? Then you know that sometimes it costs more and sometimes it costs less."

Frustrated Abdul squirmed, "Fine, fine. How much are you talking about? Just tell me."

Seeing that he had won the upper hand of the negotiations, Naji smiled.

"It is a simple matter of 3,000 dollars for the importation tax. Plus 8,000 dollars for each carpet. Not much. All in cash. You see nothing really." Naji folded his hands and looked innocently at Abdul.

Turning to his companion, Abdul said, "Tariq, go back to the truck and get the money this rug merchant wants. Quickly, traffic is building, it is getting late."

"Won't you have some tea?" Naji asked, "Please sit down and have some tea. I have just brewed some fresh. It is very good tea, just in from India. You will like it."

"No. I do not want tea. Give us our rugs and we will go."

"Yes, Yes. I understand. Bakhtiar and Ali will load your carpets for you. There is always time for tea. I shall pour you a cup. Please sit down," Naji said.

"Bakhtiar, load the boxes for our honored customer. He has decided to take these beautiful carpets."

Naji counted the money as Tariq handed it to him, "Very good, very good. You have very good tastes in rugs. I would be pleased to do business with you again. Perhaps you would like to see some Afghan wools that we got in yesterday as well."

Abdul got up abruptly, "No more rugs, old man. We must go." Turning he briskly walked out of the shop with his companion close behind.

Kabul, Afghanistan

Wispy white clouds carved scrimshaw shapes in an electric blue sky arching over Kabul. Deepening into late afternoon, a blue Toyota Land Cruiser drove quickly through the tan city. Crunching small rocks on the crumbling paved road in front of the building, the Toyota pulled up outside the Afghan Air Authority Building. Ahmed Mustapha, the rear seat passenger, finished gathering his papers together. Waiting outside the door, his driver and bodyguard stood silently surveying the street. Halfway out of the car Mustapha paused when he heard a strange clicking noise that pierced the background noise of the street. He straightened up and felt a rush of wind. The clicks were much louder and closer together.

Confused, Mustapha's driver turned toward the sky, drawn to where the noise might be coming from. A fraction of a second later a 2,000 pound JDAM GBU-31, guided by satellite GPS signals and dropped by an unseen American B-1 bomber, struck the roof of the Air Authority. Penetrating two floors in a fraction of a second it exploded when it hit the bottom floor.

The leading edge of the supersonic shockwave from the bomb's approach and violent impact simultaneously blew out the windows and doors of the building, shredding everything on the street with shattered glass and splinters. The brick walls of the building bulged perilously outward, spewing a dense cloud of dust though the broken windows. A fraction of a second, later the Tritinol explosive, buried within the bomb itself, exploded in a thunder of flame and deafening sound. Mixing metal bomb fragments and bits of the building itself creating another wave of destruction, concealing a lethal shower of bricks, mortar, shards of wood and jagged broken glass inside the ochre dust cloud spreading outward from the Air Authority building. Tearing through the building the explosive shock wave destroyed nearly everything in its path.

In a relentless march of physics, the force of the outward blast had spent itself in less than a second and the displaced air that pushed in front of the shockwave reversed course and rushed back to fill the void. The incredibly violent push/pull of the explosion was too much for the building's steel internal structure. The structure simply collapsed, leaving a pile of rubble surrounded by jagged walls of concrete cinder block.

Mustapha and his men saw nothing of this. To them the exploding bomb was sound, followed closely by a gust front that threw them to the ground. The huge cloud of dust and debris covered their crumpled forms as they lay on the street, in front of what had been a large, modern building.

Several minutes passed, silently filling the void left by the explosion of violence. If there had been anyone left to look upon the scene at that moment, they could not have believed there were any survivors. Mustapha slowly shook off his blanket of debris, with discomfort came the realization that he was alive. He sat up in what had been a busy street. He quickly felt his legs and then, with his hands, he made a quick inventory to check everything else. Finding everything intact, he rose unsteadily to his feet to survey the damage.

Confused, Mustapha stared blankly; it took everything he could do to keep his mind on the present. After the intense pain and noise of the blast, he could not figure out why everything was silent now. Without comprehension, he looked slowly around, everything was a light orange, covered in dust, including the jagged walls of what had been the Air Authority Building. Feeling something on his face, he wiped his face with his sleeve. He looked at his arm and noticed it streaked with blood, his blood. He was bleeding from the nose and ears; his eardrums blown out and it would be quite a while before he would hear again.

Mustapha took a step, catching himself he almost stumbled on the rubble covering the street. He did not have to go far before he found what was left of his driver and bodyguard, lying next to the twisted wreckage of the car. The car and his men took the brunt of the blast, protecting him from the disintegration of the building. He looked where the building had been. It was destroyed, nothing left that looked like a man made structure. Nothing else stirred in the silence, he felt that he might be the only one left alive. Growing in his mind was a tidal wave, an obsession, he could think of only one thing—to get away. Without a backward glance, or any other concern, he staggered down the street as fast as he could go.

The explosion shocked Ahmed Youseff, enjoying his lunch, a mile and a half away, in the Char Chata Bazaar. With everyone else in the bazaar, he had turned in confusion toward the source of the intense sound and fury. They all saw a rising cloud of dust and smoke coming from the direction of the old US Embassy. Not knowing what had happened he sat stunned next to his food.

The citizens of Kabul were nervous, there had been explosions since yesterday, outside the city limits. However, this was the first bomb to have dropped on the city itself and for a brief moment, no one knew what might be the next. Americans had been bombing Bagram airbase and surface-to-air weapons sites, but so far, nothing inside the city had been hit.

Youseff wondered what the target had been. Perhaps it had been an error, perhaps is was a bomb that fell short. So far, Mustapha's predictions of which targets would be struck by the Americans were coming true. When nothing else happened, gradually the silence was filled by people taking the time to breath again. He returned to his lunch and his companions, the panic of the moment gone.

Fifteen minutes after the explosion, Youseff had settled into his lunch, and the Bazaar was reaching a standard noise level. His cell phone rang; picking it up he answered seriously, "Hello, Hello."

On the other end, an excited voice was talking loud, fast and non-stop. After a few seconds, Youseff had not been able to wedge a word in when he realized that it was Mustapha and that he would not stop talking.

From snatches of what Mustapha was yelling, Youseff finally realized he had probably been in or near the explosion. Hanging up the phone, he got up at once, saying to his companions, "We must go. The Air Authority has been destroyed."

Driving north on Bibimahro Street, Youseff strained to see the Afghan Air Authority building. The dust had cleared, but all he could make out were jagged walls and rubble where the building had been. They had made the Afghan Air Authority building their unofficial headquarters in Kabul quite a few of their operations people had their offices there. Picking his way through the debris he thought of the thirty or forty soldiers and friends that had been in the building. He knew Mustapha was alive, somewhere. But for the rest? He knew Usama spent most of his time in this building when he was not in the mountains. Suddenly, he could think of only one thing, He must find Usama.

"If Mustapha is here, we must find him quickly," Youseff commanded his companions. Pointing to one of the men he had been eating lunch with he shouted, "You, you call the Kabul rescue."

Whipping out his cell phone, Youseff flipped it open and dialed Hamid Mohideen, the head of the al-Qaeda in the Tora Bora region.

"Hello," Mohideen answered his phone.

"Salaam a Likum, Hamid. Is that you?"

"Likum Salaam. Yes. Who is this?" Mohideen said.

"It is Ahmed Youseff."

"Ah, how is your health," Mohideen asked with relief.

"I am fine, I hope you're well. Listen, I am in Kabul and the Air building was just bombed," Youseff said breathlessly. "It is completely gone!"

"Was Mustapha there? Is there anything left?" pressed Mohideen.

Youseff looked around frantically, "Mustapha is alive. I don't know where he is now, but I have talked with him since the bomb exploded. What of Usama? I do not know if he was here."

"Thanks be to God," Mohideen answered, "Usama was not there. He is north in the Baghlan Province."

"We must get him to safety," Youseff pleaded, "The Americans knew of Mustapha and Usama's use of the building. Perhaps they are hunting them."

"No, it is as Mustapha foresaw. The Americans are bombing the Taliban buildings and airfields. They do not know where we are, that only happens in the American movies. Be strong and do not worry. I have spoken with Usama and he does not think it time to come hide in Tora Bora. He is busy planning to eliminate Fahim from Takhar and Badakshan. You must find Mustapha. I will call you later."

Closing his phone, Youseff announced to his companions, "We must find Mustapha and anyone else who survived. He cannot be far from this place. Praise Allah that these men were allowed to die for him."

Expanding their search, they looked around the bombed out building. Finally, they found Mustapha in the Kartayi Wali neighborhood of the city. Quickly bundling Mustapha into a car, they took him to the hospital. No other survivors from the building were found.

Other than cuts and bruises from the debris, and ruptured eardrums, Mustapha had not been seriously hurt. Resting in bed after the doctors had treated his wounds, Mustapha greeted Youseff loudly when he walked into the room, "Salaam Ahmed. It is good to see you. It was a close one for me. I heard the bomb coming and thought it was God coming to earth. Both my companions were killed."

Grimacing at Mustapha's shouting, Youseff realized that he could not hear his own voice and was shouting to feel himself talk. "Ahmed, hello, hello. It was good to find you alive. The Air building was a total loss, there is nothing left there for us. I was afraid at first that the Americans knew you were there and tried to kill you."

"I think so too," Mustapha answered. "I have been thinking a lot about that since the bombing. I believe the Americans are only bombing Taliban government buildings and missile sites. They do not know where we are. It was my fault for staying in that building."

"I agree, Ahmed. Is it time we move to the caves?" Youseff suggested.

"No, not yet. The Americans might see us move. They do not know us, only the Taliban. We should move from government buildings. We will blend into the neighborhoods. They will never find us, amidst the neighborhoods. The bulk of our fighters will be needed elsewhere and our caves are prepared. We do not need to run to them yet."

"Our caves will be safe from these bombs. We can move from there whenever we need to. The Americans do not know them," Youseff, argued.

"No, it is not time. The Americans are not looking for us. They attempt to put pressure on the Taliban. They cannot put pressure on us. If we run to the caves they might see that movement."

Youseff tried one more time, "I still think the caves are our best choice. We built them for times just like this. We should use them."

"No, it is not my will. Nor is it Usama's. We cannot abandon the cities and the Taliban, me must be close to them to make them behave as they should," Mustapha replied in irritation.

"Then it is decided. We can use the compound in the Taymani neighborhood as our headquarters. Their spy satellites cannot find us there," Youseff said in a low voice.

"And we must be careful. If we do move large numbers of volunteers, we must do so under cover of night so the American satellites do not see us. Any large movement in the day will attract their attention." Mustapha paused, rubbed his eyes, and said, "One thing we must do is conceal our remaining helicopters before the Americans find them or the Taliban take them from us."

Changing his tone slightly, Mustapha went on in a more conciliatory manner, "It is good, old friend, that we learned this lesson well. Our costs were low. Usama and the others were in the north and now we know what the Americans will bomb. We will just stay away from those things. Let the Taliban deal with those problems."

Our houses in Taymani will be a good choice," he concluded.

Arabian Sea, South of Pakistan

Marvel 31, a US Air Force E-3A Airborne Warning and Control radar control aircraft climbed steadily through the early afternoon blue sky. Eastbound, from an airfield in Oman it headed for point Blue West. The Air War over Afghanistan was only a few days old and the US Air Force had already implemented a complex airspace management plan. Blue West was the stationary orbit of Blackstone, the southern most AWACS, responsible for coordinating traffic inbound and outbound from Afghanistan. Marvel 31 was due to take over duties as the traffic cop for the southern portion of the airwar over Afghanistan.

"Blackstone, Marvel 31, point Delta at three six oh," Captain Mike Granly, Marvel's co-pilot transmitted over the radio.

"Marvel 31, Blackstone, copy, authenticate Delta Alpha," the controller on Marvel 23, the AWACS currently on duty, replied.

"Marvel 31, authenticates Zulu," Granly said evenly.

"Roger copy, Marvel 31. You are cleared to Blue West at three six zero. Be advised our orbit is at Flight Level 380. Glad to see you."

"Marvel copies Blue West at 360. Can't say we're happy to be here," Granly said with a smile. Calling out on the intercom, he told the Battle Manager in the rear of the airplane that he had the radio now.

"Blackstone, Marvel 31A, standing by for datalink," Major Mark Corbin, the battle manager, transmitted.

"Marvel 31A, Blackstone, you should be receiving now," Marvel 23's Battle Manager radioed back. In a few seconds, the color screens in front of the controllers blinked once, or twice, and Marvel 23's air activity picture appeared on their relief's displays.

"Roger Blackstone, we are receiving your picture. Our radar is up to speed; we are seeing much the same picture. Ready for in-brief anytime you are," Corbin said.

"Blackstone copies, push to frequency 312.275 and go secure," the Marvel 23 manager said.

Corbin switched the radio frequency and keyed the microphone briefly, to synchronize the crypto. After a few seconds he keyed the mike again, transmitting slowly he said, "Blackstone, Marvel 31A, in the green. How do you read?" After he was done, he was careful to let up on the mike key a second after he had stopped speaking.

"Five by," the Marvel 23's battle manager said. With secure communications established, the on duty manager briefed Corbin on the current situation over Afghanistan and the air picture over the Arabian Sea. When he was satisfied that Corbin had heard all the items he wanted to pass on he said, "Roger Marvel 31 you are now Blackstone. Have fun Marvel 23 out."

"Copy, Marvel 31 is now Blackstone," Corbin acknowledged.

Leaning back in his chair, the battle manager aboard Marvel 23 called out on the intercom, "It's Miller time. Another day, another dollar, let's beat feet." With roles exchanged, the tired crew aboard Marvel 23 turned north, on their way back to Oman. It had been a long eight hours, working non-stop directing Air Force and Navy traffic supporting the war in Afghanistan, and they had only been the entry/exit controllers.

Within minutes of taking over as Blackstone, Corbin heard the first inbound, a division of Navy flight of F-18 Hornets reporting in. "Blackstone, Knife 205, Division of Hornets, Point Blue. As fragged."

"Roger, Knife 205, authenticate alpha alpha," the Blackstone controller replied.

After a brief pause to look down the column, the lead pilot found the right answer under his thumb, "Knife 205 Hotel."

"Roger Knife 205, proceed to Kilo. Contact Horse with load," the controller directed.

"Knife copies. Cleared down track, switch Horse," the lead pilot acknowledged. Switching frequencies with his flight, the radio was silent again for a few minutes.

Lieutenant Jacy Ellis, one of the controllers aboard the AWACS, announced over the intercom, "Hey, Major Corbin, I just got a message from Horse over Fort Sandeman in Pakistan. They're saying they don't want anymore Navy guys up there. They all come out screaming for gas." Different controllers worked inbound/outbound traffic from the Persian Gulf and those from Diego Garcia and the carriers in the Arabian Sea.

"Yeah, Jacy got it. Thanks," Corbin replied.

Turning to Lieutenant Colonel Gary "TP" Salinas, the Fighter Pilot who was serving a fill-in tour as Strawboss, the Joint Forces Air Component Commander's airborne representative, Corbin said, "TP what do you want to do. I figure that if we keep the Navy guys in Mid-country we've got to move our KC-10s up to Point Lima East."

"Nah, let's not do that. We need them to do double duty at the Echo Anchor for Air Force and our foreign drogue players. Can't afford to leave those guys without tankers," TP replied.

"Well let's just feed the Navy into the flow at Echo/Fox. The south flow to Darkstar will probably save them 30 to 45 minutes. That should be enough to keep 'em from screaming, " Corbin suggested.

"Yeah, good idea, let's do it that way. Send all the Navy guys to the southern AWACS sector. If Darkstar needs 'em, they can always draw one of the KC-10s up to their entry at Golf. Is the Navy going to send any of their tankers in our direction?"

"No, there aren't any on the frag. The Navy keeps them all close hold over their own carriers," Corbin replied.

"Okay, I guess they've got short legs as well. Let's switch all the Navy traffic to Darkstar as well. I'd better give the Navy rep back in Qatar a heads up, otherwise they'll be pissed."

"What do you mean get pissed? Don't they know flexibility is the key to airpower? We'll switch 'em when the next flight checks in. Hey, something else occurred to me, these guys are showing up thinking they have a Time over Target. Last I talked with the guys in Darkstar, they had a stack going at Golf. Better tell the Navy rep when you talk to him that their times are only release times. The TOT is at our discretion."

"Sure I'll do that. How goes the flow for Horse anyway?" TP asked.

"I think pretty good, it is a long way up there. Horse hasn't said a thing about needing to stack guys up before letting them into the AOR."

"Yeah, maybe we should just keep the fighters in the south. Air Force or Navy they've all got shorter legs than the heavies," TP thought aloud.

"If we do that we'll need a few more tankers for the Karachi Hold Point. The bombers sure soak up a lot during pre-strike refueling."

"Next time I get a chance, I'll talk with the planners. I think we should send the R model tankers to Karachi. They've got a better offload capability. We'll send the other tankers, the Es and the 10s, to Golf. That way they'll be closer to their home bases, and they can flow up country as needed," TP said.

"Darkstar, Bone 21, flight of two, with 24 each," the flight lead of two B-1 bombers, out of Diego Garcia, announced on the radio.

Jacy, working the eastern traffic, confirmed the authentication and then directed them to contact Horse. She reached over and tapped TP on the shoulder.

"What's up Jacy?" TP looked up.

"Well, it's like this, I just sent a flight of two B-1s to Horse and they've got 48 JDAMs between them. Five minutes before that I sent a flight of three B-52s with 36 JDAMs. I've got three more flights of B-1s and two of Buffs due in the next half hour. I don't know how long it'll take to drop all those bombs, but the way it's going I figure there might be a traffic jam up there before long."

"Yeah, I see your point.' TP nodded. "That's the narrow part of the country.

That's all we need is a bunch of Bombers getting in each other's way. How many we got up there right now?"

Checking her clipboard, Jacy replied, "Not including those two, I've got four flights of Bone's and three flights of Buff's already in the AOR. Make that 17 bombers."

Thinking of the southern controller TP replied, "Let me ask John what his load looks like, we might start shifting them."

Leaning over, TP grasped the shoulder of the controller working the western, Persian Gulf traffic, "Johnny, how many fighters ya got in the AOR with Darkstar right now?"

"Well, sir. I've got four fourships of F-16s with JDAMS, five flights of Strike Eagles with GBU-10s, three flights of Tornados, four F-18s inbound, outbound I've got two flights of F-14s and four F-18s. That, plus a cell of three tankers at point Golf right now," John replied, running through his list of traffic. "Oh, and I've got tanker cells at Echo, the transition point Yankee and another at Bravo near Oman."

"Yeah, pretty busy ain't it. Thanks," TP patted his shoulder, saying as he straightened up, "I gotta call the JFACC."

TP Salinas needed a little time to think, he sat down at his console and rested his head on his outstretched fingers. Things were getting a little complicated. All he was supposed to do was to make sure the Frag was executed smoothly, make a few calls on the way and watch what was going on. Now things were seriously busy and definitely backing up. He had to make some big calls on his own and he felt uncomfortable about that. He was sure that the Navy guys would not be happy stuck in the southern part of the country. The biggest problem was that he just did not have the tanker assets to support them if they continued to bingo out of the AOR low on fuel. Tankers were another problem; each model carried a different amount of fuel and he did not have the offload capability where he needed it. He could make short-term calls, but that would not solve anything tomorrow. Everything really needed to go smoothly and for that to happen it had to be planned that way.

Dialing Surveyor on the secure SATCOM, TP decided that he needed to shift the burden of planning back on the JFACC where it belonged. Lieutenant Colonel "Goof" Marco was pulling the day shift as the Surveyor, the Air Commander's representative on duty in the Combined Air Operations Center located in Qatar.

"Surveyor," Goof Marco answered.

"Hey, Goof is that you? You pullin' Surveyor duty? It's TP, I'm doin' the

Strawboss on Blackstone today."

"Hey yourself TP. I saw your name on the crew roster. How ya been bud? It's been what three, four years?" Goof answered.

"Yeah, man. I'm great, just great. I was doin' a staff job in DC when I got this great TDY deal," TP said excitedly. "Last time I saw you was back at Shady J. Look at us now. Listening to the radio while someone else is flying our Strike Eagle sorties."

Goof smiled to himself. "Yeah, tell me about it. Needs of the Air Force and all that shit. What's up? What can I do for ya today? I'm showing green by the way."

"I'm green too. Well, thing is we're starting to jam up here. Have you guys got Link 16 running there at the CAOC?" TP asked. "The flow is not too bad right now, but it's starting to get backed up and I'm making too many calls. I figure we need to fine tune the frag a little bit," TP said.

"We've got it up. I don't have it at my desk though. What do you have in mind?" Goof asked.

"First, the Navy guys are screaming for fuel when they leave the AOR. I've temporarily been shifting them to a south flow to save gas, but the problem is hard TOT's and targets. Darkstar has done some target shifting on the fly and you know the Navy is raising holy hell. The sticker is that I can't afford to send my drogue tankers up country for them alone. I need them for other folks around point Golf. They're legs are just too short to go all the way up to Kabul. Even the F-16s are having trouble doing that," TP rattled off.

"Yeah, I can make that happen. Let 'em gripe, they should be happy just to be players in the game," Goof replied. "Is that all?"

"Not really. Darkstar, the southern AWACS, is stacking up their fighters before letting them into the AOR. Horse hasn't started stacking yet, but with all the bombers headed up to the north it's gonna happen soon. Plus this whole TOT hard target thing is not going to work once we get good and ramped up. We've got to smooth the flow out so things don't get bunched up. Oh, and we have to tailor our tankers to offload required, the bombers are soaking up more than the fighters by a long shot. And the fighters are coming out of the AOR low on fuel," TP said.

"Sounds like we just need to space out the TOTs a little to me," Goof offered.

"Goof, the deal is time. The Bones are dropping 48 JDAMs per flight, Buffs are dropping 36, heck, a B-2 drops 16. The F-14s are dropping GBUs as well as the Strike Eagles. All of these guys need maneuvering room and time to drop their loadouts. All I'm saying is that we need to come up with a system that'll handle the crowd that's coming. This is pretty early in the game and things are getting crowded," TP said.

"Yeah, I think I see what you're talking about. You gotta know that one of the things we're looking at is that day after tomorrow we're gonna run out of fixed targets and start hitting them all over again. When the CSAR gets going in the north we're gonna have another crowd to deal with in the northwest," Goof mused.

"Goof, you flew A-10s in Europe back in the good/bad old days. What did you guys do for Close Air Support there? It wasn't regular CAS, it was called something special, what was it?" TP asked.

"Yeah, we did Push CAS in USAFE. You just timed flights to show up at contact points with your fragged ordinance and they'd send you where they need you. It was set up as a continuous flow. But we're not doin' CAS in the AOR yet," Goof replied.

"I know, I know. With a few hard targets and little maneuvering airspace, the jets are piling up. Maybe what we need is to just send in the jets and have the AWACS controllers assign the targets. This TOT/ hard target thing is the log jam."

"Good idea. We could do the Push CAS thing with BAI. We could just Frag whatever jets to show up with ordinance and task them before going in country. Then we could relay targets to the AWACS, set priorities or even chop the air to ground FACs when those guys get setup." Goof started thinking, "But it'll take a couple of days to work into the Frag, we've already sent out tomorrows Frag and the one for the day after is almost done."

"But at least it'll smooth the flow," TP said. "Don't forget the tankers either."

"Thanks, man. Good on ya, I'll see what I can do here. But you'll still have to just deal with it for a day or two," Goof said.

"No biggie. It's my job. I'm just a traffic cop. See ya, when I see ya," TP said, hanging up the SATCOM.

CHAPTER 5

8 October 2001
33,000 Feet west of Kharkov, Russia

Pinto looked at his lineup card, checking the timing for the next refueling, "Grumpy. We're coming up on our third refueling. The divert is still that Russian Airbase outside of Moscow."

"Well I guess it's time for another rendition of the dance of the sugar plum fairies. I'd better call the wandering gypsies in and tighten up the formation. They've been chillin' since the last one over Poland," Grumpy Westin said, keying the back radio he transmitted, "Chevy, tighten it up we've got a tank coming up."

Grumpy watched the other five aircraft of Chevy flight slowly move back to the left and right wings of the KC-135R tanker. They were the third wave of 492d Fighter Squadron, all Strike Eagles that deployed from RAF Lakenheath early that morning. "You know I used to have a strike line somewhere near here, and here we are just cruising along, just like we're back in the states. It's funny, it seems like a whole other life when we used to have a checkered flag commitment in Aviano, Italy. We had a pre-planned nuclear target near Kiev."

Pinto, a Military history buff, broke in, "Hey, if we're talking history, there's a lot of it around here. For instance, the place we start our next tank was where the Russians suffered a very big defeat in '42. Just north of that is Kursk. The Germans and the Russians had the biggest tank battle ever in the summer of '43. There were over three thousand tanks in the fight; the German's kicked it off on the fourth of July. It turned out to be the last big attack the German's ever made in Russia."

"Okay, okay. Enough with World War II already. Let's think about this new war, or just this next refueling," Grumpy said, grinning into his facemask. It was always entertaining to listen to Pinto go off on a streak, but sometimes it took longer than you had bargained for.

"Whatever you say, boss. You know if you don't know history you're condemned to repeat it," Pinto replied, nonplussed.

"We're topping off on this one," Pinto said, reviewing his flight plan. "We'll be taking just shy of 20k. The plan has us landing around 10 or 11 and everyone needs about 10k to make it to Ganci min fuel."

"Okay, I think we'll cycle twice this time, take ten each, to keep everyone about the same. Just in case," Grumpy said. "I know we're doing min comm but I'm going to let everyone know."

Keying the back radio he said, "Chevy, listen up. We'll do two cycles, 10 each, Acknowledge."

"Two." "Three." "Four." "Five." "Six."

"Alright, let's get this thing going."

Grumpy eased the throttles aft slightly and rolled left. With the slightest pressure, he eased the nose down. The fighter slowed a few knots, descended 20 feet and began moving sideways in relation to the tanker. Continuing the slide aft, before reaching the centerline of the tanker, Grumpy rolled right to kill the sideways motion of the airplane and pushed the power up. It was evident he'd done this a few times before, the jet smoothly rolled out on the centerline, about 50 feet behind the boom in the pre-contact position. Usually the tanker would signal that he was ready to begin offloading, today Grumpy felt like knocking on the door.

When Grumpy's aircraft had stopped moving relative to the tanker, the boom operator rotated the boom down and extended the probe ten feet. Acknowledging the signal that tanker was ready to begin offloading fuel, Grumpy started walking the throttles, pushing one at a time up slightly to slowly pick up speed and close the distance.

In seconds, he was closing with the tanker as fast as a man could walk, slowly he closed the distance with the tanker. Grumpy added a slight backpressure on the stick, and the airplane began to climb. He was face to face with the business end of the refueling boom; he used this as a reference for height. He stopped the climb and continued to slowly move forward. As the nose of his fighter approached the boom, the operator moved the boom right, out of the way.

Out of the corner of his eye, Grumpy saw the yellow stripe underneath the tanker. Unconsciously, he lined up on it and began pulling power ever so slowly. The fighter stopped exactly in the contact position, ten feet from the big tanker. As he concentrated on maintaining his position, he could just see the inboard engines along the canopy bow. In good position for a plug, he waited on the boomer to do his job.

A yellow stripe was painted on the centerline of the big tanker as a reference for the airplanes to use. The boomer laying on his stomach shook his head, *those F-15 guys expect me to do all the work*, he thought. Unlike most other Air Force airplanes, the air-refueling receptacle on an F-15 was on the left shoulder of the airplane behind the canopy, the boomer would rather have the fighter lineup to one side, making his job easier. It would be his fault if he smacked the fighter, so he moved the boom a little to his right, extended it and moved the boom gingerly along the left side of the fighter's canopy.

Pinto watched the progress of the boom, calling its position out loud. "Boom's beside your head, it's next to me. He's reaching for it, and, we're plugged."

"You're in the apple. We're taking gas at 11,000 pounds," Pinto added.

"Okay," Grumpy said, concentrating on keeping his precise position relative to tanker. He continually walked the throttles, one at a time, to control the speed fore and aft. Slight pressures on the stick to the side to control position relative to the center stripe and even smaller up and down movements for vertical spacing. To an untrained eye, it looked like the big fighter hung motionless beneath the tanker.

Pinto gave a running commentary on the refueling, "You're doin' fine. You're in the apple."

"Your doin' fine. Come up one."

"Too far. Down one."

"Forward two. On the apple."

"On the apple, 2,000 to go."

"There's 10k."

"Ready, ready disconnect," Grumpy said, as he pressed down on the auto-acq switch to disconnect the hydraulic lock on the boom. Simultaneously, he pressed slightly forward on the stick and cracked the throttles back.

"Boom's clear," Pinto said.

Grumpy looked up at the boomer, checking to be sure he had descended a few feet below the tanker. Then looking left and right, he saw another Strike Eagle very close to his left wing. Clear to his right, he rolled slightly right and began moving toward the right wing of the tanker, going back to where he had come from. Chevy Flight was practicing quick flow refueling to minimize the transition time between aircraft on the boom. As planned, the first jet on the left wing replaced him in the pre-contact position just seconds after he was out of the way.

Grumpy passed behind and underneath the other two fighters on the right wing. As he climbed up on the wing of the second fighter, the one next to the tanker's wingtip began descending to get in position for the next refueling. He relaxed and wiggled his fingers and toes, now he could watch everyone else get their gas while he waited his turn to top off his gas with the remainder of his offload.

After two more airplanes had cycled through the boom, Pinto broke the silence in their airplane. "Hey, boss. You looked outside lately?"

"No, bro. I've been watching the show here. What's up?" Grumpy replied.

"Well I haven't looked at it on radar, yet. But, it's getting mighty dark out ahead of us. Our course line will take us right through what might be a big thunderstorm," Pinto warned.

Immediately concerned that all the jets wouldn't get their full load of fuel, Grumpy took a quick glance, "How far away is it? We've got our second look at the boom next. How much time have we got?"

Pinto, trying for a jesting note in his voice, said. "Well, we got a few minutes. I tried looking at it. Our radar may be great at taking pretty pictures of the ground or seeing airplanes almost forever, but it just ain't that good at being a weather radar."

"Let's hope the tanker boys are looking at it. Jiggy's clear of our six, so we're on deck," Grumpy said as he pulled power to descend and set up on the wing of the jet on the boom, his turn next at quick flow.

"Damn, Grumpy. This thing is getting close. I can see it plane as day on my radar now," Pinto added worriedly. "Tanker's not turning or anything, we gotta turn left thirty, maybe forty degrees."

"Just a few more minutes. Surely, the tanker guys see this thing! Jiggy is coming off the boom now and number six is the last one. He'll be done in a minute or so," Grumpy offered, trying to keep Pinto calm.

Jiggy, flying the number three position in Chevy Flight began moving right behind number one and number two. Her sole concern was the formation and she was busy looking for nose-tail clearance. She did not have time to pay attention to the approaching weather. She sensed that she had put in too much bank; the flight began to move left faster; she glanced at the fighter on the boom. She took out a little bank trying to figure out what she had done wrong, when a cryptic radio call came from the tanker.

The tanker co-pilot transmitted tersely, "Tanker's comin' left."

"What'd he say, Hustler?" Jiggy asked.

"I dunno. I think tanker dudes speak another language they don't want us to know anyway," Hustler said with a grin. He was thinking, just another hour or so, and then this fighter drag would be over. Time for some of that beer he had put in the travel pod, hanging on one of the weapons stations out in the cold air, the beer should be ice cold.

Jiggy was sliding to the right even faster, she figured that she had cleared number two's right wing and glanced up. Surprised she saw the two fighters were whipping violently up and down and rolling to the left.

On the intercom Jiggy said, "Damn, the tanker said he was rolling left. Everyone's turning away from us!" She realized that she was still going right, while they were going left, in seconds they would be far apart. Suddenly angry at the tanker's unbriefed turn, Jiggy tried to correct her spacing.

"Hey, Jiggy. Hate to rain on your parade, but there's a hell of a thunderstorm brewing just ahead of us. They're going away from it and we're going into it." Hustler said, suddenly worried.

Abruptly, the tanker and the rest of her flight disappeared into the murk and she was alone in the darkening sky. Still accelerating towards were they had been she abruptly rolled out of her turn. Desperately scanning the sky, she thought to herself, five Strike Eagles and one big KC-135 Tanker could not just disappear, could they?

"Shit. I've lost sight. I don't know where they are," Jiggy said.

"Holy shit! I've got a hack, girl, let's turn. Let's go Lost Wingman right now!" Hustler exclaimed.

"Okay, okay. I'm on instruments. Turning right, thirty degrees of bank."

"How many seconds is it? Fifteen or thirty?" Hustler asked.

"We're number three on the tanker. It's forty-five seconds."

"No, Jiggy that'll take us into those dark clouds. Cut down the time!" Hustler said, raising his voice.

"No way. I was right behind number two," Jiggy replied.

"Jiggy we can't go into that storm! It's way too black in there!"

"Okay, okay. I'll pull power, drop down 1,000 feet and roll out now."

The first heavy gust of turbulence threw Hustler up against the canopy, swallowing he said, "Yeah, yeah, Oh, that's fine. This is all a game to me. I like this ride. I'd pay money for this kind of ride."

The aircraft plowed into the blackest part of the thunderstorm, violently bouncing over 400 feet at a time. Jiggy concentrated with every bone in her body, "I'm having trouble seeing the HUD here. The velocity vector is jumping all over the place."

"You're doing fine, babe. I'm right here with you. Hey, have we made a radio call?" Hustler asked.

"Uh, no. I forgot all about it. I'm showing over two miles on the air-to-air Tacan," Jiggy said. Keying the mike on the back radio, Jiggy said, "Three's lost wingman. Two miles separation."

"Roger, three. We saw you disappear. Thought you wanted to visit the Caspian Sea," Grumpy radioed. "Say posit."

"Three is two miles away, at 310," Jiggy responded. "Somewhere in a big dark cloud."

"Chevy One copies. We're headed 050, at FL 330," Grumpy replied. "Go to radar trail. We're clear of the clouds right now."

Jiggy noticed her heading was 130 or was it 150, the airplane was jumping around so much. She was heading deeper into the storm. Jiggy quickly rolled into a thirty degree left turn. She took control of the radar and thumbed forward on the auto-acq switch to put the radar in Super Search. Where she could automatically lock onto the first target the radar detected in a cone in the front of the airplane.

Jiggy stopped the turn on a 050 heading, they were still deep in the storm, buffeted by up and down drafts raging through the thunderstorm. The radar continued to stay in Super Search and the range was approaching five miles. Raising her visor, she wiped the sweat from her forehead with the back of her glove.

Hustler observed, "Jiggy, come another thirty or forty left. We're just paralleling their track. We need to cut across it."

"Okay, sure, I knew that," Jiggy said, turning the jet another forty degrees. As soon as she rolled out, the radar resolved a lock on the Grumpy and the formation in front of them. Jiggy thumbed the back radio and said, "Chevy Three, tied, six miles in trail, 310."

With relief, Grumpy replied, "Chevy One copies. Just stay in trail. Say fuel state."

Jiggy looked at the fuel totalizer over her right knee, "Chevy Three, 25.6."

"Chevy One. Thanks, we're not in a hurry, you've got enough gas to make it so just relax. We're on the home stretch. Call the visual when you get it," Grumpy replied.

"Man, that was not fun." With a mischievous grin, Hustler said, "Why'd you do that?"

"Shoot, I was just minding my own business like I was supposed to.' Jiggy said, with a tinge of anger in her voice. "It was the tanker that jinked left."

"Sorry, Sorry. I was just kiddin'. I knew you didn't do that on purpose. I was just kidding, okay?" Hustler apologized.

Deflated, Jiggy replied, "No big deal. I guess I'm just wound a little tight right now." Opening her mask, she wiped her face.

"No harm, no foul. I was just worried about my underwear, plus the Foster's I put in the travel pod. We must have taken a couple of 5g hits in that cloud. Hey, look at it this way, we've only got a few hundred miles to go and then we get to land at some old Soviet Airbase and drink some cold beer. No worries, piece of cake."

"Just shut up and color, you're no help," Jiggy laughed.

"You're the one that always gets the tough break, and you want me to shut up. Heck you're the bad luck magnet, not me," Hustler said, trying to get her to relax.

Getting into it, Jiggy said, "I'm the bad luck magnet, how come you're always around. Funny how that is, I never seemed to get into trouble before I met you."

"Yeah, it's me, blame me. Here I am just ten feet behind you. Just minding my own business, but you gotta blame someone. So go ahead, blame the WSO," Hustler went on.

"Would you like a little cheese with your whine?" Jiggy said, with a grin on her face.

Ab Bazan, Afghanistan

A bright mid-morning sun cast fourteen shadows as a column of horses slowly snaked down a rocky, dusty trail on the ridgeline northeast of Taloqan. The river in the valley below separated Taliban lines around Taloqan from Northern Alliance positions north and east of the town. Mark's team had spent two solid days traveling from Tajikistan. They had yet to meet any Taliban or even their new ally, the local warlord, General Abdul Fahim.

Jostling on his horse, Mark mused about the tactical situation. Supposedly, Johar says we will find the warlord, maybe today or maybe tomorrow. Afghanis were the same as Arabs in this way, everything was maybe, it might happen, or it was possible. The phrase Mumpkin summed up the concept of maybe, a verbal shoulder shrug rather than an expression of certainty. The little town of Ab Bazan was one of Fahim's strongholds, and he was supposed to be there. I guess we'll see what we'll see Mark thought.

Jostling on his horse, he turned to look back at his troops; twelve Americans were riding behind him and none of them looked like they were comfortable. He was sure that none of them were happy to be riding horses, much less along narrow mountain trails, where a fall might take several thousand feet to stop. With a chuckle, he thought it best to skip the cavalry charges, better leave that to these Afghanis. They looked like they were born on horses. Suddenly, he was acutely tired of jostling around on the back of this uncomfortable, smelly horse. His back hurt and he was almost ready to walk again after this trek. You just did what the mission asked of you, it was not always easy and sometimes it surely wasn't fun. But it was always good, after it was over.

The column entered the town, if you could call it a town. By US standards, it was nothing but a collection of mud walled huts, however the view of the mountains around it was fantastic. Mark thought it did look familiar, like a movie set. It came to him, a Sean Connery, Michael Caine movie…. something about Kings. *The Once and Future King,* that's it. He was sure the movie probably had something to do with Alexander the Great. You measured fighting here by the thousands of years, not the hundreds. By the looks of this mud-walled town, nothing much had changed in the millennia since Alexander's visit.

Johar stopped, he let the reins of his horse fall to the ground, swung his leg over the low cut saddle and dropped to the ground. He walked steadily inside the nearest building. In a moment he walked out with two other men, one of them dressed in a duplicate of Johar's bed-sheet/suit coat combination, the other had a large shawl draped over his shoulders. One of them carried an AK-47, with two bandoleers of copper cased ammo draped across his shoulders.

Dave, the CIA guy, used to riding on horses, was not tired. He walked up steadily to the new men and greeted them warmly, in their own language. Mark, forgotten and sore from the ride, stood next to them, a rising tide of irritation forming within him. The pleasantries took thirty or forty minutes, at least it seemed like it. Finally, without introducing him, Dave turned to Mark, "Okay, here's the plan. These guys are going to get us a building with a few rooms where we can crash. Fahim isn't here right now, but they expect him. They expect us at a dinner in our honor tonight."

"Great, I always like being wined and dined when I get to town." Mark started peppering him with questions. "What is the situation like around here? Where are the nearest Taliban and how secure is it?"

Dave held up his hands after just a few of Mark's questions, saying, "Whoa, big fella. I've already told you about all I know of these guys. I was here a few days before coming to get ya'll. There were about two or three thousand guys here then. Tactically speaking, we should be okay, this is one of their stronghold towns."

"Sorry, I'm an info junkie. I guess I just like to know what's going on," Mark said a hint of sarcasm in his voice.

Dave pretended not to notice, pointing down the valley, he said, "The Taliban lines are on the other side of that river. Do you see the smaller ridgeline between the town and us? That's about twelve miles away and there aren't any roads between here and there."

"Where's the building we're gonna use?" Mark asked.

"We'll follow this little guy here, he'll show us where we'll crash. By the way, they say we can use this place as long as we wish," Dave said, turning to speak to the armed Afghanis. Who turned and began walking down the street to another mud walled building.

Their building only had two large rooms, one in the front facing the street, and one with windows facing the back. A smaller single room had been built outside against the back wall. A rough door in the wall led to a very small courtyard in back, framed by the outside walls of the buildings next door. A smaller mud wall spanned the gap between the buildings and enclosed the courtyard. The ground was bare dirt, covered in rocks, with broken bottles and old piles of garbage scattered here and there. An outdoor privy stood against the back wall.

The building was on top of the hill and the back windows gave them an unobstructed view to the south and west, across the valley. Dave, the SF trooper, picked the small room in the courtyard and quietly setup the commo gear, placing the small dish antenna outside. Within minutes, the back room became their sleeping quarters and the front room, facing the street, became the rec and meeting room.

Over a gourmet lunch of Chicken Loaf MRE's, Mark said, "Dave, pretty soon, we need to do a resupply. Is the only option open to us horseback or can we have choppers fly in?"

"I wouldn't think US choppers would be a great idea just yet, especially during the day. Besides, we've got a Hip; it blends better into the local area. Maybe I can talk my boss into letting you use it. But don't plan on it carrying much at these altitudes."

"Well, we really need stuff more than people, right now. I think we could pare down the load so it can get over these mountains. I'll start the wheels cranking on our end, so we'll be ready when your boss gives the okay. But as soon as Task Force 160 gets into town we'll be using our own choppers."

"Okay, I'll ask next time I check in," Dave replied around a mouthful of food.

Changing the subject, Mark continued to feel out this CIA guy, "These

Mountains remind me of Desert Ranger training with the 7th in Fort Bliss and New Mexico. Rugged. Nothing but rocks and sun. Lots of sun. Only these mountains are probably twice as high as the southern Rockies. I have to take an extra breath every now and again just to make sure I can."

Dave scooted backward and leaned against the wall. Laying his rifle across his lap, he looked up at Mark. "Yeah, I know those mountains. There is a pass northwest of us, not very far from here, that's over 15,000 feet. These are some tall rocks." Dave stirred the coffee in his canteen cup, blowing steam off the top to cool it. "Can't do thin air too quick, it's a great way to get sick."

Mark nodded, stood up and walked over to one of the men lying on the floor. Kicking Dave lightly on the foot he said, "OD, before you get your beauty rest, tell me something? Did you get the SATCOM up and check in with mother? If you've already talked with them, next check in get them to start planning a resupply. Dave is going to get us the company's Hip for transport, if we don't have any of our own lift."

"Yes, sir, I did that already. I'll get them working on a resupply. Now if you don't mind I've got to work on my wrinkles," OD replied. When Mark nodded at him, he rolled over.

Mark squatted next to his team sergeant. "Gary, when you get a chance, get a resupply list together, okay? OD is going to get with mother on the next check-in and Dave is going to see if we can get the company chopper, a Hip, to make the run for us."

"Sure, sir. We don't need much right now. Food, batteries, water tabs and fuel for the Whisperlite stoves." Gary noted, "The best thing is to get a route established. Mike, the medic, has been complaining to me about transport if we get someone hurt. Any idea of the timing?"

"Not yet. I'm reasonably sure that the resupply will happen in the next few days. But, I'm sure not taking bets on when we'll meet with this Fahim guy."

Dave, overheard the conversation between Gary and Mark, couldn't resist adding his two cents. "Mark, we've been in country about two weeks now and this Fahim guy is awfully happy to see us. Or shall I say, he's real happy to see my boss' plain paper bags. So far, we've spread around nearly three mil with these guys. So, right now we're pretty good friends and since the Zoomies started bombing to the south, they all think we're close to the end of the war."

"I don't know how close the end is, but right now I'd settle for just meeting this guy. Maybe then we can get into this war ourselves," Mark said.

Enigmatically, Dave said, "You should be honored. We've been invited to dinner with the Man, himself. But take it from me, I wouldn't get too excited about solving the problems of the world all at once."

Mark stood up, "You may be right, we'll see. These dinner things always seem a bit too formal to me. Long on talk and short on action." Dave did not reply, in the silence that followed, Mark stepped outside into the courtyard. Gary got up and joined him a few minutes later.

In a low voice Gary leaned close to Mark and said, "I haven't heard that CIA dude talk so much, you must have scratched a nerve."

"Yeah, he's the life of the party. But as spy's go, he's our spy," Mark said with a smile.

A big commotion in the darkening streets attracted Mark's attention. Looking out the front door, he saw a large group of horsemen rattling up the street, a big man with a large black moustache in the lead. Calling inside he said, "Hey, Dave. Think this is our host?"

Dave stood up, "Could be, let's head on over there."

Picking up his gear, Mark asked conversationally, "What's for dinner anyway? "

Catching Mark by the arm, Dave confided, "The menu is probably rice and goat. And you eat with your hands, don't forget, it's your right hand!"

Mark flashed him a big grin, "Dude, I've had Kepsa before. I'll keep my left hand in check and the soles of my feet out of sight."

"Good, I'm no Miss Manners. Who's going?"

"I think it'll be just me and Gary." Mark glanced at Gary "We're ready."

Kabul, Afghanistan

Ahmed Mustapha rolled on his side; he stopped there for a minute, wincing in pain. Sitting up slowly, he was sore all over, every muscle in his body screamed with every move. Standing, he walked slowly to the table next to the wall and picked up the ringing cell phone.

"Hello, hello."

"Salaam, Ahmed. How is your health?" Mohideen said.

"I am better. I can hear better each day, but you must speak up! Every time I move I hurt," Mustapha said precisely.

"Yes, I know. God spared you. You should count your blessings," Mohideen said solicitously.

"I give thanks every day."

"That is well. I am sending you several of my men to replace those you lost.

You must get your operation running again as soon as you can, we must reestablish communications. With your building in rubble, where will you work from?" asked Mohideen.

"We will be working from the compound in the Taymani neighborhood."

"That is good, I will send you ten men. Some will be guards, but the rest know something of communications. Muqtar bin Laden still wants to work out of Kabul. If this is what he wants then you must get the communications system up and running again. It is very important."

Mohideen's words upset Mustapha, in frustration he said, "I will do this. It has not been long since the bombing at the Air Authority. It takes time to get going again, I barely survived with my life."

"Yes, yes, this is true. I am sorry for your pain, but we must go on. Overall, the American bombing hasn't hurt us very much. Your section is the only command center that has been bombed."

"I know this. Do you not remember that it was my suggestion that the American bombing would not be effective against us, in the first place? This was my fault, though, I should have moved out of the Taliban building. It was a mistake to stay," Mustapha said.

"Perhaps. But it is done. Now we must figure how to keep going. Last week you ran Usama's nerve center, he still wishes to operate from Kabul. Therefore, it is simple. You must get going again, no anger or blame will help you do this."

Mustapha, beginning to lose his patience, replied indignantly, "I will do this. I have not been idle."

Sensing his anger, Mohideen tried a different tack, "You are a brave fighter. I know you have done well. All I am saying is that you now must get back to work, not that you haven't done what is required of you."

Deflated, Mustapha replied, "It is hard. I lost everyone and everything."

"No. This is not true. You have lost much in our battle. But you still have your health and best of all you can continue the struggle. You can look forward to fighting and killing Americans!"

"Yes, you are right. I am ready. When will you send these men?"

"They are already on the way. I think they will be in Kabul later today," Mohideen said. "How will they contact you?"

"Do they have cell phones? That is the best way to meet."

"What about reestablishing your communications network?" Mohideen asked. "Do you have any thoughts?"

"I think it best not to use Taliban phones, or radios, anymore. The Americans will be able to find us that way. It is better to use cell phones and move frequently, like Muqtar bin Laden."

"Yes, everyone has cell phones. That is well," Mohideen answered.

"I will need weapons as well. Do they have weapons?" Mustapha asked, "Are there any I know?"

"You know Asif Yameen, well. He is their Mudier and will work well for you. They all have weapons and I will send you whatever else you need."

"This is good. Before this happened, our Muqtar told me that he wishes to make another video, and get it to the west. I think we should do this tomorrow, or the next day. You must make arrangements to get the video to Pakistan," Mustapha said.

"I will do this. Call me when the tape is made," Mohideen said.

"I will call you as soon as it is done," Mustapha asked. "I have been out of touch with our people. Have you heard from Hassan since the bombing?"

"I have heard from him. He told me that the rabbits have been delivered and are on their way to their hutches," Mohideen said.

"Thanks be to god, this is good news. I will call you tomorrow," Mustapha hung up.

Mohideen turned to Samir Mohammed, one of the top al-Qaeda commanders in Afghanistan, "He will recover. He is having trouble, but will not give up on our cause."

"This is good. He has done much for us in the past. I would not like to eliminate him now. But watch him closely, the fight may have left him," Samir said in a conspiratorial whisper.

"I will care for him closely. He did mention that Usama desires to make a tape and get it to the west."

"I have heard of this. When it is done, we must get it to Al Jareeza. It must be defiant. The Americans are not hurting us and they are afraid to fight us on the ground. We will spread the word around the world," Mohammed concluded.

Mustapha walked into the sitting room of his house, where his wife and Said, his fourteen-year-old son, were sitting quietly. He looked at them grimly for a long moment. Finally, he said, "You must pack and leave for Pakistan immediately. It is no longer safe for you here, go quickly. Wait for me in Quetta."

Without giving them time to reply, he turned his back on them and went back into his room. Mustapha dressed slowly and called for his new driver, Nabil Zahrah. He did not know him well, but he had come highly recommended. He was the nephew of a friend killed in the Air Authority bombing. Short, wiry, with curly, greasy hair, he had come from Pakistani madras and had trained with

Youseff in the south. Mustapha thought that for an Egyptian he was very attentive and mostly quiet.

Moving slowly, Mustapha left his house, stopped in the compound, looking slowly around he squinted in the sun. A short wall, encircling four houses and several outbuildings, surrounded the compound. A private courtyard, formed by the front of the houses facing inward, was framed by small trees growing between the houses. There was no grass, only bare dirt. Several four-wheel drive vehicles stood haphazardly around the compound. Guards, armed with AK-47s, walked around the perimeter. It was safe here in his fortress.

He approached his Land Cruiser, "Hello, Nabil. I must get out; today we go to the Bazaar. It is lunch time."

Pausing at the gated entrance, Nabil carefully looked left and right. Seeing no traffic, he accelerated quickly out onto the streets of this sleepy section of Kabul.

An hour later, in a Char Chata café, Mustapha was drinking coffee and reading a newspaper. His cell phone rang and interrupted him. Answering it, he said, "Hello, hello. Yes, it is me. How is your health, Muqtar?"

"Good, good. I am doing well, I hear better every day, but it still hurts to move."

"Yes, I will come tonight. I will bring Youseff. You are in the mountains? Yes, I know this place. I will be there this afternoon."

"Likum salaam," Mustapha said and hung up.

Youseff drove into the Taymani compound in mid-afternoon. He got out of his car and walked towards Mustapha's house. Before he reached the door, Nabil opened it, letting him in. Inside he saw Mustapha sitting uncomfortably in a chair, touched he said, "How are you old friend? Are you feeling better? Obviously, you are moving around and this is good."

"I am better. I hear better and can move about on my own. I still hurt all over, it is like I was beaten very badly."

"Yes, you were beaten. Being that close to a large bomb, it is amazing you are alive. You look much better than when we pulled you from the rubble." Nabil closed the door behind him.

"It is a small price to pay. Others have gone to Allah."

"Yes, yes. It is still better to enjoy life while you have it," Youseff observed.

"I suppose this is true. But they say there is much gratification in sacrificing for Allah."

"Why have you asked me here? We have spoken much in the last days, it is good to see you in person, but why must we meet?" Youseff asked.

"It was not me, it is Usama that wants your company, and he did not tell me what was wanted. He wants to make a video and tonight we are to meet with him for dinner."

Distracted, Youseff's gaze wandered to the window, "It is probably for an update on training in the southern mountains."

Turning abruptly, Youseff continued, "Is he coming here?"

"No, we will meet him in the mountains. He likes to live in the traditional way. We need to leave soon, when will you be ready?"

"I am ready now. We will take my driver?" Youseff asked.

"No, Nabil will take us. He knows the way," Mustapha answered.

Getting into the car again, Mustapha leaned forward. Speaking in a low voice, he instructed Nabil, "Go west from Kabul on the way to Ghanzi and stop in Maidanshar. It is about 35 kilometers."

"Yes, Mudier," Nabil replied.

When they reached the small town of Maidanshar, Nabil stopped. Mustapha leaned forward again, and told Nabil to turn right and head towards Wonay Pass. Passing through the small town of Jalez, Mustapha directed a right turn up a narrow valley with 13,000' mountains on each side. As they approached a spectacular 14,000-foot peak, Mustapha directed a left turn off the paved road. Several miles later, bumping violently along an unimproved dirt road, they turned once again and saw a large Bedouin tent with horses and vehicles parked outside.

Nabil stopped the car and Mustapha got out. Two armed Arabs walked up to him, after speaking briefly, Mustapha motioned to Youseff. Youseff slowly got out of the car and joined Mustapha. The two of them walked across the dirt toward the tent; pausing they lifted one of the folds, stooped and went inside.

"Salaam a Likum, Muqtar," Mustapha said, bending slightly at the waist. He faced a tall, thin man wearing a white Kefya, sitting serenely on a large Persian prayer rug. Youseff greeted Usama bin Laden the same way.

"Likum salaam, my friends. How is your health? It is a great day," Usama said in return.

"It is indeed Muqtar. We are well. How does this day find you?" Mustapha replied, straightening up.

"I am very well. It is good to be here in the mountains. It is good for the soul." Speaking slowly, bin Laden went on. "One can get closer to God and nature by living like our ancestors."

"Yes, this is true," Youseff replied.

Sweeping his hands towards the rug in front of him, bin Laden said, "Come, come. Sit down beside me and tell me of your family. It has been a long drive, would you like some *chai*?" Usama nodded at a servant that had followed the two visitors, the servant nodded deeply and went out again.

Moving towards Usama, they sat down on either side of him. The guard that had accompanied them went to the far end of the tent and stood by the tent flap.

"Ahmed, tell me of the American bombing. I have heard that you were almost trapped inside the Air Authority building when it was bombed," Usama began.

"Yes, yes. I was very lucky, a matter of a few minutes and I would have been inside. We had just driven up when the bomb hit the building. I had just gotten out of the car and was still in the street. As it is, I lost my driver and bodyguard. Both have been with me since we were in Africa," Mustapha explained.

"That is lamentable. Praise be to God that you survived."

"Yes, God still has things for me to do," Mustapha agreed.

"Yes, God is great and our task is hard. Ah, a moment, here is Jamiel with our *chai*. Let us enjoy our refreshment," Usama said. The servant placed a small rectangular metal box in front of Usama. Inside the box was a small pile of burning charcoal and a teapot. Usama picked up the pot and poured the hot tea into the glasses Jamiel had spread on the rug.

"Please, my friends. Enjoy your tea. Help yourselves if you would like more," Usama said in his slow sweeping, grand manner.

Mustapha and Youseff each took a glass of tea each, raised it to their lips and saluted Usama.

"Now my friend, please tell me of what you are doing to get our control center back on track in Kabul," Usama said.

"Muqtar, we will be able to restore some of our capability and communications. I lost everything in the raid. Mohideen is helping me restore our facilities. I do not think we can easily replace the Air Authority building. In a matter of a few weeks, we can support your needs. I think the primary control should be in Tora Bora. The Americans will target anything above ground and we cannot afford to expose ourselves in that way."

"So, is the American bombing hurting us as much as it is the Taliban?" Usama asked.

"No, Muqtar. We have spent much effort getting our cave complex operational. Our camps are abandoned and the Americans bomb empty places. Only the Air building has been targeted. We do not need to go underground, but we should shift the bulk of our communications to the Tora Bora complex. It is what we built it for," Mustapha replied.

"Then you are saying that we can proceed as we had planned and not run and hide in the mountains?"

"Yes, Muqtar. The Americans are hitting governmental buildings and are hurting the Taliban. They do not affect us. It is time that we should not be dependant on Taliban phones and buildings. We can use our cell phones, our safe houses and if we keep moving, the Americans will not find us," Mustapha went on.

"That is good. I like to keep on the move, it comes to me easily and I like to be close to my ancestors. I will stay with my tents." Usama turned to look at Youseff. "What of you Youseff? How is the training operation?"

Excited, Youseff was ready to tell bin Laden of his success, "It is going well Muqtar. We have over 12,000 new people in training and over 5,000 experienced men to train them. We are building an invincible Army that will last for centuries in the Afghan mountains."

"This is good news as well. I believe that we will have need of those brave fighters very soon. But we will discuss this later, perhaps over dinner." Turning back to Mustapha he said, "Ahmed my friend I forgot to ask you of Hassan, is he doing well?"

"Yes, Muqtar. Hassan has very good news. Our next great strike against the blasphemous infidel is almost ready. The last shipment has been delivered and is almost in place. They will be ready soon. It will be a glorious day."

"Yes, Hassan is a brave fighter. It will be a wonderful stroke. When the center of evil, the US falls, Europe will be easy prey. No one will doubt our power or dare to confront us," Usama said with satisfaction. "We are close to expanding the kingdom of God."

Airborne over the Arabian Sea

"Bone 71, Diego departure, contact Blackstone on frequency 257.725. Good luck and good hunting!" the controller said as the B-1 left Diego Garcia's airspace.

"Diego, we'll send one for you. G'day, Bone 71," Captain Kyle Loffler said in reply.

"Bone 71 switch 257.725," Major Barry Carmody, the Aircraft Commander transmitted on the second radio.

"We're pretty heavy right now, Barry. What does the flight plan say we'll have at our pre-strike refueling?" Kyle said, reaching for a copy of the flight plan lying on the console between the two pilots. He had crewed with Barry for over a year, but this was only the third time they had flown with the Weapon System Operators or WSOs in the two back seats, Captain Mary Whitman, and First Lieutenant Johnny Nall. They were headed for their second combat mission over Afghanistan and were intent on their jobs.

"I think we'll have about 80K, our divert is Oman all day," Barry said.

"We've got 48 JDAMs today. How many targets are we supposed to cover, Mary?" Barry asked the Offensive WSO.

"Well, we're fragged for 30 targets, but 15 of those are double hits. So we'll have a few spares," Mary replied.

"So, Mary, tell me again how you guys worked out those double hits. This sounds like a weird tactic to me," Barry said.

"Well, it's pretty cool. I was in the Mission Planning Cell yesterday when they cooked this one up."

"We were wondering where you were. We all went down to the beach and no one could find you. You know you're supposed to stick together as a crew don't ya?" Barry said, half in jest. Mary was 28 years old; she cut a very attractive figure, even encased in a green bag. With short black hair, dark eyes and a sharp sense of humor, she was a lot more fun to talk to than the guys were.

"Sorry, boss," Mary said, "I was just doin' my job. It's not all fun and games, tryin' to keep you out of trouble. Some of us have to work between sorties, ya know."

"I know, I know. Just kiddin'," Barry said apologetically. "Tell us about this new tactic."

"Well, it was like this. The weapons guy was checking out the BDA that came in from the first strikes. The JDAMs have been hitting real good; he figured we were getting a better CEP than the Laser bombs. We're hitting whatever coordinate we squirt into the bomb. Anyway, today's frag was for the cave complex at Tora Bora."

"So, it should be simple, we'll just hit those and shut down the caves, right?" Kyle said.

"Not really. You see most of our bombs in Diego right now are the Mk-84s. And the Weapons guy says that they would all go off second order before getting any penetration," Mary explained.

"Yeah, I've heard of that," Kyle said. "Something about the bomb exploding on impact before the fuse sets it off, right?"

"Yeah, that's right. The bomb body isn't strong enough to stay together and get any penetration on hard targets. As the case deforms it sets off the tritinol before the fuse times out," Mary said.

"So, anyway. The Frag says to penetrate and go for a K-Kill and there just aren't enough Blu-109 penetrator bombs to go around. To shut down the caves the weapons guy comes up with this plan. We've got coordinates for the cave mouth and we're gonna hit that with a Mk-84 JDAM. Our bombs are fused for instantaneous and we'll spray rocks all over the place. That way we'll at least get the entrance. Then our wingman Bone 72 will come along a minute in trail and drop a BLU-109 JDAM about 100 yards back from the cave mouth on a one second fuse. Their bombs will penetrate into the cave itself and shut down the entrance and maybe blow out a few eardrums."

"Yeah, that sounds like a good idea," Johnny offered, "How will we do battle damage assessment? How will we know if we did any good?"

"I don't know, but the Weapons guy is pretty sure that the overpressure from the bomb exploding will screw up the cave structure and collapse them," Mary replied. "I guess we should be able to see where the roof collapsed."

"Sounds like all we have to do is keep a tight system and drop off a JDAM on each street corner. Is that right?" Barry said.

"Yeah, that's right," Mary said, after explaining it she was slightly uncertain whether the plan would work. "I guess there are folks that watch these caves and they can see if there is anyone using them. That way they'll know." She hadn't thought of follow-up or BDA. During planning, it seemed like a great idea to make the caves fall in on themselves.

She realized that it might be possible that the second bomb might penetrate into solid rock and explode. Rock would not transmit an overpressure shock wave as dirt would. Dirt was almost like water, somewhat compressible, but it transmitted a shock very well. These were not underground bunkers in dirt where the shock wave of the exploding bomb might be enough to crack open the structure, they were caves hewn out of solid rock.

She had seen a tape of the 5,000 pound GBU-28 Bunker Buster bombs that F-111s had dropped on some of Saddam's bunkers during the Gulf War. It seemed simple in the video. The WSO had just lased the middle of the bunker complex. It had to be the roof; you could see the vents and the door area clearly in the IR image. When the bomb hit it just threw up some debris from the roof and it seemed like a fraction of a second later the door blew off and stuff came spewing out of all the vents after the bomb exploded. A direct hit and it was easy to tell that the bunker was a hard kill. The BDA was right on the screen. This time they would not have an IR target pod to watch the bomb go off and she had no idea where the vents were anyway. What if the penetrator missed the rooms or halls of the cave? Just how much shock would be transmitted to the supports inside the cave?

Shrugging her shoulders, she thought it was worth a try anyway. Better than wasting BLU-109s on regular targets. Maybe if they could figure the BDA out the Strike Eagles would bring in those Bunker Buster bombs. She thought it would be fun to drop one of those.

"Blackstone, Bone 71 flight of two, as fragged." Barry transmitted on the front radio.

"Blackstone copies, Authenticate X-ray, Charlie."

Scanning the crypto sheet Kyle said, "It's X-ray."

"Bone authenticates X-ray," Barry replied over the radio.

"Bone 71, try again. Authenticate Hotel, Zulu," the Blackstone controller said again.

"Shit, it was the wrong code." Barry shot a glance at Kyle. "Dude, read that right, we can't afford a fuck up here."

"I got it right, see. Run the columns yourself. It comes out X-ray," Kyle said defensively.

"Check the time, Kyle. It's supposed to be in Zulu. Check the time on the sheet. Maybe you got the wrong one," Mary interjected.

"Shit, you're right. We just changed times and I forgot to change sheets," Kyle quickly started shuffling the crypto sheets until he found the one matching the current Zulu time. "Barry the new code is Yankee. Tell him Yankee."

"Yeah, I thought so. Blackstone said Zulu in that last authentication. I think he was trying to give us a hint," Mary said.

"Bone authenticates Yankee, I say again Yankee," Barry said pensively.

"Roger copy, Bone 71. You are cleared down track contact Horse on 223.5. See ya on the way back!" the Blackstone controller said merrily.

"Bone 71, Horse. You are following two other flights. Fly 420 knots ground and maintain FL310."

"Roger, Bone copies FL310 for the altitude. We have a hard TOT, unable 420 knots," Barry replied over the radio.

"Sorry, Bone 71. Your TOT is out the window. It's rush hour here today. You don't want to run into anyone else's bombs do you?" Horse asked.

"No, sure don't want to do that. Bone 71 will fly 420 ground."

"Sorry about that Bone. You are cleared in the AOR. Check out with me on 320.4"

"Out on 320.4, Bone copies."

Over Khost, Barry noted, "Okay, boys and girls, were over the dark side now. Keep your heads up, now's no time to take a nap."

"Barry, I've got a tight system. Bomb Bay doors are coming open," Mary said as she concentrated on her target attack. "We've got our first target coming up. I'd like the consent switch now so I can get a hot pickle button."

"Okay, Mary. My consent switch is hot. You've got a hot button. Let's do some good," Barry said over the intercom. "I'm flying this manually today. Kyle tell me if you see me drifting."

Kyle looked over at Barry, checked the displays and then looked outside again at the rugged terrain.

To keep Bone 72 in the loop, Kyle transmitted on the second radio, "Bone 71 is over the IP. Bombs away in two minutes."

"I'm on the pickle button," Mary said as she watched the delivery system.

Matter of factly, Mary intoned, "Ready, Ready, bombs gone." Then, "I'm sequencing to the next target."

"Scope's clean, nobody's looking at us," Johnny said.

To no one in particular, Barry loudly proclaimed, "Hey, you rag-heads. Special delivery for ya. You don't even have to answer the door. Hope you enjoy it."

"Yeah, when it just absolutely has to get there overnight! Roll the Bone's," Kyle joked. Everyone laughed.

A minute later the AC in the second aircraft called, "Bone 72, bombs away."

CHAPTER 6

Four-thirty in the morning on a cloudless night, the headlights of a U-haul panel van illuminated a pool of light in the slow lane. Few other cars were on the road and the van was trying to blend into the sparse westbound traffic, doing exactly the speed limit.

The passenger nervously looked inside and outside the van. Abdul Zadeh, looked at the driver, "Tariq, do not drive faster than the traffic, we must not bring attention to us. As a matter of fact, you must drive the speed limit, no faster. We will be entering Dallas very soon."

Tariq Israni, illuminated in shadow from a passing car, glanced at his friend, "Abdul, I am not speeding, I am driving the speed limit. Soon we will be there, do not be nervous. We must work today, I am worried that you have not had enough sleep?"

"I am not nervous, and besides, I cannot sleep in this truck. I must be at work at seven this morning; I will just have to go. What time will you have to be at work?" Abdul asked.

Tariq stared straight ahead into the darkness, his right hand limply gripped the top of the steering wheel. "I must be there at eight and I will most likely be late. But I do not think they will care, they are happy when cab drivers show up for work."

Settling back into the rhythm of the road, they fell silent once again, deep in thought, staring out the front of the windshield.

Commuter traffic started picking up, as the truck approached 635, the loop around town. The two men rode in the empty silence of being on the road for several days straight. Passing the I-635 exit signs, Abdul blurted, "You must turn south on 635. We should not go directly to the storage center. We should back track before dropping off the truck."

"I think it is fine to drive straight through. We do not have time to waste," Tariq replied.

Sitting up, Abdul gestured towards the exit, "I said we should exit 635 south. Do as I say. It will take little time and attract no attention."

Tariq made no reply; stubbornly he did not turn, continuing straight towards downtown. Fifteen minutes later, he exited at Hampton Road. Stopping at the light, Tariq turned right onto West Commerce and pulled into the U-Lock-it Storage unit. Tariq wheeled the truck smoothly up to one of the small storage spaces and stopped very close to the door of one of the units. Both men got out. Abdul opened the door of the storage room while Tariq slid the door of the U-Haul truck open. Before reaching inside, they both looked around them, checking to see whether they were being watched. Silently, they pulled a wood box out of the truck; together they carried each box from the van into the storage room. Taking the rest of the blankets and boxes they had used to hide their cargo, they threw it hastily into the storage room, littering the floor of the crowded space.

The transfer complete, Abdul locked the door of the storage shed without speaking a word. Tariq closed the door of the U-Haul and Abdul got into the drivers seat. Driving out of the parking lot, Tariq looked at his watch, they had taken less than ten minutes to unload the truck.

Turning westbound on the freeway, Abdul headed for the Dallas U-Haul rental center on I-35E to turn in the truck. Pulling into the parking lot, he paused briefly to let Tariq get out of the passenger side. Tariq half ran towards his car, parked in the strip center parking lot next door. Abdul parked at the front office and went inside, he was the first customer of the day. Abdul had paid cash for the truck's one-way rental from Washington, DC. Too early for conversation, the attendant gave him a surly look, and went outside to look over the van. Abdul followed him outside.

Tariq started his eight-year-old Chevrolet Impala and drove into the parking lot, as Abdul walked out of the door. The attendant watched dully, as Abdul got into the car. Thinking that the two probably owed him money, he strained to see the license plate as the car squealed out of the lot, but could only pick out the first letter and two numbers.

"Quickly, Tariq. Turn out your lights until we get to the road. I think that U-Haul man back there suspected me. I do not know why, but we must not give him any more clues than he already knows," Abdul said, as he began tearing up the credit card he had used for the deposit on the U-Haul truck. "We must not use that credit card again. Money is getting tight, we must get some cash for travel after our mission."

"Yes, but we shouldn't do it all at once. That will attract attention as well. Just use the ATM and take money from the account in Atlanta."

"Yes, yes, we should use mostly cash from now on. Drop me off at the transit office. I will go to work now," Abdul said. "I will meet you at the mosque after work."

Alan Baumler, the Dallas Area Rapid Transit morning shift supervisor, spotted Abdul walk in the door and head for the time clock. Quickly getting up from his desk, he intercepted him in the hallway, "Abdul, you're an hour early. Trying to make up for not showing up to work Sunday or Monday?"

Avoiding eye contact with his supervisor. Abdul said, "No, I am early because it is the only time I could get a ride to work." Ignoring the older man, he fed his time card into the clock and stamped it.

"Is that so. What's your reason for skipping work the last two days? Did the dog eat your homework?" Alan said sarcastically.

"No, my car broke down. I was visiting my cousin in St. Louis on my days off and my car broke. I could not fix it and it took two days to get home. I only just now made it here," Abdul said.

"Car broke, uh? Well you look terrible." Alan asked, "Are you fit to drive this morning?"

Abdul shrugged and pushed past Baumler, "I am fine. I will go to my bus now."

"Go ahead," Alan said, as Abdul walked out into the lot, he added, "Abdul, that's the second time you've not shown for work. Either use the telephone next time or you'll be looking for another job. Got it?"

Nodding, Abdul, turned and walked away. "Yes, Yes. I understand, it will not happen again." Abdul said as he went out the door to the bus parking lot.

At six p.m., Howard Bowman, silently let himself out of the house. Without a word to his mother, he got into his car and drove down the street. His parents' house, a nice colonial with a well groomed yard, was a block west of Preston Street, a couple of miles south of I-635. More and more these days he felt that he wasn't related to his parents, he felt like they didn't even know him. They worshiped things, and did not even go to church on Sunday. They did not even want to know what Howard did, and that was fine with him.

Diving to the mosque in Addison he worried about his friends Abdul and

Tariq. They were true believers and were helping him understand the moral failure that was America. At the mosque he was known as Ahmad Mohammed, perhaps one day he would be able to go to Madras in Yemen or Pakistan and study at the foot of the mullahs. The others at the mosque were dedicated to Islam, but they accepted life here in America. They did not really understand that America was evil and upset the balance of the world. They were fat, lazy and slothful trying to live off the sweat of their brothers. Abdul and Tariq were not like that. They were from Egypt and Saudi Arabia; they understood what life should be like. He felt a kinship with them, as he had not shared with anyone else, he had ever known.

Ever since the glorious attacks on America's decadent financial district, and the symbol of American power, though, it was hard to be a Muslim in the open. He had not heard from his friends since last week. Just a week ago, another mosque in Arlington had been fire bombed. Perhaps they had been caught in a police dragnet, or were victims of American hate. He hoped that he would hear from them today; he was worried. Looking at his watch at a stoplight, he suddenly realized he was late.

Pulling into the parking lot, he noticed Tariq's car parked near the back as it usually was. With satisfaction, he hurried inside, just in time for the first call for prayer.

After prayers, Tariq came up to Howard and slapped him on the back, "Ahmad, it is good to see you. How is your health?"

"I am well. It is good to see you. I have not seen you for several days and have been worried about whether you had fallen victim of American intolerance," Ahmad said quickly. "I had no word from you and was worried."

Tariq laughed, "We are fine. Abdul and I had to visit his cousin in St. Louis. We had car trouble and were just a little late getting back. We are fine."

"Yes, but with the attack on the Arlington mosque last week and the FBI picking up innocent Muslims, I was worried that you would be unfairly caught and held against your will."

"Thanks be to God. We are fine. But have you heard anything, any rumors or anything with our names? What has been on the news in Dallas?" Tariq asked, suddenly nervous.

"I have heard nothing about you. That is why I was worried. The police are picking up what they call suspicious Arabs. This makes you vulnerable to misguided Americans. You need to be careful. Please don't disappear without telling me where you are going."

Relieved, Tariq smiled, "I will not leave you alone next time."

"You and Abdul are the only true believers here, you are my only friends. I do not know what I would do without you," Ahmed replied, petulantly.

"These are fine Muslims but they do not have the fire that God lights in your belly. They have not seen what the evil American society has done to our people. You are a dedicated Muslim, with a desire to learn much. It will be awhile before we are needed, but I promise, you will come with us on our next trip. Until then, we have much to teach you. We only serve Allah. Now be quiet, the Muqtar himself is about to speak on the news and we must be attentive."

The buzz of conversation fell quickly, as one of the worshipers turned up the volume on TV along one side of the wall. The newscaster was talking about a tape of Usama bin Laden that had been released and shown by Al-Jareeza. Everyone intently watched bin Laden listening for the message he had for them. The tape opened with bin Laden seated in front of a rock face, dressed in an American camouflage jacket, with a white turban covering his head. Next to him were his second in command Ayman al-Zawarhiri and Ahmed Mustapha.

Bin Laden began speaking, his voice drowned out by a translator a few seconds later. "The Americans have no proof to justify their cowardly attacks on Afghanistan and its people. And those who claim to be Arab leaders, but remain in the United Nations have become unbelievers and have forsaken the teachings of the Koran.

"The American bombing is not hurting us. The evil Americans are not destroying us. They are cowardly attacking women and children. The Americans have no courage and fear to attack us directly. They choose to destroy the homes of millions of women and children, leaving them homeless before the cold winter months."

Rearranging his microphone, bin Laden paused for a moment, took a brief drink of water, and began speaking again, "Thanks be to God! The greatest buildings of the corrupt Americans were destroyed. America reacts by bombing Afghanistan because they are afraid. They are full of fear from the north to its south, from its west to its east. And now America will not live in peace."

"What America is tasting now is something insignificant compared to what we have tasted for scores of years.

"If inciting honest god-fearing people to strike the World Trade Center is terrorism, and if killing those who kill our sons and families is terrorism, then let history be witness that we are terrorists. We fight for ourselves and our way of life. America is the great Satan and it is not a sin to kill Americans, it is only just and right. They are evil and represent everything that is wrong with the world.

"We say our terror against America is blessed by God, and is justly required in order to put an end to suppression, in order for the United States to stop its support of Israel.

"We have taken up the cause of fighting for our way of life; we have the courage to face great evil. We will not be squashed into the dust alongside the road. I call all good Muslims to take up arms against the infidels. To fight for what is right and just. Kill Americans wherever they hide.

"This is a matter of religion and creed, it is not what Bush and Blair maintain, that this is a war on terrorism. There is no way to ever forget the hostility between us, and the infidels. This is an ideological war so Muslims have to ally themselves with Muslims.

"The Americans have no courage or they would fight us on the ground. Soon they will collapse upon themselves, as they deserve. Muslim's will have a place in the sun, that cannot be attacked and it will endure forever. If Americans think they have paid enough, they will learn they have not. Thanks be to God. Allah Arkbar."

The newscaster began speaking as the translator trailed off. Someone turned the TV in the mosque down and everyone began speaking at once. In the sudden rush of voices, Tariq turned to Ahmad, "You have heard great words from a very great and courageous man. How do you feel after hearing his words?"

"I feel as if I must join the jihad, that it is my duty. We must make sure Muslims are heard as one voice in the world," Ahmad responded, slamming a fist into his open hand.

"This is good. Soon you will be called. Until then do not attract attention or you will never get the chance to become a martyr and live in heaven." Getting up to leave, Tariq concluded, "I will see you again soon."

Ab Bazan, Afghanistan

Uncomfortable, Mark sat cross-legged on top of his feet; he had already shifted his position three or four times. Whatever he did, his knees would start hurting very quickly and one of his feet would go to sleep. To Afghanis, and most Arabs, it was rude to show your feet to strangers making it impossible to stretch out. There was simply no easy way to stay comfortable for long, sitting around the Kepsa plate. Mark already knew that, but it did not change the fact that his knees were killing him. The Americans had arrived a little late after greeting their host they had been shown to an open spot near the back of the room.

Mark observed the crowded room. The cooks had brought in large circular aluminum plates, nearly four feet in diameter. Filled with rice, tomatoes, and onions each plate was topped with the skinned body of a goat. No head or entrails, just muscle still on the bone. Still uncomfortable at the thought of digging in, Mark watched Gary, who was obviously at home and had obviously had done this before. Without a second thought Gary reached in, tore off some meat from the bones. He dropped it onto the rice and mixing the meat with tomatoes and onion he balled it all up into a ball. Hesitating, Mark watched those around him. Without comment, one of the Afghanis next to him pulled off pieces of meat and tossed them in front of him. Nodding at his benefactor, he rolled it into a ball of rice like the one Gary had. After finishing his first rice ball, he reached for the goat, not thinking that it had just been pulled off the fire. Digging deep he tried to get a good-sized hunk of meat, in a few seconds he realized that it was still hot. He pulled his burning fingers out and blew on them for a few minutes. Smiling at his laughing neighbor, he began eating as if he had been doing this for years.

There were three platters in the room, each one was surrounded by men sitting, or kneeling with their legs tucked under them, all of them engrossed in eating. There was very little talking; they were all busy digging in, anxious to get theirs before it was all gone. Dave glanced at Mark between bites, smiled briefly and went back to furiously stuffing his mouth. Mark thought he was obviously much at home or very hungry.

The food on the plates was mostly gone after fifteen minutes. One of the cooks brought around a towel, stopping at each diner for them to wipe their hands. Finished, they moved to sit with their backs against the wall, again tucking their legs to the side or underneath them. A traditional Kepsa dinner progressed in phases now was the time for conversation. The noise level in the room began to rise as small groups began talking animatedly back and forth. Dave left Mark and Gary alone with their neighbors, and went to talk with Fahim on the other side of the room. Mark found it hard to chat in a language he did not quite understand. Feeling it was rude to talk in English, they both just nodded and smiled when addressed, happy to study their new friends.

Dave began making his way back to them, stopping every so often to exchange a few words with someone he knew. Approaching them he squatted next to Mark and whispered in a conspiratorial tone, "Fahim is ready to talk. We're going to another house and have some *chai*. You guys ready?"

"Yeah. It's too bad though, we were just getting the hang of conversation here with Ali. He was telling us about his lawn mower. I suppose we can make an allowance for you though," Gary replied. He and Mark stood, looking expectantly at Dave and then each other, Mark broke the ice. "I guess we're ready."

The three of them trailed Fahim's entourage out the door and into the house next door. The front room was bare and unoccupied. In the middle of the floor, a small charcoal fire burned around a pot of greenish looking tea. Several lumpy cubes of sugar, and six unwashed glasses, on a piece of dirty brown paper sat next to the fire.

They all sat down in a circle around the fire, much as they had for dinner, but smaller. In this new, private setting, Mark expected that they would quickly get down to business and discuss plans for their operations.

With both hands, Mark accepted a glass of tea, vigorously blowing on it and taking tiny sips of the hot liquid. Surprisingly strong, it burned all the way down. He picked up a cube of sugar, dropped it in the tea and watched it dissolve. With a dirty spoon lying on the brown paper, he stirred the thick sugar into this tea.

Finishing his tea, Dave said quietly to Mark, "I will introduce you now and will translate what he says." Grinning, he continued, "You'll just have to trust me that I won't get too wild about those stories of you sleeping with your sister."

"Great, all my secrets revealed and I won't even know about it. Before we do any negotiating, we need to talk. Dave, I gotta know the score before I can commit to anything."

"Sure, sure, but this is just flowery intro stuff, it doesn't mean anything. I'll make sure and check with you. I won't agree to anything without you."

Dave put his glass down. For a long moment he stared into it and then suddenly, as if coming to a decision, quickly looked up at Fahim. He cleared his throat and with a sweeping gesture of his hand, he pointed at Mark and Gary. In Dari he loudly proclaimed, "General Fahim, I would like you to meet my friends from the US Army Special Forces. Their names are Captain Mark Goode and Sergeant Gary Wilkerson. They are the leaders of the Americans that have come to help you."

Listening politely, Fahim smiled at the introductions. With an amused look on his face he began speaking right after Dave was finished.

Leaning towards Mark, Dave interpreted Fahim's remarks, "He greets you and welcomes you to his country. He offers you his hospitality and anything he has is yours."

Before Mark could reply, Gary gripped Dave's upper arm, "Dave, please do us a favor and just say his words. I've been in situations like this before and we just need straight scoop. Don't filter it for us, and don't interpret. It's confusing enough without trying to figure out your spin. I don't want to piss you off, but it'll work if you just say his words. Thanks, man."

Mark nodded at Gary's comments, adding, "I agree, Dave. When it's about me I'll talk to him directly and you just interpret the words. I'll speak slowly so you can keep up."

"Okay, okay. Sorry, I didn't mean to piss you off. I haven't done this interpreter thing very much," Dave back peddled.

"It's okay, we're not pissed. I just know how confusing it can get. Mark and I both speak Arabic and Farsi, but we need you to translate Pathan. It just works better if you do it straight."

Realizing that everyone in the room was looking at them, Mark nodded uncomfortably. Smiling at Fahim, he said, "General Fahim it is an honor to meet you. I am impressed with your troops and how well you have led them against a numerically superior foe for so long. I am Captain Mark Goode and," waving his hand towards Gary, "this is my second in command SFC Gary Wilkerson."

Pausing as Dave translated, he went on, "We are honored to represent our country and fight alongside such famous and dedicated fighters. We look forward to teaching you ways to overcome our joint enemy."

Dave finished translating Mark's words, and waited patiently for Fahim to speak. Fahim leaned to one side and spoke with his Lieutenants, just like Mark and Gary had done before replying, then he spoke directly to Mark. Dave translated quietly, speaking in Mark's ear as he did so.

"It is an honor to meet two American Special Forces soldiers. We also look forward to fighting with our new American friends. We have heard much of your exploits and your bravery. Today, we are interested in you and what battles you have fought."

"Sir, our mission is not really about me, it is about what we can teach you. I would be happy to tell you anything. What is it you would like to know about me or the Army?" Mark said.

"I wish to know how long have you been in the Army? How came you to be in Special Forces? Were you in the Persian Gulf War?" Fahim asked.

"I have been in the Special Forces for two years. Before that, I served a tour in the Rangers and another as a Platoon Commander in a Mechanized Infantry unit. I have spent years training in all aspects of warfare and my team can do much to teach you," Mark replied.

"Yes. How many years is this? You were not in the Gulf War then?" Fahim asked.

"I have served just over eight years and no, I did not serve in the Gulf during the war. I have not seen action in a war of that scale."

Fahim leaned over to his colleagues and said something in private, most of the men around him burst into laughter. Trying not to laugh, a few of them looked at Mark and Gary furtively. Mark spoke quietly into Dave's ear, "What did he say? Was that a joke on me?"

Before Dave could answer, Fahim spoke again, "Excuse me, I was discussing another matter. My question to you was about your experience and your mission here. You come to us saying you would teach us how to fight war. I say most of the men in this room have been fighting for nearly 20 years, what can you teach us?"

Embarrassed, Mark turned beat red. Where had he gone wrong? What did he say? "I am sorry. I did not mean to belittle how well and hard you have fought here in Afghanistan. You are good soldiers and have fought the Taliban with courage. What I meant to say is that we are here to help you."

"I too am sorry if I have made you feel uncomfortable. But you only brought 12 men with you. America does not offer much of a fighting force. You bring no more weapons than 12 men can carry. I need troops and weapons you offer neither. My friend Dave brings US Dollars, these I can use to buy weapons. With dollars, I can pay my men, so that they can make sure their families have enough to eat. When my men are paid, they are happy and word spreads, soon more men will come to our cause. Winter is coming soon and my men have not had time to work their fields. Some have not been able to live in their homes for years because of the Taliban. Their families are living close to starvation, for them there is little promise of a future. To fight the Taliban we need food, money and weapons. Twelve men by themselves, we do not need." Fahim said, looking appreciatively around the room. It was obvious that all the other Afghanis agreed with Fahim.

"I understand, General. You are faced with difficult decisions and conditions. It is extremely hard fighting in the mountains without support. We are here to help you." Mark tried hard to smooth his ruffled feathers.

"Yes, yes. Words." Fahim waived his hand dismissively. "I have had help from the Americans before. When we fought the Russians, the Americans came to help. They offered many things, weapons, ammunition, stinger missiles and money. We beat the Russians and won the war. When that happened the Americans were through with us. They helped us win that war, and then left before the sun was down. Because of this, the Taliban were able to gather strength. We still needed your strength and you abandoned us."

Feeling he was losing control of the meeting, Mark tried to steer it back to the future and what they could do now. "Again, General I am sorry for the mistakes of the past. I cannot fix those mistakes. I can assure you that my country is here now for the long term. We realize our mistakes and are here to fix them. We are serious about helping you defeat the Taliban."

"I see. My friend Dave is giving us the help we need. For the moment, I do not see how you can help us. You are my guests please make yourselves at home. Whatever you need you may get from Ali Ahmeen." He motioned to one of the men beside him. "He is one of my senior commanders, and will supply your needs."

"Thank you, sir. We want for nothing now. You have provided us with a house and water. Our main wish is to help you in your fight with the Taliban," Mark said.

"Maybe this is so. I will give you permission to travel within my territory. You may go where you wish. Perhaps you can find a place where you can help us fight," Fahim said, abruptly standing up. Obviously, the meeting was over as the rest of his entourage stood up as well.

Staring at Mark, a smirk flashing across his face, Fahim said crisply, "You are welcome here. Do not think I have no appreciation of you and your intentions. We will talk again soon. In the meantime make yourselves at home." Turning, he walked quickly out of the house.

Mark looked at Dave in bewilderment, "It looks like I really hit a home run here doesn't it."

"Don't worry about it. He took some pretty hard hits after their provisional government fell apart and the Taliban took over. He's been fighting a guerrilla war in these mountains ever since. I think he's just trying to make a point, he'll come around."

"I agree," said Gary, "When I was in the Gulf, it was the same bullshit. The Saudis, the Egyptians, and the Kuwatis they all spent more time talking than they did anything else. Heck, the Syrians were the worst, those guys even threatened to fight us instead of Iraq before the war started." He gripped Mark's shoulder. "It's just gonna take time, that's all."

"Maybe, but if we don't get something going soon and get these guys fighting the Taliban then this whole thing is going to go to shit. We're not going to bring in huge numbers of troops. Man, this is the show, it's gonna be Special Forces and Zoomies."

"Mark, these things take time. He doesn't know how to use you yet, and besides you're not throwing around a bunch of bucks. It'll work out, just wait and see." Dave assured him.

"I hear you guys, but time is something we don't have a lot of. We've almost got a direct line back to DC and they're breathing down our necks pretty hard."

Dave shrugged his shoulders, "Well maybe we ought to take Fahim's advice. The best thing is to check out the Taloqan area and see what's going on."

"Sure, that's a good idea. You know Fahim's right in one way, there aren't enough of us to make a big impact by ourselves," Mark said, "We are force multipliers, not cannon fodder. Trouble is how do we tell him that."

The last one out the door, Gary said, "Yaas, sir. I think we oughta head out in the morning. Check out those frontlines, that'll give the boys something to do!"

Jalalabad, Afghanistan

A precise man, Samir Mohammed left his house outside of the bazaar district of town. He made sure to lock the door before he got into his Range Rover. Driving south, he headed towards the White Mountains. Negotiating the rough roads was not always easy, surprises lurked around every curve and he wanted to make sure he got to his destination without trouble. The White Mountains formed the border between Afghanistan and Pakistan; they were some of the most rugged mountains in the country.

Samir's specialty in al-Qaeda was politics and religion and he often had to work closely with Pakistanis. As he drove, he worried about the toll the American bombing had so far. The reason for his trip, he wanted to see for himself the new measures they had developed and the result of the bombing. Living underground may seem like a good idea to some, but he wanted to check it out for himself. He was to meet Ahmed Mohideen, the al-Qaeda leader at the Tora Bora cave complex. He drove quickly through the town of Parchir, headed east for a few miles, then turned south on a rugged dirt road.

Climbing slowly into the mountains, his British built four-wheel drive barely labored on the rough, rocky road. He stopped at a small collection of mud-walled huts, just past the outskirts of a nameless small town. Getting out, he walked to one of the huts. Before he got there he was intercepted by several al-Qaeda, each dressed in robes wrapped around their shoulders and armed with Kalashnikov AK-47s. With his new escort, they changed course and began climbing the rough footpath that led to the Tora Bora cave complex.

It was at least another hour of hiking the rock-strewn trail before they reached the midpoint of the mountain ridge four thousand feet above the town. They had stopped at another small group of four small mud walled huts, without ceremony he was ushered into one of the buildings.

Inside he found Ahmed Mohideen waiting for him. Mohideen stood up and greeted him warmly, "Hello my friend. I hope your drive here was a safe one."

"I am well. How is your health?" Samir replied.

"I am well, thank you. You have not been here before. If you are willing I would like to show you the complex," Mohideen replied.

"Yes, I am very interested in seeing what you have done here. The Americans bombed our training camp at Garmabak Ghar last night and there is nothing left. I have never seen such destruction. All those buildings, everything, just gone. Nothing but piles of rock and twisted metal. There were forty buildings there and the only things left are the houses at the end of the field. No one was killed, we were fortunate that we had moved most of our training into the mountains," Samir said, shaking his head slowly.

"We are ready for American bombs. They will not find us here in these mountains. Come, I will show you," Mohideen said, as he led the way outside, up the mountain slope.

"Our first line of defense is the mountain itself. These slopes are very steep; it is hard to find anything in these mountains. Right now we are over 9,000 feet and our caves go almost up to the 13,000 foot level of the ridge line." Rounding a bend in the trail, they entered a new ditch. "Here are the entrances to our first caves. Trenches are spread out one kilometer either side of where we are standing. All of these trenches are connected to caves where we have stored ammunition for rifles and RPGs. From these trenches, we can shoot at anything that moves down below. It would be suicidal to attack us here."

Samir followed Mohideen's gaze, they looked down into the valley and could easily see the town of Parchir spread out far below. Looking to the north, Samir imagined he could see Jalalabad. To the east, the Khyber Pass, the Gateway to Afghanistan. "It would take a very brave man, or a foolish one to attack up this mountain," Mohideen concluded.

Satisfied, Samir observed. "This is a very impressive fortress, Mudier Mohideen. My expertise is that of politics and religion, not that of operations. I can easily see how difficult it would be for an enemy to attack up these slopes. It is hard just to walk up, much less to fight up this slope."

Mohideen nodded with satisfaction, "Come, I will show you some of our caves."

He strode down one of the trenches, pausing at a small outcropping of rock. With a knowing glance at Samir, he stepped through the small opening at the back of the trench. Samir noticed they were suddenly in front of a small rectangular opening in the rock. The entrance was framed in square lengths of timber and filled with broken rock. Together they stooped, bending low to enter the cave.

Mohideen reached for something on a table inside the entrance. Holding it out he said, "Samir, take this flashlight. In a few moments your eyes will adjust to the darkness and this will make it easier for you to see."

In the dim light of Samir's flashlight he said, "Follow me."

Samir followed Mohideen into the dank entrance, down a dimly lit twenty-foot passage. His eyes had not yet adjusted to the darkness when they abruptly reached the end. Too narrow for a man to walk normally, the passage required Samir to turn a little sideways to avoid scraping the walls. He did not realize Mohideen had left him, but he found himself alone. He noticed an opening to the right; Mohideen must have already gone inside. He went through the short passageway and found a rough wooden door; he opened it and brushed through a blanket hanging from the ceiling. Squinting, he was suddenly in a large, well-lit room, perhaps 15 feet long and six feet high. It was packed with Soviet AK-47 ammunition boxes.

Mohideen, stood inside waiting for him; he began describing the room, "This is one of our weapon storage areas. We have mostly rifle ammunition in here. The next room has RPG rounds. If you go through that door on the left, the corridor slopes down for thirty feet and there are sleeping rooms and food storage. There are eight caves for this section of trenches; most of them are interconnected. All the corridors are on different levels and have sharp bends for blast protection. We can move fighters from one area to another, below ground."

Samir, still blinking in the brightly lit room, observed, "That is a very good idea to isolate an explosion. Also, if one cave is discovered or a tunnel is collapsed, there is a way to get out to another area of the mountain. You have done a lot of work in building this complex."

"Thank you, it is true. Many smart people have been working on it for quite awhile, some of the ideas we got from the bunker the CIA built to fight the Russians. Let us go back outside and go up the mountain to another level. There are more caves up there, some with prepared positions to fire mortars on the slope below. Plus, there is our communications cave, from it we have radios and cell phones that can cover the world." Leading the way back into the tunnel, Mohideen went back into the sunlight.

On the surface, they followed another trail uphill to another tier of trenches and caves. One of them, much larger than the one they had just visited. They entered the door, a small one, low to the ground. The entrance passage went straight into the mountain for ten feet, made a sharp turn to the right, and ran another thirty feet before dropping again. At the end of the tunnel, large enough for to man walk normally, there was a very large room, perhaps thirty feet long and over eight feet high. Chairs and tables were arranged along the walls. Telephones and radio receivers were arranged on most tables, a few had computers with bright screens. Samir noticed a clump of telephone cables that ran into the room from another door, he walked closer to examine them.

"Those telephone cables connect our communications center to the Afghani grid and from there to the outside world. We also have HF radio antenna and satellite to get the Internet from here. We can talk with our fighters and send email around the world. Most importantly, since Ahmed Mustapha's communications center was bombed in Kabul, it is up to us to take over all the outgoing communication needs," Mohideen said proudly with a thin smile on his face as he turned slowly around the room. "From here we are secure from prying eyes, and bombs."

"In the rooms next to this one we have people monitoring operations in America and Malaysia, and the Philippines against the infidel. We will execute our next attacks and we will have a glorious victory," Mohideen enthused.

"This cave is connected with sleeping quarters and storage sites. Plus, we have another complex above this. In the next ravine, the American CIA built a cave. This cave, which will take about an hour to walk to, is dug deep inside the mountain. It has ventilation and power systems. The ventilation shafts alone can be used for entrances and exits." Mohideen continued excitedly, "You could stay inside for months."

"The generators have stopped working, however, and now we must use gasoline powered standby generators outside. It is large with many rooms for sleeping and storage. It even has a pool to collect rain and snow for drinking water. In the cave entrance is a passage large enough to hold ZU-23 guns left by the Soviets. With these guns we can shoot down airplanes. There is enough food and water for everyone on the mountain, plus more for visitors."

"The walls of the CIA cave are concrete, with real blast doors inside the cave. This works well against bombing. It is a very nice place and is where our senior leaders will come. You have space in there if you desire it," Mohideen said, clapping Samir's shoulder with pride.

"I believe you. Mustapha was right about the caves, out of the sight of Americans, we do not have to worry about their bombs. What they cannot see they cannot destroy. I have not seen Youseff's training camps in the mountains of the north. But your operations center is very formidable, I am impressed," Samir said.

"We are prepared to fight for years from our caves and mountains. None will ever defeat us here. If they do, well, the Pakistani border is just over the ridge behind us. As a matter of fact, the CIA built us another set of tunnels that lead across the border. You can emerge in Pakistan and never be exposed to the sun."

Back in the sunlight, after their tour underground, Samir was relieved to smell the clean air again. One of the guards pointed excitedly to the southwestern. Three contrails stretched across the blue sky, arranged roughly in a triangle. Mohideen and Samir watched intently, they could barely see the little black dots at the front of the contrail. Suddenly, the dots turned to the right, they lined up behind each other, joining the contrails into one long plume of white smoke, like the head of an arrow. They headed straight over the town of Parchir. Watching, the al-Qaeda leaders stood fascinated as the B-52s opened their bomb bay doors. As if in slow motion, Mohideen saw a large number of small black objects falling below the contrail.

Mesmerized, they watched 54 500 pound bombs fall from each airplane, onto a complex of Taliban buildings just outside the small town. Stunned by bombs exploding continuously for over a minute and a half, the town and entire mountainside were completely obscured in a huge cloud of orange flame and black smoke.

Overhead Gardez, Pakistan

"Tom, we're coming up to the pre-IP at Gardez. I've got an update and a good system. The GPS is tight." Captain Terry Hunter, the Navigator on Chivas 51, the lead B-52 of a flight of three.

"Copy, Terry. How about you Johnny? Are you ready for delivery?" Major Tom McCall, the Aircraft Commander, asked the bombardier.

You could almost here the grin when Captain John Erdmann replied, "Yeah, man. I've got everything tied up nice and tight. And I've got 54 of the prettiest little eggs ready for their breakfast. Special delivery."

Chivas 51 flew past the pre-IP to the Initial Point, a 14,000-foot mountain peak southeast of Kabul. The target for the day, was a Taliban maintenance complex, next to the airport outside of Jalalabad. Resembling the first three fingers of your hand, the traveling Vic formation began to break up as the left aircraft began spreading out wide and dropping back. The aircraft on the right pulled power and began dropping back as well. At the IP, the lead aircraft turned east northeast, the outside aircraft immediately began turning to follow the lead. There was a big gap between the two aircraft. The aircraft on the right wing, number two, hesitated until lead had crossed his nose, then turned to follow, smoothly dropping into the gap left behind by the last aircraft.

"Chivas 51, ten minutes from target." Captain McCall transmitted blindly on the radio.

"Tom, there's another flight ahead of us coming off a target to the south of ours. It's Mash 55. I don't know if they're coming off left or right. Keep a lookout for them."

"Okay, Terry. Arnie, keep your eyes peeled, they're on your side," Tom said.

"I got 'em out at about 2:30. They're in trail and marking," Lieutenant Arnie Bergman said, barely out of flight school he was enthusiastic about everything. Peering out the co-pilot's right window, he gave them a running commentary. "Man, do you think we're dragging contrails like that? It's like we're telegraphing our bomb run. Like a great big advertising sign, saying, get your bombs here, cheap with free delivery."

"Yeah, in a few minutes when we turn again, look behind us and you should be able to see our trail. It's like an arrow of death and destruction," Tom replied. "Hey Arnie, how's our gas doin'? Will we have to do a post-strike refueling?"

This was Arnie's first combat mission and, really, his first deployment in the venerable B-52 Buff. This particular Big Ugly Fat Fucker was almost twice as old as Arnie's 25 years. Arnie recalculated the fuel. "No we won't need it. But we'll have to do a fuel check with two and three to check the wingman's fuel state." Tom's question brought Arnie's head back in the cockpit and the game.

Soon, he was looking outside the window again, "Man, these are the biggest mountains I've ever seen. It is so rugged here, much more than the Rockies. And jeez, it's so brown."

"Five minutes out," Terry Hunter said, "It's time to go air-to-ground."

"My system's tight. I've got a good designation," John Erdmann chimed in.

"Our Nav systems are good. The GPS is tight; I just froze a radar map of the mountain near Jalalabad. We're good to go," Terry said.

"Bomb bay doors coming open," Captain Erdmann said. "Door's are green and open. I'm ready."

"Okay, the consent switch is hot. Johnny it's your airplane," Major McCall said.

"Ready, Ready, drop," Captain Erdmann said as he squeezed the button to fire the bomb release. The string of bombs loaded in the bomb bay, or hanging from the wing racks began falling away from the airplane like a giant zipper. One by one, at 100 millisecond intervals, another bomb dropped off the bomb racks. In the aircraft, the effect was similar to driving along a road paved with bricks and no shocks.

It seemed like an eternity, when the last of the explosive squibs released the bomb shackles and punched off the last bomb into the airstream, Major McCall called out on the radio, "Chivas 51 bombs away."

"I'm showing all the bombs gone. Nothing hung." Captain Erdmann said, "I'm closing the bomb bay doors."

The airplane shuddered as the bomb bay doors closed and Erdmann reported, "Doors are closed, in the green." Looking at Terry he grinned and said, "I'd say it's Miller time."

On the radio, they heard Chivas 52 report their bombs away. The trail aircraft, Chivas 53, had inadvertently opened up spacing a little more than planned and it was nearly a minute later that they called their bombs gone.

The 108 500 pound bombs of the first two aircraft created a firestorm across the maintenance complex. No-one could see in the hell created as each bomb exploded a fraction of a second after the previous one, walking across the target area, smashing everything in its path like the hand of a giant. Everything within a half a mile of the center of the bomb blasts was completely destroyed. Anything within thousands of feet, buildings, vehicles, people, anything was severely damaged. The shock of each bomb added to the previous ones, creating a thunder that seemed to go on for minutes, throwing dust and debris over 2,000 feet into the air.

The last aircraft had dropped CBU-89 Gator mines. The bomblets, housed in Wind Corrected Dispensers sensed the wind drifting them away from the target. The aft fins swung, flying the dispenser toward target. At a pre-determined altitude above the target, the bomb casing split open, fluttered away and the bomblets spun out, creating a pattern on the ground. Each mine, capable of exploding if touched, would self-destruct at random times over the next two weeks. The Taliban would not be able repair the damage or use the airfield and maintenance complex for a very long time.

Hearing the last aircraft call bombs away, Tom turned the lead aircraft ninety degrees to the right, exiting Afghanistan airspace as quickly as possible. Once in Pakistan, he slowed down so the three B-52s could reform into their traveling Vic formation.

"Horse, Chivas 51, checking out with three hits," Major McCall transmitted.

"Roger copy, Chivas. Good work. Cleared direct Dera Khan. Contact Blackstone outbound." The Horse AWACS controller responded. "You're thirty in trail from Mash flight. He's doing 280 knots."

"Chivas copies, thanks, have a good one," Tom replied.

CHAPTER 7

10 October 2001
Kowkcheh River, Afghanistan

The gray light of dawn was breaking over the Khvajeh Mohammad Mountain Range as sixteen horsemen, strung out over a half mile with the morning sun at their backs, approached the Kowkcheh River. Making their way slowly down the shallow hill sloping toward the river, they looked like a throwback in history, or a scene out of a western movie. Most of the riders dressed in tan desert camouflage uniforms with OD green web gear, were wearing black watch caps and sported fuzzy new beards. The others wore western pants and a mix of jackets, long shawls, turbans or fur caps on their heads and all of them had full beards. This 21st Century cavalry was heavily armed with automatic rifles and pistols, most American, some Soviet AK-47s.

Johar led the team as he had when they first came into the country. Dave let his horse follow Johar into the water as he started across the river. The horse jostled on the rocks that littered the riverbed, gradually descending to its belly in water. Dave leaned back, lifting his feet into the air to keep them dry. Behind him, Mark, and the other members of Team 225 were catching up as the group bunched together, waiting to cross the river.

The team was out scouting the Taliban lines around Taloqan. The Northern Alliance held the mountain ridge north and east of town and the Taliban held the valley east of the road. Mark and Gary were there to eyeball the enemy and see how their defenses had been arranged.

As the dawn brightened, Mark could that see they were in very rugged, but open terrain. Feeling uncomfortable and exposed, he could see for miles. Unbroken sight lines were easily 10 to 20 miles. Other than rocks, there was very little cover. Scraggily bushes, trees, some low grasses and very little else covered the light brown landscape.

The terrain was a two edged sword. If they could see the enemy at such long distances, they could also be seen. He had hoped to get across this open terrain before sun up, but travel by horse was slow and complicated. At the very least, Mark hoped that it would be hard to distinguish Americans from Afghanis from a distance.

If they stuck out as he felt they did, they were bigger targets. That would make them defensive and if they were, they stood no chance of being effective. He felt frustration at not being able to do his job the way he knew he should. Being here, right now was a mistake. If this broad open valley, between two rugged ridges, was typical Afghanistan terrain, then it would be impossible to operate covertly. He thought about how he could make the NA let him operate on his own, and then remembered that his primary job was to get the NA to act. His team was not supposed to be the shooters.

Deep in thought, Mark was not paying close attention as his horse sloshed through the river. Without warning, it stumbled, pitching him forward almost into the water. Almost going over the horse's head into the water, Mark grabbed onto the horse's mane as tightly as he could. Losing his seat, he slid down the horse's wet flank, his legs in the water. Mark quickly circled his left arm around its neck. With his right, he desperately hung on as the horse recovered its footing. Dismounting as soon as they had crossed the river, he took stock of his gear and his wet boots. Passing him on the bank, some of his team joked about his riding skills, others just smiled at him glad it had not been they who had been pitched into the water.

Mark took a quick inventory. He had not fallen in, but he had lost two magazines for his M4 and an MRE. Getting back on the horse, he cursed the fact that he had also forgotten to bring replacement socks on today's one-day mission. Suddenly hungry, with wet feet, he rejoined the column, a grumbling tale end Charlie.

The string of horses wound their way across the western edge of the valley and began climbing the opposite ridge. Before long, the slope reached nearly thirty degrees, the trail switching back on itself as they slowly climbed the mountainside. Approaching the craggy top of the ridge, Johar stopped and the column of men and horses began slowly bunching up together. Mark picked his way around those in front of him, making for the front of the column. Passing Luke, he told him to disperse the men, setup lookouts and keep an eye on the terrain around them. Reaching the top, he found Johar, David and Gary already dismounted, scanning the valley beyond with binoculars.

Pulling out a pair of Steiner 7x60 binoculars he kept in his daypack, he began scanning Taloqan, 15 kilometers away in the valley below. At first glance, there appeared to be little movement of any kind.

"I don't see much in town," Mark said. "Where are the lines?"

Dave spoke to Johar, translating his response he said, "The Taliban have trenches dug in on either side of the road entrance into the town and in the low hills above that. They have bunkers that bulge out from the main line at regular intervals, and these have interconnected trenches in the valley leading up to the town."

"Oh, and he says they have tanks dug in on the low hills surrounding the town," Dave added.

"They must be T-54/55s. I don't think the Soviets used anything else in this country. I can't imagine them leaving anything late model, like T-72s," Gary observed.

Johar spoke again, Dave translated, "And don't forget the heavy machine guns in those bunkers at the ends of the trenches."

"Hmm, interlocking fires from heavy machine guns, supported by tank guns. Even if those things can't drive, they're still a big threat and hull down they will be hard to hit," Mark mused. "They've setup a pretty good static defense."

Grinning, Gary said, "I can see why Fahim doesn't want to make a charge of the light brigade in there. Dave, does Johar have any idea how many Taliban are down there?"

Dave translated again, pausing as Johar spoke, "He says around 4,000 Taliban and al-Qaeda in the town. And, ah, around two to three thousand in the ridges around the town."

When Mark did not respond right away, Dave added, "So, how do you think we can take these guys out?"

Sitting down on a rock he took out a notepad. "Well, we sure ain't gonna do it with 12 SF guys. We're gonna have to go about it in another way," Mark said. "I suppose they have a good water supply with that river down there?"

Continuing his halting interrogation, Dave asked Johar about the river, their food supply, as well as Taliban troop locations. When they were done Johar finished staking his horse down, taking a bag from his saddle he pulled out some hard bread. Taking a bite, he just stared at the Americans without expression.

Dave squatted next to Mark, on a low voice he said, "Johar says that the river provides plenty of water and they get their food from Kunduz along the road. Also, the Taliban appear to like the villages. There aren't very many of them outside of the villages and the towns and they rarely come out of the village. There is a small garrison at Khanabad and more than 10,000 in the town of Kunduz."

"Sounds like these guys here at Taloqan are the leading edge of Indian country, from their perspective," Gary observed. "Good for us."

Dave nodded, and continued, "Johar says there are more around Mazar and this type of defense is typical. When the Northern Alliance has attacked in the past, they go in at night, hit a small section of Taliban lines hard and fast. Then they run away before the T get a chance to respond."

"Yeah, but if we cut off their food supply, it would probably still be a while before they were softened up enough to give in," Mark said. "It would be better to get them involved in a fight. We'd have to take out their heavy weapons, hitting those tanks and machine gun posts first."

"Yeah, boss. I see where you're goin'. Take out the tanks and the machine gun pillboxes, that would leave the field open for the NA boys to make a cavalry charge," Gary said.

Taking out his map, Mark folded it, showing the northern end of the country, all the way south to Kabul. "Yeah, in a way. I was thinking on a bigger scale. I think we oughta isolate this whole end of the country. Taloqan is just the beginning. There's only one road and only one pass from here all the way west to Herat."

Mark poked the map with his index finger. "That's the Salang Pass just north of Kabul."

"If we can close that pass, then all the Taliban in Mazar e'Sharif, Kunduz and Taloqan are essentially cutoff. It would take days, maybe even weeks, for any Taliban convoy to make its way through the mountains or around the west end through Herat."

Looking at the map, Dave rubbed his chin, "So, we cutoff the T in the north what then? It doesn't take away their weapons?"

"Maybe not their weapons, but it might impact their will to fight. The first thing it'll do is bring a shiver a fear into their hearts. Then we pin them in place, take away their ability to move and then shoot; it'll make it easier to mop up those that choose to stay."

"I still don't follow you here, Mark. This is the problem facing Fahim," Dave said, gesturing towards the Taliban lines. "Right here at Taloqan. How does it help him by closing Salang Pass?"

Mark dropped his binoculars onto his chest and sat back against a rock, slipping easily into lecture mode. "Dave, it works this way. First, you gotta know that we don't have the troops or firepower to take out those tanks by ourselves. My team just isn't enough."

Gathered in a semi-circle, Gary and Dave sat down in unison. Gary opened an MRE, while they listened to Mark. Pausing, Mark looked at the rest of the team, arrayed on the top of the hill, in clumps of twos and threes, all facing different directions.

Satisfied with security, he took a pull from his canteen, shook his head, and went on. "Second, the best way to fight these guys is not to confront them head on. We're a force multiplier and that's what we want to do here. If we cut off the T in the north then they are isolated from their lines of supply and reinforcement. It simply makes them weaker. It'll also make each town less likely to help the other one out. That way we can concentrate on each one individually."

"Those guys in the trenches wouldn't be much of a threat for a Mech Infantry Company, but the NA are pretty far from anything like a modern Army. Any softening up we can do before they fight them in a pitched battle is all to the good."

"Third, we're not interested in capturing a little ground. Fahim may be, but we need to find a way to collapse the whole Taliban command structure. We need to find a way to deflate the whole country. From a ground pounders point of view, the Salang Pass is *the* choke point for the whole northern part of the country. Winter is not that far away, maybe it's time to be bold," Mark concluded.

"Maybe you're right, but I think it'll be a hard sell to Fahim," Dave concluded.

Gary, poking his food with the white plastic spoon, observed, "The way I see it is if Fahim buys that strategy, we still need a plan on how to deal with local T. Are we gonna call in the Buffs to carpet bomb these guys?"

"No, too big of a hammer. I think the best thing would be to call in TacAir and have them drop those Laser guided bombs like they used for tank plinking in Iraq. I'd bet if we took out the tanks and the machine guns the Taliban wouldn't be so brave," Mark said.

"Fahim will want to know when can we make this happen?" Dave shot back.

"I gotta be honest. I don't know the situation or when we'll get air. But I just know it'll happen."

"But when," Dave pressed. "That's the key. You have to know when."

"Sorry, dude. I don't know when. I know the Air Force is targeting Taliban infrastructure right now. I assume that as soon as they're done then they'll release air to us," Mark equivocated.

"Boss, we do have to come up with a plan on how we're gonna do this. When it does happen, we can't just make this up. We gotta have a plan," Gary said.

"When we do get air, I think we've got to split up the team so we can run different targets."

"Gary, I tend to agree. I think any detailed planning on how we're gonna support Fahim here at Taloqan is premature. The thing is we don't even know how he'll fight, or even if he will, so far it looks like he doesn't like direct confrontations. The way I see it, any plans we make to support him in the field are liable to be wasted, we'll have to wait until we know what he'll do. I think the most important thing, right now, is to isolate the whole area. That will change the whole dynamic for Fahim. From a strategic point of view, we've got to do something now, we've got to close the Salang Pass."

"Okay, boss. I just don't want to get caught flat-footed. In the Gulf a lot of us ended up not doing anything because the Air Force couldn't integrate us into the plan," Gary said. "I just want to be a part of the plan from the beginning."

"We'll get to it. We might just need a Zoomie to help with this. I'll talk with the B Team tonight about it. You're right, we need to think about how to do this thing, rather than make it up as we go along. But for now, we've got to figure out how to get Fahim to close the pass."

Dave sat cross-legged, playing with a couple of rocks at his feet. "Well, some of my buds are clearing the old Soviet airfield at Golbahar. That's pretty close to the Salang Pass. Fahim's people are all through that area. The logistics could be easier there."

"Now you're talkin'! Looking at the map, he doesn't have very far to go. If he can just push out a bit, occupy one ridgeline he could close the pass. Maybe the choppers they're moving into Dushanbe can fly out some supplies, or maybe we can get that turbine DC-3 you guys have to bring in a load of stuff. Let's find out what Fahim might need to mount an operation against the pass," Mark said.

"It sounds good coming from you, but I still think it'll be hard sell. But we can try," Dave shrugged.

Mark moved to lower himself to the ground; leaning against his rock, he took a long swig from his canteen. Wiping his mouth on his sleeve, screwing the top back on the green plastic bottle he got an impish look in his eye. "Tell me something, Dave, why are you here? You're a civilian, but you're living large like an Army guy. What's the deal, don't you like hotels?"

Dave quit playing with the rocks at his feet and with a slight smile looked at Mark. "Yeah, I just love living close to dirt and skipping a shower for a few weeks, it's my life. Mark, I didn't think you were the type to want to hear my life story? Why all the curiosity?"

"I dunno I've never met a real spook before. I'm curious. So why are you here? What did you do before?" Mark said with a bit more force. He was more than curious; in the back of his mind, he had not really trusted this CIA guy since they met the first time. He was a civilian, he was not a professional and the bottom line is that Mark was worried whether he would cut and run when the shit began to fly. He had to know a little more about him.

Dave leaned back and replied with a grin, "Man, if I told you I'd have to kill you. The simple story is that this is the family business; my dad was in the OSS back in World War Two. What about you?"

"For me it's simple, I didn't want to follow in the big man's footsteps. My dad was an Air Force Commando in Vietnam; his dad was a flyer in World War Two. For me, the Army was a better deal." Shrugging his shoulders he went on, "I guess, I just don't like flying, but I was raised to believe in something bigger than yourself. I bought all that profession of arms shit, and I still believe it. Besides, I like being a pro, and I like my job. That's why I'm here. What about you?"

Sensing the undertone of Mark's question, Dave's smile faded from his face. "This is my job too. I don't drive a bus, I don't peddle stocks and I don't order people around. It's up to me to make sure we don't see anymore 9/11 shit."

"Yeah, well, we need to start back and see Fahim," Mark said. He was miffed that Dave clammed up, they were thrown together for this mission and he needed to know something about him.

Dave walked off stiffly. When he was out of earshot, Gary observed, "That dude's wrapped pretty tight."

Tajikistan Refueling Anchor, 28,000 feet

"Exon 55, Cylon 23, inbound with two, noses cold," Jiggy transmitted over the front radio. On the intercom she said, "Hustler, explain to me again why is it that we aren't doing comm out procedures on the tanker? Why do we have to broadcast to the world what we are doing?"

"Fuji told me that's the way the host nation wants it. Some BS about Air Traffic Control or something. Besides, everyone knows what we're doing here, they just don't know exactly where we're goin," Hustler replied. Glancing at his flight plan he crosschecked times with his watch. "We're right on time for the tanker. The winds are in our face and stronger than predicted. We'd better make this tank quick if we're gonna hit our TOT."

"Okay, I'll see what I can do. But I'm not going to do the whole radio drill with this guy."

132

"Roger, Cylon. Exon copies, cleared down track for a fighter turn-on." The Tanker's co-pilot replied to Jiggy's radio call. "Contact the Boomer on this Freq."

Jiggy responded by simply transmitting, "Cylon."

Hustler had been working the radar, not only clearing the airspace for unwanted intruders, but also painting the tanker to get an idea of where he was and what he was doing. Satisfied that there was not any factor traffic that could be a problem, he locked up the tanker so they could finish the rejoin. "Jiggy, there's the lock on the tanker. His aspect is changing, I think he's already started his turn."

"Shoot, he's 23 miles out. That'll put us about two to three miles in trail. What's he doin?" Jiggy said as she looked at the data block for the air-to-air target.

"Remember the tanker said we're cleared for a fighter turn-on. He's just flying around a circle and doesn't care how we get in. Fat, dumb and happy— what a life!" Hustler joked.

"Yeah, I'd bet he did it on purpose. He knows our range; I tuned in his air-to-air TACAN. He knows what he's doing to us. Screw that!" Jiggy said heatedly. Looking over at her wingman, she held her clenched fist up, about head high, so that he could see it. When she saw him looking at her, she pushed her fist forward to the canopy rail. Satisfied that he had seen her visual signal, she put her hand on the throttle and pushed it all the way forward. The jet started accelerating, in less than a minute they had gained 100 knots.

Jiggy used the target box in the HUD to try to find the tanker. She picked up the plan form of the wing as the tanker was still in its turn. "Hustler I've got a visual. Say range."

"Tanker is about five miles now, he's about to roll out. Do you mind if I ask you how long we're gonna scream in here at 400 knots?"

"It's a zen thing. Do you expect me to do math in my head? I was told there would be no air-math." She grinned in her oxygen mask.

The range had closed to almost four miles. Looking out at her wingman again she noticed that he was looking at her closely. Holding her fist up near the front of the canopy she brought it back slowly behind her head. Then, slowly, she reached for the throttles, with a big head nod she pulled them to idle. Her wingman was hanging in position, so she held her hand up again for another visual signal. She held her fingers out straight touching her thumb, then opened and closed her fingers. Without looking at her wingman, she nodded her head again and deployed the speedbrakes. The huge speedbrake on the F-15E sprang into the airstream from the top of the airplane. Other wise known as the boards, the speedbrake was twice as big as the door of a house. The jets began slowing down quickly.

Jiggy looked at the range again; at one-mile back, they were still doing 50 knots more than the tanker. The two big fighters fluidly closed the distance to the tanker like boats on the sea. At a half mile to go, Jiggy gave the visual signal for speedbrakes again and closed the boards. With the throttle still in idle her jet matched airspeeds with the tanker just as it reached the pre-contact position, about 60 feet behind.

Opening the refueling door, she pushed the throttles up slightly to close the distance, over the intercom she said, "Radar is going Standby."

She was very comfortable on the boom and the boomer had plugged her easily. The planned offload was only 10,000 pounds and should have gone quickly. Sensing that they had been on the boom longer than they should she spoke up, "Hustler, how much gas do we have? Are you still showing flow?"

"Jiggy, we're full and up until a second ago we were still showing a little flow. I'd say we're done."

"Copy that, disconnect now," Jiggy said as she pressed down on the Auto-Acq switch to disconnect the hydraulic jaws that held the refueling boom in the airplane's receptacle. Out of the corner of her eye, she watched for the boom to fly up and to the left out of her way. When it didn't she said, "I'll try it again. Ready, disconnect now."

"The boom is still hooked up. It won't release," Hustler said. Twisting in his seat, he looked closely at the refueling probe connected to the airplane just a few feet from his left shoulder. "Jiggy, it's leaking a little gas on the outside of the airplane."

Disgusted Jiggy said, "That's just great. The boom goes out of commission and our wingman doesn't have his gas. This tanker is the only one around. If he doesn't get his gas we'll have to abort."

"We have to get that boom out first," Hustler replied.

"I'll call the tank and have him do the disconnect," Jiggy said as she glanced up at the boomer's window about twenty feet from her canopy. She saw him waving at her, a concerned look in his eyes.

"Jiggy, that won't work. The 135s can't do that, only the KC-10 can. We'll have to do a brute force disconnect, it's no big deal. You just pull power and slowly drop aft. The boom will pull out easily," Hustler offered.

"I guess you're right," Jiggy replied. Breaking her vow to maintain radio silence she wanted to tell the tanker and her wingman what the problem was.

"Exon, Cylon cannot disconnect. There is a malfunction and our system is not working. We'll do a brute force disconnect."

"Exon copies. Drop down ten feet and take it slow," the boomer replied.

"Okay, Hustler here goes," Jiggy walked the throttles back slowly and the jet began dropping aft. At the same time, she eased the airplane down a few feet, working very hard to maintain the centerline on the tanker. Murphy's Law took over as they hit a patch of turbulence. Bouncing around Jiggy concentrated very hard to maintain relative position and move slowly aft. Quick movement now could damage both aircraft.

"The boom is fully extended," Hustler said. Jiggy walked one throttle up to slow their drift aft.

"There it goes," Hustler said. "Oh, shit."

"What?" Jiggy replied suddenly on edge.

Hustler did not respond. Instead, Jiggy heard a dull *Pow*, immediately followed by frigid swirling air filling the cockpit. The inside of the canopy frosted over. Jiggy's first concern was where the tanker was. With her glove she reached up to the front windscreen and tried to wipe away some of the frost. She could see they were separating from the tanker when the *Master Caution* light on the instrument panel caught her eye.

The utility hydraulics were RLSing. She realized there must be a leak in the system and it was trying to isolate the leak. She made up her mind that they would have to turn for home immediately, she punched in the steer point and turned to put it on the nose.

Her mind was racing furiously. She tried to figure out what she had done wrong, or what had happened and what she had to do next. Slowly she became aware of the cold and the noise. She realized that she had not heard from Hustler. Normally he was always right there, in her ear. "Hustler you okay?" Trying again she said, "Hustler, I can't hear anything on the intercom. If you can hear me wiggle the controls." On pins and needles, she held the controls lightly and felt the rudders wiggle slightly. She was relieved, but worried about his condition. "Hustler, we're headed for home right now. It'll be about 45 minutes, but I think we'll be okay."

She continued to watch the Utility hydraulics as it slowly continued to lose fluid. Before long the pressure read zero and she realized that she would have to run the checklist. Turning to her right she tried to reach for her flight bag to pull out her checklist. As she did, the wind almost ripped off her visor, panicked at the thought of having no protection for her eyes, she caught it with her hand and snapped her head back forward under the protection of the front windscreen and HUD. She tried to think of what to do next and realized that since she could not hear the radio she had better have her wingman do all the coordination. Transmitting in the blind she said, "Face, this is Jiggy in the blind. I can't hear anything on the radio or intercom. It looks like we have a hole in our canopy and we've got a utility hydraulic failure. I'm steering for home base right now and slowing to 210 knots. You need to do all the talking."

She descended to 18,000 feet, too high to warm it up much, but better than the frigid below zero air of 28,000 feet. Running the checklist over in her mind she thought about the things she needed to do to land with a hydraulic failure. She glanced at the hydraulic gauge once again to see if there was any pressure left at all. The fuel gauge caught her eye. They had lost about four thousand pounds and must have fuel leak. Concerned that fuel might be a problem; she decided to jettison the bomb load. She rotated the Selective Jettison switch above her left knee to A/G. She wanted to keep her wing tanks and the air-to-air missiles, but get rid of all the bombs.

She could see out of the windscreen a little and looked for a craggy mountain peak to drop the bombs, best not to drop these weapons on friends. Seeing a likely spot, she put her forefinger in the protected Jett button and pressed it purposely. The jet shuddered as all the bombs released from the airplane. She tried to call up a PACS page to see if they had separated cleanly, but could not read the screen. She scanned the instrument panel again to check the status of the airplane. Shocked, she could not bring herself to believe that they had lost 7200 pounds of fuel. The first thought that crossed her mind was the fuel leak was worse, but then she realized she had punched off her fuel tanks with the bombs. They might not make it.

Aboard Cylon 24, Face Davis watched Jiggy's jet closely. He was surprised when she jettisoned her bombs, but realized that it was a good idea. He had called Ganci and everyone there was prepared for Jiggy's arrival. "Dono, get out your Pod and see if you can see Hustler. I think he's still in there, but he must have run his seat all the way down."

"Okay, I'm tracking 'em right now. I can see Hustler. He's huddled as far down as he can get. It must be well below zero in there. Man, it's unbelievable. The entire canopy is just gone, it's a fuckin' convertible. Jiggy is scrunched behind the HUD. I hope they were wearing their jackets!"

"Jesus, I can' t even imagine being in that cold wind. They've gotta be freezing! I can see the jet is wet on the top and the bottom of the wing. That must be were that hydraulic leak is coming from."

"We're only a few minutes out now, Face. Do you want to land first, in case she shuts down the runway?" Dono asked.

"Good idea. We'll do that, but I want to line her up and get the gear down first."

Jiggy saw Face shoot ahead of her and she wondered where he was going. Slowly, she realized that they must be close to base. Checking the INS, she saw they were about 10 miles out and lined up with the runway. She started to slow down to gear speed and ran the checklist from memory to get the gear down safely. About five miles out, Face started pulling ahead of her slowly and she began concentrating on her approach.

She could see out of the front much better and lined up on the runway centerline. She placed the velocity vector past the runway threshold and flew as efficient an approach as she could. She flared the airplane and touched down smoothly. Knowing that she only had emergency brakes and no cable, she aero braked the airplane to about 80 knots. Dropping the nose tire on the runway she pulled the emergency brake handle and stopped the airplane in one fluid motion.

Shutting down the engines, she unstrapped as fast as she could and opened the canopy. Only then did she realize that the entire canopy was shattered, the frame only held a few jagged shards of Plexiglas. She had to check on Hustler, climbing out on the engine intake she scooted back to his seat. He was huddled as close to the floor as he could get. Several of the maintainers joined in and they all reached in and gently pulled him out of the seat.

Seeing his ashen face, she grasped it in both hands. "Hey, dude. I thought you were warm blooded. What's this about you being cold?"

"I, I, I, neeeverr said I wassss cold." Hustler shivered.

"Well, we're gonna call you Eskimo from now on. Let's get you out of here," Jiggy said as she helped get him off the airplane and into the makeshift ambulance.

Jiggy walked into the 492d Squadron Ops, holding her flight gear as well as Hustler's. Trash Cannon was on the desk and asked, "So Jiggy, I heard you had to do a brute force disconnect and the boom smacked the canopy, is that right?"

"Yeah, I didn't realize until later that the boom had shattered the canopy completely. We got a Utility Hydraulic failure along with it. I think we had a fuel leak as well. Do you know where Fuji is, I've got a bone to pick with him over the jett program."

"Fuj is over in flight planning messing with the AFMS. Jiggy, I've got a question for you. Have you ever done a brute force disconnect or refueled anything else but the F-15E?"

Jiggy had already started moving towards the room they were using for flight planning. Pausing, she turned back towards Trash. "No, that's the first time."

"Well you remember that the boom is on the centerline of the tanker and I'd bet you lined up on there, didn't you? Am I right?" Trash asked.

"Yeah, I always line up on the centerline and stay there," Jiggy replied. She was confused about where Trash was going with his questions.

"Jiggy, the thing is that the refueling receptacle on the Eagle is on the left shoulder. That puts a significant side load on the boom. Did you consider that when the boom released it tried to snap back towards the centerline?"

Flushed, Jiggy realized that the emergency might be her fault. "No, I didn't even think of that."

"The boomer should have been controlling the boom, sure, but you gotta think of that next time. Don't put all your eggs in someone else's basket."

Feeling hollow, Jiggy went back towards the flight planning room. Inside she found Fuji. He looked up and asked, "So Jiggy, I heard of your adventure. Glad everyone made it out okay. How'd it go?"

Jiggy was mad and could only focus on one thing, the fact that Fuji had mis-programmed the Selective Jettison routine. "Fuj, didn't you setup the basic program for the AFMS load? Didn't you do the jettison program?"

"Yeah, I did that before we deployed," Fuji replied.

"Well, you fucked it up. I tried it today in Air-to-Ground and it jettisoned the wing tanks as well. I barely made it back to the runway. What were you thinking anyway?"

"Whoa, I'm sorry. I'll look at it, but don't yell at me."

"You put me in a fuckin' bind and all I needed was another problem because you fucked it up!" Jiggy said. She felt her anger beginning to rise.

"Look I'm sorry, but why didn't you check the PACs before you punched the button? You should have looked."

"Yeah, I fucked that up. I trusted you. You're just a fucking Seagull anyway!" Furious, she spun on her heel and picked up Hustlers gear.

"Hey, I said I was sorry," Fuji replied, stunned at her attack. Suddenly mad he yelled at her back. "You never listen, you're just a fucking Ice Princess!"

North of Bellpat, Pakistan

"Shit, I thought, temper tents were bad. This old garage they got us staying in is worse than just sleeping outside. It's cold, drafty and it sure doesn't give much protection against the rain. Plus taking a crap in a hole in the ground is barbaric,"

Sergeant Martin Erdmann announced grumpily to no one in particular. Throwing his blanket over his head, he rolled over and finished his tirade. "And to top it all off they won't even let us shoot anything. This is bullshit!"

"Yeah, when you're right, you're right, Marty. At least the officers have to sleep in the stock room, sooes we don't have to listen to 'em snore. At least we got that goin' for us," one of the gun loaders agreed from his cot.

"We've been here two days and those bomber dudes have been having all the fun. If we're gonna be TDY we might as well be doin' something," Erdmann continued from under his blanket.

"We oughta complain to the boss. Do you think Skeletor could do anything about it?" the loader asked.

Erdmann's muffled voice wafted up from the cot, "Nawh, man. He wants to fire someone up as much as we do. I guess we just gotta wait on the MIFWICS to make up their minds. You know there's gotta be a lot of good we can do there. But it's the same old shit."

"Military way." The loader laughed. "Hurry up and wait."

Major Skeletor Saloman lifted the flap on the GP Medium tent the squadron had erected to serve as the Operations Center next to the parking area. Stooping slightly he ducked his head inside the tent and shuffled inside. Approaching the Field Desk set up with HF radios and the STU-III secure telephone, he grabbed a chair and sat down.

"Hey Johnny," he addressed, Lieutenant Colonel John Arthur, the Gunship detachment commander, "anything good off the wire? Have we made the Frag yet?"

"As a matter of fact it's your lucky day," Lieutenant Colonel Arthur replied. "We're on for two airplanes tonight. It looks like a road recce/interdiction, working with Horse."

Skeletor could barely contain his excitement. "Shit hot. We've been sitting around ever since we got in theater. First Doha and now in this godforsaken rock desert. It'll be good to fire a few rounds downrange!" Skeletor said.

"Yeah. We've only got two tails, so we can't cover the AOR all night. We're gonna run two shifts, early and late. Since you're here, I'll give you first dibs. Which one does your crew want?" Johnny asked. "Oh, don't forget this is Allah's country. Be careful what you say."

"Yeah, sure, I was just kidding with you. Far be it for me to impugn a foreign culture or people. I am just an unfrozen caveman; your technology scares me," Skeletor said, fluttering his fingers in the air, a grin on his face.

"So, Keerock, what's new? Which shift do you want?" Arthur asked again.

"Oh, heck decisions, decisions. I guess I'll take the first shift. Do these guys stay up late or get up early?" Skeletor said.

"No idea. Should I put you down for a wake-up call as well?" Arthur asked.

"No way, the boys will be too excited to take any naps," Skeletor said as he got up out of his chair. Walking to the entrance of the tent he raised the flap and looked back at Lieutenant Colonel Arthur. "I'll send someone to pick up our section of the frag. See ya, when I see ya. QSY"

"Same here," Arthur said, Saloman chuckled again, and disappeared through the flap. Arthur laughed to himself, remembering the old German ATC term, *"Happy to quit speaking to you." I'd almost forgot that term, it fits- QSY.*

Skeletor headed back to the maintenance bay, the billet for his crew. He was slightly distracted thinking about the mission for tonight. For a road recce, they would be assigned a section of road and look for activity and traffic. The published rules of engagement, the ROE, prevented them from attacking any single vehicles without confirmation from the ground or other sources. Moreover, they had to be cleared hot for the sector by the AWACS controller. Other than that, they would be on their own, free to develop and prosecute their own targets. Essentially that meant they would be on their own for tonight. It was good to be back in the saddle. Better check on which tail would be first up tonight, and get the boys into planning mode.

Approaching the building, he saw Jason sitting in a chair outside. "Jason, we're on for tonight, a road recce. Better take the Nav over to Ops and breakout the frag. I'll go shake the Flight Engineer and preflight the airplane."

"Sure boss, we'll get on it," Jason said, jumping up. He zipped his flight suit and went inside to get Captain Larry Maravola, the navigator assigned to their crew. He made his way through the maintenance bay and then the stock room, finally, in the former offices of the office building he found Maravola watching a movie in the makeshift crew lounge.

Maravola looked at him when he came in, Jason said happily, "Hey Larry, we're up. Let's get over to Ops and see what the frag has for us. Skeletor said we've got a road recce."

"Verrrry niiiice. You know it's goood to be wanted. Just where is this road we're supposed to be looking at?" Larry grinned.

"Don't know, let's go check it out." Together they headed out of the maintenance building, making their way to the Ops Tent. It was early afternoon, and the sun was perched high in an arch of electric blue. They walked quickly across the dusty ground. They had been in Bellpat two days; they flew into the airport when the Pakistanis agreed to let them in country. So far, they had not been included on the frag or in any supplements, leaving them nothing to do but sit around. Boredom and frustration showed on everyone's face. To make it worse, the Paks would not let them off base. Their world was the flight line and the makeshift barracks. If one of the crew dogs hadn't brought a TV and VCR, most of the guys would have started to fight with each other or died of boredom. They had come over to establish a forward operating location, planning to fly two or three Gunship missions over Afghanistan and then rotate back to Qatar. Free time was not something they had bargained for.

The silence of their trek to Ops was broken when Larry spoke up, "You know, I was looking at the map of Eastern Afghanistan and they've got more than a few tall mountains. If we're gonna be at 10k above the target we'll be below some of those mountains. Some of those valleys are big enough to turn around in, some aren't. I think it's going to be hard to do our standard left orbit. Instead, I think we'll have to do some trolling passes."

Laughing, Jason replied, "I just want you to keep us away from those rocks. Could you do me that favor? I've got this thing about rocks, especially in the dark."

"Oh, yeah. I see your point," Larry said disdainfully. "That's my job. But you'll have to get over that rock aversion, or at least learn to live with it."

Slowing his pace, Jason said thoughtfully, "I hadn't really thought about it before. But I guess we'll have to do things a little differently here won't we?"

"Yeah, we're not in Kansas anymore," Larry said, reaching for flap of the Ops Tent.

The sun had dipped below the Suliman range as the crew of Spooky 45 gathered around the left wheel blister, just aft of the crew door, for tonight's briefing.

Skeletor cleared his throat to get everyone's attention. "Hey guys, if you can spare a moment of your time, I'd like to tell you what's on the plate for tonight. We're going to do a Road Recce along the A1 highway between Jalalabad and Kabul. We're just working with Horse tonight, no one on the ground. I'd like to remind you the ROE has us first getting clearance from AWACS and that we can't attack single vehicles unless we have an outside confirmation. The weather is going to be clear, all night, with light winds."

"The terrain around Jalalabad is fairly open and around 3-5,000 MSL. The highway passes along a ridgeline to the south that reaches 7300' and the town of

Kabul is bracketed northeast and southeast by peaks nine and eleven thousand feet high. Terrain will definitely be a factor for us. Given the higher ridge along the south side of the road we'll be trolling on the north side. Around Jalalabad we can do orbits. Well, that's the highlights for tonight. Oh, I almost forgot, one of the MC-130 boys will be dropping a Daisy Cutter on Tora Bora tonight. That's just south of Jalalabad and our section of road." Looking up from his notes, he asked, "Anyone have any questions?"

"Yes, sir. What time is that big boy going off? That's a fireworks show I'd love to see!"

"It's scheduled for about mid-way into our Vul time. I'll let you know Mike, wouldn't want you to miss your show." Skeletor grinned. "Let's get this thing rolling."

"Horse, Spooky 45. We've got a convoy of six vehicles crossing the A1 Sorkh Rud River Bridge, west of Jalalabad. Request permission to engage," Jason transmitted.

"Spooky, you are cleared to engage the target. Report BDA."

"Roger, Spooky 45 cleared to engage six vehicle convoy," Jason replied, un-keying the mike, he looked at Skeletor. "Okay, boss. Horse cleared us hot."

"Thanks, Jason. FCO get the 40 and the 105 ready. We'll shoot the front of the convoy and get 'em to stop," Skeletor said. "Then we'll tag the tail-end Charlie on the way down the other side."

"Right boss, guns ready," the Fire Control Officer said.

"We'll be in position to shoot in about two minutes. I'll hit the lead car and then we'll rake the convoy with the 40."

"Sounds good. We're ready," the FCO said.

The lead car was approaching the crosshairs of Skeletor's gunsight, mounted on the left window of the airplane. "Ready, ready, fire!" Skeletor said as the car bisected the sight. The aircraft lurched when the big gun fired.

Looking through the infrared sight system the FCO saw the lead car explode, two following cars swerve to avoid it, and the last three crash into the each other. "Shack, boss. The tail end Charlie crashed into the guy in front, no need to bottle them up. They did it too themselves."

"Great, hit them with the 40," Skeletor ordered.

Skeletor watched the video as the bright blooms of the exploding 40mm rounds enveloped the remaining vehicles of the convoy. The third truck seemed to explode twice as a much larger bloom rapidly covered the first blast of the shell.

The FCO observed, "That third truck had some good secondaries. Looks like we got 'em all. We can see some T running around. Boss you want us to take them out too?"

"No, let them go. Our targets for tonight are the vehicles. Besides it's getting close to Mike's fireworks show. Let's head back to Jalalabad," Skeletor said.

"I'm all over that!" Mike, one of the gun loaders said.

Skeletor looked at Jason's dark form, his face illuminated by the instrument panel lights. "Jason let's come off right and go north of Jalalabad. We'll fly past it a bit and then turn back over the city so we can let the boys see the blast from the left side." Jason nodded in response. Concentrating, he rolled the airplane into a thirty degree right bank. Glancing at the situational display, he rolled out on an easterly heading. Jalalabad was dark but only 12 miles in front of them. Passing Jalalabad, he flew another four minutes before turning back to a westerly heading. The entire crew gathered at the weapons ports and cockpit windows to watch the explosion.

Out the corner of his eye, he saw a few of the crew at the window, looking aft of the airplane, "Hey, the TB area is about twenty miles just forward of the left wing. Their TOT is in thirty seconds."

"Spooky 45, Horse, traffic, left 9:30, opposite direction, two thousand below."

"Spooky 45, copies, we are hold fire, and will hold this heading," Jason replied.

Out in the darkness, heading east two thousand feet below them, was an MC-130H carrying a BLU-82/B. The seven and half ton bomb, filled with 12,000 pounds of explosive and mounted on a pallet in the cargo bay of the C-130. When it came time to drop the bomb, the 130 crewmen would release the shackles and push the bomb along the rollers until it built up speed and fell out the open cargo door. As it entered the slipstream, a small parachute would deploy to stabilize the bomb during the descent. A radar fuse would detonate the bomb at a pre-determined altitude.

"Hey, Jason when is it going to go off," one of the crewmen asked.

"Any second, just wait for it, it should be just aft of the wing now," Jason replied. He strained, but still could not quite see out the left window. Besides, with the rest of the crew pressed against the glass it did not leave any room for him to see. Somebody had to fly the airplane; he relaxed and sat back, looking out the front.

"God Damn! Did you see that?" one of crewman said excitedly. "A bright flash, for a second or two lit up the whole area of the mountain. Damn that was a big one."

The others chimed in excitedly about what they had seen. Jason just kept flying.

Tora Bora, Afghanistan

Ahmed Mohideen suddenly found himself on the floor, thrown out of his bed, he couldn't see in the dark. Confused, he sat up, a long moment passed before questions began to race through his head. Where was he, what had happened, what was going on? He groped for the light switch. He was sure light would reveal the tear in his world. He had been sleeping soundly and all of a sudden his head hurt and his ears rang. The light did not come one, he fingered the light switch back and forth, several times. It dawned on him that the light wasn't going to work. Fuzzily, the thought came to him that the generator must not be functioning, maybe it was the generator that had made the noise. Suddenly, he realized where he was and what must have happened.

He opened the door and stumbled into the hall shouting for his bodyguards. The second he shouted, he winced in pain from the pounding in his head. For no reason, an image of what had happened to his friend, Mustapha, in Kabul shot through his mind. He knew it was not a generator, it had been an explosion, an enormous bomb. He worked his way outside, feeling along the wall. In the dim starlight, he could see the house next door was blown totally flat. He turned slowly around; the roof and one wall of his own house was lit with a flickering light and heavily damaged. Turning to look up slope, he could see that the light came from several other houses burning furiously.

Stepping over the rubble strewn everywhere, he went toward what had been the front of the compound. All the buildings and trees were down; everything was flattened or splintered into thousands of pieces. As if pasted in the scene of destruction, a few men wandered listlessly, endlessly looking in the debris for something they could not see.

Mohideen shouted, trying to get their attention. Moving closer to them, he could see that they were all in a daze, still stunned by the explosion. Recognizing the nearest man as someone he knew, he grabbed his arm and said, "Saleh, Saleh. Listen to me. Where were you when the bombs dropped?"

Saleh Zaidi looked at Mohideen blankly; slowly, almost painfully, he said, "I was in the kitchen with three others. There was only one explosion. It was bigger than any I have seen. It was bigger than the sun. I cannot find any of my companions. Do you know where they are?"

"One explosion, not many. Not like we saw yesterday? Are you sure only one bomb?" Mohideen said.

"Oh, yes, there was only one explosion. One huge flash, like a message from

God, and then the house was on top of me. Have you seen Kalid and Ahmer? I have been looking for them, they were here a minute ago." Saleh, asked, his eyes wandering jerkily around what was left of the compound.

"No, I have not seen them. Where did the bomb go off? Was it right on top of us?" Mohideen asked.

Saleh's gaze returned to Mohideen, slowly he pointed up the ridgeline. "The flash came from up the mountain. It was not right here."

"How far up the mountain did it explode?"

"I do not know. I saw the flash and then when the sound reached us the house was on top of me," Saleh said. "I could do nothing."

Thinking to himself, Mohideen said aloud, "It must have been several kilometers away. It must have gone off near the caves. We are still alive so it must not have been a nuclear bomb. But I have never heard of one bomb so big before." Saleh just looked at him, expressionless and lost.

As if wading through a fog, Mohideen began to gather his wits; he was desperately trying to think of something to do, suddenly he said, "We must look to the caves. We must gather those of us left alive here and see if anyone in the caves is still alive. Quickly, Saleh, gather others and we shall go to the caves."

Less than a half hour later, Mohideen led 15 stunned survivors up the mountainside to the cave complex to search for survivors. A bomb that big must have made a huge crater, destroying everything in its path. Climbing the mountainside he began to despair that they would not find anything left. The ground was scoured by a flaming wind, everything was burnt or broken, nothing was recognizable, even the dirt was charred. The shock wave had destroyed everything in its path. Even the rocks were thrown here and there, torn from their resting place.

The trenches of the lowest set of caves were the first things he recognized; they were filled with debris from the explosion. The mouths of the caves were covered in rock and dirt. At the mouth of the first cave, he set the men to digging. Frantically, they began to uncover it. It seemed like hours before the occupants burst out, coughing and gasping for breath in the clear air. Breathing dust in the dark halls of the caves, they believed they were trapped and soon to die.

By mid-morning the searchers determined that most of the caves had not suffered much damage and they had very little casualties. Surprisingly, the men in the caves were better off than those who had been outside on the mountain. They were dirty, some scratched and bruised, but for the most part, no serious injuries. The epicenter of the explosion had occurred nearly two kilometers up the mountainside from Mohideen's house. An airburst, blast and shockwave had done most of the damage. Sending tons of dirt and debris down hill in an avalanche of destruction.

The only al-Qaeda killed in the blast were in the cave closest to the center of the explosion. Horrifically, the shock had not collapsed the cave on its occupants; it was much worse. The explosion had sucked all the air from the area around the bomb. It was obvious that the men had died without knowing what had happened.

After assessing the extent of his damage, Mohideen made sure the wounded were taken care of and then went to the communication center.

One of the operators was there working on the equipment, Mohideen said, "We must tell the others what happened here. Have you been in contact or told anyone yet?"

Shrugging his shoulders, the radio operator replied, "No, Mudier. We have not been able to talk with anyone on the radio or the phones. We have tried, but there is no one awake this morning."

"Have you checked your equipment? Do we have a problem with our equipment?" Mohideen asked, shaking his head.

Wide eyed with a dirty face, the operator abruptly said, "No, we have never had a problem before with bombing. Our equipment has always worked. It cannot be our problem."

"Go and check your system and your antenna quickly. And have someone trace the phone lines." Mohideen directed him, irritated at his claim; "There is probably a break in the wires.

Taking a bottle of water from one of the tables, Mohideen sat down. It had been many hours since the bomb had broken his dreams and he was not sure what to do next.

Mohideen had begun to relax when the radio operator rushed in to report that the entire antenna farm was blown down. On top of that, they could not find the phone lines at all. Perhaps somewhere below them on the mountainside they still lay on the rock. Here, they definitely were no longer connected to the Afghan phone system in Parchir.

Drawn with fatigue, Mohideen could not bring himself to look at the radio operator, "We cannot remain out of communication. Repair your antenna as quickly as you can, find the phone lines and repair them. I must report to Kabul what has happened, I will go down the mountain, the cell phone it is the only way to communicate now."

Without word, he strode out of the building and went quickly down hill, looking for a vehicle he could use to drive within range of the cell phone network.

Driving recklessly down the rough mountain road, Mohideen looked down at his phone to check the cell signal indicator. Finally, when the bars showed a good signal, he stopped the car and dialed Samir Mohammed.

"Hello, Samir. It is Ahmed. I have driven down the mountain to talk with you on the cell phone," Mohideen said breathlessly.

Surprised to hear his friend this late at night, Samir asked, "Yes, old friend. What is it? Why do you call me so out of breath?" Samir asked.

"We have been bombed," Mohideen said simply.

"Yes, Ahmed, you have had a lot of attention from the Americans. You have been heavily bombed. So far, I understand they have not penetrated your caves. Was it very bad last night, what happened?"

"Samir, the bomb they used last night was bigger than any I have ever seen. Always the bombs are dropped, one after another, but this time the Americans dropped only one bomb. There was a huge explosion that destroyed everything above ground."

"How many caves were collapsed? How many men were killed?" Samir asked.

"We had few men killed and none of the caves were collapsed. Rocks and debris buried many of the cave doors, but we have been able to free them. Only a few were killed."

"Ahmed, it sounds like relatively light casualties to me, even if the bomb was bigger than before. Is your operation still working then?"

"Casualties were light, but the blast cleared away all of the antennas for the radios. It was a foul wind that scoured the ground and blew everything down the mountain. We do not know where they are; perhaps they are in your backyard. The phone lines are all broken as well; it will take a long time to repair them. There is no doubt we cannot operate as a control center until they are repaired," Mohideen said glumly.

"Ahmed, we cannot wait that long. The rabbits must be tended and the crops must be sown. We must move your communications," Samir concluded.

"Yes, I agree. Even if we can repair the radios and phones quickly, the Americans will continue to bomb us. They know we are in this area and they will not stop."

For a moment Samir was silent, he was trying to come up with a plan to move the communications. They would need trucks and a secure place to put them. "Ahmed, we shall move the communications equipment to Kabul. First, I shall gather trucks and drivers. I will meet you above Parchir this afternoon and we will begin."

"No, Kabul is not good. Mustapha cannot have had enough time to recover and I am sure he is not ready since the bombing of the Air Authority building," Mohideen said.

"Yes, I suppose you are right. Then we should move it to Salang Pass. Youseff can handle it. Usama is near there right now."

"Good, I shall have my men and all the papers ready. Have the trucks here this afternoon and we will move tonight," Mohideen said.

"No, Ahmed, we cannot move at night. Last night a convoy was destroyed after it crossed the river west of Jalalabad. Others were attacked on the road to Kabul. Night is a dangerous time."

"I see, I will be ready. I will bring men and weapons as well as my radio and telephone people," Mohideen asked.

"Ahmed, I will send my people and trucks. I will not be there today, I must meet with the Pakistanis tomorrow." Samir asked, "Will you go north and abandon Tora Bora?"

"No, I will only send a few men. The Americans did not destroy our caves. We are safe and strong in the caves. We cannot abandon this strong position. Our radio antennas are vulnerable to American bombs. They will bombs us, but we will not lose our caves here."

"Good, I am worried most about keeping contact with the rabbits. I am sure Usama will agree that we need to get back on the air as soon as possible," Samir concluded.

11 October 2001
39,000 Feet over Peshawar, Pakistan

"Spooky 52, Cadillac, I've got new traffic for you. Target is moving north on the road from Parchir to Jalalabad. Large target, how copy?" the controller aboard the Air Force JSTARS aircraft called.

"Spooky 52, copies. We're retrograde now. Sorry, but we're RTB, unable to investigate." Dawn was chasing the second gunship sortie of the night over the mountain range north of Jalalabad as they headed home. The AC-130 gunship is a large slow moving four-engine turboprop; with weapons, poking out in the breeze it was even slower than a standard C-130. Without darkness to shield them, they were very tempting targets for anyone with a shoulder-fired surface-to-air missile or a large caliber machine gun. In the Gulf War, a gunship tried to operate past dawn and they had paid the price with the loss of all hands. Gunship crewmen very much preferred to operate where they could see, but not be seen, in the dark.

Aboard the JSTARS radar surveillance aircraft, the controller abruptly pushed her seat back on the rails, "Shit, all we've found tonight has been onesies and twosies. Now we've got a big target, it's gotta be ten or twelve trucks and my only shooter goes away."

Lieutenant Colonel 'Buffalo' Herd, the mission commander aboard the JSTARS, had been standing behind her seat. "Lisa, relax, this is our first sortie. We're not going to win the war on our first mission. Heck, this is even the first time we've worked with the Spookies in a hot zone. Both of the gunship sorties found several targets. All things considered, we've done pretty good for a first time out."

Lisa folded her arms, looking morosely at the multi-colored screen in front of her. "Yes, sir. This is such a good target. Small convoys are one thing, but this the first big one. It's just frustrating, that's all."

Shifting his coffee cup to his left hand, Buffalo patted her on the shoulder. "Let me take a look at the frag. Maybe there's someone inbound that we can redirect. Keep a close eye on these guys and see where they go."

Back at his station, he set his coffee cup down on the console and typed a command into the computer. Seconds later, the days Air Tasking Order flashed up on his screen. He paged down to the current time block and scanned the callsigns and aircraft types. All were big bombers, B-1s and B-52s. There weren't any fighters for another four hours or so.

He went back to 1st Lieutenant Lisa MacKay's station, where he leaned over her. "Lisa, there aren't any fighters for another four hours. Only bombers. The only fighters are Navy and they're fragged for the southern part of the country. We're not gonna get them up here."

"Well sir, let's just re-target one of the big boys. They've got JDAMs don't they? They can reprogram on the fly."

"Yeah, their carrying JDAMs but that doesn't mean they can hit a moving target with 'em. They can reprogram the target coordinates for each bomb. For a moving target, you've got to be able to see it and predict where it's going to be. Strafing a moving target is one thing, hitting a moving target with a bomb is a whole lot harder," Buffalo said.

"Sir, I just hate to see this target get away. These guys are already getting close to Jalalabad. They're hauling ass. I read something once about a Strike Eagle guy that shot down a helicopter in the Gulf War with a bomb, why can't we do the same thing?"

"Yeah, it's a true story. But it was a laser-guided bomb, not a JDAM. The WSO in the back was able to re-designate the slow moving chopper as a target with the targeting pod, when they dropped it, they guided the bomb onto the chopper."

Glancing over her shoulder at her boss, Lisa asked, "Didn't you fly Strike Eagles back then?"

"Yeah, until I hurt my back. I was an Instructor WSO at Shady-J, I even knew the guy who shot down the chopper. The Strike Eagle is good at re-targeting on the fly. So to speak."

"But, why can't a bomber do that too?" Lisa asked.

"The biggest reason is that they need coordinates. If it's a fixed target, like a building or a bridge, they can use their radar to either see it or update on something else. If it's a mobile target, they've got to have coordinates from somebody else. They don't have anything like the Target Pod the Strike Eagle has. They can't actually see a target with their eyes."

"So, we're up the creek without a paddle until tonight?" Lisa said.

"Yeah, looks that way. I'll call Horse just to see if they've had something show up that we can use, but for now just keep an eye on where they go. If you can keep track of them, maybe we'll get some eyeballs on them tonight."

Buffalo sat down to raise the AWACS mission commander on his radio, "Horse, Cadillac, on secure."

"Cadillac, Horse in the green, go ahead." The AWACS mission commander replied.

"Horse, I've got a really good target. A large, fast moving convoy that originated in the Tora Bora area. It's currently in the outskirts of Jalalabad. We're watching it closely, but we've got no shooters."

"Horse copies. What about Spooky 52, you guys were paired weren't you?" the AWACS commander replied.

"Affirmative. But they're keeping vampire hours and they had to RTB before they turned into a pumpkin," Buffalo said.

"Well I can offer you a two-ship of B-1s. They've got 48 JDAMs between them. You should be able to have fun with them."

"No thanks, I don't think they'll work. The shooter has to be able to get eyes on target. Got anything else?"

"Not until next shift. The next flight we've got are Buffs. The only fighters

I've got scheduled are a four ship of Strike Eagles due in about four hours. Sorry, I can't help you."

"Yeah, I looked at the frag too. I didn't see anything, but it never hurts to ask," Buffalo said, a little disappointed.

"Cadillac, say again, your last was garbled," the AWACS commander asked.

"Horse, Cadillac copies, negative on the request. Thanks for your help," Buffalo said, slowly and clearly.

"Lisa, where is our convoy now?" Buffalo asked, leaning over the screen.

Pointing to the individual crosshair markers that represented each moving target on her screen, Lisa said, "They're already through J-bad and headed north on A1 towards Kabul."

Tracing the image of the road between Jalalabad and Kabul with her finger she continued, "I guess the word got out that we've been shooting up trucks that move at night. You can see that the convoy is growing, there are fourteen now, two more joined as they went through J-bad."

"Maybe. Or maybe they just like to get up early in the morning."

Lisa looked up at him and asked, "I doubt it. Any luck talking to Horse? Did you get any shooters?"

"Naw, it was like I said. Nothing on the frag that can put eyeballs on the target. We'll just watch them. If they stop where we can get a good posit, maybe we can hit them with a JDAM."

"I'll keep tabs on 'em. I don't have anything else to do!" Lisa said with a shrug. "They're already across the bridge where Spooky 45 hit that convoy last night. At this rate they'll be in Kabul in less than an hour."

Buffalo nodded, patting her shoulder again, he said, "Keep up the good work. I'm going to check on what's happening around the rest of the country." With a distracted smile, he left to look at the other screens.

After checking with the other controllers in the airplane, Buffalo went back to his screen, to page through the frag. It was a slow time and he had begun wondering where his old unit was, maybe they were deployed as well. Looking through the frag, he found the 335th and the 336th Fighter Squadrons from Seymour Johnson AFB deployed to Qatar. Sipping his coffee, he remembered that the Eagles, his old squadron, had been converted to a training unit, they would not be deployed to this operation.

An hour passed and from the corner of his eye Buffalo noticed 1st Lieutenant MacKay waving at him. He got up and walked over to her. "What's up?"

"My target blew right through Kabul and now they're headed north on the

A76 towards Charikar."

"Strange. I would have bet money that they would stop in the city. They must be carrying something important or headed to a particular place." With a nod he added, "This is good news. Are they still moving fast?"

"Yes, sir. They're still hauling the mail and they added three or four trucks passing through Kabul."

"In the Intel briefing I heard yesterday they were talking about possible reinforcements of the Kunduz, Taloqan area. Maybe that's where they are going. Keep a close eye. This is the kind of stuff that we've got to send back up channel. Right now these guys are good intelligence for us."

"I'll keep my eyes peeled, boss. We're going off station in another three hours aren't we?" Lisa asked.

"Yep, do you need a break? You've been at the console for, what, nearly three hours already?"

"No, sir, I'm okay. I've got water. I'm fine," Lisa said.

"Well if you need to go to the can let me know," Buffalo said. "Keep me posted if these guys stop or anymore trucks join the convoy. I oughta see if I can get the ELINT boys to see if they hear anything from them. They've gotta be communicating, either by radio or cell." He left to go and see if he could get some electronic snooping support to shadow their convoy. He would try to raise the AWACS or Rivet Joint controllers, or maybe a Commando Solo was airborne.

Before Buffalo had started getting ELINT involvement, one of the controllers tapped him on the shoulder, "Hey, boss. Lisa is over there waving at you like mad."

"Yeah, thanks, I guess I'd better see what she wants." Getting up again he went back to MacKay's station.

"Any changes?" he said as he approached.

"You bet, there are nearly 20 vehicles now and they blew right though Charikar. They're climbing the mountain towards the pass at Salang," she said excitedly.

"Well, they're getting bigger. Sounds like Intel was right about reinforcements for Kunduz."

"I wouldn't know about that, sir. I'm going to lose these guys as they go through the pass. With the orbit we're in, I won't be able to reacquire them until they get to Baghlan. That's another 60-80 klicks through the mountains."

"I don't figure they'll let us move our orbit to over Afghanistan. You'll just have to let 'em go. Nobody is flying over that side of the mountain range.

There's no CSAR to cover that area for another couple of days."

Disappointed, Lisa said, "Okay, sir. I'll keep a lookout, but the odds are I'll lose them. That's a lot of area I'm blind in. Is there anyway for someone to get sensors on the area?" She hated to lose such a big target; she almost felt as if it was her target, her convoy and these guys were obviously up to something. If she lost them, they might never be able to reacquire the target.

"No, sorry. That's the ROE right now. Just do what you can. Remember we're not going to win the war in one sortie." Buffalo stood up.

Debriefing the Intelligence Officer after the mission, Lisa played the tape showing the convoy, and how it got larger as it approached the Salang Pass.

Pointing to the image, she said, "And here they enter the pass. You can see the road out of Pol-e Khormi about 60 klicks north of the pass. We extended our orbit to the east up to the Afghani border as far as we could, but I couldn't see any further south than Pol. I never did pick up the convoy again. That's it, I passed the target along to the guys that took over from us."

"So, would you say we lost a large convoy of approximately twenty trucks somewhere between Salang Pass and Baghlan?" the Intel Officer asked.

"I'd refine it a bit. They're somewhere south of Po-e Khormi. They were lost in the shadow of the mountain," Lisa replied. "Is there anyway you can get some eyeballs up there to see where they've gone?"

"I don't know. I'll pass the contact along to the CAOC, maybe they'll task the U-2s or have the overhead boys look in the area. But you know, I can't do anything other than that myself?"

"I know, I know. It's just that I know these guys were up to something, I could feel it. I want to find them," Lisa said as she stood up.

CHAPTER 8

Ab Bazan, Afghanistan

Dave paused at the plain wood door of the SF hooch. Leaning with one hand against the whitewashed mud wall of the building, he kicked the wall with one foot and then the other in a vain attempt to knock some of the dust off his boots and jeans. Dissatisfied, he shook his head, opened the door and stepped inside.

The team had gotten back from their Taloqan survey less than an hour previously. They had just begun to settle in and rest. Inside, Dave looked slowly around the front room at the sleeping bodies, sprawled next to the walls. Not seeing Mark or Gary, he headed for the back. Entering the kitchen, Dave saw Mark and Gary cooking the team's dinner. Two kerosene heaters served as the stove top, Mark tended a pot of boiling spaghetti noodles on one and Gary was frying a pan of some tough looking meat on the other.

Dave sat down on the floor, loosened his web gear and cradled his AK-47 in his lap. Suddenly tired, he leaned his back against the wall and watched the cooks. After a few minutes he said, "That looks like the best Italian food this side of the Med. Is there enough for a third wheel?"

"No way, dude. Thing is, what do you bring to the party? Everybody's got to bring something," Luke replied, barely suppressing a smile.

Dave opened a small paper bag by his side. "Well, I got some tread bread from the *Muj* down the street. Does that count?"

"Sure, dude. That's a score, you're in." Gary joked, "Although, I think we all would have preferred it if you'd brought wine instead."

Laughing, they all smiled with a quick flash of memories of home and anticipation of a tasty meal.

Mark stirred the boiling water, looking evenly at Dave, he asked, "So, did you catch up with Fahim? Are we gonna get to talk with him sometime soon?"

"Yeah, I saw him. He sent his respects and would love to see his American friends after breakfast tomorrow. I think he's looking forward to hearing how to win the war and route the Taliban from his cherished Military advisors."

"Yeah, right. Thanks for your support." Mark said with a smile, "Got any land in Florida I can buy as well?"

Mark turned serious, "Did you really tell him what I want to talk about?"

Waving his hand dismissively, Dave replied, "Naw, man. I wouldn't rat you out early. It's probably better to catch him by surprise anyway. That way there is less time to figure out why your idea won't work."

Gary opened a can of tomato soup and sat it down by a small gas fired stove. He pumped the plunger several times, lit a match and twisted the burner valve. The stove burst into smoking yellow flame as Gary hastily adjusted the flame. When it was burning steadily, he carefully placed the tomato can on the stove.

Turning to look at Dave, he said, "Hey, bud, if you want in on this dinner you gotta flip the meat on that other heater. I'm going to heat this sauce."

"I'd be happy to flip. What kind of meat is this?" Dave asked as he picked up a fork.

"Don't ask, don't tell. Cook it enough and it won't make you sick. But you'd be better off not knowin'." Gary replied.

"What do you want anyway, Dave? A menu and a napkin in your lap?" Mark said with a laugh. "Perhaps a candle on the table?"

Gary pulled a glove on his right hand and stirred the contents of the can with a spoon. To himself he said, "Ahh, this sauce is gonna be better than Mama Rosie's back home."

Gary pulled a large bottle of McHiennile's Tabasco sauce from a bag on the floor, holding it up for Dave to see he grinned and said, "Only the finest of ingredients and spices in this restaurant. Not to worry, I got the great leveler right here. With this you can eat anything!"

"Just asking. Don't want to seem like an ingrate or anything," Dave replied.

"No offense. After that Kepsa dinner we had, I figured you'd pretty much gone native," Gary replied. As an afterthought he added, "We won't make you eat with your fingers though."

Since they were the cook team, they were the last ones to eat. They filled their plates with spaghetti noodles, put a few pieces of what resembled hamburger meat on top of that and then poured what was left of the tomato soup over the whole thing. Gary generously sprinkled his plate with the tabasco sauce and then shoved the bottle at Dave, "Here. A few drops add a little flavor, a lot of drops add a lot of spice. Go ahead, have some spice."

With an uncertain look, Dave took the bottle, sprinkled several drops over his dinner and handed the bottle back to the grinning team sergeant.

Taking their food to the rear courtyard they sat cross-legged on the ground to eat. In the dim light of the evening sky, Mark ripped open a small foil pouch from his pocket, and poured it into his canteen. Shaking it up, he offered it to Dave, "Here, Kool Aid is better than the water around here."

Gary took a swig, after handing it back to Mark he wiped his mouth on his sleeve. He twirled his fork in his spaghetti and lifted it to his mouth.

Mark swallowed his first bite, and asked, "So, Dave. What did Fahim say when you talked to him?"

"Nothing really. He was talking to one of my buds about weapons. We're buying a bunch of Russian stuff and shipping it here for the NA to use in their next offensive. The supply line is a lot closer. They were busy talking about that when Fahim interrupted for a minute to ask what I thought of the Taliban lines."

"What did you tell him?" Mark asked.

"I just told him we saw tanks, buried hull down, along with some heavy machine gun emplacements."

"You didn't tell him what I said about attacking those tanks, did you?" Mark asked leaning forward over his plate.

"No, but I'd bet money that he knows it. They're smart enough to figure out that going in at night makes it almost impossible for the tanks and guns to shoot them easily."

"Yeah, I figure he already knows about those positions and that he can't take them head on. I just don't want him knowing what I think, or what we're planning, before we talk that's all."

"It's cool, I only spoke in general terms. I can keep a secret, I work for the company, you know?"

Searching his spaghetti, Mark said, "I know, I know. Sorry. After that lecture I got from him the other day, I just want to play my cards close, that's all."

Mark put his plate down, carefully balanced his fork on the rim. Talking with both hands, he began, "See, it's like this: Fahim can't deal with those tanks and neither can my team by itself. The only way to do it is with TacAir, and until we get air support, we can't do anything about Taloqan. The biggest problem there is that I'm not really sure when the MFWICs will release the air to us. But, and this is the big but, it is vitally important to build on our momentum, we've got it rolling now and if we squander it, it will be hard to get it going again. That's why I think closing the Salang Pass is a strategy that will do us some good. Right now!"

"The Salang Pass, right, I remember." Dave, moving sideways, stretched out his aching knees, "Hey, what's this MFWICs? What does that mean?"

Without looking up Gary deadpanned between bites, "It means 'mother fucker what's in charge.' You never heard of that before?"

Not missing a beat, Gary speared a piece of meat with his fork, sloshed it around in tomato tabasco sauce. Pausing before lifting it up to his mouth, he said, "So, how we gonna talk this Fahim dude into going for the Salang Pass anyway. You figure he'll have a grasp on Army issue strategy?" He popped the meat into his mouth triumphantly, looking between Dave and Mark for their reaction.

Dave leaned his back against the wall and stretched his feet out. Crossing them at the ankles he said, "No, first time I've heard that line, it's a good one though. Well, I don't think he'll respond to the argument that closing the Salang Pass would be a strategic move. His war against the Taliban has been a hit and run; survive to fight another day kind of thing. To him, strategy is keeping the supply lines open. You gotta understand he's a warlord and is stuck in his area. Heck, even his Army is mostly made up of villagers called in for a particular battle."

Frustrated, Mark shot back at Dave, "But don't you see that by closing the pass, it will be the T that is cut off from resupply and reinforcement He's bound to see that as a good thing. Noone can mistake that it'll be easier to deal with the T piecemeal one at a time."

Dave reached for Mark's canteen, raising it to his lips; he slowly took a sip of the Kool Aid, savoring the flavor. Finished, he unhurriedly said, "Mark, look at it from his perspective. He's never had enough gear or men to meet the Taliban head on; survival has meant that he was winning. Even if we we're able to isolate the T in Mazar, or Kunduz, or Taloqan, from his point of view, if they are still there, then they are every bit as strong as they were before. And his guys on horseback simply can't deal with them."

Dave continued, "For all his experience in fighting, it's only been in this country, and in reality, it's only been on a small scale. That's all he's going to see. To him that's the world. For my money, if you press that strategy line of reasoning, he's just going to clam up and then it's going to be hard to get him to do anything."

Mark stared at the floor for a few seconds and then abruptly waived his hands in front of his face. "Okay, okay. I give up. I won't argue grand strategy or OODA loops with him. I still think it is vitally important to close the Pass now. How do you propose we try to talk him into this?"

"I don't know. Man, I'm not a Military thinker. I'm just telling you my read of him as a person. Don't you have any other ideas?" Dave asked.

Mark looked despondent; he was desperate to do something constructive.

In the heavy silence, Gary spoke up, "Why don't we think about playing to his strengths?"

"What do you mean, Gary?" Mark asked, hopefully.

"Well, the way I see it is like this. From what Dave says, I gather Fahim isn't a big picture thinker. He sees the threat in front of him and that's fine, but he doesn't have the resources, or the motivation, to do anything but deal with it piecemeal." Getting into the subject, Gary rubbed his hands together. "Our strategy will be to convince him that closing the Salang Pass is the thing he can do to hurt the T the most right now with what he's got. Dave you said yourself he understands supply lines."

Dave nodded.

Stroking the stubble on his chin with his thumb and forefinger, Mark gazed at them both, lost in thought. "So, we've got to convince him that closing the Salang Pass is the path of least resistance. There aren't many Taliban or AQ there so they will be easier to dispose of than the T around Taloqan."

"Yeah, that might work," Dave, observed. "I still think he'll be a hard sell. For all his flourish, he pretty much sees what's in front of him as black and white. He'll probably figure out what you're trying to do."

Waiting outside the mud house where they were to meet Fahim, yellow light filtered the dusty streets. Stomping their feet, the three of them were the only things moving on the streets; their breath, fogging in the morning chill. Several minutes passed on the lonely street before the door opened. Ushered into the bare room where they had first met Fahim, they found him seated alone next to a small charcoal fire.

"Hello, my American friends." Seated he waived towards the rug next to him, gesturing for them to sit down. "It is my hope that your stay here be as pleasant as we can make it. Is there anything you need? Are you getting food and housing without problems? Are you comfortable in the house we have provided?"

Mark stood in front of the older man, trying to be as formal as he could. "Thank you, sir. We are comfortable and have plenty of food and water. The bread is especially popular. Thank you."

Doing his best to translate, Dave tried not to make himself part of the conversation.

Not looking up, Fahim stared into the fire. Picking up a small burning stick, he stirred the coals. After a long moment of silence, he nodded, "That is good. We believe in hospitality; it is very important to us."

Lapsing into silence again, Fahim idly arranged four glasses in front of him. Pouring *Chai* into each, he held them up to each of his visitors in turn. When they all had glasses, he took a sip of his own and sat it back on the ground. Straightening up, he looked at them decisively, "My men tell me that you went out to see the Taliban lines around Taloqan yesterday. Tell me what you think of the Taliban and their defenses?"

As Mark began to speak, Gary and Dave exchanged furtive looks.

"Yes, sir. We spent most of yesterday looking at the defenses to the east and north of Taloqan. We found the Taliban well prepared to defend against a frontal assault. We saw trenches that connect machine gun nests and several tanks buried hull down."

Fahim twirled his long gray mustache with his gnarled hand, "Perhaps, you have a suggestion for me? Did you develop a good way to attack these breastworks?"

"With the forces you have at your disposal? I think a frontal assault in daylight would likely result in failure. An attack at night, or in daylight after the tanks have been destroyed, would stand a better chance of succeeding," Mark answered.

Taking another slow sip of tea, Fahim pondered. "Perhaps. We do not have heavy weapons that would take those tanks out easily. It would take sticks of TNT or some other explosives placed against the side of the tank to destroy it. The US has weapons that we could use I am sure."

Glancing at Dave, Fahim continued, "My friends here are buying us weapons from the Russians. They bring no Sagers, I have asked for anti-tank missiles. We have nothing to use on tanks and buried tanks are very hard targets indeed. Their turrets are the only things that show above the ground."

Nodding, Mark said, "You are right. Tanks hull down are a tough target for anybody on the ground. From our trip yesterday, I have no idea of how good the Taliban are as fighters or how well they would coordinate. But I do know they are well dug in."

"I assure you that they do very well fighting. You can see my needs. I have no weapons that can destroy those tanks. I must deal with them, and the machine guns, before my men can attack the town. I know their defenses are brittle, as an old dried up tree. Once those tanks are destroyed, the Taliban will collapse within the town and we can clean them out easily."

Mark gazed at the older man without blinking, "Pardon me for asking, sir. But what would be your plan of attack once the tanks are taken care of?"

Suddenly energized, Fahim spat, "All of my men are mounted on good mountain horses and carry their own weapons. Is it not obvious that we would attack on horseback? Will you destroy the tanks, and the machine gun trenches? Have you big bombers that will bomb the town and the tanks?"

"Yes, sir. The bombers and fighters can and will drop bombs, but I cannot promise you that they will drop on the town. For two reasons, first, our country does not want to destroy civilian targets if it can be avoided. Second, I'm sorry to say, we cannot get TacAir for our own targets for a few more days," Mark said, as formally as he could.

"The Air Force is currently bombing Taliban infrastructure targets and have not begun hitting other targets." Gary quickly added.

"So. You offer me no support. Perhaps, in the future. Someday. But no help now, no help now with the tanks in front of Taloqan?" Fahim said with a grimace. "You will not bomb Taloqan."

"Sir, I do not have an input as to when the TacAir will be released to our targets. It will happen, I'm sure in a few days. Even then, we must pay attention to collateral damage; we must be careful not to hit civilians accidentally. Until that time, my superiors are very interested in things that you can do. They feel that there is another place you can attack." Mark worried that he was losing the sales battle, much like he had in his previous meeting with Fahim.

Mark paused to take a breath. Fahim, taking advantage of the momentary silence, said, "Where do you think we could attack, if not here? The Taliban threaten the routes into our mountains. This is where our strength is!"

"Yes, sir, I know that. We think it would be a very good thing to close the Salang Pass. The Taliban are not expecting you there, they are not in prepared dug-in positions, and it would be very easy to close the pass to traffic," Mark said, putting all his cards on the table.

Fahim looked as if he was speaking to a wayward child. "So, Captain, if I closed this pass what good would this do for me? The Taliban in the pass are not threatening the villages of my men. It is true we control land very close to the Salang Pass, *but that is because our villages are there*. The American CIA is helping us prepare a Russian Airfield at Golbahar to fly in supplies. It will take more than that to keep the Taliban away from the villages near the Salang Pass. It is a long way away from here, it would take many weeks to move men there and it would be dangerous for the villages here. I see no advantage in taking that risk."

Struggling to keep in the game, Mark asserted, "Sir, it is a place where we can attack the Taliban, where they are weak. If we close that pass, they cannot use it to reinforce the towns of Mazar, Kunduz and Taloqan. With no supplies, it will make it easier for you to deal with the Taliban in the towns. If this war lasts through winter then we will have choked them off in the north."

"Captain, do you realize that I would have to move most of my men away from the lines around Taloqan to do this?" Fahim asked.

"Yes, sir, I know that. But if we cut off the pass, the Taliban would be unable to take advantage of your temporary weakness around Taloqan."

"There are 6,000 Taliban around Taloqan and another 10,000 in Kunduz. This is more than I have in my whole Army right now. I cannot expose my men and my villages to chase a will-o-the-wisp at the Salang Pass. My problem is Taloqan. We must solve this problem first and then we can look at your pass."

Suddenly standing, Fahim said, "Besides, did you not know that the al-Qaeda drove twenty trucks full of men into the Salang Pass yesterday. These men have not come out. Therefore, the pass is more heavily defended than you know. I choose the risks I know, rather than the unknown."

With that comment, Fahim walked purposely towards the door. "Captain, I appreciate your desire to help. Figure out how to help me in Taloqan, if you desire to do so."

Pausing at the door, he turned and looked at them still sitting on the floor, "Farewell for now, talk to me when you are able to help."

South Brooklyn, New York City

Mike Lambert drove his Ford Taurus, carefully negotiating heavy traffic headed south on Washington Avenue. He stopped at the light at Atlantic and turned right. His partner, Charles Bonner, was in the front seat pouring over a Mapsco flip map of Brooklyn. Glancing at the traffic in his rear view mirror, Mike looked at his partner and asked, "So, found where the turn is yet?"

"Yeah, man. No worries. Let's cruise the neighborhood before we stop. Just to get a feel for what it's like," Charles answered.

"That's fine. What's the turn?" Mike asked again.

"Turn left on Hoyt Street. It's about five blocks past Flatbush. Bond is the block before it."

"Okay, how many blocks is Bergen from Atlantic?" Mike asked.

"It's three blocks south and two over. Go down to Wyckoff Street and turn left again. We'll just sorta circle the block."

Turning left on Hoyt Street they passed through a neighborhood that had long since passed its prime. The streets were busy and there were many people, but it was just run down with trash littering the street and abandoned cars scattered around each block. Hoping to blend in with their plain white car, two white guys in a new sedan cruising the streets stood out like a neon sign. Turning left on Nevins, they passed a Bodega, crowded with men hanging around at the curb hooting at them as they drove by. Northbound, they crossed Bergen Street where it was no different from any of the other streets in this area. They circled the block at Dean and finally turned east on Bergen.

"This is it. On the right, 238 Bergen Street There's a spot on the right just past it. Pull over," Charles said as he pointed out first the apartment and then waived towards the parking spot.

"Okay, okay. Keep your shirt on. I'll make it. You goin' in or do you want me to? In this neighborhood, I think only one guy should get out and talk to the landlady here. What do you think?" Mike said.

"That's fine, I'll go. Let me put my ear piece on so you can hear what's going on," Charles said, gently fitting an ear bud into his ear. In a low voice he said, "Check, check, Check." The ear bud was a wireless transceiver, a microphone and speaker that he could wear without attracting attention. The microphone picked up the vibrations of his voice in his ear, as well as conversation close to him, and the transmitter amplified the signal and relayed it to the receiver in the car.

Mike, his ear bud already in, said, "Loud and clear."

Mike adjusted his rear view mirror to see the front door of the apartment, as well as the sidewalk. Turning to his partner he said, "Ready to go?"

Charles pulled on a sweatshirt, adjusted it so that it covered the radio on his belt and the tell tale bulge of the pistol on the inside of his pants. Sticking his badge and ID in his pocket he nodded to Mike and stepped out of the car.

Dressed in jeans, sneakers and a Giants sweatshirt he did not look like a businessman or a cop. However, he still managed to stick out in the crowd. He was a little self-conscious, but decided not to let it bother him. Let them wonder who he was he did not care. Walking down the sidewalk, he took in the rest of the people around him and smiled. This was a good job after all. He loved being outside, on the move and doing something different everyday. This was a lot better than working a desk, shuffling paper for no good purpose. At least here, he was making a difference, even if it was a little one, everyday.

He stopped at the stoop for 238 Bergen Street Looking around at the neighbors he registered the scene and the characters on the street. Reaching for the bell, he pressed the button for the land lady.

A small, tinny voice answered the bell, "Who is it? What do you want?"

Leaning in to the speaker Charles said, "Yes, ma'am. Mrs. Anthony, you called us yesterday afternoon. I'm here to talk with you."

"Yes, young man. Who are you with? What do you want?"

"Ma'am. I'm here in response to the complaint you called in yesterday. Could you please open the door?"

"Oh, yes. I'll be right there. Wait a minute," the voice trailed off.

A few minutes later, the door creaked open. An old lady with thin graying hair, wearing a nondescript housecoat poked her head out of the door. She was heavy set and wore dirty house slippers that barely covered her swollen feet and varicose veins. Squinting in the sun, she adjusted the glasses on her nose with one hand and tried to brush a few strands of gray hair out of her face with the other. Looking like an owl, she looked at Charles expectantly.

She didn't say anything and after a short strained silence.

Charles said, "Yes, ma'am. If you could invite me in, we can talk about your complaint. I'd be happy to show you my ID inside."

Holding the door with one hand, she gathered her smock with the other and looked nervously past Charles into the street. Glancing left, she followed the plume of smoke still smudging the sky from the attack on the World Trade Center.

"Come in, come in. I'm sorry. You can't be too sure in this neighborhood. Please come in. Please come to my apartment." Turning, she left Charles to hold the door open, as she disappeared down the narrow dimly lit hallway. Stopping at her door, she put her hand on the knob, and looked nervously at Charles over her right shoulder.

Stammering, she said, "I don't usually do this. But this time I thought it might be very important."

Reaching into his back pocket, he removed his ID wallet and opened it. With the badge and ID in front of her he said, "I'm Agent Charles Bonner, ma'am. I'm with the FBI and I'm here to talk with you about your call yesterday."

Peering intently at the ID in the gloom she said, "Alright, young man. You can come in. But please be quiet. Folks around here talk." Shakily, she opened the door and went in, with Bonner close behind.

Mike watched Charles as he made his way down the street. He noted that only a few people looked at him when he stopped at the front door. He could see that the old lady was obviously nervous and hesitated to let him in. Mike spoke into Charles' earpiece, "Just tell her you're working your way through college selling magazines. Or better yet, oxy-clean." Expecting no reply, he chuckled under his breath at his wit, and continued looking around at the street traffic.

The land lady sat down on a dusty old couch covered with a heavy brocade fabric that had once been brightly colored. Charles followed her into the sitting room. The apartment was stuffy and still, with a musty odor. Hot and close, Charles could barely see in the dim light coming from the heavily curtained windows.

"Mrs. Anthony, you called in with a tip of a suspect individual. I'm just here to follow up on that call. I promise not to make a scene with your neighbors. Was this person one of your tenants or a neighbor?"

"I hope this won't take too long." Gathering her smock at her throat again, she looked around the dark room nervously.

"It won't take long, ma'am. If you could just tell me about the person you called about." Taking out a note pad he sat down on an equally musty stuffed chair across from the couch.

"Well, I suppose it's for the good," she said slowly. "It's my tenant in 2B. It's right above my apartment."

"Yes, ma'am, what's his name again?" Charles said gently.

"His name is Hamid Farouk. He's been here for about nine months. Pays by the month. He's always on time and usually very quiet. But I don't like him, I don't trust him at all," she said quietly.

Shaking her head, she continued, "I don't know where he came from, or what he does. He claims he's a delivery truck driver and he always he pays me in cash. He's never late. But I know he's got a secret, you can just tell. He doesn't like anyone around here and scowls at everyone. I just don't trust him."

"Could you tell me where he works and what he does every day?" Charles said.

"Well he says he drives for Brinks Delivery. But I don't know for sure. He's usually gone during the day and never leaves at the same time. Always odd hours—coming and going. Usually, with one or two others. One of them has very mean eyes. And they always walk very heavily on the stairs and stomp around on the floor. I don't know what else, oh, he gets up very early in the morning."

Looking around again she said, "He's never done anything wrong or bad to me. But with the Trade Center and all. He's from over there, he has that accent. I think he said he was from Egypt. I just wanted to make sure somebody knew about him."

"Did he show you a passport or any identification or anything?" Charles asked.

"No. He didn't have a passport. He said he was a refugee. He did have a driver's license," she said nervously.

"Is there any particular time we might be able to catch him at home?" Charles added hastily. "So we can ask him some questions."

"Mostly he's home around five o'clock. Sometimes, he goes out again around seven, I'm usually asleep when he gets back. He's always up at four a.m. He plays this wailing record and thumps the floor." Nervously, she got up and paced the small room, "Is that all you need? I really think you should go."

Flipping his note pad closed, Charles got up and followed her to the door. As she opened it, he fixed on her eyes and said, "Thank you for calling. You did the right thing. It's probably nothing, but we'll check it out. It's better to be safe than sorry these days."

"Thank you for coming. Please don't tell anyone that I called you. I don't want anyone to know," she said with a fearful look in her eyes.

"Don't worry, ma'am. It's just between you and me. We might have to call on you again, but we'll do it on the phone. Thanks again," Charles said, turning his back he walked quickly down the hall and out into the street.

"Dude, you missed your calling. You shoulda been a door-to-door salesman. You got that soft soap working on that old lady. You had her in the palm of your hand, I bet you could have sold her the Brooklyn Bridge," Mike said into Charles' ear bud, laughing aloud as he walked back to the car.

"You're so funny, a regular comedian. If I gotta put up with you hassling me while I'm on the job you're buying lunch!" Charles replied, gritting his teeth, trying not to attract attention from anyone else on the sidewalk.

Charles quickly got into the car and opened the screen on the laptop computer mounted on the console in the front seat. Typing he said, "We got a name and a work location. Let's run a check on him and see if he works were he said he does."

"Where to now, boss? I'm just a driver," Mike said, wheeling out into traffic.

"I know you're a big spender. Head to KFC, I saw one back on Atlantic." Intent on the screen he looked up at his partner grinning, "Do you think you can make it that far without directions?"

"No problem, GI. You getting the kids meal?"

"No way, I'm going for the gold. And don't whine about paying, it's unbecoming a professional," Charles said.

Mike found a parking space on the street in front of the restaurant. Before they got out, they removed their ear bud radios. Locking the doors of the car, they silently walked across the dirty sidewalk.

"Do you think this guy's dirty or maybe just an INS collar?" Mike asked as he opened the glass door to Kentucky Fried Chicken.

"We'll soon see, most of them have just been low level illegals so far, maybe we'll get lucky," Charles said. "I know we'll have a reply by the time we're done with lunch. By the way, I feel like the most expensive thing on the menu today, do you feel rich?"

Coming out of the restaurant after lunch they quickly got back into the car. Charles flipped open the laptop. "We've probably got a response on this guy."

Logging on to the network he picked up the incoming message. "It looks like we hit the jackpot. He's wanted by the INS, his work visa has expired. His driver's license checks out for upstate New York, but he doesn't have a commercial. Let's see, hmm. He's no political refugee either. Plus—you'll like this. There is no record of him working for Brinks Delivery. His credit report shows a bank account of nearly 20k. Sounds to me like he's covering up something."

"I think it might be a good thing to talk with this Farouk guy. What time did the old lady say he would be home?" Mike asked.

"She said he comes home off and on around five. We should setup surveillance and catch him when he comes home this afternoon. She also said he's always home at four a.m; from her description, he must be doing the four o'clock prayer call. I'd prefer to get him this afternoon, I hate getting up early."

"Okay, let's call the boss and set it up." Mike pulled out onto the street, grimly he said, "Just one question Hamid, just one more question."

"Arif, go and pick up Hamid and Jamiel. You must move the rabbits; they have been to long in one place. Move them tonight. Load them into the van and put the whole thing into the storage room," Hazim Zakko said. "You must hurry. Make sure the van is full of gas. Go now and call me on the cell phone when it is done."

"Yes, I am leaving now," Arif Hassan replied as he got up to leave the apartment.

Zakko was the leader of their group and had a very short temper; Arif did not want to give him a reason to start yelling at him again. It was most unpleasant, very much like his father yelling at him.

He would take the subway over to Bergen Street stop and get Hamid. Jamiel was usually there; they were together most of the time. With three of them, it would not take long. Two could load the rabbits and one could be the driver. It would be longer waiting for sunset so no one would be suspicious of the stolen van with new plates. Better to blend in he thought as he went through the subway turnstile.

Four thirty that afternoon, Mike and Charles were in a van watching the street traffic. With their windows closed, it was hot and stuffy in the vehicle without the air conditioning running. Mike sat up quickly, when he saw two Arabic men in blue jeans, running shoes and black leather jackets, cross Bind Street and continue east on Bergen. "Hello, do you think this is our boy?" Mike said. He steadied the digital camera on the steering wheel and snapped a few pictures of them as they came up the street.

"Mumpkin," Charles replied. "If they go into Mrs. Anthony's place, I'll call her and ask if these are the guys."

Snapping a few more pictures, Mike said, "There they go, waltzing inside bigger than Dallas. Give her a call." Picking up the radio handset, he transmitted to the other two cars supporting them on the stakeout. "Mark has been sighted, waiting confirmation now. We should be moving in a few minutes."

Hitting the redial button on his cell phone, Charles called the land lady who had reported the suspicious individual. "Hello, Mrs. Anthony. This is Charles Bonner. We spoke this afternoon about Hamid Farouk."

"Yes, yes. I'm calling because we were wondering if that is Hamid going up the stairs right now? Is he going up to his apartment?"

"That's great, thank you very much."

Hanging up the phone, he turned to Mike and said, "That's our boy. We'll use those pictures out on the net. Meantime, let's pick him and his brother up for some questions. Ready to go?"

"Ready. Are we going to take our jackets or just look like undercover cops?" Mike asked.

"Let's just look like cops today. That way folks on the street will just think it's a drug bust or something."

"Fine by me, let's go," Mike said as he got out of the van. Walking up, the landlady was already at the door of the apartment looking more nervous than before, if that was possible. Behind the two FBI men, a police van pulled up to the curb.

Arif was happily walking along the sidewalk on the north side of Bergen Street. He liked having something to do that took him away from his boss. It would be fun working by himself for a change. Surprised, he slowed down when he saw the NYPD van pull up in front of Hamid's apartment building. Not knowing what to do, or whether the police were going to pick up Hamid, or if they were after someone else, he stopped immediately and looked into a shop window. He began to panic. *Should I run? Do they know of us? Are they arresting Hamid? Am I next?* After a few minutes, staring with unseeing eyes into the window, he realized no one was running across the street to get him. He breathed a sigh of relief and turned slowly back to watch the activity across the street.

Two New York City policemen were at the door of Hamid's building. In a few minutes, Hamid and Jamiel were hustled out of the door by two other men with short hair, wearing blue jeans and sweatshirts. Holding their heads down, the policemen pushed them into the van. Arif began feeling the blood pounding in his head. He was getting hot and could barely hear anything with the rushing noise in his ears. Sure that the cops were after him too, he slowly turned and walked back the way he had come. Most of the people on the sidewalk were not paying attention to the drama across the street. He turned the first corner on Bond Street and briskly walked several blocks before stopping at a pay phone.

Hazim scowled at the caller ID, answering the call he reluctantly said, "Hello, Hello."

"Hazim, it is Arif," he said thickly.

"Arif, what is it you want? Where are you calling me from, is it a pay phone? What are you thinking? You know you should be using a cell phone!" Hazim replied angrily.

"Hazim, it is Hamid. He is arrested. I am calling from a pay phone so I can watch the street. I am right across the street."

"Arif, you fool of a camel. You must not use a payphone. You must get away from his apartment, now," Hazim said earnestly into the phone.

Arif ignored him and repeated in a daze, "It is Hamid. He is arrested. Jamiel as well. Both of them were led from the house in handcuffs. They were taken away in a city police van. But the cops did not look like city cops."

"Arif, listen to me. Hang up the phone and leave that place. Quickly make your way to the subway. Change trains at least three times. Meet me in Manhattan in three hours. In the park, you know where," Hazim said.

"What are we to do? Are they after us? Do they know? What do I do Hazim?" Arif said plaintively.

"I have told you, you fool. Leave that place, now! Go to the subway. Change trains at least three times. We will meet in the park at eight pm. Go now. We will know soon if they are hunting for us."

"Yes, Hazim. You are right. I will meet you."

"Wait, Arif. Have you moved the rabbits? Are they vulnerable? We must not lose them!" Hazim said.

"No, they are safe. I have not moved them yet," Arif replied.

"Good, I will meet you in the park. This phone will no longer work. Come alone," Hazim said as he hung up.

Damn the evil Satan. He wondered who had exposed them, and whether the whole cell was in jeopardy. Their mission must succeed! Grabbing a backpack, he stuffed it with money, passports and some incriminating documents. Without a second thought, Hazim rushed out the door.

Sar e-Raqowl, Afghanistan

Two Toyota trucks careened west on the A-77 highway, no other traffic was on the road carving through the steep mountain valley. The first one was a Land Cruiser, with four men in it, closely followed by a pickup truck with a Soviet DshK14.2mm machine gun mounted in the bed. One man grimly hung onto the gun as the truck sped along the road carelessly. Approaching the small village of Sar e-Raqowl, the two vehicles slowed down. Spotting another Land Cruiser, the driver pulled off the road and stopped next to it.

Ahmed Mustapha leaned forward, rolled down his window and squinted at the occupant of the other vehicle, "Is that you Youseff? I can barely see you."

"Yes, it is me. We have been here for more than an hour. We came through Ghanzi and Qargha."

"We were delayed. Are you ready to travel?" Mustapha asked.

"Yes, what do you want to see me about?"

"It is not I that called for you, we cannot talk right now. We must go. Tell your driver to follow us and he must drive quickly," Mustapha said nervously, scanning the darkening sky furtively.

"We are ready."

"Good. Then follow us. It is not far." Mustapha tapped the driver on the shoulder, rolling his window up as the SUV accelerated back onto the road. The pickup with the machine gun and the second Land Cruiser strained to keep up as Mustapha hurried west.

Forty-five minutes later, they crossed the Helmand River and passed through the disheveled town of Navor, peasants stopping to stare at the rushing convoy. Climbing the mountain, the convoy's speed dropped considerably. Mustapha's vehicle turned left suddenly onto a gravel road leading to the Ruins of Markhana. Reaching the end of the road they stopped in front of several tents, erected on one side of the ruins.

Mustapha got out of the first truck and waved hurriedly for Youseff to follow him. Before Youseff reached him, Mustapha turned, and walked briskly towards the first tent.

Youseff joined him as Mustapha talked to the guard in a hurried staccato conversation. Finished, Mustapha spoke to Youseff. "Usama will see us in a few minutes. We are late. I was delayed in Kabul. The roads downtown were closed."

"Has there been much bombing there lately?" Youseff asked. He had not seen his friend so flustered since almost being caught in the bombing of the Air Authority building. "Have they gotten close to you again?"

"Not me," Mustapha sighed. "No it was the TV tower. The tower in the middle of town on Kohi Asamayi. The Russians tried to bomb it for years, and others have tried to take it out, and missed. I was eating lunch a few blocks from there on the other side of the river. We heard a roar, and then seconds later the tower just exploded. I was looking right at it and it just went up in smoke. When the smoke cleared the tower was no more, it was like the finger of God had smashed it into the ground."

Mustapha continued nervously, looking around furtively, "A few minutes later the bridge across the Kabul river was bombed. The Taliban closed the roads out of town and we could not cross the river for several hours."

At that moment, a guard waived at them. Following him, they threaded their way between several tents and trucks scattered across the rocky ground, to a small tent at the back of the ruins. A guard inside opened the flap of the tent, stepped outside, and held it open for them as they ducked inside.

"Hello, my friends. It is my hope that you are doing well! Please sit down next to me." Usama bin Laden motioned to them to sit down. Three others were gathered on the large prayer rug inside the tent. "We were just talking with our friends from Herat. Please join us. Mustapha, I believe you are late, why is this so?"

"I am sorry, Muqtar, I was delayed leaving Kabul. An American airstrike destroyed the TV tower downtown and took out the bridge over the river next to the Women's Hospital. The roads out of town were closed," Mustapha replied as he sat down across from bin Laden.

"I am aggrieved to hear of this. How is the bombing in Kabul and how are our good friends the Taliban handling it?" Bin Laden asked.

"Muqtar, the roads are clear, and the city is largely intact. The Americans are bombing every Taliban building and most structures. I heard the barracks next to Fort Kalacheh outside of Kandahar were all flattened, but the fort is untouched. Our places are not being hurt very much around Kabul, because we are moving away from Taliban buildings. Since the Air Authority building was bombed, I have not been able to rebuild my communications center, so that was moved first to Mohideen in Tora Bora. This is our biggest problem," Mustapha said.

"I have not heard from Mohideen for several days. Tell me of the bombing around Tora Bora."

"The Americans have bombed Tora Bora very hard. It is obvious they knew of the area already and were able to pick out many of the other caves. Their first attacks were on the entrances of the caves, when they tried to collapse the caves themselves. Most of our caves do not go directly back into the mountain, as you know they turn left or right after the entrance. Most of the American bombs were dropped right behind the cave entrance and blew up in solid rock without damaging the cave itself."

"What of injuries? How many have been hurt?"

"Many have been hurt, but few killed. The bombers that leave marks in the sky dropped many bombs on the surface and it was not safe to be out in the open. Mohideen told me the worst was one single blast yesterday. It destroyed the antenna for the radios and telephone lines. The bomb did not collapse the caves; many were killed inside the ones nearest the explosion. The air was sucked out of their lungs and they died as if they were sleeping," Mustapha continued.

"Mohideen was only able to communicate by cell phones. To do that, he had to go down the mountain. Samir, in Jalalabad, sent him many trucks and they moved his communication equipment and technicians to the Salang Pass. I sent several of my people with him when his trucks came through Kabul. We will rebuild the communication center in one of the caves in the pass."

One of the men on Usama's left stirred, "What of the trucks? We have heard that they were blown up by one or two shots. Is there a plane overhead attacking them?"

"Yes, any convoy that travels by night is being attacked. One of three vehicles was destroyed going from Kabul east to Jalalabad, yesterday night. I have heard reports of an airplane noise, but the explosions are not like the bombs that have been dropped. We are traveling by day, in small numbers. It is the safest way." Mustapha cleared his throat and looked at the other man. "What is the news from Herat?"

"The Americans have been busy bombing Taliban targets around Herat. The airport has been hit repeatedly. All the taxiways and runways have craters in them. Every airplane and building is destroyed. Our people are moving out of buildings and into the villages. It is not safe to be in buildings anymore," Nadir Mohabbat, the man who had questioned Mustapha replied.

"It is true," Ahmed Youseff added. "Our training camp outside of Kandahar was totally destroyed, just like that, except for a few small buildings on one side of the field."

"Ahmed, you have moved our new recruits from that field, have you not?" asked bin Laden.

"Yes, we moved most of our training into the mountains. It was a good decision. Mustapha could see far when he told us this would happen. There was a Surface-to-Air missile site on the hills north of Kandahar. The Americans attacked it. The missiles are still there but the control and firing center is gone, the ground beneath it broken, black and burned. I wanted to preserve the Mi-8 helicopter, so we parked it next to the Mosque in Kandahar. This morning the helicopter is no more, all that is left is a few blades from the rotors."

"The Americans are hitting the Taliban very hard. Will they fall? Is the Northern Alliance moving to take advantage of this bombing?" Usama asked.

"No, Muqtar. The un-believers of the north have not moved from their positions. Mazar e-sharif and Kunduz have not been hit at all. Their general Fahim has not moved an inch. However, I heard from Taloqan that Americans were spotted outside the town to the north," Youseff answered.

"We have only suffered injury in Tora Bora. Have we reestablished communications outside of the country?" bin Laden asked.

"Yes, Muqtar. Communications are operating in the Slang Pass area again. As I said Samir, Mohideen and I have transferred men and equipment there and have set up in a well-protected cave not far from the town of Kehnjan. I know you are concerned with our next strike. We have been in communication with them," Youseff said quickly.

"This is good. Our primary concern is with our next strike on the Americans. These men on the ground concern me as well. From other reports I have heard, the Taliban are holding, but are somewhat shaken. The north is the crucial point. If the Americans get a foothold on the ground in the north, we will be vulnerable. It is possible that they could drive a wedge from the north to Kabul. If they succeed, the whole of Afghanistan might fall. We must defeat the Northern Alliance once and for all. Before the Americans bring troops on the ground," bin Laden observed evenly. "Youseff, what can we do to help the Taliban in the north?"

"I think we can easily move two thousand men to Kunduz tomorrow. That is most of the men in the Slang Pass caves. Within a week we can move as many as twelve thousand into the area," Youseff answered.

"With that many men, the Taliban would have enough strength to attack Fahim and drive him into the mountains. We could secure the Russian border from American infiltration. We must do this thing. I will discuss it with Omar. Youseff, start moving your men to Kunduz. Do this tomorrow. We must move quickly to keep the Americans from exploiting the bombing. We must prevent them from getting on the ground." Bin Laden got up suddenly and began pacing back and forth. "What of these Americans spotted around Taloqan? Who are they and what are they doing?"

"I do not know who they are Muqtar," Youseff offered. Mustapha shook his head when bin Laden glanced at him.

"We must find out who they are. They must be killed," bin Laden said. "We cannot let Americans roam about on the ground in Afghanistan. They must all be killed. Where are they staying? Who are they working with?"

"I heard reports of ten of them and they went back across the river towards Ab Bazan. This is one of Fahim's strong points. We cannot attack them in that town. Perhaps we will kill them when we start the offensive to cut off Fahim," Youseff answered.

Usama stopped pacing, "Yes, that is a long way behind Northern Alliance lines. We have no spies that will go that far. We must kill them before there are more. If we kill them then others will be scared to come to Afghanistan. It might be too long before that can happen. We must strike them soon."

"Perhaps we can offer them a target to bring them out in the open, where we can catch and kill them," Mustapha offered.

Bin Laden stoked his beard, "Catch them. You are right; it would be better if they were captured. It would be better to catch them. We do not need them all. Kill all but a few of them. We must have a few on TV, with the rest dead. To have those criminals on TV, that would be a message for the world!" He began pacing excitedly again.

"First we need to get our men to Kunduz and Taloqan to help the Taliban crush Fahim. Youseff, start doing that right away. Mustapha you are right, I must think on this for a while. We must find a way to catch these Americans." Usama waived with his hand. All the men on the rug stood up at once.

Ushering them towards the flap of the tent he said, "Go, drive Fahim into the hills or bring his head to Mullah Omar. I need to think how to catch these Americans."

Mustapha ducked out of the tent first, bin Laden held Youseff's arm before he could follow. "Tell me Youseff. Do you think Mustapha is about to crack? I see much strain and fear within him."

Youseff, who had no family and was fanatically dedicated to only one cause, replied, "I still think that Mustapha has his uses. He will perform, but I too see him wavering in the faith. If it were me, I would no longer trust him with critical operations. But he can still handle the Kabul area."

"Perhaps. I have known him a long time. His reaction to the bombing is what worries me. Perhaps I need to make a change. Go now, guard always against danger."

CHAPTER 9

12 October 2001
White House Situation Room, Washington, DC

"Ladies and gentlemen, the President of the United States." A Secret Service Agent at the door announced as the President walked briskly into the oak paneled room. Everyone present hastily stood up and turned towards the President.

Brushing past the agent at the door the President perfunctorily said, "Thank you, and please take your seats."

The president sat down in his place, at the exact center of the far side of the long wooden conference table. Settling into his chair, he picked up the days agenda. He glanced around the silent room crowded with his war cabinet and their assistants; fixing his gaze on the Chief of Staff, he said curtly, "Let's begin."

The Chief of Staff cleared his throat, "Sir, I'd like to begin with a summary of the campaign so far with inputs from CIA and Defense on the progress of the war in Afghanistan, followed by an update on the hunt for al-Qaeda. Finally, FBI will give us an internal picture. Mr. Director if you please."

The CIA Director stood and smoothly grasped the remote slide controller an assistant held over his shoulder. Pointing it at the plasma video screen that dominated one end of the room, he displayed his first slide. Scanning the room once, he smiled thinly, settling his gaze on the president.

"As you know, sir, we have had Special Activities Teams on the ground with elements of the Northern Alliance for several days now. The Army has deployed one Special Forces A Team, Team 225 I believe, to join with my guys. To this date, they have engaged in no combat operations. I received reports that Team 225 conducted a reconnaissance of the Taliban lines around Taloqan, but I do not have a summary of the forces they observed there."

Thrusting one hand towards the screen, the director thumbed the wireless remote, advancing to a new slide on the big screen. The room remained silent, all eyes concentrating on the screen. Each picture the Director showed were digital images, sent directly from the field, of Northern Alliance troops and the targeted areas. Pictures of the people and the villages gave a sense of immediacy.

"We asked that the NA stand down from any ops until the air campaign had gotten underway. They have complied with that request. My SA Teams have begun to resupply the NA with weapons, clothing and food purchased from the Russians. We were able to restore the abandoned Russian Airfield at Golbahar to accept helicopter traffic and expect to be able to operate small aircraft soon. Resupply is primarily by ex-Russian Helicopters that are company owned. We expect the Northern Alliance to be able to resume operations against the Taliban in a very short time."

Continuing, he showed an ancient walled city, "This is Mazar e-Sharif, and to support the NA leader here, General Dostum, we have another CIA SA Team already married with an Army SF Team, ready to be inserted. The plan is to insert them tomorrow night. We expect great things from our relationship with Dostum, he comes with a very good reputation and a big desire to fight.

"Early tomorrow morning, Kabul time, the Army will insert elements of another A Team to re-enforce those already with Fahim. Air Force personnel are with that team in anticipation of releasing Air Force assets to support NA operations. I will leave it to Defense to describe elements of that effort.

"We have made some progress developing contacts with insurgent forces in the east and north of Jalalabad. They are Pashtuns and are closely related to the tribal forces allied with Fahim. General Fahim has provided those contacts. We expect to have a team ready for insertion there within a weeks time."

Showing an overhead slide of Kandahar, he concluded, "There has still been little progress developing contacts in the south. As you know, Kandahar is the main stronghold of the Taliban and its allied tribes. To date, it has been, shall we say, difficult to establish a relationship with anyone that we trust there. At the moment, we are pursuing avenues through Pakistan. We feel that these are most likely to help us achieve our goals of creating and aiding a resistance movement in the south. Otherwise, our operations, with respect to Afghanistan, are going as expected. The next phase of the operation will begin when the Air Force begins flying out of the northern bases provided by Kyrgyzstan, Turkmenistan and Uzbekistan."

Looking quickly around the room, he said, "If there are no questions, I will turn the floor over to Defense." Gesturing towards the Secretary of Defense he said, "Mr. Secretary."

The CIA Director resumed his seat and held the remote control over his shoulder; a runner took it and passed it to the Secretary of Defense. Without standing up, the Secretary of Defense took the remote and carefully placed it on the bare table in front of him. Obviously he would be speaking without notes, he took a sip of water and looked confidently at the president.

"Mr. President, our operations are broad and ongoing. The Air Force has begun sustained operations against the Taliban infrastructure over the entire country with exception, of course, of the northeast quadrant. Our Combat Search and Rescue forces are establishing a capability based in Dushanbe, they will become operational as of midnight local, Kabul time. We will commence combat operations in the northern area at that time."

"The Air Force is currently operating out of bases in Diego Garcia, Oman, UAE, Qatar as well as forward deployed locations in remote areas of Pakistan. We have forces arrayed in the countries the Director mentioned and, as stated previously, will shortly begin operations in the north. The CENTCOM command and control elements are fully operational in Qatar at this time."

Picking up the remote, he casually directed it towards the screen and brought up his first slide. "The majority of targets identified by Air Force planners as of strategic and military value to the Taliban have been hit and destroyed. As you can see from these slides, we have significant bomb damage assessment video of these targets."

He slowly paged through the BDA slides, announcing the target name and location for each one. First showing a pre-strike photo of the target, and then the post-strike BDA photo, he described the extent of damage.

Moving through twenty different target sets he stopped with the BDA photo of the Fort Kalacheh at Kandahar. "As you can see from these BDA photographs, we have severely degraded the Taliban infrastructure. These are a small sample of the 450 targets identified and struck in the last few days. Using 95 percent precision guided munitions, I might add we have taken every effort to reduce or eliminate collateral damage and civilian casualties. In a very short time, we will have struck and largely destroyed all of the Taliban infrastructure targets on our list. This does not mean that our air mission is complete, far from it. We are only beginning to move to a new phase. Our next task will be bringing in support of ground operations.

"As per our previous discussions at this table, we are concerned with the proximity of winter and how it might inhibit future operations. In particular, the ground operations of our Northern Alliance allies, they provide the overwhelming bulk of forces on the ground. With that in mind, we believe that we should make it a priority objective to close the Salang Pass. If this pass is closed, it will inhibit Taliban and al-Qaeda efforts to reinforce their strongholds at Mazar e-Sharif, Kunduz and Taloqan. If we are successful at this effort, we can dissect those strongholds one at a time, on our own terms. Our SF A Team commander on the ground proposed this and by this time will have met with Fahim to discuss this operation.

"Regardless of whether we can direct Fahim's energy at the Salang Pass, the next phase of the operation will incorporate what is essentially Close Air Support. The targets will be against Taliban and al-Qaeda in support of Northern Alliance operations. We are preparing more Special Forces A Teams for insertion to support these NA operations. There will be Air Force Air Liaison Officers, and enlisted men, included to coordinate air operations with our teams and the NA. As the Director mentioned, we will be inserting the first one of those integrated teams to support Fahim's forces tonight. Over the next few days we will be inserting another team to support Dostum's operations around Mazar e-Sharif.

"This does not mean that we will turn our air operations completely to CAS. There will still be strategic targets to strike; some emerging and some preplanned. For example, we exhausted the targets suited to B-2 attacks yesterday. However, they are still serving a purpose in the air campaign. Their unique 3D radar has been put to use mapping out the cave complex at Tora Bora.

"Tora Bora, by the way, has received extensive attention in the last days. We have been unable to confirm damage assessments in the complex. Photos do not show the same roof collapses evidenced in the underground storage complex west of Kabul. Attacks against Tora Bora have included JDAM strikes against known caves, the entrance and the cavity. In an effort to collapse the caves near the surface and kill their occupants, B-52 area attacks with conventional munitions have targeted the complex. We have also dropped the BLU-82/B Daisy Cutter weapon in an effort to collapse and kill personnel in the caves. Afterwards, we had reports of a large convoy leaving the area and past ELINT has shown that it had been a very busy communications complex. Overhead imagery shows accurate hits. We are still having some trouble evaluating the actual depth of damage to the complex. With no personnel on the ground for observation, it has been very difficult to assess battle damage, therefore, we believe the complex is still operational and robust.

"The B-2 radar has provided us with intelligence that shows the entrances to cave mouths that have either survived our previous attacks or are in the process of being repaired. We have planned a large Laser Guided Bomb attack against those targets for tonight. These will be the first fighter sorties flown from our new northern bases.

"I am optimistic that this attack will severely degrade, or neutralize, the contribution the Tora Bora complex will make to the war effort for the near term. It is a strategic area, however, because of its proximity to the unguarded border with Pakistan. At some point, we will have to mount an offensive on the ground into that area. Without forces on the ground, we cannot make sure that we have eliminated the Tora Bora complex. However, I feel confident that we have degraded their operation.

"The proximity of winter cannot be downplayed. It will severely hamper if not terminate NA operations against Taliban and al-Qaeda forces. It remains to be seen how the NA will conduct their operations even with our heavy application of air support. We are prepared to do what it takes to see the war through the winter with both logistical support and combat power. It is critical that we get the NA moving soon if we are to leverage the impact of our air support. I just want to mention, I know some feel that the success of relying on the Northern Alliance to provide the combat power on the ground may be a little shaky by itself. I think that our strategy of marrying them with Special Forces is the only real way of winning this war. Conventional forces would take 6-9 months to put in place even considering we could overcome all the diplomatic problems that represents. Time is a factor.

"Cold weather will also degrade the Humanitarian effort. We have had C-17s dropping Humanitarian rations for the last several days over the southern and eastern parts of Afghanistan. There have been some problems with the relief packets themselves, but we are working to overcome them. As we can confirm the destruction of the surface-to-air threat over points further north, we will expand these airdrops. I will leave it to the Secretary of State to discuss the Humanitarian relief effort on the ground."

He looked silently around the table, like an owl peering at everyone behind his big glasses. Sitting down he slid the slide controller to the Secretary of State, sitting on his left. The Secretary began to stand up only to be interrupted by the Chief of Staff.

"Excuse me Mr. Secretary. Before you speak, we would like to hear from the Director of the FBI. I believe several of his issues will be under the purview of State. With your permission?" He looked expectantly at the Secretary of State.

The Secretary, half out of his chair, sat back down with a big smile, and replied, "I yield the floor to my esteemed colleague at the FBI. What do the spook hunters have to tell us today?"

Standing up the Director of the FBI addressed the President, "Sir, we have had several dozen specific threats against internal targets in the United States. We are working closely with Justice and are currently identifying and detaining foreign nationals that meet the terrorist profile we have developed. At the moment, those detentions are restricted to personnel that are illegally in the US and do not hold legitimate resident credentials. We have picked up for questioning over 400 in the last few days. It will take several more days to process these detainees and or link them to the information of specific threats we have received through our own sources and through foreign support.

"Let me go through a short list of specific threats we have received since our last meeting."

Ab Bazan, Afghanistan

Mark stepped out the back door of their hooch, a two-room mud house with an enclosed backyard located on a side street of the rugged mountainside town. The town was on a wartime footing; the streets were crowded with native soldiers on foot and horseback. To Mark, the soldiers looked more like pirates or outlaws, they were all dressed in robes wrapped around their heads as turbines, baggy pants and western shirts and coats. They all had beards of varying lengths and colors, but most importantly they were all heavily armed with automatic assault rifles, mostly Soviet made. Everywhere they went, their weapons were strapped on their backs.

In the back courtyard, Gary was brewing *chai* over a charcoal fire. He greeted Mark as he sat down. "I've brewed some tea for you. Relax, have a glass and let's solve the problems of the world."

Picking up a dirty glass, Mark wiped it out with his T-shirt and held it up for Gary to fill. "Gary, you're turning native on me. Drinking *chai* every chance you get. Eating nothing but tread bread and goat. Dude, you're gonna forget the states before long."

"No, sir. I just figure that if I've got to live here, it's better to just settle in and get comfortable. I think that if you're going to be in the boonies for a spell, it just makes sense to accept it, to go with the flow. Keep you socks clean, change your underwear every once in awhile and relax. I just can't think of home, pizza, my kids and my honey and keep my mind on the job too. It just doesn't work, that's all. For me it's just survival mode. Go with the flow." Gary replied, filling Mark's glass from the pot. Finished, he moved back to make himself comfortable and sit with his back to the wall.

"Kinda of a sixties philosophy, isn't it?" Mark asked, sipping his tea.

"Yes, sir. Peace, love and harmony. We'll all get along, just don't forget your bullets and your NOGs," he said with a big grin.

"So, what's your take on Fahim's reaction to our suggestions? What do you think he'll do?" Mark asked.

"If you're asking my opinion, I figure he won't do shit. Strategy stuff, like closing off the Salang Pass, is a bit beyond him. To Fahim, and even the Taliban, war is just going out and beating the shit out of your enemy. When you've kicked his ass sufficiently and he gives up, well, that's when you win. I hate to say it but their point of view is immediate, none of them thinks about things really long term. They're all about what's in front of me right now and how do we deal with that. You know, their enemy today may be their cousins or neighbors tomorrow. They all think alike. Comes with the territory."

"Tactics and strategy are just words, not ideas. Hell, these guys have been fighting that way forever. Genghis and Kublai Khan rolled through here with some pretty brutal cavalry. Overwhelming brutal force was their tactic. Kill every man who stood before them was their strategy. The last guy to really do anything around here was Alexander the Great, and that was over two thousand years ago. He beat these guys by using cohesive units and some degree of maneuver. Beat 'em good, set up a local government and then he went away. Before long they were right back to where they had started. Your choice as to who really won. These guys have held the field for a pretty long time. Tends to color your perception," Gary mused.

Looking up from his tea, he laughed and asked Mark, "Sorry you asked, huh?"

"No, I wanted to know. I just didn't figure on a history lesson on top of the deal." Mark smiled and changed the hot tea glass to his other hand.

"Yeah, don't get me started. I've got an opinion about most things, but no pressing need to share them with the world," Gary said with satisfaction. "History is how we got here. I think if you ignore it you'll never figure out how to do things better."

"Okay, fair is fair. How do we make this better? How do you think we ought to make it better?" Mark asked.

"Don't say I didn't warn you," Gary said, he poured a little water in his tea glass, swirled it around and threw out the dregs of his tea on the ground.

Suddenly, it was important to Mark that he hear Gary's opinion, he pressed him, "I admit I'm not all knowing here. Look, I tried to make Fahim see the importance of the Salang Pass, it just didn't work. Dave said he wouldn't buy it and sure enough, he didn't. How do we get this guy moving? How do we achieve our goals here? Time is a big issue. I'm really interested in what you've got to say."

"Okay, sure." Gary picked up a short stick from the fire and stirred the dirt in front of him. "The deal is this. Fahim won't move against the pass and he told you exactly why. The biggest threat he has is the Taliban forces around Taloqan. They threaten his base of operations. To him, force must be met with force, the biggest threat first. For him there is just no threat at the Salang Pass."

"On top of that he doesn't really trust us. The only way to get him to move is to use airpower to take out the Taliban heavy weapons. He hasn't got the firepower and Luke's 50 cal won't take out a T-55 tank. We sure don't have the means by ourselves. The reality is that we must deal with the Taliban here first. I think it's time to get together a plan to use air to take out those Taliban positions. I'm pretty sure that once we take them out of the equation, Fahim will attack."

"Okay, I agree with you. We've gotta do something soon; the word is that air will be released to non-strategic targets after tomorrow. I haven't done this close air support thing. I had a two-day Familiarization course at Hurlburt Air Force Base a few years back, but that doesn't mean I can run it. Didn't you do this kind of stuff in the Gulf War?" Mark asked.

"Yeah, in a way I did. But, that was ten years ago. A bunch of our teams were assigned to the Arab forces that were sent to help the coalition. There were Egyptians, Kuwaiti's, Syrian's and even the Saudi's. SF Teams were assigned to all those guys and each one had an Air Force Air Liaison team with them as well. We lived with those Air Force types and worked with them. Before the war began, we got a lot of training calling for air strikes." Gary, paused took a sip from his canteen and put on his sunglasses. He looked around the courtyard.

In the silence Mark said, "So you know how to call these pilots in to strike targets?"

"Well, let's say I know it isn't as easy as it sounds. Roughly, it works like this. You say, 'Hey you, this is me. Find this place, call it the IP.'"

"Then you say, fly so and so from the IP for X miles. See this and that feature; tell me when you see them. I'm here; the bad guys are there. When you see that, tell me and I'll clear you to drop. The hard part is the stuff the pilots see doesn't look like it does to us on the ground. I know it won't be easy."

"So, we just use our laser designators to show them where we want to hit. Should be easy," Mark said.

"Yeah, except most of them can't see our laser spot. Some can, some can't. The A-10s are the only ones I know for sure that can see a spot. For the rest, we'll have to let them know our coordinates. They probably won't be dropping Laser Guided Bombs anyway," Gary replied, racking his brain trying to remember how to be a Forward Air Controller. "We've got to put together a nine line brief to let them know what the target is and how to hit it. It all takes time to setup. And if we don't have big features on the ground that the pilots can see it makes it a lot harder."

Sitting in the circle with them, Mike Yakoob, one of the troopers, spoke up, "Well why can't we use GPS? That's as good as a laser spot, isn't it?"

"Yeah, we can use GPS. The biggest trouble with that are our maps. Have you noticed that the GPS coordinates from the box don't match the map?" Gary said.

"Yeah, it's true," Mark said. "The GPS operates under a coordinate system called WGS 84. The maps we have are based on a survey from the thirties. They are way out of date."

"That's right." Gary finished, "So all we can really do with the GPS is tell the pilots where we are. We can't figure a good coordinate for where the targets are."

"Well, that's not entirely true," Mark said. "My Steiner binoculars give us bearing and we've got those laser range finder binos as well. They'll work out to twenty klicks."

"Okay, so what we do is give the pilots our location and then tell them the bearing and range to the target. It'll work," Mark continued. "You got the format for this nine line brief? We need to start putting that together."

"Sure, I brought a pamphlet with me. I'll setup the initial planning. The biggest problem I see is what are these guys dropping? You know they'll be fast movers like F-16s or F-15Es, or even Navy F-18s. They won't be moving slow like A-10s."

"We gotta do what we gotta do. Anyway, I talked with the B Team a little while ago and they're sending a Pave Low in tonight with supplies and a couple of these Air Force types you were talking about."

"Shit hot, I'd rather those guys put the plan together anyway. Maybe they've got good maps. When are they due in?" Gary asked.

"They are supposed to be in just after midnight at that LZ we setup on the other side of the mountain. Sorry I didn't tell you. We'll have to leave in about an hour to get there before dark," Mark said, "I'd better go scrounge Johar and see if he'll take us. You goin' with?"

"Yeah, I'll go. I'm sure Mike here will want to go as well. I'll get one more guy and we'll be ready in a few minutes."

Later that night they crouched on the windswept mountainside, waiting for the inbound helicopter. About twelve-thirty, they heard the faint THWWOOP-THWOOOP, made by the rotor blades of a heavily loaded chopper making its way up the mountain. The team switched on their night vision goggles, looking down slope, they could easily see two CH-53 Pave Low helicopters approaching from the north. One headed directly their way and the other held off and began a slow circle about a mile away.

Gary broke three infrared chem sticks and handed one to Mike and OD. The three of them spread out into a triangle with Gary at the middle of the LZ, the others forming the base. The helicopter would use the V to navigate into the landing zone. As the helicopter hovered closer, the rotor wash beat them with gusty winds, stinging their eyes with dust and pebbles. They pulled their dust goggles over their eyes.

The helicopter touched down and relaxed the rotor pitch slightly, reducing the volume of dust and wind, but not by much. The rotor RPM did not slow down, this would be a combat unload, with power on to make it easier to takeoff again at this high altitude. The rear ramp was already down when the chopper touched down and the crew had begun throwing gear and supplies out the door before they had touched down. Two men ran out the back of the helicopter and hit the ground, joining the mounds of supplies the helicopter had dropped off.

Less than a minute had passed and the helicopter crew had offloaded all the supplies and equipment they had brought. The pilot pulled pitch and the hurricane force winds began beating them harder as the helicopter lifted into a hover four feet above the ground.

Those remaining on the ground crouched as low as they could, while the helicopter spun around pointing its nose down hill. Stopping, the chin dropped slightly and the helicopter accelerated down the hill. In a few minutes, the crushing noise and winds were gone and the mountainside was quiet again.

Mark approached the two new arrivals. In his NOGs he could see them crouching on the ground, they hadn't yet turned theirs on. To keep from scaring them he said in a low voice, "Hey, you guys. Relax, we're Americans here, we're here to pick you up. Welcome to ancient Afghanistan. Did you have a good ride?"

Spinning around the first man said, "Yeah, Hey how are you? You guys with Team 225?"

Mark said, "Yeah, I'm Captain Mark Goode, the CO of 225. Three of my guys are picking up the stuff the chopper brought so don't worry about that.

We've got horses for you to ride."

"That's good news! I'm Captain Woodrow Campbell. This is my ETAC, Staff Sergeant Brandon Ray. We're Air Force. We were sent here to help out with the CAS war."

"Yeah, I was expecting you. We've been trying to figure out CAS and we're sure happy to have you guys. We figure our biggest problem is maps. All of ours are old and don't match the GPS coordinates. We hope you brought new maps with you."

Woody cleared his throat and peered at the dark figure in front of him, "We did bring new maps and stuff, we're all set. We are supposed to get air the day after tomorrow. Err, I guess it's tomorrow now."

"Great, we'll be able to do the nine lines then and figure out where the targets are. One other thing we've been curious about is what kind of bombs are the fighters going to be dropping?"

Caught a little off guard, Woody hadn't expected to be talking tactics and delivery strategy two minutes after jumping out of a helicopter in the middle of the night on an Afghani mountainside. "Uuuhh, humm. We're not getting fighters for our support. What do you mean, "what kind of bombs?""

Mark was incredulous, "What do you mean no fighters? No F-16s or A-10s for us?"

"No, sir. We're not fragged to get fighters, at least not for awhile," Woody said as he shifted from one foot to another, a little uncomfortable standing on the steep slope and being interrogated in the darkness. He decided that he needed to see who he was talking to, he reached for the velcro bag attached to his belt; pulling out his night vision goggles, he switched them on and snapped them into the carrier strapped to his head. "We're probably only going to get B-1s and B-52s, at least for quite awhile."

"How the hell do they expect us to talk a bomber guy onto a CAS target? We don't have enough batteries for our lasers to do this CAS thing very long," Mark said indignantly. Nothing personal, but he was beginning to dislike this Air Force guy. Forcing himself to relax he said, "By the way, call me Mark. We all go by first names here on the team."

"Woody, call me Woody. No, we're not doing the classic nine line brief. Things have changed. We're not talking the pilots onto the target anymore. At least that's not how we plan to do it here. We still do it a little, but we've got gear that reads out coordinates for us. That's what we tell to the pilots."

"Besides," Woody went on, "The bombers are dropping JDAMs for this operation. They'll probably never get below twenty, twenty-five thousand feet.

We'll just call 'em with the target and tell them where we are. Then the target goes boom."

"I see, you just plot the targets and relay that to the bombers? That'll take a little time to do. What if the bad guys are moving?" Mark asked. "What are these JDAMs anyway, is it some new laser guided bomb?"

"A JDAM is a GPS guided bomb, all you have to do is squirt the coordinates of the target in and it'll guide onto the target. To answer your question no we don't plot targets anymore. Not usually. We've got a spotting scope that reads out your position and the position of the target. We either just read that out over the radio or, with some of the airplanes, we can data burst the info on a radio and it goes right in to their system. Bingo, no need for a nine line, or five line or confusion on the radio," Woody said.

Gary appeared next to the two of them and said, "We're all saddled up boss. Ready to go. What's this about a spotting scope?"

Woody shifted to look at the newcomer and said, "We've got this high power optical scope that uses a laser range finder. The scope knows its GPS position and when you laze a target it figures the bearing and range and calculates the GPS coordinate of the target. It also works at night. In clear still air it can see about 10-15 klicks. I've seen targets out to 20 klicks at Fort Irwin."

"Man, that's cool shit. Did you bring a couple of these high speed, low drag doofers? If I was a betting man I'd say it's going to be a popular item around here!" Gary enthused. "Soon as we get back, let's set it up and play with it."

"Sure, it weighs about 20 pounds. It is a little hard to lug around, but it comes off the tripod. Some of this stuff the chopper brought with us are batteries for the scope," Woody said.

"Well, that's a relief. We've been worried how we're going to talk pilots onto the targets around here. And until we hit a few, our hosts won't do a thing," Mark said. "Hey, your horse is over here. We've been here to long, let's head back to Bazan."

"Johar, let's go, bud. Lead the way," Gary said as they mounted their horses.

Ganci Airbase, Krygistan
492nd Fighter Squadron

Captain 'Squeaky' Klein, helping to fill out the forms necessary to get the jets properly armed for the night's first combat sorties, looked at his partner, "Hey Cheese. Did you say the frag had us dropping BLU-109s with the Paveway II guidance packages?"

Major 'Cheese' Knutson, who was leading the Mission Planning Cell for the 492d Fighter Squadron that evening, replied, "Yeah. We're dropping GBU-10Is and we need FMU-143 fuses set to one second delay. Make sure you write down BLU-109s. We need penetration and we don't want Mk-84s going off low order. We're fragged for two flights of four, with four GBU-10Is each. Standard load of AIM-9s, AIM-120s and tanks each side."

"Okay, I'll get Weapons cranking. I think they had most of the BLU-109s setup for GBU-24s. They'll have to switch. But no big deal," Squeaky said.

"Cheese, do you want us to breakout the frag and plan the attack as well or let the crew plan the attack?" 1st LT Rat Arnold asked.

"Who is scheduled for tonight?" Cheese asked. The squadron's aircrews were paired up as formed crews in two ship flights, assigned to fly on a rotating basis by flights.

"I think Grumpy's flight is first up. Jiggy is number three. The next four-ship is Dweeb and Lurch," Rat answered.

"Naw, let's just call them in early and let them work out the deconfliction. TOT won't be a problem; they've got a half hour to get the bombs off. Since they'll have to fly it, it'll be easier if they figure out to how keep their eight jets away from each other," Cheese said. "Tiger has the desk right now doesn't he? Give him a call and let him know."

"If you don't need me right now, I'll just run over there, okay?" Rat asked, heading out the door he added, "I'll let him know what we need on the jet's tonight."

"Go ahead, we're fragged for only eight tonight. I'm sure it'll get busier tomorrow," Cheese replied, "I'll be in Intel if you need me. Go on back to the crew room when you're done. I don't think we'll be busy tonight." The aircrew on the Mission Planning Cell would spend four days on the MPC before they could go back to flying the line; when others were flying it is hard to keep your spirits up.

Lieutenant Colonel Tiger Markusan had his feet up on the makeshift duty desk in the operations room. He was in full swing, talking about his favorite game, Golf, with the enlisted technician that was manning the desk with him. The technician was busy writing on the grease board, keeping track of the days schedule when Rat came in the small room. Their makeshift operations room was an old office on the side of the hangar that served as the squadron area for the 492d while deployed to Ganci.

Breathlessly, Rat began speaking, "Sir, we've been breaking down the Frag.

It came in a few minutes ago. We're up for two four-ships tonight. Cheese says the targets are all basically in the same place so he thinks it best if the crews plan the attacks so they can figure out the deconfliction."

Holding up his hand, Tiger said, "Hold on Rat, you talk too fast, wait a sec. Say it again slowly. I thought we would be up for 16 lines tonight, not eight."

"Yes, sir. Cheese was breaking out the Frag. We're only tasked for two four-ships. All the targets are in the Tora Bora cave complex. He's got weapons switching over to 10Is with penetrator warheads," Rat said again slowly.

"Okay, I'm with you so far. Only eight sorties," Tiger said. "What else?"

"Cheese figures that it would be best if the crews plan the attack. Instead of having the MPC do it. All the targets are within 10 miles of each other in Tora Bora, all within the same TOT block. So he figures that the deconfliction would work best if the crews that fly it plan it."

"Okay, I get ya. Go on down to the crew room, they're probably there." Glancing over his shoulder at the grease board, Tiger said, "The first flight is Grumpy and Jiggy, Dweeb and Lurch have the second. Let 'em know they need to get hoppin' on the plan. Thanks for the heads up."

Leaning forward he pressed the transmit switch on the VHF radio used by the squadron maintenance. "Sergeant Gaudette we've got the frag in for tonight. Drop by and let's talk about it."

"Roger, sir. I'll be there in a couple of minutes," the Maintenance Super replied over the radio. "By the way I've got a full line up and two spares."

"Roger, see you in a minute," Tiger answered.

"There's no friggin' heat in this dingy room. I thought these guys were civilized. Modern, twentieth century and all that," Captain Face Davis complained while zipping his flight jacket; he sat down on a box in the crew dog's TV room. "You should see how the maintainers have setup their rooms. Man, they've got Stereo, VHS, DVDs and a big screen TV. Plus their own grills and shit. Look what we got?"

"Shit face, if you hate it so much, change it. I never saw you lift a finger or sweep the floor. Why didn't you bring a DVD player?" 1st Lieutenant Stick Mason said. "Just shut the fuck up!"

"Get a grip, bud, I wasn't bitching about what you've done. It's the shitty rooms, man. I just hate living on a cot listening to you snore," Face said. "If the Snacko can't scrounge some good stuff, I'll see what I can do. A good friend of mine is a Tanker from Mildenhall. Those guys swap out every two weeks, they can be our delivery boys."

Rat breezed into the room and looked quickly around. Face quit talking when he came in. Stick spoke up, "Hey, Rat. Got the frag in yet? What are the targets for tonight?"

"Yeah, frags' in. It's kinda light though. Only eight lines. Seen Grumpy or Dweeb?"

"Eight lines, shit what a waste. We've been here for days and they can't figure out how to use us yet. Those Buff and Bone guys are having all the fun, while we're sitting here watching *The Fugitive* for the thirteenth time," Face complained.

Waiving his hands at the screen, Stick Mason shouted, "Man, just *shut* up. All you've been doing is complaining today. Can it! The doctor is fixing to get hit by the train!"

One of the other loungers in the TV room said, "Grumpy is outside getting a suntan and Dweeb is asleep, Jiggy's over at Intel."

"Thanks man," Rat said over his shoulder as he left the room.

"Hustler, have you seen Grumpy or Pinto?" Jiggy asked as she entered the squadron flight planning room.

"Yeah, I told 'em both that we've got some targets to plan. They'll be here in a few minutes. How about Dweeb's flight, they coming too?" Hustler asked.

Jiggy stared at the map in front of her; it was a Russian 1:200 thousand topo map. There were very few US detailed maps available. Absently she said, "Rat hooked up with Dweeb after he got me. His flight will be in here in a while as well. Let's go ahead and get started. It looks like we've only got thirty minutes over the target area before the AC-130s come in for a road recce behind us. Splitting that between two flights that only gives us 15 minutes to get 16 LGBs off."

"Yeah, I think so. The biggest problem is bloom time when the bomb explodes. I think we ought to hit this in a racetrack pattern with every jet 45 seconds in trail. We can stagger targets front to back to get a little more separation, but the best deconfliction will be in timing. That way the bloom of the previous bomb will be gone before the last 20 seconds of laze time for the next bomb. Plenty of time to reacquire the target and get the laser on in time to guide the bomb," Hustler observed.

"Okay, okay. If everyone is just setup in trail, all they have to do is stay in position. Everyone just flies the same track and they'll be deconflicted from the previous jet. You know we'll need a zone the guys can float in so it'll be easier to keep station," Jiggy suggested. "I don't know anyone good enough to stay within a tenth of a mile."

Jiggy kept talking as she developed the idea in her head, "Yeah, a zone will be easy. If we fly at 420 knots then 45 seconds is 5.25 miles. Each jet can float between 4.5 and 5.5 miles, that'll keep the last 15-20 seconds of the time of flight clear for the dropper. We'll just pick out update points so guys can check their systems prior to making each bomb pass. As they come off the lasing leg, they can go right into a mapping leg and follow the leader around for the next bomb pass." With a smile, Jiggy looked at Hustler. "What do you think?"

"Sounds good. It'll have to be a fairly tight pattern. The whole thing will have to be about 24 miles around. I sure hate flying the same pattern for that long, that's a lot of exposure in a small place. That pattern is more like a night sortie around Dare County Range back in North Carolina," Hustler said.

"Exactly, nothing like training like you'll fight. Fortunately, the threat level is low and the bad guys don't have any serviceable SAMs that can touch us above 22k," Jiggy replied. "Don't worry about it. Let's go see V and see if he has anything for us." Together they went to the Intel shop to see Mike Griffin, the Squadron Intelligence Officer, otherwise known as V.

The Mad Hatter's Intel shop was just a small room next to the Duty Desk; the only access was by a door behind the desk. V was staring intently at the computer terminal connected to the Air Force intelligence network. He was spinning a trackball and looking at a radar image when Jiggy and Hustler entered the room.

"Hey, V. got any pictures of our target for the night?" Jiggy asked as she bent down to look over V's shoulder.

"Yeah, what pics I've got are on the table in the folder. They don't really show the DMPIs very well. I'm not sure how much help you'll find them," V said.

"Great. Compressed delivery times and poor target definition. Let me take a look," Hustler said picking up the folder.

"Hey, we do have something neat just coming over the net though. That's what I'm looking at right now. See," V said pointing to screen, "these are 3D pictures of the caves and the pixels are GPS tagged."

Hustler and Grumpy bent down to get a better look at the screen. V pointed out the different items on the screen. "See, here and here, are the DMPIs that you guys want to hit. The 3D picture shows the cave entrance pretty clearly."

"Where did this come from anyway? I've never seen a 3D radar picture, that's way cool," Jiggy asked.

"Yeah, it's pretty slick, but I can't tell you. It's a secret and you don't have any need to know. If you say anything I'll have to kill you," V grinned at the two of them.

Straightening up Jiggy laughed, "Okay, keep your secrets. Just print us copies of these things for the targets. Single copies are okay for now until we figure out how to split up the targets between the flights."

"Well, cool as they are they won't help me guide the bomb. There's still nothing that's IR significant about the cave mouth. The GPS is cool, but we don't want to drop this thing ballistically, we want to give it a little guidance. We're going to have to offset track something else that might be hard to do and get it into the field of view. V, I thought we were supposed to hit the cave mouth and then uphill to go into the cave, what's up with that?"

"I called the CAOC about that and they said to offset the second hit to the right 100 meters. They already tried dropping straight uphill 100 meters and didn't get any results," V said.

"Okay, great. Can you produce the coordinates for that offset?" Jiggy asked.

"Yeah, I can do it. But you can do it too can't you?" V asked.

"Yeah, you're right. AFMSS can do that conversion. We just thought you'd like to make yourself useful for a change," Hustler said as he picked up the 3D radar pictures off the printer. "Sitting on your butt doesn't count as helping the war effort."

"So, you want I should take these pictures back then?" V said, tugging on the folder.

"Sorry, what would we do without Intel to keep us in line." Taking the folder in both hands he grinned at V, looking at Jiggy, "I'm going back to Flight Planning, you coming?"

"Yeah, I'll be there in a minute. I just want to check on what else is going on around the AOR."

CHAPTER 10

13 October 2001
Duane, Tajikistan

Major Tom Collins stepped outside the door of the makeshift Operations/ Flight Planning room of the 333 HMS Special Ops Helicopter squadron. They had set up operations in the warehouse next to the Army Special Forces at Dushanbe Airport. Collins scanned the deserted parking lot; pulling out a cigarette, he put it between his lips. Cupping his hands to shield the flame, he lit his lighter and held it to the end of the cigarette, squinting in the smoke as the butt ignited. Taking a deep drag, he looked around again as he breathed out a cloud of smoke. He shook his head and started walking across the forlorn lot. He liked his job, always going to new and different places, being a helicopter pilot in the Air Force was like being a bastard stepchild, but at least the Brass left you alone. He thought about the jarring difference between the sophisticated American presence and the dilapidated Russian façade. He had joined the service at the end of the Cold War and the Russians had always put up a fearsome front. It was easy to tell that for all their bravado they were only putting on a good show. Every one of these Russian buildings had been decaying for decades. Here they had dropped in with technology the Russians couldn't buy or steal, stuff the Russians didn't even have in Moscow. Reaching the edge of the buildings, he paused briefly to stub out the cigarette on the ground. Grinding it into the dirt with his foot, he started out again for the flight line.

A few minutes past midnight and he was to lead two of the squadron's helicopters on the first combat insertion mission of this new war. They would be going in to support one of the Afghan tribal warlords of the Northern Alliance. Their mission was to lift twelve Army Special Forces troopers from Team 228, accompanied by an Air Force Forward Air Controller team. The Air Force team was made up of a frustrated Air Force Fighter Pilot, stuck in a ground job during a hot war, and an Air Force Enlisted Terminal Air Controller. The two of them would direct air strikes in support of the ground war. Two CIA Special Activities Operatives would also be on the flight; they were supposed to join others already with General Dostum.

Feeling confident, Collins walked briskly across the dark tarmac. He could only see a few feet in front of him and he studiously ignored what lay beyond the inky blackness. In his mind, he re-examined all the unknowns and risks that this mission presented. They would be doing a combat insertion over unfamiliar enemy terrain to an unknown location. To top it off, they didn't have any good maps of the area. The last map survey of Afghanistan had been done in the sixties and he was sure those outdated coordinates would be very different from the WGS-84 GPS coordinates used by the helicopter. Their GPS system would only get them close to the target, they would have to visually navigate the last few minutes of the mission reading the map. Not an easy thing to do using night vision goggles in a bouncing helicopter, at night, over unfamiliar terrain. The high workload, combined with the potential of flying into a hornet's nest of a hot LZ worried him. He sensed, more than saw, a shape approaching in the dark. He tried shifting his focus and scanning his eyes to either side of the object. He began to see the dark shape of his MH-53J looming in the dark.

Earlier that afternoon, they had thoroughly briefed the loading, the landing and the off load. Whatever happened, he was confident his crew could handle it, they had been flying several years now and were comfortable with each other. He was worried about the Air Force and CIA passengers. They were not used to operating in this lights-out environment, a mission like this was high risk and you didn't need guys like these screwing things up. He didn't like taking risks he couldn't control, and these guys were a big risk, if they didn't follow orders things could get ugly quickly. Hell, if anything, the tribals were an even bigger unknown. Had they picked an unobstructed landing zone? Would they keep clear during the landing and offload event? Murphy's law could always reach out and bite your ass when you least expect it; "whatever could go wrong, will go wrong."

He skirted deftly around the refueling boom of the helicopter, jutting out the nose of the aircraft. Without thinking, he reached out with his right hand and lightly drug it along the rough aluminum and the smooth Plexiglas of the cockpit as he passed. The Army SF Team was already in place, checking over their gear for tonight's mission.

Master Sergeant Evan Marks, the Helo's Crew Chief, spotted him coming around the right side of the aircraft first, "Hey, Major, the Army guys just got here and are loading their shit. The Air Force dudes have been on board for about a half hour; they're locked and loaded. But I haven't seen the company guys yet."

"Thanks Evan. We'll need to pimp those guys, real quick. We gotta crank in 20 minutes." Peering at his dark shape, Major Collins tried to see Marks' face. "How does the Helo look for tonight?"

"I hear you, sir. The Helo's good to go. FMC, of course. The Maintainers fixed the FLIR and the gearbox checks okay. The book is already signed off, do you want to see it?" MSgt Marks replied, "Plus you'll be happy to know that I scrounged a whole box of batteries for the NOGs. We'll see tonight!"

Nervously, Collins drummed his fingers on the skin of the helicopter. "That's good news. I don't need to see the book. Hey, where's Tully?"

Marks turned his attention to the fuel tank attached to the sponson on the side of the helicopter. "Sir, the co-pilot is just finishing the pre-flight. All the rest of the crew is here and we're all good to go. Don't worry about us."

Collins pursed his lips together, looking at the ground he kicked at something on the pavement, "Okay, I'm going over to Berry 22. Back in a minute." Collins began his brisk walk to the second helicopter crouching nearby in the dark.

At the Pave Low helicopter, Collins saw his friend, Captain Arnie Zimmerman, Berry 22's Aircraft Commander, and his wingman for the night. "Hey, Arnie. I just checked the weather and talked with the boss. We're go for tonight with a return via the FARP north of Boskala. The CO wants us to validate Boskala as a refueling point, in case we need it for a search and rescue capability in country. I expect we'll probably be on the ground there for an hour or two."

Captain Arnold Zimmerman grinned at his friend, "That's just great, but you know we don't really need the gas? What are we gonna do, just drop in and jaw jack for a while? Every time we shut down, we risk breaking the bird. You're not trying to make me miss this great hotel we've got here. Are ya?"

Zimmerman turned serious, "So I get to lead the RTB to Boskala as briefed?"

"Yeah, we'll switch after the insertion lift. Speaking of the insertion, make sure the entire crew is using their NOGs. I don't trust these tribal guys any farther than I can throw 'em. If anybody shoots at you, you're cleared hot to return fire. Anybody!"

"Yes, sir! You can bet we'll all be scanning. Maybe the bad guys will get one free shot, but that's it! Everyone will be tethered, mini-guns in each door will be off safety, the M-2 is locked and loaded and the observers will have their M-16s. Dude, we're ready to rock and roll." Zimmerman nodded happily. "Let's just do it."

"Good, don't forget this will be a silent departure and op. For the insertion, make sure to hang back in wedge left. I'll be coming off target to the right so you can follow without repositioning as I lift off," Collins said.

Arnie nodded slowly, "Yeah, Hoss, as briefed. You nervous or something?"

"Yeah, sorry. I guess a little. Night. Combat insertion. Unknown terrain. Working with tribals that have a track record of shooting down Helo's. To top it off, I've got these amateurs along for a joy ride. I just expect one of these light foot dudes will run into a blade."

"Relax, Hoss. It ain't nothin'. Besides 45 did last nights insertion and it went off without a hitch, didn't it?" Zimmerman said, clapping Collins on the shoulder. "Besides, you signed up to see the world. Right?"

"Yeah right, it ain't nothin but a thing." Collins nodded and turned to walk back to his chopper. Looking back, he said, "But 45 went to a friendly LZ. We're going to Indian country!" Without another word he turned his back, walking purposely back to his chopper.

Arnie couldn't help laughing at his retreating form. "Hey, do you guys need some extra barf bags for the civvies?"

Collins didn't acknowledge Zimmerman's comment; he just flipped Zimmerman off over his shoulder, and kept walking.

Collins boarded Berry 21 through the back ramp. He scanned the troop seats inside the dark chopper, counting 14 passengers strapped in and ready to go. He leaned close to the Crew Chief and spoke into his ear; "Chief, no company guys yet?"

"Well, sir. Some guy dropped off their gear and said they'd be out a few minutes before start. So, I guess they'll be here on time."

"Shit, what prima donnas. I'm not going to wait on those clowns. Don't they know they're just a small part of this op?" Collins groused, "I'm going to strap in. Tell me if they get here, if they don't we're going without 'em."

Collins made his way to the cockpit and sat down. Without looking at Tully, he strapped in. Finished, he looked to his left at his co-pilot. "Tully, how's it goin' dude? Are we good?"

Nodding, Tully stowed his checklist in a pocket on the left sidewall. "Yeah, man. Isn't it engine start time?"

"Yeah, let's do it," Collins replied as Tully reached up to engage the starter to the number two motor. Intent on watching the gauges, he was slightly surprised when Marks tapped him on the shoulder and flashed him a thumbs up signal. He nodded at Marks grimly and looked back at the engine instruments.

Once both engines were started and the rotor blades were coming up to speed, Collins began adjusting his night vision goggles. "Tully, we're gonna run dim steady tonight. Make sure the running lights and strobes are off and the form lights are on half." Looking at Tully to his left he said, "You ready?"

"Yeah, Hoss. We're ready and 22's form lights are on, they're ready. Rotor's up to speed and everything is in the green," Captain Tully Broadshear said.

"Okay, here we go." Collins rotated the collective and the auto throttle increased engine rpm to match the increasing load on the rotor blades. Slowly, the big helicopter began to shake a bit as Collin's approached the pitch/power liftoff point. As the helicopter broke free of the ground, the ride became noticeably smoother, the weight completely suspended by the eight blades of the 72 foot diameter rotor.

"Gear up," Collins called as he pressed the rudder pedals to the left and rotated the helicopter to the left. The tail rotor responded by adjusting blade pitch to push the tail to the right. Scanning the takeoff area in his night vision goggles he stopped the turn on the outbound heading. He eased the stick forward at the same time as he gently twisted the collective; the helicopter rotated the nose down ever so slightly and the big chopper began to accelerate.

Berry 22 followed Collins in a cloud of dust about two minutes later. As they emerged from the gloom of the airport, they climbed to just over 100 feet above the ground for the transition to traveling formation.

An hour and fifteen minutes later, they crossed the Madera River that formed the border between Turkmenistan and Afghanistan. Collins descended to less than fifty feet above the terrain flying 160 miles an hour. There wasn't time for him to do anything other than avoid the terrain and manipulate the controls. Tully monitored the navigation as well as kept tabs on the terrain following/avoidance radar; just to make sure Collins avoided the terrain. It was always best to have two eyes outside, whatever might kill them would come from the outside. The Crew Chief, MSgt Marks, sat in the jump seat and kept a sharp eye on the engine instruments and the fuel state, as well as scanning the forward looking infrared display. As far as he was concerned, there was no way they would be surprised by an engine problem on the dark side, but just to make sure, he watched each little jiggle of more than a dozen needles.

The two dark helicopters crossed the frontier over a swampy area between the towns of Keleft and Dali, both in the hands of the Taliban. He planned to circle west over the flat plains of Jowzjan province and cross the A76 Highway between two medium sized villages. The LZ they were headed for was a ridgeline above these plains about 50 miles southwest of Mazar e-Sharif. The passengers hoped to meet a group of Dostum's Afghani guerrillas.

Collins reviewed the insertion in his mind. It should take no more than two minutes to approach the LZ, make the hot drop and exit. Their plan was to follow the ridges held by the Northern Alliance to the east until they could cut back to the north and pass east of the town of Mazar. Flying low, fast and blacked out on their exit, they would be over a hundred miles away from their inbound path. By going back a different way Collins hoped to avoid anyone he might have awakened on the way in. Look for a green triangle and all he asked for was two minutes, then they could be on their way.

"Five miles out," Tully announced.

"Tracers falling aft," the rear gunner, manning his M-2 .50 caliber machine gun, called over the intercom. Looking out the rear of the aircraft with the ramp down he could clearly see Berry 22 and the source of the tracers with his night vision goggles.

"Copy," Tully replied as the helicopter sped only a few feet off ground.

Collins tensed a little on the controls and the helicopter bobbled ever so slightly in response. As an afterthought he said, "Sorry, sweaty palms."

"Half mile, approaching the target. Mile a minute forward, 20 down," Tully Broadshear said.

"Copy," Collins replied. "Gear down."

"Gear down," echoed Tully. "I've got the sticks."

"Copy the sticks, I see 'em too. Are they the right color?"

"Can't tell yet. Keep going," Tully answered.

"Tell me when you can see the color, I'm worried about these guys."

"Sure Hoss keep going. You're at 15 feet, 100 forward," Tully said.

"Okay, okay."

"Ten feet, 50 forward," Tully said.

"The lights are blue, they're blue," Marks said breathlessly.

"They're wrong, they're supposed to be green," Collins said, tightening his grip on the collective; he was ready to abort.

"There's only four guys on the ground, I say they just made a mistake, go ahead and land," Tully interjected quickly.

"Gunner's heads up for bad guys," Collins said to the men manning the mini-guns on each side of the helicopter. "Okay, Tully. I'm going to land. Tell

22 to orbit and look for bad guys, forget Wedge Left."

For those on the ground the first helicopter blacked out the stars as it began spreading dust as it settled onto the ground. Arnie, in the second chopper, began circling the LZ. He was using the FLIR to look for concentrations of bad guys to target in case the LZ was a setup and they were ambushed.

As soon as Berry 21 touched down, Marks lowered the ramp at the rear of the aircraft and the passengers ran out carrying all their gear. The two Air Force guys were just clearing the door when Marks heard Berry 22 report taking fire from down slope. Quickly, he scanned the interior of the chopper. Seeing it empty of passengers, he said, "We're clear."

"Go, go, go. Fire from down slope," Tully called. "We'd better come off left instead of right."

"Fuck that, we're gonna go right over this ridge," Collins said as he lifted off and accelerated for the top of the ridgeline. As the chopper began moving Berry 22 opened up on the shooter with one of its mini-guns, a bright streak of light reaching like an angry finger from the helicopter to the ground.

"Berry flight bug out south," Tully called over the radio as Collins maneuvered the helicopter over the ridgeline.

The passengers rushed to throw their gear out the back of the chopper in the limited amount of time Collins had allowed them on the ground. The last SF trooper stumbled as one of the Air Force guys landed on him as he jumped to the ground. Three of General Dostum's Northern Alliance irregulars quickly loaded their equipment on their horses. Within a few minutes, after the noise of the helicopters had disappeared over the ridge they were all loaded and ready to mount their horses. Hastily, they departed the LZ to avoid any Taliban that might come looking around this part of the mountain.

In the early hours of dawn, the caravan of newly arrived SF Troopers, Air Force Forward Air controllers and the company men made their way into the town of Kariz, where General Dostum greeted them.

"Welcome, welcome. I am very happy to have you here. All of you. Please make yourselves at home," Dostum said as he gripped the hand of each man in turn.

"I want to know each and everyone of you. We have not much to offer but whatever we have is yours. We are very happy to have you as allies. We are very happy to have your help in our war to free our country. With you, we will be able to defeat the Taliban. I am sure we will be able to do this in short order." Beaming broadly he said once again, "We are very happy to have you."

Dostum looked at all the Americans. "One thing is very important. Very important. I need you to remember this, please listen to me. You are not used to operating in this country or with this enemy. Please follow the instructions of my men. I could not bear it if one of you were shot or captured and my men have been told that it is most important to safeguard our Americans from the Taliban. It is more important than their own lives."

"It is most important. Please no wandering about, no fighting on your own. You are our connection to America. You are very important; it is with you and your radios that we will win this war. We must keep you safe, please help me in this matter."

"Please make yourselves at home. You have been traveling, I have a house set aside for you to use. This morning you shall rest and perhaps sleep. This afternoon I shall show you our battlefield and perhaps tomorrow we can start destroying the Taliban in earnest. Please rest now," Dostum said as he greeted his American Allies enthusiastically.

Ganci, Kyrgyzstan

Twenty-four F-15E Strike Eagles of the 492d Fighter Squadron were huddled in the dark on a huge expanse of concrete on this former Soviet Air Base. They were parked tail to tail with a common taxiway behind them. Spread like branches of a large gray Christmas tree, the noses of each airplane pointed away from all the other airplanes and there was more than 100 feet between airplanes, just in case an errant explosion from one might destroy the others.

Four of them, Marker 21 flight, were alive in the dark with beacons and position lights flashing. They were preparing the first fighter sortie to be flown from the north side of Afghanistan. To the left of the nose of each aircraft, straining impatiently for flight stood a crew chief wearing a headset. In a few minutes, they would disconnect and the four airplanes would taxi out to the end of the runway in radio silence, turn their lights off and take off into the night sky.

A van with parking lights flashing moved quickly down the flight line, it stopped with a jerk in front of Lieutenant Colonel Grumpy Westin's jet. The passenger jumped out and ran around the van to the crew chief, standing at the edge of the red flashing pool of light created by the jet's lights. He bent down, shouted something into his ear and then just as quickly ran back to the van and jumped in.

"Sir," the crew chief said, "that was the super. She just told me they've passed a 10-minute Rolex. She said that they would pass the word to the other jets. Do you want to just wait here before you taxi?"

"Yeah, thanks Chief. We'll just wait here," Westin replied as he flipped two switches on the left console. "I'm going to go dim/steady on the lights."

"Sure, sir. That'll be fine." To the crewman standing by to pull the chocks, he pointed to his watch and flashed ten fingers.

Ten minutes later than planned Grumpy turned his lights on bright/flash and the crew chief asked him, "You ready to go, sir?"

"Yeah, Chief. Are the other three jets on bright/flash?"

"Yes, sir. I see all three jets have their lights going. Does that mean they're ready to taxi too?"

"Yep, we're going comm out tonight. You can pull chocks and disconnect. Thanks for the start, see ya when we get back," Grumpy said over the intercom.

The Crew Chief bent over slightly and looked at the crewman under the wing, next to the left wheel. Once he had his attention he put the tips of his thumbs together with his fingers balled up into fists and then flipped both of them up to signal the crewman to pull the chocks. He pulled the headset plug from the comm cord and dropped it on the ground. The crewman pulled the chocks off to the side and then disconnected the comm cord from the airplane, rolling it up as he walked clear of the left wing. The Crew Chief came to attention, waiting for the pilot to begin taxiing.

Grumpy looked left and right and then pushed the power up slightly. With the airplane rolling, he wiggled the rudders left and right to check the nose gear steering and stepped on the brakes lightly to test their operation. With the nose bouncing slightly, he returned the Crew Chief's salute with his left hand, and, as he brought his hand down, he extended his thumb and little finger and flashed him a "hang loose" signal. As the jet turned onto the taxiway, the Crew Chief reached up to pat the wingtip as it went by.

Slowly the other three jets in the formation followed Grumpy at roughly 300-foot intervals as they taxied along the parallel taxiway to the end of the runway. The taxiway that led to the end of the runway was only standard width and would not allow Grumpy to turn the jets away from the buildings that surrounded the airfield. He taxied up close to the edge of the runway and turned about thirty degrees to the left to allow the other jets to do the same. He wanted them to point their ordinance towards an open area on the opposite side of the base. He left the lights on bright, but turned the flashers off.

Before the last jet stopped, a crew of four enlisted men was swarming around Grumpy's jet. Checking for leaks, cuts in the tires and other abnormalities they also pulled the safety release pins to arm all the weapons on the jet. As soon as they finished his jet, they ran to the next one to give it a last chance look over before it took the runway.

Tracer Nelson, the pilot of number four, turned off all his lights and turned on his formation lights as soon as the ground crew was finished checking over his jet. In turn, each jet up the line turned off their regular night navigation lights and turned on their formation lights to signal that they, too, were ready for takeoff.

Grumpy turned off his lights as well and flipped his formation lights on full. Over the intercom he said, "Pinto, you ready to go?"

"Born ready. Let's do it," Pinto said.

Pushing up the power, he turned the jet towards the runway and with the jet rolling slowly, he looked at the tower. Seeing a green light, he flipped on his taxi light and continued onto the runway. Without stopping, he briefly checked the engine instruments at 80 percent rpm, pushed the throttles into afterburner and pulled the stick full aft. The jet quickly began accelerating down the runway and as the nose began to rise, Grumpy released some of the backpressure he held. The jet gracefully lifted off the runway into the dark sky and he quickly retracted the gear.

Twenty seconds later he heard a buzz and looked down at the radar warning receiver, he saw that number two had locked his aircraft up with his radar, he knew that the others would soon follow in the radar trail departure.

Grumpy climbed into the clear night sky, headed directly for their first steer point near Dushanbe. Holding 330 knots he waited for his number two, Sly Stone and Tally McGoldrick, to join in a loose spread formation on his left. Checking his RWR again, he could see two more lock indications. Pinto must have been thinking the same thing because he said, "Grumpy it looks like we're all joined up. Sly's on the left and Jiggy has a lock. air-to-air TACAN says four miles. I'd say we're good to go. Better check in with Magic soon."

"Yeah, in a minute," Grumpy replied. Sliding his clear visor back on his helmet, he looked at the stars, bright points of light covering the rugged sky. Engaging the autopilot, he twisted in his seat and moved his head to the left and right to get the full view of the Milkyway. Whistling under his breath he said to Pinto, "Dude, check out the Milkyway, that's something you just don't see back in the states anymore."

"Yeah, man. It's cool. Better check in with Magic."

"Kill joy," Grumpy snorted.

Keying the microphone for radio one, Grumpy slowly said, "Magic, Marker as fragged."

"Copy, Marker, Rolex ten minutes and contact Horse 330.15. Good hunting,"the German controller aboard the NATO AWAC's aircraft replied.

Pinto typed in the new frequency and said, "You're up."

"Horse, Marker as fragged," Grumpy said again. Three distinct transmissions of two clicks each followed his radio call. The other three aircraft in the flight were checking in with a zipper to acknowledge they had made the frequency change.

"Horse copies Marker. You are cleared on station. SAR is in place and holding."

"Pinto, what do you think he means by that?" Grumpy asked.

"Dunno, maybe that's why we got the Rolex to begin with," Pinto replied.

"Maybe. As we cross over Kunduz, I'm going to drag the boys. Eight mile trail will give us a minute separation," Grumpy said, talking more to himself than Pinto.

"You doing okay up there? I want to take another look at the target photos."

"Yeah, I'm fine. Go ahead," Grumpy replied. He pushed down on the castle switch on the stick and flipped it to the left to take control of the air-to-air radar. Bumping the cursor at the top of the screen, he extended to range to see all the traffic meandering around Afghanistan.

"Marker, Drag," Grumpy transmitted over the back radio. He watched the air-to-air TACAN begin to count up as Jiggy slowed and began opening up the distance between flights. He pushed the power up to expedite the spacing operation. Accelerating to 480 knots true airspeed, he watched as Sly began slipping aft. Satisfied that the formation was settling into the proper attack spacing, he bumped the cursor on the radar to display a range of 40 miles.

In the first jet of the train, Pinto said over the intercom, "Hey Grumpy, I'll need the radar to check the system. Can you spare it a minute?"

"Sure, you've got the radar," Grumpy replied. Pulling the radio switch aft he transmitted, "Three's mapping."

Pinto took control of the radar and started a patch map of the airbase at Bagram north of Kabul, the update point for tonight. Freezing the map, he fine tuned the cursors, squeezed off an update, and then designated it to refine the target steering.

"System's tight," Pinto announced. "Radar's yours, you've got a good designation. I'm going to the pod."

Sliding the coolie switch on the right hand controller, he took control of the Target Pod on his right MPD display. Brushing the TDC with his thumb, he moved the Pod to the left to look into the valley where Jalalabad lay as they passed it. He stirred the Pod around for a few minutes, both to check the operation of the pod and to familiarize himself with the neighborhood. Reaching up, he wiped the sweat from his forehead with the back of his Nomex glove.

"Five minutes out. I'm going air-to-ground," Grumpy said.

"Copy," Pinto said absently. He pulled the Autoacq switch aft briefly to return the pod to the cue point. Pushing the Autoacq switch forward briefly, he switched to narrow field of view to see if he could breakout the target area; seeing nothing, he pushed forward again to switch back to wide field of view. Staring intently at the screen, he ignored the stars and the lights reflected on the inside of the canopy.

"I don't see the target. I'm going to the offset track point," Pinto said, trying to keep Grumpy in the loop. He brushed the TDC again to move the cursor over the bright spot they had planned to use as an offset point if the target wasn't IR significant. Thumbing forward, he went narrow to check the offset.

"Two minutes. Designation looks good," Grumpy said.

Centering the cursor over the offset, Pinto pulled the trigger on the hand controller halfway to initiate track. With the tracking stabilized, he pulled aft on the Autoacq again to cue back to the target and then forward to switch back to wide field of view so he could keep the offset and the target in view. He pulled aft on the castle switch to go to TGT mode in the pod and quickly glanced at push button seven to make sure the pod had shifted.

"Good track, cleared to pickle," Pinto said as he stared intently at the display. Not actually seeing the target made him nervous, he checked the coordinates the pod was looking at and then glanced back to his photo, checking one more time that he was looking at the right target. Happy that they matched, he looked back at the stability of the target track. Pressing the laser fire button with his little finger he said, "Laser's on. Good ranging."

"Ten seconds TREL. I've got the release cue," Grumpy intoned.

"Cleared to pickle," Pinto repeated.

"I'm on the button," Grumpy said as he pressed the pickle button on the stick with his right thumb.

Suddenly, the aircraft lurched as the 2,000 pound laser guided bomb was kicked off the airplane's bomb rack.

"Bomb's gone. One's checking left." Grumpy said over the back radio. Rolling into a left bank, Grumpy pulled the stick to get some G on and turn the jet. Approaching the rollout heading, he relaxed the G and rolled out steady on the new course.

As soon as Pinto felt the bomb release, he thumbed the laser fire button and said, "Laser's off."

He continued to watch the track intently throughout the turning maneuver, he saw the IR picture change a little as they rolled out on the new heading. Worried about the stability of his track, he quickly checked the offset track point to make sure it was still looking good.

It was drifting a little to the left, so he gently brushed the TDC. The picture was more washed out than on their previous heading, without contrast in the picture he had to keep brushing the TDC to keep the crosshairs in place. With twenty seconds to impact, he turned the laser back on a little early, but he hoped it might stabilize the track. Worried about drifting off the target, he glanced quickly at the displayed target coordinates; they were still very close. He squeezed the trigger switch full action to redesignate the target. The track settled down and he watched the TIMPCT numbers count down.

As the bomb exploded Pinto said, "Laser's off. Well, we hit whatever we were aiming at. I hope it's the target."

"Two's bomb's gone. Checking left," Sly said over the radio.

"Hustler, I think Sly is late. That's going to affect us isn't it?" Jiggy asked. Looking at the air-to-air TACAN, she saw they were exactly 16 miles behind Grumpy. Right where they were supposed to be. With that spacing, each bomb should be on target, one minute apart. One minute spacing would prevent conflicting flight paths and the bloom from the previous bomb from washing out their picture.

"Yeah, if they're over four miles out of position, go to twenty miles on the radar and check," Hustler suggested.

"Can't do it. They've already checked left after the bombs away call. Range will be screwy until we roll out behind them," Jiggy said.

"Yeah, you're right. I guess we'll know soon enough if we get caught in the bloom."

Pushing the power up, Jiggy accelerated the jet. "Hustler, I'll put a few more knots on and when the bomb comes off, it'll have just a hair more energy. Maybe that'll be enough for you to bring its nose down at terminal," Jiggy said.

"Yeah, maybe. If the bloom goes away with enough time to reacquire the target and get the laser on, and enough time to avoid stalling the bomb, and…"

"Ten seconds TREL, cue's on," Jiggy interrupted.

"Laser's off," Hustler said. He thought it would be better to drop ballistic, with the laser off there would be no chance that it might try and guide on an early signal. He would try to guide the bomb in the terminal phase.

"Three, bomb's gone, checking left," Jiggy chimed in over the radio.

"You were right, can't see a thing," Hustler said, as the bloom of number two's bomb obscured the infrared image. He thumbed the castle left to cue and set the offset track point in the steer point. Ready for when the bloom died away, he would reestablish the offset track, switch to target, slew the pod back to the target, redesignate and get the laser back on

"Twenty seconds to impact," Jiggy said.

"Fifteen."

"Twelve seconds."

"I'm just making out the track point," Hustler said as he reestablished the track. "Going target," he said as he thumbed aft to target. "Redesignate. Laser's on."

The bomb, traveling on a ballistic path, is supposed to need a minimum of twelve seconds the properly follow a laser designation. Hustler got the laser on in the last eight seconds of flight. It could not quite keep up with the guidance packages commands to pitch down and land short of its ballistic path. The combination of the sudden flight control inputs and the commands to pitch down caused the bomb to use a lot of energy and, in fact, impact a little short of the intended target.

"Not a shack, but definitely a hit. The bomb fell just outside the cursors a little short." Hustler said after replaying the strike in his mind. "Too bad the only hits that count out here are direct hits."

"Shit, all that because we had a little positioning problem. I'm going to watch two like a hawk. I don't want to do anymore of that," Jiggy said disgustedly.

North of the Salang Pass, Afghanistan

Squatting on his haunches, Ahmed Youseff threw the dregs of his tea into the small campfire at the back of the cave and stood up. Making his way around the Russian ZU 23-2 gun, he walked to the cave mouth. Rayshid Sayed, his Lieutenant in charge of the Salang caves, followed him closely.

Standing on one side of the cave entrance, Youseff looked out over the narrow valley and then pointed at the peak on the other side of the deep gorge.

Seeing where Youseff was pointing, Sayed quickly spoke, "The unwashed Afghanis that follow Fahim hold that peak, and the other side of this pass. We have always been able to use this road during the night; by day, it has been more of a problem. Have I not heard reports of the Americans shooting our trucks south of Kabul at night?"

"It is true. When an American airplane drones overhead it is not safe to drive on the roads—even without lights," Youseff replied.

"If we have people out listening, can they not distinguish the noise of this airplane?"

"Perhaps. It is a different sound from the jets that fly overhead. It is probably the Spooky gunship that we have seen on TV. We do not know where it flies and the Taliban can no longer use their air radar. Each radar site still working has been attacked by the Americans. No matter where it was placed, they found it like they could smell it."

"Perhaps we could draw this airplane into a valley like this one. With people in the mountains, on the ridges we could point out where it is and shoot it down," Sayed suggested.

"Perhaps. Right now I have another problem. Muqtar bin Laden has told me to send most of our fighters to attack Fahim at Kunduz and Taloqan. He wants us to send ten to twelve thousand men."

"This will be hard. We have not completed the training of many of those men. Many have just joined us since last month. Some barely know how to hold and fire a gun," Sayed observed.

"They joined our cause to fight for Islam against the unbelievers. God will guide their hands. I am not worried about training or weapons. We have plenty of both. What we do not have a lot of are trucks. It is getting through this pass and traveling at night that is the biggest problem."

Picking up a pair of binoculars from a makeshift table, he raised them to his eyes and scanned the ridge and peak across the valley. Following his eyes Sayed said, "There have only been a few of their guards watching us. We do not see many fires from their camps. My men think that most of their people have been called somewhere else. I think you may not have as much problem driving this pass as you might think."

"Have you heard there is much construction and dust at Golbahar? Is that not south of here?" Youseff asked.

Staring into the distance Sayed replied, "I know this place. It is only a few miles east from this road. It is in a small valley near Charikar."

"Some of my men say that helicopters are landing there at night and bringing in troops and supplies. This is a big threat to the road. This road is the only one from Kabul north to Mazar e-Sharif and Kunduz," Youseff said.

"Ahmed, they may be landing there. But there cannot be many. It is only a few miles from here and we have heard one or two helicopters over the last nights, but there is not much traffic. The mountains are like record players.

Sound travels far along these valleys. I would be more worried that these helicopters bring in supplies, weapons and ammunition which are a greater threat than a man on foot in these mountains."

Youseff dropped his hand, the binoculars dangling from his fingers as he walked slowly back to the cave mouth and sat down at a makeshift table. Setting the glasses on the table, he put his fingertips together and gazed into the hazy blue across the valley. "I see, that is even more reason to attack at Kunduz and Taloqan, it would prevent the Northern Alliance from building up forces here. Moving our men is still our problem, how do we move our men from these caves and in the valley west of us. We need trucks and do we move in the day or the night?"

Sayed still stood at the cave mouth and turned slightly. "It is as you say. Trucks are the biggest problem we face, whether we use the day or the night. First, we need to get trucks here. We need to do this before we can think of moving the men to Kunduz."

Continuing, Sayed said, "I have only a few trucks here for me to use. I do not have enough to move these men to Kunduz, even if we had two weeks."

Crossing his arms, Youseff looked down at the table. "Yes, we need to bring trucks here as quickly as we can. And we must do it in a way to keep this Spooky from finding them."

Sayed moved to a chair next to Youseff. Sitting, he stuck his feet out in front of him staring at his toes poking through his sandals. After a minute, he spoke softly, "The trucks must move night and day. There are many, so that if they come through Kabul during the day, tongues will wag and the Americans will find them. Also, if they come all at once at night the Spooky will find them. Surely, one or two will not attract attention from the Americans."

"That must be true. One or two trucks would slip by without notice. We could gather them here in the mountains and in a few days we would have enough and we could drive the men to Kunduz," Youseff said.

Leaning forward, Sayed put his arms on the table. "There is plenty of room in the mountains to hide trucks easily. When everything is ready, all could be sent. I have not seen these Spooky airplanes come north of Kabul. We could drive day or night. And if they come into our valley looking for our trucks, they will die."

"Yes, I am confident that your plan will work. Plus, any nosy Americans that fly into the valley will die. That makes it even better. It is a good plan, but it will take several days to gather all the trucks needed. I will arrange the movement of the trucks, you make sure they are safe and then move the men when you are ready."

"Yes, Ahmed. I will do this, I have the honor of God to do this. How many men shall I leave in the camps?" Sayed asked.

"None. Perhaps only a few to make sure the unwashed locals do not move into our caves. Muqtar bin Laden has said he wants everyone in Kunduz and Taloqan. Move everyone," Youseff said.

Putting his hands flat on the table, Sayed took a deep breath and said, "Ahmed, we cannot do this. Mohideen moved his communications and radios here from Tora Bora. These men need support and protection; they control our fighters throughout the world. Plus we must continue to man these caves above the pass. If for no other reason than to prevent Fahim from using the pass."

"Then leave only a few men to watch the pass and a few more to hold the hands of the radio people. But everyone else must go to the defense of Kunduz. Make sure that you send them," Youseff said forcefully. "It is bin Laden himself that has decreed it."

Nodding his head, Sayed acquiesced, "Mudier, I will do as you wish. Two vehicles will go to Kunduz to check the way and report back to me on the state of the road and the problems that our men may encounter. I will be ready when the trucks are here; our men will be safe from bombs until it is time to fight."

Turning to the men grouped around the 23mm Russian gun he said, "Ali, you are from Baghlan? Is this true?" Sayed asked one of the men lounging next to the gun.

Standing quickly, Ali Najad, replied, "Yes, Mudier Sayed. That is my home village."

"Go and see Hassan Nasir on top of the ridge. I want you to take two vehicles and drive the road from here to Baghlan and then to Kunduz," Sayed said.

"But, Mudier, I only need one vehicle for that drive. It will only take a few hours," Najad replied.

"No, take two. One of them should be the truck with the Russian heavy machine gun on the back. You might need it if you meet some brigands from the Northern Alliance. Look carefully at the road and make sure to leave signs for drivers that may follow you so that they might also be able to travel the road as if they grew up here," Sayed instructed.

In the rocky valley west of the Salang Pass, a dark brown Toyota Land Cruiser bumped slowly along a gravel side road that branched off the A76, the main Kabul highway. Inside, Ali Najad peered nervously up the steep, narrow valley. He was looking for a small track that led off the right side of the road.

About five miles from the main road, where the road skirted a bubbling stream on the west side of the valley, he shouted and pointed to the left.

The Toyota turned left onto a narrow track that emerged onto a cleared area two-thirds of the way up the ridgeline. At the back of the clearing was the entrance of a small cave. In front of the cave, and for several meters above it, several tall antennas were scattered. One vehicle was in the clearing, parked at the mouth of the cave. It was a small pickup with a Russian 12.7mm DShK heavy machine gun mounted on a tripod in the bed.

Najad jumped out of the Land Cruiser and jogged over to the pickup. Out of breath, he spoke quickly to the driver. "Hassan and Sayed told me that you and the truck must come with me to Kunduz. Come, we must leave right away."

"I have been told to guard this cave. I will not leave when a Afghani runs up to me and cries for help," the driver retorted.

Insulted and suddenly angry, Najad gritted his teeth. "I have been ordered to go to Kunduz and to take this truck with me. If you are afraid and cannot drive with me to Kunduz, then you will have to face Sayed and explain your fear. I heard Sayed and Youseff talking and this is a job ordered by bin Laden himself. Who would you like to complain to now?"

Abdul Saleem, a little less courageous when confronted by an order from bin Laden replied quickly, "I was only talking to you in jest. You have no sense of humor. We are ready to leave and drive to Kunduz with you. Give us a few moments to gather our belongings and we will be ready." Gesturing at his comrades, he barked orders to get the truck ready to leave.

Ab Bazan, Afghanistan

"Dave, it's time we talk with Fahim again. Now that we've got Woody, and the Zoomies are going to release air to us, we just have to work out with him how we're going to do it. We gotta work out a plan," Mark confided. It was approaching noon and Mark knew that soon they would be getting the details of their first sorties of air support. Tomorrow it was up to him to take the Air War to the Taliban and al-Qaeda on the front lines.

"Yeah, you're right. Get Woody and tell him to be ready. I'll go and track down Fahim and see if he'll talk to us," Dave replied. Finished with lunch, he wiped his mouth with his sleeve and stood up. "You know, all we seem to be doing lately is sitting around, shooting the shit and eating. Wouldn't be so bad if we had ice cream…maybe a little Blue Bell."

"Yeah, it's time we earned our pay. We've got air coming tomorrow and right now nothing to use it on," Mark said.

"I'll see what I can do," Dave said over his shoulder as he left their hooch.

Getting up, Mark walked through the door to the back courtyard. Seeing Woody and Brandon, by a campfire he went over and squatted down next to them.

Picking up a rock, he tossed it up and down a few times. "Woody, Dave is going over to talk to Fahim. He's the Northern Alliance General in these parts."

"Yeah, you were telling me about him. Not really happy to have us, right?" Woody interjected into the brief silence.

"Well, maybe I'd say more reluctant. Or maybe he just doesn't like me, or the Army. He seems to like Dave and the other company guys. Anyway, Dave is going to try to setup a meeting with him. Since we're going to get air support tomorrow it would be good to have some targets we are cleared to hit," Mark said.

"Yeah, man, it would be damn shame to send them home with ordinance left over!" Woody said.

"It would at that. Kind of embarrassing too. We have to work up some targets. Tell me again how this JDAM thing works, I'm not familiar with it."

Woody poured some coffee into his canteen cup and cupped both hands around it to eek a little warmth from the hot liquid. "Okay, a JDAM is a 2,000 pound class weapon. It's an Mk-84 bomb body with a GPS guidance package. Technically, it's called a GBU-31."

"So, it has more HE than say a 500 pounder?" Mark said.

"Sure does. More than twice. Some of the weight is taken by the cast iron case, but most of it is this stuff called Tritinol. Pretty stable, but a very good explosive. Anyway, the weapons guys put a fuse on the back end. Sometimes the fuses are wind driven, or electrically operated. The fuse only has to work for a few seconds after release from the airplane. The delay is settable; so when it senses that the bomb has hit the ground it can set off the warhead, say in a small fraction of a second, like a tenth. Or maybe as much as a whole second," Woody said.

Woody had been an F-15E pilot stationed at Seymour Johnson Air Force Base in North Carolina. He was sent overseas to Europe to be an Air Liaison Officer with the 173d Airborne in Vincenza, Italy. The assignment folks considered being an ALO a career-broadening job. To Woody, it was a rotten deal to not be flying. Especially for a good war, like this one. To be stuck on a mountainside, eating goat, while his buds were flying was just a crappy deal, no way around it. The enlisted man on his team was Brandon Ray whose career field was working CAS with Army units. Very rarely did he ever spend time on an Air Force base. To him Italy was good duty.

"Okay, okay. I've got the explosive and fusing thing down," Mark said, waiving his hand. "We use different stuff like that all the time. What I want to know is how this GPS thing works?"

"Fair enough. Have you worked with Laser Guided Bombs before?" Woody asked.

"Yeah, some. We've heard that our laser illuminators don't work real well with them. No one ever told us quite why, but it really puts a crimp in our capability," Mark replied.

"I know why, let me tell you how an LGB works and then I'll explain the GPS bomb," Woody said, taking a sip from his coffee.

"Okay, I guess I asked for Lecture 101. Go ahead." Mark said as he put his back to the wall and sat down to make himself comfortable.

Picking up a small stick, Woody drew a small square in the dirt, placing his canteen cup in the center, he said. "You see it's like this. This cup is our target. My hand is the airplane and this stick is the laser beam, or a short part of the beam." He paused and looked expectantly at Mark.

"With you, man," Mark said, a little annoyed.

"Okay. Say you are with a team over on this hill, my foot. What's the range of those handheld lasers? Say, a little more than a klick or so? Anyway, less than a mile." He put the stick on the toe of his boot and aimed it at the cup.

"Yeah, with fresh batteries they're usually good out to a klick and half, maybe two on a clear day," Mark replied.

"The scatter range on the reflected beam is little farther, but no matter. The deal is that these bombs are going very near supersonic by the end game phase. At this altitude and temperature, they are doing better than 12 miles a minute. The bomb really needs 10 to 12 seconds of good solid, stable guidance to zero out errors as it approaches the target. At those speeds that means it needs to have good, stable, guidance from about two and a half miles out."

Mark, looking intently at Woody's hand, nodding his head slightly, said, "So, you're saying our lasers don't have enough power to guide the bomb out that far?"

"Yeah, that's part of it. The other part is that for a handheld laser, the bomb really needs to come in from a thirty degree cone around your azimuth, or line of sight to the target, to stand a chance of guiding. Remember the bomb guides on reflected laser light and since you're so close and at a low angle to the target, your beam's reflections are very limited. Add that to the lower power of the reflected beam and the bomb has real problems seeing your beam," Woody said, lowering his hand.

"Yeah, I see your point," Mark said. Still annoyed to be getting a lecture from a zoomie.

"One other thing about a handheld laser. It's like a rifle, isn't it? By that I mean you hold it like one and it's hard to keep it on the target without moving it around a bit."

"Yeah. You gotta control the movement, kinda like a figure eight, and relax, but you can't just keep it stock still, if that's what you mean," Mark replied.

"Well, each of those movements results in large displacements of the guidance fins as the seeker tries to adjust the aimpoint. What happens is the bomb wiggles around as you move the laser spot around."

"So, you're saying I'm screwing with the seeker as the spot moves around," Mark asked as he was beginning to see the limitations of his handheld laser, but not to the point that he was ready to consider this guy an equal.

"Exactly, and depending on the bomb, it may not have enough energy left after a few of these wiggles to make it to the target. It may fall short."

"Oh, shit. You said the bomb has to come over my shoulder, right? If it falls short it's gonna be closer to me!" Mark whistled lightly through his teeth.

"Yeah, man. Now you see the problems with that thing. The danger area for a 2,000 pound bomb is well over 3600 feet. How far away can you lase again?" Woody asked, matter of factly.

"Okay, so what good is my handheld anyway? And how do you get around that jerky problem in an airplane?" Mark asked, a little frustrated.

"A handheld is good to use as a pointer. You can shine it on a target to positively ID it for the guy in the air. That is if he can see it. Some airplanes, like the Strike Eagle can't see the spot. One of these days, maybe, but not right now."

Picking up the stick, he stuck it in his fingers at an angle. "As for the jet. This is how it works. The jet flies a ground track and releases the bomb. After it's gone, the jet turns to one side, mostly to slow the apparent rate of movement of the target with respect to the sensor. When it comes time, the jet will turn the laser on and illuminate the target. Angles are a problem here as well, but as long as you illuminate the target from the rear quadrant or from the side, the seeker on the bomb will see a reflected beam. The sensor on the airplane is stabilized, and the laser is way more powerful than anything you can carry on your back. Plus, it can see much farther, say 12 miles or so." With a slight grin, Woody finished, "I can't actually tell you the range, or I'd have to kill you."

Smiling, Mark replied, "My line by the way. So, it's a bigger laser and it's stabilized too. What you're telling me is that the guys who drop LGBs like to do their own thing. It makes it a little hard to deal with them for our targets."

"Well, yes and no. It's an improvement over the classic eyes on target thing, but it is a little cumbersome. Remember, the system was designed for bigger targets behind the lines, not CAS targets."

"Fine, fine, you've told me more than I want to know about LGBs. How about my original question about JDAMs?" Mark asked.

"Okay, the bomb body and fuse are pretty much the same. It's the guidance that's different. One more thing on the LGB. The LGB uses steering fins on the seeker, which is on the nose; the fins at the back are just to stabilize it during flight. When the seeker sees a laser spot in its eyeball, the computer tries to center the spot in the eyeball using the fins to do it. The fins, on most of the packages, slam from stop to stop. This uses energy. It's a continuous thing, kind of a feed back loop."

Taking a breath he continued, "The GPS guided JDAM leaves the airplane with the target coordinate and altitude in its brain. It also takes a snap shot of the point where it left the airplane, a point in space. The computer essentially computes a bunch of points along a ballistic path to guide the bomb to hit the target. As the bomb falls, the computer compares the actual position with the computed course and if it is off, it displaces the wings at the rear a small amount to get back on to course. Its brain continually updates the course during its fall to the target. But since it doesn't slam the fins around, it doesn't use as much energy, which is a good thing. It also doesn't care about clouds or being able to see the target. It just follows a course."

"I can see that not needing to see its target is a good thing, you can use it in bad weather and all. But how does that make it easier for us to use?" Mark asked.

Getting into it, Woody clapped his hands together, "Yeah, man, this is it! All we have to do is make sure the guy in the air has a good GPS coordinate for the target and we're good to go. I've got a doofer that reads our coordinates and with a laser it figures bearing and distance and then gives you the coordinates of the target. We just relay that to the guy in the air! It couldn't be easier!" Woody said with enthusiasm.

"Now you're talking, that is cool. That kind of techno-shit is what we like. Show me this high speed, low drag doofer. Why don't we have one of these things?" Mark said.

Dave walked into the hooch and took off his hat. Searching for Mark inside he finally found Woody's impromptu study group around the campfire.

Squatting he said, "Mark, I talked with Fahim. He said he doesn't have time to meet today. He said he wanted me to tell you and the Air Force man that he wants you to take out the Taliban in the town. He said it's simple, he wants you to hit all of them and then he'll go in."

"You gotta be shitting me. He won't even talk. Didn't we already tell him we couldn't just lay down bombs all over the town? Didn't we tell him we needed to coordinate the bombs with his attacks?" Mark said, trying to control the rage and frustration boiling inside.

"Yeah, we told him that shit. But he wants you to take out the T. I guess he doesn't think you're serious. If you do that, maybe he'll believe we're here to help," Dave replied.

"Shit. I'm near my wit's end with this guy. Does he even want to fight? Did you tell him we're getting air tomorrow?"

Shrugging his shoulders, Dave replied, "Hell yes, I did. He said he might meet us above the Taloqan tomorrow in the morning, but you've got to show him some shit first. I know you're skeptical, but I think he'll fight. They just do everything slowly around here."

Mark grimaced and said disgustedly, "You hope he'll fight. You guys have spread around enough money, you ought to get something for it." Angry, he fell silent.

Dave just shrugged his shoulders awkwardly.

Into the strained silence, Woody cleared his throat. "We'll get out there. When we get the air, we'll show him what it can do. Even the T will be surprised." With a big grin he finished, "This ain't your Daddy's air war anymore. If they're gonna make me eat MREs and sleep on the ground, at least I get to blow stuff up! This is gonna be fun!"

CHAPTER 11

14 October 2001
Golbahar, Afghanistan

A crisp gusty wind battered the two CIA Special Operatives; mercilessly, it sliced through their civilian clothes like tiny knives. Bitterly, they fought the wind and the darkness, wrestling with a broken power supply cable for their predator ground control station. They were in a hurry, trying to setup operations on a hastily repaired, barely adequate airfield northeast of Kabul, the only plus side of the Golbahar Airfield was that it was in the hands of the Northern Alliance. Nothing was easy. First, the diesel generator wouldn't start; a quick shot of ether solved that problem before they killed the battery. Now, no matter what they tried, the power cable wasn't transmitting electrical power and to top it off they couldn't get the quick release to release at all. Craig, one of the two CIA Special Activities Operatives finally wrested the connector off and held it up so his partner John could shine the flashlight on it. At last, a break, instead of a broken wire or a short, it looked like a simple bent pin.

Time was a factor, it was pressing on them heavily. Tonight they were supposed to fly the first remote controlled Predator sortie of the war and the power supply problem had cost precious time and threatened the whole mission. They had yet to check out any of the systems on the Predator, it had been delivered that afternoon by the team's Hip helicopter, bought from the Russians. In a rush, they had only had time to mount the wings and tail of the Predator, they were assigned to launch less than a half hour from now. Hoping for the best, they hurried through the initial BIT checks.

Sweating in the cold unfriendly wind, Craig was relieved that they had finally gotten the GC station up and running. "John, we gotta get this thing going. You go ahead and get the bird ready, I'll finish getting the GC station up. We've got to get on the air pretty soon. The Spooky we are supposed to work with will be

215

on station in less than a half hour."

John realized Craig was right, with a long expression he stood looking down at his partner. Finally he said, "Okay, so you're good? Use the walkie-talkie if you need me. I'll call you when I've got it ready for takeoff."

John got into the battered Toyota pickup that their Allies had given them and slammed the door. True to form with the ancient truck, it took two tries to keep the door shut. He cranked the engine for several seconds until it caught and settled into a rough idle. Engaging the clutch, John accelerated down the dirt road as fast as he could. Threading down hill he headed for the end of the runway where they had left the Predator parked under guard. Skidding to a stop at the rear of the UAV, he leaped out of the truck and ran to the Predator. The Tribesmen he had left standing guard was standing next to it with a blank expression on his bearded face. John just imagined what he was thinking; probably never even seen an airplane before and this one didn't even need a pilot. Stepping back as John approached, the tribesman squatted out of the way at the edge of the recently bulldozed runway. In silence, he watched as John fussed with the strange aircraft.

Using a small bulldozer flown in for the purpose, John and Craig, the only CIA Special Activities Team at Golbahar, spent three days re-grading the old Russian runway. John tried to be careful, but without a roller to compact the dirt and gravel, he was worried about how the rough repairs would affect the composite prop of the unmanned vehicle. They didn't have a spare prop or the equipment, much less the time, to smooth it out any further. He'd just have to go for it and hope for the best.

John shined a flashlight into the fuel tank, leaning against the fuselage; he jiggled it back and forth to check the fuel one more time. Given the high altitude of the Golbahar airport he had decided to operate the RQ-1L drone at a reduced fuel load. Close to the battlefield, they didn't need quite as much loiter time and the reduced weights made it much easier to takeoff and climb in this terrain.

He pushed down on the fuselage, just forward of the tail, swinging the twenty-seven foot long airplane around to aim the nose down the runway. Changing his grip, he pushed on the front of the inverted tail and began walking the drone to the very end of the runway. For some reason, the wind had let up slightly, still gusting but not as strong and from different directions. *At least the runway sloped downhill,* he thought. In a few minutes, he was panting and beginning to struggle to push the 1900 pound aircraft up the gentle slope. Gesturing to the guard, he pantomimed for him to come and help push it.

Reaching the end of the gravel and dirt runway, he aligned the nose with the far end of the runway. The guard, yet to speak a word, held the aircraft as John quickly threw chocks under the main tires. As if on cue, Craig called him on the walkie talkie radio, "John, GC is up and running. I'm good to go. Is the bird ready? If you're ready, it's time we launch."

John wiped his sleeve across his face, pulling the small radio from his back pocket. He held it to his lips and answered breathlessly, "Sure Craig, we're ready."

"Start it up and let's go through an abbreviated checkout," Craig replied.

Walking to the left side of the aircraft, aft of the wing, John opened the panel covering the 'on-airplane' controls. He flipped the battery switch on, set the servo switch to local, the throttle to idle and switched the magnetos on. Standing behind the propeller arc, he grasped the tail with his left hand and rested his right hand on the prop. With as much energy as he could muster, he quickly flipped the composite propeller down to start the engine.

The prop jerkily rotated for two or three blades, but the engine did not start. John stretched to reach the control panel to prime the engine one more time and checked to see that the mags were on. Switching them off, he rotated the propeller until he found a compression stroke and carefully positioned the prop. Switching the mags on, he took up his stance and flipped the prop down again. This time the engine caught and accelerated quickly, nearly to full power. Leaning further back to get away from the spinning propeller, he held onto the inverted tail. After a moment, satisfied that the UAV wouldn't jump the chocks under the wheels, he took the two steps back to the control panel and pulled the throttle to idle.

With the engine ticking over at idle, he pulled the radio from his back pocket and transmitted to Craig, "Engine's running, brakes are still and I have it chocked. I'm switching the servo control to auto now. Go ahead and run the flight controls and sensors."

"Roger, here goes," Craig said, settling down on the stool in front of the operator's console. He began moving the joysticks, first the flight controls and then the sensor suite; hopefully there would be no connectivity problems.

Doubling the safety factor, the first thing Craig did was to set the parking brake. Then he checked the ruddervators full left and right. When the six foot long inverted flight control surfaces, mounted at the very back of the drone, were deflected in opposition, or together, they operated as rudders or elevators to control yaw or pitch. Next, he checked out the ailerons mounted at the far end of the trailing edge of the 49-foot wings. The aircraft was controlled primarily by autopilot, but he had to make sure that the controls responded in the right direction.

Satisfied the flight controls would respond to his commands, Craig then checked out the electro-optical and infrared visual systems. During the day, the EO system would serve as a gyro stabilized television camera that could transmit a signal back to the operator and even relay it via satellite anywhere in the world. At night, the EO sensor could see very little so Craig switched to IR. Slewing the small turret on the chin of the Predator, he turned the IR sensor to scan the left and right side of the runway. It was past midnight and the IR imager was working very well, Craig could see the Afghan guard sitting on a rock at the side of the runway. Finished with his checkout, he stowed the sensors to protect the lenses from rocks and dirt on the takeoff roll.

Picking up the walkie talkie, Craig transmitted, "John, I've got the systems checking out fine. Are you ready to launch?"

"Ready, we're already lined up with the runway," John replied.

"Okay, here goes. Half throttle, brakes and I'll takeoff," Craig replied. John hopped to pull the chocks out from the main wheels. The sun still painted the mountaintops, but in the valley, it was nearly pitch black.

The turbocharged 914 Rotax accelerated quickly and strained against the brakes. Craig released the brakes, the drone jumped forward and before Craig could shove the throttle fully open, the unmanned vehicle was in the air. Craig let the UAV climb steadily, turning right to fly down the valley in the general direction of Charikar. Tonight he would be looking for a Taliban compound near Bagram Airport. If he could find it, they would work with Spooky, the AC-130 Gunship, to destroy the target. Craig leveled off at about 2,000 feet above the ground; before the UAV reached Bagram, John had rejoined him at the ground control station. Sitting down on a box, John turned on the UHF speaker and picked up the microphone.

"Easy 22, Spooky 35."

"Easy 22, Spooky 35." The co-pilot of the AC-130U gunship transmitted again. He was trying to raise the ground controller who they had been fragged to work with tonight. Their backup mission was road recce and there hadn't been many vehicles on the road during their flight to the Bagram area; he was hoping the ground FAC would be up on frequency soon.

"Easy 22, Spooky 35." He tried again without enthusiasm.

"Roger Spooky 35, Easy 22 here, have you been calling long?" Craig replied.

"Only an hour or so. Not bad, how are things going down there? Any traffic for us tonight?" the co-pilot asked.

"Spooky we're doin' great, the weather is balmy and we've got a really nice hotel. Money for nothing and chicks for free. But you wouldn't know about that.

Hey, I do have some targets for you. Standby for the coordinates," John replied. Panting he looked at Craig painfully, "I'm getting too old for this shit. You do the running next time!"

"Yeah, if you could stay on your diet you might not be sweating so much. You gotta get in shape. It ain't my fault," Craig shot back.

"Shit, I'm a technician. I'm 55 years old and I sure ain't no spook. These are supposed to be my golden years or something, you know!" John said.

"Yeah, you're just an adrenaline junkie. Get those guys on target, we ain't got fuel to last all night you know," Craig said, trying to change the subject.

"Go north up the road from Qarah Bagh. Midway on the road before the ridge there is a group of buildings in the northeast side of the road," John transmitted on the radio. Staring intently at the Ground Control Station's wide field of view IR display, John tried to talk the AC-130 onto the target using the IR sensor from the Predator drone.

"Roger, north up the road from the town. Does the road make a wide curve to the south at the midpoint?" the pilot said. He was watching his repeater display that showed the Fire Control Officer following the FAC's directions with the aircraft's onboard IR sensor.

"Yes, Yes. The road makes a bend to the south. The group of buildings is on the other side of the road," John said, nodding his head hurriedly.

"I see a large square building and a smaller rectangular building northwest of it," the Pilot said.

"Roger, does the square building have a square holding pond right next to it. Do you see that?" John asked.

"Roger, we see the pond. It's just west of the square building."

"That's it. Confirm that you see the rectangular building northwest?" John asked.

"Affirmative, we see the rectangular building."

"Copy, that rectangular building is the mosque. Do not engage the mosque. Copy, do not engage the mosque?" John said.

"Copy, the rectangular building is the mosque," the pilot acknowledged.

"In front of the mosque are three large vehicles oriented east-west, do you see that?"

"Roger, we see the three vehicles. There is a fourth moving out from behind them right now," the pilot said as he saw the vehicle moving in real time.

"Copy, that, I see it too. You are cleared to engage it. You are cleared to fire."

Craig put his finger on the screen and said, "Hey, John don't you think that truck is a little close. We've never worked with these guys. Let's see how well they work before we clear them to fire that close to a mosque, okay?"

Quickly hitting the transmit button again John tried to stop them, "Spooky 35, standby, standby. Hold fire, you are not cleared to engage."

"Copy, hold fire," the Gunship pilot replied. "The vehicle stopped in front of the square building and there are several people walking around it."

Seeing the truck had finally stopped in front of the Taliban Headquarters, John transmitted, "Copy, you are cleared to fire. Cleared to engage that truck."

"Cleared to fire," the pilot answered. Over the intercom he said, "Two to three rounds on the 40. Cleared to fire."

Less than fifteen seconds later the first round exploded on the right side of the truck, followed by one on the left side. The third round hit the truck dead center, obliterating it in a plume of flame and smoke.

"Good hit. I got good secondaries on that one," the FCO exclaimed on the intercom, counting two additional explosions as the truck tore itself apart.

John saw another truck begin to move. "Another truck moving from in front of the mosque. You are cleared to fire on that truck."

"Copy, we see the moving truck," the pilot said.

"There are also people coming out of the mosque towards the vehicles. Concentrate on those vehicles," John said.

"Roger, copy."

Peering at the screen, Craig said, "Man, we're going to town. Look at those boys go. They can sure shoot that thing."

"Yeah, man that's the shit. This is fun!" John answered. The vehicles disappeared in bright spots, an after image of death on their IR screens. In minutes, the AC-130 had all the vehicles in front of the mosque burning, as a bonus, stored ammunition was exploding in the flames adding to the confusion.

"Are we cleared on the square building?" the pilot asked.

Looking at Craig and seeing his nod of agreement, John transmitted, "Cleared. You are cleared on the big square building."

On the Gunship intercom the pilot said, "FCO, use the 105 on the big square building. Cleared to fire, go ahead and level it."

Craig rolled the Predator out of its turn, heading the UAV back on a northerly track of its orbit. Seeing a bunch of little white dots appear from a dark section of terrain above the building complex, he pointed them out to John. "Hey, look at those people running. They came from nowhere; they probably came from a cave or a tunnel. See, they're running towards the mosque."

"Yeah, look there's another one coming from that spot. You're right it must be a cave complex. Let's get 'em."

"Spooky, easy. Popup target. Go east from buildings. Follow the dirt road along the small hill. Approximately 200 meters on the north side of the road is a dark spot," John transmitted over the radio.

"Roger, the spot where those runners are coming from?" the pilot asked.

"The same. Those are bad guys going to hide in the mosque. Get 'em if you can, but let's hit the dark spot. It's a cave entrance or tunnel complex."

"Copy, spot in sight," the pilot said.

"Cleared to fire on the spot," John replied.

Seconds later the explosion filled their screens, additional rounds following it in rapid succession. Suddenly, a huge secondary explosion filled their screens, it was so bright that Craig could easily see John's face. They had hit a large weapons cache. "Yeah, right there. Good hit Spooky," John transmitted.

"There are still a couple of guys moving down there," the FCO said. "Look at that one running."

"Get 'em. Get 'em. Don't let that guy get away," the pilot said. The crew manning the 40mm put several clips of ammunition into the gun, keeping it working as they chased the running Taliban.

"Good hit. That one was less than two feet in front of him. He's gonna have a headache tonight," the FCO said into the intercom. "There's nothing left at the cave entrance, boss."

"Permission to go back to the compound?" the pilot asked over the radio.

"Yeah, go back to the compound. Take out the rest of those trucks and make sure you level that square building," John replied.

Northwest of Taloqan, Afghanistan

Woody sat cross-legged on the rocky ground. He tried to stabilize the high power binoculars he was using by wedging his elbows into the crook of his knees. Still shaking a little, he pressed the Steiner 8x30s into his eyes harder. His back started to feel warm as the welcome sun poked above the ridgeline behind him. To him, he hoped it would soon shine on the town below. Without taking his eyes from the Taliban lines, he spoke to his Enlisted Terminal Attack Controller, "Brandon, set up the laser scope on the tripod. As soon as the suns up we need to get some good target coordinates."

Pulling the boxy scope out of the protective case, Brandon attached the tripod and set it on the ground. He connected the power supply cable to the battery. "Sir, do you want me to turn it on and go ahead with the coordinate acquisition?"

"Not yet, let's save the battery until we can see just what target we want to hit.

Might as well get 'em all in one swoop," Woody replied, turning to look at Brandon, he added. "Thanks for setting it up, it won't be long now."

Looking back down the mountainside, he settled back into his survey of the town. Gradually, the Taliban lines were becoming visible in the gray light of dawn. "Hey, Mark. I see two T-54/55 tanks buried hull down and what look like trenches connecting them to small houses on the flanks. Is that the target area you were talking about?"

"Yeah, man. Those are Fahim's. We must hit the targets, because he won't do a thing until we take them out," Mark replied.

"Good, we'll spot the two tanks and the buildings for a start. Brandon, how you coming with the scope?" Woody asked.

"Set up and leveled. It's ready to turn on," Brandon responded.

Dropping the glasses down to his chest slowly, Woody glanced at his ETAC. Brandon was watching him expectantly. Woody nodded his head slightly and said, "Go ahead, fire it up. Look on the north side of town. That's where the valley sort of opens out onto the plain. Just before the town, there are two T-54/55 tanks flanking the town, buried hull down. Pull the coordinates for those tanks and the two pillboxes connected to them by a trench line."

Gazing down at the town Woody continued, "Those targets will be our pre-plans for this morning. After that we'll just see what develops."

"Can do easy, sir," Brandon replied. He put his face to the viewfinder and toggled the display to wide field of view. Looking in the corner of the display, he could see the numbers that told him the unit was running and had figured out where it was. Scanning the town, he easily located the valley and the pillboxes/houses that Woody had described. But he could not find the tanks. Switching to narrow field of view, he concentrated on the terrain between the two pillboxes.

"Sir, I'm pretty sure I've found the pillboxes, but I'm having trouble seeing the tanks. They are just not breaking out. Where are they in relation to the houses?"

Woody put the glasses up to his eyes again and looked for something to lead Brandon's eyes to the targets he wanted. "Okay, see the road leading into the town from the right? Before you get to the town, you'll see a group of what appear to be irregular piles of dirt with some darker lines behind them; those are trenches. After that, there are two regular shaped dirt piles and then at an angle, say about 30 degrees, back to the town you can see the houses. That regular shaped dirt pile on the right, nearest us, has a MG barrel protruding out of the window. I don't see anything in the left one right now."

"Okay, so the tanks are those irregular shaped piles? I don't see much definition."

"Yep, in between those piles, or pointing out of them are the barrels of the tanks, long and thin. All you'll probably see is the shadow, not much of an IR target this time of the morning. If the light is right, you can make out the markings on the tank itself. Lase the turret, don't worry about trying for a better place," Woody directed.

"Okay, I think I see the tank tube." Brandon pressed the laser button and the first set of numbers to appear were the GPS coordinates of where they were standing. He quickly wrote those down on his notepad, and then toggled to the next set of coordinates.

In the few minutes it took to find the pillboxes and the tanks, the morning sun had fully illuminated the valley before them. Mark heard a growing noise behind them as he turned around abruptly. In seconds, the entire team was looking expectantly up the ridge, some of them picked up their weapons. Over the ridge rode 100 Northern Alliance riders on horseback. At the lead in the cloud of dust was Fahim with a tight group of men around him.

Pausing, Fahim gestured left and right and then continued riding directly towards them. Without further word, the riders behind him split silently into two groups and stopped their horses below the ridgeline. For several minutes riders kept streaming over the ridgeline joining the Afghanis below them on the ridge.

Mark, watching the Afghani cavalry ride over the ridge, couldn't help but feel he was standing in the middle of a Hollywood movie set. Or, maybe he had been transported back in time, anything but getting ready to fight a war in the twenty-first century. Fahim stopped near them and dismounted.

Mark stood and greeted Fahim, "Good morning, General. It is good to see you and your men. It looks like they are ready to fight."

"It is a good morning. I wish you joy in it. We have come to see what it is you offer and what you can provide. They all want to see for themselves," Fahim said, gesturing down the slope. "What do you think of the defenses the Taliban have prepared for us?"

"I think that your assessment of the Taliban defenses is correct. Those tanks and the heavy MGs would be more than a match for mounted cavalry," Mark replied.

Stepping forward Woody was ready to start lecturing on how air support would make quick work of the tanks. He immediately sensed a palpable tension between Mark and Fahim; before he opened his mouth, he stopped himself from speaking.

Fahim stared at Mark unblinkingly and in a testy voice said, "Yes, they have many men with those tanks in trenches as well as in the town. See the tops of the two story buildings on the edge of town?" He paused dramatically to make sure Mark and Dave were following his out stretched arm. "There are machine guns and mortars on the roofs."

With a sinking feeling, Mark glanced quickly at Dave; they had missed seeing those targets. Woody raised the binoculars and scanned the rooftops. He nodded to Brandon who swiveled the scope and quickly took readings of their coordinates.

"You would have me charge that town and those machine guns? My men are brave, but they are not fool hardy," Fahim said in disgust.

"No sir. We do not ask that you charge that town without our help. We are here to help. We want to help and we will," Dave quickly replied.

"Then destroy the Taliban in the town and we will take what is left," Fahim replied.

"Sir," Mark said. "I must tell you that we cannot just level the town. Our orders prevent us from attacking purely civilian targets. We have to avoid damage to civilians as much as possible. What would you have us hit?"

"What specific target would you have us destroy? Which one poses the biggest threat to your men?" Mark quickly corrected himself. He realized it was very important to be precise in what he said and didn't want to be misunderstood again.

Fahim did not reply immediately, he squatted on the ground and pulled an old set of binoculars from the folds of his robe. Bringing them to his eyes, he slowly scanned the town. After a few minutes, he took them from his eyes and slowly looked at Mark. Standing behind Brandon's scope, Woody watched the developing scene expectantly.

Fahim addressed Mark, "Very well, Captain Goode, when you can destroy those tanks in front of the town, perhaps then we can see the help you promise." He stood up and put the binoculars back inside the folds of his robe.

Mark held Fahim's eyes in a steady gaze and replied, "Then we will hit those tanks. If there are any other targets that you need us to hit before you attack, please let me know."

Dismissively, Fahim said, "I will let you do your work." He then turned and walked towards a small charcoal fire his men had made amongst the rocks. "In the meantime I shall have some tea."

Turning to Woody when Fahim couldn't see him Mark rolled his eyes. "Woody, Let's do it man. Call some air in on those tanks."

"Wilco, buddy. One air strike coming up," Woody replied. Spinning on one foot he headed for the radio. "Brandon give Tango a call and brief him on the coordinates. Let's hit the far tank first."

"Tango 23, Mako 51," Brandon keyed the microphone of the PRC-117 VHF/UHF radio. Releasing his thumb he waited for a reply. Keying the mic again he repeated, "Tango 23, Mako 51, we have a target for you.

Crackling over the static on the radio, Brandon heard the reply from the B-52 orbiting overhead, "Roger, Mako 51 this is Tango 23. We're on station as fragged. Authenticate Foxtrot X-ray."

Subconsciously, Woody gripped Brandon's shoulder very hard as he listened. Brandon winced as he looked at his crypto sheet. "Mako authenticates, Bravo, I say again, Bravo. We've got an immediate; tanks in the open. Are you ready to copy the target coordinates?"

"Uhh, sure Mako. Go ahead. Ready to copy."

"Man are those guys in a hurry or what?" Tango 23's Bomb Nav said over the intercom.

"Yeah, maybe he wants to get back to his luxurious tent; let's humor him guys. It sure doesn't sound like some AQ fucker on the radio to me," the pilot said.

"Mikey, I've got the coordinates. Did you write them down as well?" the co-pilot said.

Mikey Wellington, the Bomb Nav said, "Yep, I got 'em. Want to compare?"

"Let's do that, get the TACP to read them out one more time and we'll compare that with what you guys have written down," the aircraft commander said.

"Mako, Tango would like a read back of the coordinates," the co-pilot transmitted.

"Tango, Mako copies. Here come the coordinates again." Brandon concentrated on reading them one more time on the radio, slowly. After he was done he looked at Woody and then Mark who was standing above him on the hill. Nodding, he said, "I've made contact, they'll drop soon."

Mark nodded, glancing at Dave he asked, "Should we tell Fahim the fireworks are about to start? Once the ball gets rolling it'll happen pretty fast."

"No, let him enjoy his tea. Maybe it'll be a wakeup call for him," Dave replied sarcastically.

"Sir, Tango says bombs away in about three minutes. They are in a turn and they'll be headed back to the target in a second. We caught them on the outbound leg of their holding pattern," Brandon said with satisfaction.

"Man, that's service. You call, we haul and deliver 2,000 pounds of high explosive faster than Dominoes brings the pizza!" Mark laughed.

Brandon gazed into the valley with the handset to his ear, out loud he said, "Tango is inbound."

Woody smiled at Mark and conspiratorially said, "Here she comes." Raising the binoculars to his eyes, he wanted to see the tanks up close.

"Inbound," Gary said loudly, listening silently to Woody and Brandon. He wanted to reorient the men's focus. The rest of the Special Forces Troopers stopped chatting, in unison and looked down the mountainside.

Less than two minutes later they heard the faint tearing noise of jet engines as the B-52 passed by overhead. Straining against the binoculars, Woody thought he could just hear the clicking noise as the fins of the JDAM made its final corrections before the bomb hit the target. He didn't want to blink, in case he might miss the explosion. He wasn't sure he heard the fins, but he thought he did. He did not see the first bomb, but the huge fireball that engulfed the first tank was unmistakable. Out of the cloud, billowing black smoke and flame, the turret of the tank was plain to see as it came flipping end over end trailing bright flames.

Woody followed the turret intently for what seemed like several minutes before it arced into the ground. Suddenly, they were engulfed in the report of the explosion. Woody calmly took the glasses down and said, "Brandon, tell Tango the first bomb was a shack. Cleared to drop on the other three targets immediately."

"Mickey, Mako says cleared to drop on all three of the remaining targets. First bomb was a shack," the co-pilot said.

"Man, that's a relief. The first JDAM dropped in the CAS role and it's a shack. Who woulda thunk a Buff would be doing CAS," the aircraft commander broke in. "The miracles of heathen technology."

Mickey was excited. "Shit hot! You said it. I've got the next three targets programmed in. We're already six miles outbound, we could turn in now and be off our first axis to drop all three in one pass. I figure we'd be parallel to the coordinate they gave us for their location if we turn right."

"Rock and Roll, I'm witcha. Too bad the tail gunner will be the only one to see the show!" the aircraft commander said, as he began turning the bomber in a wide right turn back towards the target.

Najid Moussaui snapped his head up, his heart thundering, ears ringing. Surprised, he didn't know what had happened, he looked quickly around to find out where the noise had come from. He saw the unmistakable black cloud and flame billowing from the other tank.

"What was that? Did Hassem blow his own tank up? Is there something wrong with the ammunition?" He asked of no one in particular. He was one of two tank commanders in the valley in front of Taloqan. He and Hassem had been talking with each other on their radios about the large group of Northern Alliance heathens on the ridgeline. They were preparing to shoot at them to let them know they saw them and that if they came any closer they would most certainly die.

Sliding down the hatch, he shouted, "Hassem's tank blew up. Start the engine. We will shoot at the unwashed heathens on the hill. We cannot let them think we are without teeth, if they think we are weak, they might try to attack us."

The ancient engine of the T-55 tank started with a cloud of black smoke. With the engine running, Najid now had hydraulic power to lift the main gun and swing the turret. To align the gun with the group of horseman on the ridge, he peered down the barrel and bore sighted the largest mass of horsemen. Then he raised the gun to its maximum elevation. He knew his round would probably fall short, but at least he could get close to them and make them worry.

Gesturing excitedly, the gunner said, "Najid, the range is too far. Those horsemen are too far for us to shoot them. We will waste our ammunition."

Trembling, Najid almost choked with anger. "It is not important. We must shoot at them to let them know they can get no closer. If we are lucky we might hit them." Resting his hand onto the handgrip Najid lightly touched his finger on the trigger guard.

"The gun is ready," the gunner announced.

"Perhaps the wind will be with us and the round will reach them. It is Allah's will." Najid put his finger on the trigger, squeezing slowly the gun barked when the round fired. The tank jerked violently backward and a wisp of smoke wafted into his face as he stood up through the commander's hatch.

With satisfaction, he looked toward the ridgeline to see where the round would hit. As he waited for the impact he heard a strange click, click noise, coming from the sky, he could not find where the clicking was coming from.

On the mountainside, the quiet tranquility of the morning was suddenly broken by the explosion of the first bomb abruptly interrupting the background noise of men talking and brewing tea. After the blast echoed down the valley, it was followed by a total lack of sound. All of the sound sucked from the mountainside with the blast.

Fahim and his commanders were stunned into silence, staring in the general direction of the town below. Woody glanced over at Mark and Dave and then at Fahim. Calling loudly he asked, "Is that what you guys wanted?"

Standing up he gestured towards the billowing smoke in the valley. "That ain't nothing. Watch this, there's more coming."

A few seconds later, as if on cue, three more explosions erupted on the plain. Within seconds of each other, the remaining tank and the machine gun posts were totally obscured in smoke. Before they heard the reports from the bombs in the valley, Najid's tank round exploded less than a thousand feet down the slope from them.

Brandon, watching the scene in the spotting scope, announced to the crowd, "That last one was fired by the second tank. Don't worry he's a mort."

Slowly, Fahim got up and made his way towards the small knot of Americans. Silently, Mark watched Fahim approach. Before the Northern Alliance Leader could say anything, Mark extended his hand towards him—in his fingers a pair of Steiner 8x30 binoculars. Fahim took them without a word, his face the picture of stone, and raised them to his eyes.

Fahim scanned the town as a slight breeze blew the smoke from the Taliban strong points. Like an incoming tide, Fahim was surrounded by his men, every one of them chattering, excitedly discussing the scene below.

With his spotting scope, Brandon could see the town easily. The tanks were just gone; they had been replaced by holes in the ground. The turret of the first tank lay next to the smoking hole where it had been. From this distance, they could see nothing of the second tank. The machine gun posts were smoldering piles of rubble. Dozens of Taliban were running about, in confusion, trying to figure out what had happened. Chaos ruled Taloqan.

Slowly, lowering the binoculars, Fahim turned to look at Mark; several bad teeth revealed by the wide grin that split his face.

Mark could see that the arrogance was gone from Fahim's eyes; he decided to be magnanimous. "As you can see, General, we can hit precisely what you asked for. You see what we can do and now that we have air support, I am sure that we can support any request that you have."

"Captain Goode, I am impressed. I had thought it would be hours before you would be able to hit any target, much less destroy it as you have done. And you did it before I had my morning tea. Very well, you keep your promises. If you can continue to do so we just might be able to make our arrangement work."

"Yes, sir, I think we can do that. But we still have to pay attention to collateral damage. Now we can declare open season on the Taliban and al-Qaeda. One thing though, sir, it would work best if we could coordinate our airstrikes with your ground operations. We can hit targets that are a problem for your troops and then you can attack them. I believe that even those strikes will serve to demoralize the resistance. That will make it easier for your men to carry through the attack," Mark said, happy to be making progress for once.

"Perhaps you are right about the morale of the Taliban. I think that remains to be seen, but I can see that you are right about taking out difficult targets and this will make it easier for my men to defeat them," Fahim responded. "We will fight!"

"General, what target do you want us to hit next? Can your men take the town now?"

"You have kept your word, now we will keep ours. We will attack the town," Fahim said, turning to his men he cried in a booming voice, "To your horses, we ride on the town. Allah Arkhbar!!"

Woody, who had been watching the drama play out, took the PRC-117 handset from Brandon's hand, holding it to his mouth he transmitted, "Tango, Mako, Three shacks. Excellent job. I've got another target for you, standby for the coordinates." Releasing the mic he said, "Brandon, let's give Tango the coordinates for the trenches in front of the town. Let's hit those ASAP before the attack."

The Taliban who were living in Taloqan were in total disarray. Most of them had not realized that the explosions had taken out the tanks and machine guns guarding the town. Or that soon there would be Afghani warriors riding through the billowing smoke, riding down to kill them. They ran about trying to put out the fires and take care of the wounded. A few noticed the large group of horsemen gathering in the plain just in front of the town.

Raising the alarm, some of them picked up weapons and rushed towards the trenches in the front of the town determined to kill as many Northern Alliance men as possible. One of the leaders had just begun organizing the defense of the town when four more huge explosions rang through the air. Hundreds of Taliban in the trenches were killed outright or just disappeared in the violence of the explosion. The survivors were stunned by the blast, surprised by the rush of the Northern Alliance Horsemen galloping towards them. Panicked, they broke and ran, only to be cut down by the tribesmen, flushed with the nearness of their victory and the devastation of the attack.

With no heavy weapons to destroy the Afghani Cavalry, the Taliban did not last long. The fight for the town was over in minutes, leaving the men of the Northern Alliance to celebrate their lightening fast and overwhelming victory.

CHAPTER 12

Kabul, Afghanistan

The morning sun was bright, overpowering the pale blue sky; the air crisp and cold. Mustapha breathed shallowly, a cloud of condensation followed him as he walked outside. Squinting, he dialed his cell phone, standing in the sun trying to collect any stray warmth. Pushing aside his Kefaya, he raised the phone to his ear. The still air resonated with the slap of his feet as he twisted and stamped, trying to generate a little heat. He stopped moving when the call was answered, expectantly he said, "Muqtar bin Laden, how is your health? Do you want anything? Are the Americans causing you any problems?"

"No, Ahmed. God has seen fit to provide me with everything I need. I am comfortable and want for nothing. How does our fight progress?" bin Laden answered.

"Muqtar, last night was not a good night for us. My new communications area, northeast of Kabul, was hit very hard last night and most of my men were killed. It seems as if they knew I was there, and once again, the Americans have destroyed my communication site. I am afraid I have failed you."

"Mustapha, this may be a setback, but it is not the end of the war. The Americans are spineless and have no patience once things become hard. Do not worry, their initial victories will ring hollow. We have history, the force of will and the power of Allah on our side. In the end, they will be defeated. But it is important to communicate with those brave ones who tend our rabbits? They are in America and it is very important that we remain in contact with them," bin Laden replied.

Wiping his brow with the back of his sleeve, Mustapha listened intently, waiting for bin Laden to pause. "Muqtar, I believe the Americans are able to detect our location, I am worried that they can hear our radios when we transmit or that there is a spy amongst us. In every case, they have targeted our communications areas, especially those in fixed buildings. Perhaps we should rely on cell phones. That way we can be mobile and by fading into the background of Afghani traffic, the Americans will not be able to identify our location by radio or tapping a telephone."

"Cell phones are a good idea, mobility is how I stay alive. But you do not answer my question. My concern is that we must remain in contact with the rabbits. Has this been done? Tell me you have been in contact with them?" bin Laden asked again firmly.

"Yes, Muqtar. I have talked with them. All is ready. Except in the north. Things are not quite in place there. Perhaps tomorrow or the day after."

"Ahmed, the rabbits must be released. They must strike the next blow, and they must do so soon. If you are lost, who shall call them with the execute order?" bin Laden asked.

"Yes, Muqtar, I understand. I have told Mohideen, and he knows of this operation. He can take over for me if something happens. Their mission shall succeed," Mustapha answered. "It must."

"This is good. Do not make a mistake, their mission is very important. On another issue, I have heard rumors and tales of American spies operating with the Northern Alliance. Are these rumors true?" bin Laden changed the subject suddenly.

"I also have heard these rumors. Also, that Fahim's Tribal followers have rebuilt the old Russian airfield at Golbahar and have begun flying small planes. I think that they are responsible for the attack on my new communications site yesterday," Mustapha said.

Mustapha began pacing across the rocky ground as he continued talking, oblivious to his surroundings. "Last night, just before the attack on our building there were sounds of a small plane coming down the valley north of Bagram. It must have been an American plane."

"It is these spies that I am worried about. We must catch them soon. Especially if they intend to incite the Northern Alliance to attack."

"Yes, Muqtar, I understand. I have also heard reports of Americans near Taloqan since I last talked with you. There are definitely Americans assisting Fahim," Mustapha said.

"This is news, I have not heard of Americans near Taloqan, this we cannot allow. What do you think attracted the Americans attention to your communications site?" bin Laden asked.

"I am sure it must have been the radio transmissions coming from the building. It had to be that. We must stop using radio and rely on cell phones to avoid this," Mustapha asserted.

"Perhaps. I agreed with you that it is good to use cell phones. It is impossible to track us. But as for the radios, perhaps we should not stop using those, with radios we can reach our friends around the world. We must still be able to use those. Youseff said in our last meeting, that Mohideen was moving his communications people to the Salang Area. Is this true? Has it been done?"

"Yes, Muqtar, this is true. Mohideen has moved his equipment and communications people to Youseff's caves. I know they are ready to transmit. That is why I can assure you that we are still in contact with our rabbit farmers, I used them last night," Mustapha replied.

"Do not tell Mohideen's communication people to stop what they are doing, we need our radios to stay on the air. They are in caves and are protected from the American bombers in the air. This gives me an idea for our American spies. If the new radio site attracts their attention, then perhaps the spies will come to see for themselves. Then Youseff will be able to handle them. I will speak to him. Tell me more about the bombs against you last night? Tell me what is it that happened?"

"First we heard the drone of a very small plane, we looked for it but could not find it. Shortly after that, the first explosions occurred amongst the vehicles outside. The explosions were not as large as the bomb that took out the Air Authority building. There were usually two, three, or four explosions at a time and much smaller explosions. Even my men who ran away could not escape the attack. Soon, all the cars and people in front were attacked and then the main building with the radios and telephones was totally destroyed," Mustapha related.

Without hesitation bin Laden asked, "It is too bad you did not use a building next to a Mosque? The Americans would never destroy a Mosque, this would be very good on TV."

Mustapha stopped pacing, staring off into the valley in front of him, he could see Kabul in the haze. "No, Muqtar. We were right next to the Mosque, but it was not hit. They did not target the Mosque and it received no damage."

Bin Laden sighed, "This is a disappointment. We must look for the barbarism of the Americans mindless attacks. Is there anything usable left at Qarah Bagh?"

"No, nothing. Everything is destroyed. And now I believe it is not safe to move during the night on the roads. Soon they will bomb our people in the hills. What is next?"

"Do not worry, we must continue with the plan as agreed. The key is eliminating the Northern Alliance and Fahim. If we can split his occupation of the north then this bombing by the Americans will fail as well. Perhaps even now they are gloating over what they think is the success of the American bombing. They underestimate us. Bombing will not stop us. The Americans have no courage and little character; they will not face us on the ground. They send spies to hound our borders, but cringe like dogs at the edge of town. Drive them away from Salang and Golbahar. Split them by driving north from Taloqan."

"Muqtar, if we wait too long to pry them away from Golbahar and try to defeat them at Taloqan they may have time to become strong. If they continue to fly their small airplanes, they will be able to attack us more and more frequently. Perhaps even our caves will become uninhabitable," Mustapha said.

"Stop this. You bleat like a woman. You lose faith and begin to believe in, and raise the possibility or even the certainty that we will fail. We will not. Go and do what I say. If you cannot stand the heat of battle and spend all your time worrying about cowards, then your life is at an end. Do not cry to me anymore," bin Laden said angrily.

Mustapha hurried to apologize, it would not be good to get bin Laden angry with him. "Forgive me, Muqtar. I did not mean to say we were defeated. We will kill the craven heathens God has ordained it. God will help us drive the tribal barbarians from Golbahar."

"Good, have courage, Allah is behind us. We will destroy them. Now go and fight the war." Bin Laden hung up.

Closing his cell phone, Mustapha slowly dropped his arm to his side. His eyes, unfocused, gazed into the rugged distance. He turned and surveyed the carnage of the night's attack. He began picking his way through the destroyed trucks and debris from the attack on the building. Walking towards the Mosque, he thought to himself that it was easy for bin Laden to say he talked like a woman. Bin Laden had not been bombed and barely escaped with his life. Bin Laden had not had to run into the mosque last night to avoid death from the silent killer. He, on the other hand had been bombed before and had almost lost life several times for Allah."

Everywhere the Americans were pushing them very hard. On the roads, their training camps, in Taliban buildings, and Taliban Military installations. Even Tora Bora had been heavily attacked. He feared that they could not move anywhere the Americans could not find them. Perhaps bin Laden was right about driving a wedge into the Northern Alliance. But Youseff and the Taliban in Mazar e-Sharif and Kunduz could handle that.

By himself, he got into the only car left in driveable condition and started for Kabul. For him it would be best to move back into the city.

Kesendeh, Afghanistan

"Ah, Captain Steve and Captain Frank. It is good to see my American friends. Have you been treated well? Is your house all you would have hoped?" General Dostum asked, holding out his right hand in a gesture of friendship.

The two entered the dark room in single file and they both returned Dostum's greeting and handshake. Captain Steve Farrell was the 125 A Team Commander and Captain Frank Karnow, the leader of the Air Force Tactical Air Control Party, stopped next to the General, their boonie hats in their hands. Staff Sergeant Tom Biggins, the Enlisted Terminal Attack Controller, the other half of the Air Force TACP and some of the other A Team members crowded into the small room.

"General Dostum I'd like you to meet some of my men. This is SFC Mike Edson, we call him Fast Mike, he's the team sergeant. And this is Little John, communications, and Big Ed, weapons."

After introducing all of his men, CPT Steve paused and nodded to Captain Frank. Speaking up, he introduced Tom Biggins. "General, this is my other team member SSgt Tom Biggins. He's been controlling air strikes since the Gulf War."

"It is very good to meet you. I am sure you are all fine professionals and I am very glad to have you here to help with our war on the Taliban." Gesturing to a rug spread on the dusty floor he continued, "Please sit down and we shall talk. I believe we have to talk about the first attack where we shall need you."

Sitting down on the rug they all folded their legs Indian style to avoid showing their feet to their new hosts.

Speaking first, Captain Frank said, "General, we have air support available today and with your permission we would like to run the first strikes independent of a supporting mission for your troops."

"Is this so? Please tell me why I should not coordinate my movements with your attacks?" General Dostum asked.

"Sir, it is primarily because of training. Sergeant Biggins and I are currently the only people qualified to call in air support from the Air Force. We have been teaching our Army brethren how to do this job and would like to use the first few sorties to have them practice with real live targets. That way we could qualify a few more teams to support your operations and then we can operate in more than one area," Captain Frank argued.

"I have heard that others are not anxious to work with the Americans, I assure that this will not be true here. But, I understand what you say and this sounds like a reasonable request. More teams that are qualified would be good. This is also good, because I am not quite ready to attack the Taliban today. But we plan to move very soon. Therefore, it is my desire that you begin working Taliban positions around Shulgareh. This might work well for your training."

"That's the town just south of Mazar e-Sharif, is it not?" Captain Steve asked.

Dostum grimaced, struggling with a cold, he covered his mouth; unable to control it any longer, he coughed twice violently into a closed fist. After a moment he went on, "It is the town along the Balkh River. To approach Mazar e-Sharif we must remove the Taliban from there and any positions on the Alborz Ridge. This is the 1500-meter ridge that overlooks Mazar from the southwest. Right now there is Taliban artillery on that ridge."

"Those two sites would make good training targets for us. I would like to scout those positions this morning and attack them today?" Captain Frank asked.

"Yes, this would be acceptable. But you will take some of my men as escorts and to protect you. Please do not take risks. Bazan will lead you, if he feels you must retreat, then please do so. We cannot afford to lose you," Dostum said. "Tomorrow, God willing, perhaps we will attack to the very gates of Mazar e-Sharif."

Jiggy's flight of F-15E Strike Eagles, Goblin 21, was fragged for a mixed load of cluster bombs and unguided Mk-82 500 pound bombs. Finished refueling from the tanker in the Taj track, Jiggy climbed to the top of the stack and settled into a holding pattern, prepared for a long wait. With this load of ordinance, they could attack a convoy or a large area, but cluster bombs and 500 pound bombs had not been real popular in the war so far. "It's just great, we get to cool our heels in a cap and no-one want our bombs. I'm tellin' ya, Hustler I sure don't want to carry these things home!" Jiggy griped over the intercom.

"Just have patience, Jiggy. We're lucky to be flying after your argument with the scheduler last night. Sometimes you just gotta shut up and color. Not everyone wants to know what you think all the time," Hustler remonstrated.

"What do you mean? He asked me a question, I told him the truth. What's the harm in that?"

"Maybe it did, maybe it didn't, but what difference did it make? Never pass up the chance to keep your mouth shut. Forget it, at least we're flying and not cleaning out the latrine."

"I suppose you're right, maybe it won't be too long before we get a tasking or a dump target. I'd just rather be carrying Laser Guided Bombs or even JDAMs, that's all."

An hour and a half of loitering in the stack passed before Magic called them. "Goblin, Magic, I've got tasking for you."

Sitting up from the slumped position she had adopted, Jiggy replied, "Roger Magic, Goblin ready to copy."

"Goblin proceed to point Key and contact Tomcat 01 on Tad 203. Your mission is CAS today. If you need a tanker come back to me on this Freq," the Magic controller directed.

"Roger Goblin copies," Jiggy transmitted. "Hustler did you get that down? Tomcat one on Tad 203, point Key."

"Got it! We're steering to Key right now, I've got faster hands than you and I can chew gum at the same time. The new frequency is in Radio One, giddeyup," Hustler replied.

"Tomcat 01, Goblin 21," Jiggy transmitted. After a short pause, she said it again, "Tomcat 01, Goblin 21."

"Goblin 21, this is Tomcat. Ready to copy the brief?" SSgt Biggins replied.

"Goblin 21, mission 2A405, two F-15Es with mixed 82s and 87s, One plus hours, Freeze out."

"Goblin, Tomcat copies your brief. Standby FAC brief," Biggins transmitted. "IP at eastern bend of North/South Road between East/West Ridge and North/South River. Bearing 195 for 30 miles from Key. Target area bearing 195 for 13 miles, 1200 feet, description to follow. Friendlies five klicks west. Egress south. How copy?"

"Jiggy I got the IP, the friendlies and the Egress. I need more on the target," Hustler said over the intercom.

"Goblin copies, the IP, friendlies and Egress. Say again target description," Jiggy replied over the radio.

"Goblin, Tomcat. Target is tanks, trucks, artillery and personnel in open. There are some buildings in the target area. We'll have to talk your eyes onto the area," Biggins replied.

"Goblin copies. Proceeding to IP now," Jiggy answered. "Tomcat, Goblin would like to circle overhead the target area during talk on. We'll wait your clearance to attack."

Biggins looked up at Captain Frank, who nodded, keying the radio he said, "Roger, Goblin you are cleared down track. Weapons hold."

"Copy, down track, weapons hold," Jiggy replied.

Frank stepped forward and took the radio handset from Biggins, "Goblin, Tomcat. Target area is a town two thirds of the way down the eastern side of a 15 by 18 mile rectangular valley. The eastern side of valley is bordered by a river that runs from IP south."

Cruising high above Mazar, Jiggy headed southwest. Peering over the nose, she saw the IP on the left and a semi-circular ridge to the west with a broad rectangular valley beyond it. "Goblin sees the IP, ridge and valley."

"Tomcat copies, see the town on eastern side of valley?" Frank asked.

"Goblin has the town," Jiggy replied, pulling the radio transmit button aft she said back radio. "Goblin, drag, eight mile spacing. We'll do a left hand 10 mile triangular pattern around the town."

Setting up the first leg of the pattern around Shulgareh, Jiggy dipped the wing to get a closer look at the town, while Hustler scanned the town with the infrared LANTIRN Targeting Pod. "Tomcat, Goblin is in orbit around the town," Jiggy said.

"Copy, Goblin see the north/south road run through the town and the open square in the center of town?"

"Goblin sees the road and square," Jiggy answered.

"Copy, see the large building on north side of the square?"

"Goblin has a large square building with a smaller rectangular building east of it," Jiggy said.

"Copy. That building is your first target. In the courtyard, two Triple A pieces are parked. With good target ID, that large building and the courtyard as targets, you are cleared hot."

"Goblin cleared hot on the large square building and courtyard," Jiggy replied, on the back radio. "Goblin Two, I'll drop one 82 in the courtyard, when you swing around on the northeast leg of the pattern you attack the building with one 82."

"Goblin two drops on the large square building," Lurch Copeland acknowledged.

"Jiggy, I've got the courtyard in the Pod. You've got a designation," Hustler said on the intercom.

"Thanks, bro I'll drop on the next leg of the triangle and come off right. We should be able to keep the target area in sight the whole time. I'm going air-to-ground," Jiggy acknowledged.

Reaching the end of the southern leg of the triangle, Jiggy pushed the power up to Mil and rolled into a sliceback to the left. On the radio she transmitted, "One's in on the courtyard."

Lining up with the azimuth steering line to the target designation she let the nose fall gradually. As the speed built up, she let the target drift further down the pitch ladder in the heads up display. Once the target reached thirty degrees down, she thumbed aft on the auto-acq switch on the stick to switch to a Continuously Displayed Impact Point display in the HUD and pushed the nose over. With CDIP, she would manually control when the bomb was released.

Passing eighteen thousand feet Hustler said, "You've got laser ranging on the target. Looks like you'll have to shallow it out. Remember 10k is the floor."

"Yep, Spatial Disorientation, sorry," Jiggy replied as she pulled the velocity vector up to 20 degrees to get the CDIP pipper closer to the target. As the pipper rose to the target she said, "Ready, Ready, pickle."

Pressing and holding the pickle button down Jiggy felt the jet rock slightly as the explosive cartridges pushed one 500 pound bomb away from the airplane. The bomb began falling on a ballistic path to the courtyard below. Pulling back on the stick, Jiggy put a five g safe escape maneuver on the jet, more to get back to altitude quickly than to get away from the bomb. With the nose reaching twenty degrees, she relaxed the pull and rolled right to turn back towards the triangle, as the speed bled off she pushed the throttles into min burner.

The sleek gray F-15E arced gracefully through the sky. Inside both Hustler and Jiggy were looking intently at the targeting pod display. They were trying to catch a glimpse of their target when the bomb went off. Jiggy looked outside and leveled the jet at the twenty-two thousand foot orbit altitude. They could still make out the courtyard when suddenly the heat signature of the exploding bomb obliterated it. "Looks like a good hit." Hustler said laconically, "Hey, I captured the winds on that pass, just incase we drop the CBUs."

"Always thinking, thanks man," Jiggy said. She twisted in her seat, scanning the sky for the others in the flight. She could see a fast moving black dot in the center of the triangle, number three was in the middle of his bomb run, and the others were near the corners of the triangle orbit at altitude in their trail positions.

"Three's off," Lurch called as she climbed back to the pattern.

Captain Frank handed the radio microphone to SSgt Biggins, "Thanks Tom, the next one is yours. After that we'll let some of our SF buds call in a few."

"Good hits Goblin. I've got another target for you. Tanks and troops in the open and in trenches. In lines, southside of town. Tanks are in dirt revetments flush with terrain," Biggins transmitted.

"Copy Tomcat. Tanks and troops in trenches south of town," Jiggy replied.

On the back radio she called, "Lurch, you take these targets. Dive toss your CEM as briefed."

"Tomcat, Goblin Two will be dropping CBU-103. Confirm your distance from target area?" Jiggy asked.

"Goblin, Tomcat is approximately three klicks southwest. No long bombs please." After a short pause Biggins added, "Recommend west/east run-in. And say again the weapon type."

"Goblin copies, west/east run in. CBU-103 is just CEM with wind corrected canisters."

Biggins turned to all the onlookers standing around him on the ridge. "Goblin is going to drop CEM, it's a cluster bomb. It shouldn't happen, but if one of the canisters don't open it might be a problem. If they run in from the west it shouldn't be a problem at all."

Putting on their Kevlar helmets, the rest of the on-lookers laid down to watch the attack. Steve, lying down next to Frank asked him quietly, "What's this CEM?"

"CBU-87 is combined effects munitions. It has bomblets for tanks and APCs, an incendiary and a frag warhead for soft targets and personnel. It's a bear. The footprint of one bomb is about 200x250 feet; anything in that area is toast," Frank replied. "And it makes a nice long boom. Trust me, it's a good show."

"Cool, but I sure wouldn't want to see one of those long bomb like Biggins was saying." Steve said as he rolled on his side to move a sharp rock.

"Oh, a long bomb probably wouldn't open up. For long ones the clamshell usually doesn't open, so when it hits it'll go off like any other general-purpose bomb. Good sized explosion and lots of frag."

"Great. Does that happen often?" Steve laughed nervously.

"No, not really. It's one of those bad things that can happen. It's a risk; you just have to consider those things when you control air. I figure most of the stuff we'll control will be GPS bombs. So, the drill will be to just get a good coordinate and let the fighters know where you are so they won't drop over your heads. We'll do that kind of CAS when we move on to the Arty on the ridge; this is more conventional."

"Two's in from the west," Nugget called as he rolled his Strike Eagle into a 120-degree bank; pulling four g, he rolled out of the turn twenty degrees nose low on the azimuth steering line.

"Redesignated on the middle tank, good laser ranging." Flight Lieutenant Jack Calder told Nugget. Calder was a British RAF exchange Weapons System

Operator from England, speaking with a clipped accent he added, "Don't cock it up."

"I've got the cue. On the pickle button. In the pull." Nugget chanted as he went through the delivery profile.

Two CBU-103 dispensers separated from the airplane as they fell, a fraction of a second apart, two small cables attached to snap rings on the airplane stretched out. When each bomb reached approximately two feet from the airplane, the cables pulled free, activating the Fuse timers in each canister, and extending small wings from the rear of the bomb casing. The bombs had small GPS guidance systems embedded in the casing that sensed the wind drift away from the intended fall line and steered the winglets to correct.

Approximately forty seconds later, the timer extended two additional sets of wings and the bomb casing began to spin up to its pre-planned spin rate of 2,000 rpm. A few seconds after reaching the spin rate, the fuse sensed that the bomb was 1200 feet above the ground and blew apart the clamshell casing causing the bomblets inside to be slung out away from the casing. Some of the bomblets found a tank and exploded, killing the tank with a shaped charge. Other bomblets exploded on reaching the ground, spreading a lethal cloud of fragmented metal and flame within a cauldron of hell.

Kandahar, Afghanistan

On the outskirts of town two small boys, eight and eleven, herded two cows across the road from Dahla towards a small community pond. Almost across the road, something attracted the older boy's attention. Looking north, he began shouting and whipping the cows with the stick he carried, frantically trying to get them across the road. Moments later a convoy of two Toyota Land Cruisers and three pickups with machine guns mounted on the back went rushing by in a cloud of dust.

Storming through narrow streets of the town, the convoy reached Zor Shar, the old city. Dominated by the octagonal mausoleum of Ahmad Shah Durrani, one of the founders of the Afghan Kingdom in the 18th century, it still retained a few of its walls and gates. The convoy slowed to make its way through the market gate. In the lead Toyota, a tall gaunt man in the back seat with a black and white beard and a white turban looked out of the widow with dull eyes. Returning his stare, two women passing through the gate, a mother and her daughter, out collecting cow dung for fuel, looked intently at him through the slits of their burqas.

To the women of Kandahar he was just another in a long line of conquerors dating back through history; the Taliban, the Russians, the Indians, the Turks, Ghengis Khan and Alexander the Great. They were all the same. They bring destruction and promises, but nothing ever changes. Life was hard, but life always went on.

Passing by the Charsuq, the market where sheep, wool, cotton, grain and fruits were sold, the convoy headed towards the square that held Kheroqa Sharif mosque. The shrine that held the cloak of Mohammed was at the center of the religious area of town. Streaking through the square, the speeding convoy went directly to the gate of a small compound; as it approached, the gates swung open and all five vehicles disappeared inside. The gates closed swiftly behind them.

The tall man got out of the first Land Cruiser, quickly followed by three men in civilian clothes carrying AK-47s. They walked purposely through the courtyard towards the door of the main house. Again, the door swung wide as they approached, and they entered wordlessly. The man who had opened the door led them down a narrow hallway to a large sitting room. Inside Mullah Omar, the spiritual leader of the Taliban sat cross-legged next to a small fire.

The tall man approached, bowing ever so slightly at the waist, he said, "Greetings, Mullah Omar. I hope your health is good and you enjoy the riches of life."

"Indeed, my health is good. I hope yours is as well," Omar replied.

"Yes, I am well."

Gesturing with his arm towards the rug beside him, Omar said, "Sit down here, beside me and tell me of your travels. I expect you are weary and thirsty. Have some *chai* and perhaps some fruit."

As bin Laden sat down a small man in traditional garb, a dark turban on his head, calf length cotton trousers, a thigh length cotton shirt and a sleeveless waistcoat hurried quickly to him, offering a plate of dried fruit. Taking a small piece, bin Laden waived him away dismissively.

"I do not get out often, I wish for you to tell me of your travels and what you have seen," Omar repeated as he leaned over to pour tea into a glass in front of bin Laden.

"I come to speak of the Americans bombing and the progress of the war with the Northern Alliance," bin Laden said. Ponderously casting his gaze right and left, he leaned forward slightly and said in a lower voice, "Perhaps, we should discuss this matter between ourselves."

Wiping his lips with the long end of his turban, Omar followed bin Laden's gaze around the room. Nodding, he said, "Perhaps you are right. This is a matter for us alone."

Raising his arms, he clapped his hands once, the servants and others in his court silently left the room. Following his lead, bin Laden made a dismissive gesture with his outstretched hand; his attendees also left the room.

Mullah Omar picked up a date from the tray of dried fruit and before he popped it into his mouth, he paused and looked at bin Laden. "Muqtar, the American war does not go well. What news do you have of the Northern Alliance?"

"Mullah, the Northern Alliance have done nothing since the war began. They sit on their haunches like a pack of dogs waiting for the spoils of war. You are still strong in Mazar-e Sharif and Kunduz. The tribal fighters under Dostum and Fahim will not withstand a strong attack," bin Laden began.

Interrupting, Omar blurted out, "Yes, we are strong there because the American planes have not attacked us there. They have destroyed almost everything else my people have and use to govern. All our buildings, our trucks, airfields, our power generators, even hidden bunkers in the mountains have been destroyed. It is just a matter of time before the cowardly Americans attack our men in Mazar and Kunduz."

"Yes, it pains me to admit that the American bombing has been accurate. It has taken out the trappings of society. But it has not affected our courage, our faith or even our men. These things you speak of, are just buildings," bin Laden leaned forward, speaking in a strained voice, "*We* have Allah on our side, with Allah we shall not lose. The Americans do not have courage, and will not let their men on the ground to fight. Even if they did, we have defeated a greater enemy on this very land not so long ago. Without courage, or men on the ground, they cannot win. Perhaps the Americans can destroy all the buildings, but they cannot kill our people. They cannot take away our faith and courage. They will lose and fade into history."

"We can keep the infidel out of Afghanistan. If we defeat the Northern Alliance, the Americans will not be able to set foot in Afghanistan. The key to their war is Kunduz and Mazar-e Sharif, and there we are still strong." Bin Laden paused, shook his head and took a sip of *chai*, after a brief moment he began preaching again.

"My military commanders are even now moving towards Kunduz to allow you to attack Fahim at Taloqan. We can push them back to the pass at Turghan. If we take the land from there to the Tajikistan border there will be no safe haven for the unbelievers. The Americans can never invade us over the Hasretisi Mountain Range; invasion has always been over the flat lands of Chatlon

Province south of Dushanbe. Now is not the time to be weak, it is time to be strong. Let them bomb empty buildings; they cannot destroy our hearts. We can make sure the Americans have no foothold or any way to invade our country."

Mullah Omar silently gazed at bin Laden Omar. After a long pause, he said, "Those filthy dogs in the north are only good at Buzkashi, dragging a goat or a calf is nothing. Games do not prepare you for war, perhaps you are right. You are the expert in military matters. I leave the defense of Afghanistan to you and it is a sacred charge. You must fight the devil from outside, as well as the weakness within our own people. Proceed with your plan at Kunduz. The majority of my followers are already there, I can spare no more men to place in Mazar-e Sharif, Kunduz or Taloqan."

"I understand exalted one. I shall do as you ask. I am but a servant of Allah, I beg to do Allah's will," bin Laden replied, casting his eyes down and spreading his hands open in a gesture of acquiescence.

Omar again paused, longer than before. "Muqtar, I see the wisdom in your plans. I see also the wisdom in planning for the future. Things do not always work as we intend. Even you have had to change plans when unforeseen things happen. Are you prepared in case things do not happen as you suggest?"

Bin Laden stared at Omar with his heavy, unblinking eyes, "I have survived a long time with many enemies hounding my footsteps. I always have plans and means to survive. I live a simple life and am always ready to drop it on a moments notice." Omar had been an ally for a long time, while he didn't want to offend him, he also didn't want to give away any options for his own survival.

Omar's façade of civility was showing signs of crumbling. Testily he replied, "We have been friends a long time. I have afforded you the hospitality of my country when no others would take you in. I believe you should share with me your plans; generalities are for children. I know you lead a simple life, always on the move, always in the mountains or the dessert. You live closer to the ground than I do. We need to have an understanding between us, just you and I, a safqua, just in case something happens which we can no longer control."

Taken aback by Omar's suddenly sharp edge, bin Laden paused to consider this secret agreement. From a calculating standpoint, bin Laden did not think the Cleric held much value if he and his Taliban movement lost the war in Afghanistan. The Taliban had protected him from the ravages of the outside world for several years, but outside Afghanistan, they held no sway. He finally realized that Omar was waiting expectantly and he must offer something to the Mullah. Soon.

Stroking his gray-black beard, he said slowly, "There is a valley south of

Sorkh Ab, which is on the road between Kandahar and Herat. In this valley of the Seyah Range there are several helicopters waiting under cover. I presume you know this valley. It is where we have had one of our secret training camps. I put them there after Clinton began sending cruise missiles."

Impatient, Omar rocked back and forth on his knees, "Yes, yes, I know the valley well. Then these helicopters are for travel to Iran. But Iran is hostile to the Taliban, they will not provide a haven for us."

Bin Laden continued in his even tone, like he was speaking to a child, "I have arranged it, the Iranians will take us in. They hate Americans more than they hate anyone else. The Pakistanis are in bed with the Americans and we cannot move about there. The helicopters are for crossing the Dasht E Barang. Once in Iran, make your way to Mashad, it is in the northeast. There we have a safe place," bin Laden said.

"It is well. I knew you would have a plan and a place to go. I know this will not come to pass, but it is a great comfort in these times of trouble." Omar nodded with grave satisfaction.

Suddenly bin Laden was ready to end the interview. "Yes, it is always good to have a way out. But we mustn't lose heart. Now is not the time to think of running. We are close to defeating the Americans and driving the Northern Alliance from your borders once and for all. Together we shall see them run like dogs and watch their children consumed in fire."

Standing up slowly, Omar waved at his followers, hovering out of earshot in the doorway. As they bustled in, bin Laden got up as well. Omar grasped bin Laden by the arms and feigned a kiss on both cheeks as farewell. "Goodbye my friend. Thank you for coming and keeping an old man informed. Farewell and good luck with the attack at Kunduz. Together we will defeat the cowardly American. Together we shall see the triumph of Allah," Omar said forcefully for all to hear.

"Farewell, Mullah Omar," bin Laden replied, arranging his Kefaya around his head. He turned quickly and left the room. In the hallway, his bodyguards joined him and together they move quickly to their trucks.

Emerging into the sun, bin Laden made his way towards the first Land Cruiser and Ahmed Mustapha emerged from the third Toyota and walked to the first vehicle. He slid in after bin Laden closed the door. The convoy started their engines and as quickly as they had come they sped through the town.

"Muqtar, how did your meeting with the Mullah proceed? What is it that the Mullah wanted to discuss? Was it the war in the north?" Mustapha asked.

"No, Omar is only interested in his own skin. He wanted to talk about escape routes. I told him about the opportunity to defeat Fahim in the north and he approved of it, but he is not interested in it. He can see only defeat for the Taliban, he is of no further use," bin Laden replied, disgusted.

"Then did you give him our escape to Iran?" Mustapha asked.

Holding part of his Kefaya in his hand, he idly twisted it as he stared out the window. "Yes, it is no matter. We still have Pakistan and we can always go to Iran if things turn out badly. Right now, we must focus on the future. I will go see Youseff and see about the defeat of Fahim. Ahmed, go back to Kabul and make sure the rabbits are harvested. It is time to sow the seeds of hell and bring down the American economy. If things are rough here we might not be able to start it, and therefore you must do it now," bin Laden concluded. Abruptly leaning forward, bin Laden tapped the driver on the shoulder, "Stop the car, immediately."

Mustapha got out of the car and stood in the dust beside the road. The convoy sped off, covering him in a cloud of dust before he could move towards his car.

Frankfurt, Germany

A cold blustery wind curled around the fussganger in front of Abu Fakhim's shop. A cold wintry day and few shoppers were braving the spitting rain. It was almost lunchtime and Fakhim did not feel like going out into the wind himself.

Stirring from his desk, he walked idly into the shop. Seeing his helper, he pulled some money from his pocket and said, "Mahel, here is thirty marks, go and get us lunch. Don't forget to bring me the newspapers."

"Yes, right away. Do you wish the American papers this time?" Mahel asked as he put on his coat.

"No, but bring the London Times and the Financial Times as well," Fakhim answered.

Back in his office, Fakhim brewed a pot of strong coffee and turned his satellite receiver to Sky News. Glumly watching the news, he brooded on his problems. Time passed slowly and the door ringer startled him as someone came in the front door.

"Herr Fakhim, here is your lunch and the papers you asked for. If you don't need me for the moment can I go to lunch now?" Mahel asked as he put down the plastic container with Fakhim's lunch from the Pakistani restaurant nearby.

"Mahel, it is a slow day today. Perhaps we will not have customers for the rest of the day. You can go home to your family this afternoon. I will not need you until tomorrow," Fakhim answered.

"Thank you, Mien Herr. Do not worry our customers will come back. They are just nervous about the war and the terrorists. Soon that will be over. Things will be good again, you will see," Mahel said, trying to encourage his boss.

Fakhim looked at him in a grandfatherly way and gently said, "Tschoos, see you tomorrow morning."

Fakhim closed the door behind his helper as he stepped out. Picking up a newspaper, he sat down and began reading. Business had fallen off dramatically; perhaps it was a mixed blessing that he could get no new rugs in from the Middle East. His customers had disappeared. He got up to pour himself more coffee.

Pacing the floor, he watched the latest news update from Afghanistan. The papers and the television readers say one thing, but he was long used to looking beyond the official words. He knew of the truth behind the public face. Despite what the media said, he could tell things were not going well.

Sitting down again he picked at his lunch. He had not received a call or talked with Mustapha in weeks. There were no supplemental shipments, no communication. The longer this went on, the worse he imagined that it meant. Over all this, was the fact that he had loaned them money. He hated loaning money to anyone. With the financial freeze imposed by the Americans, it was almost impossible to move money anywhere; the German authorities were cooperating and there was no way to access any of Mustapha's money here in Germany.

He worried about the rising hatred towards Turks, Pakistanis and other Middle Easterners in Germany. In some places, there had been violence towards foreign workers, there is a backlash coming and he didn't want to get in the way.

The worst thing was that either way the war in Afghanistan worked out, it would be bad for his profit margin. If the supply of rugs dried up, he would not have anything to sell; if the supply became easier, then prices would fall. Glumly, he began thinking that there would be no future for this business. And if the rug business was no good, then Germany may not be the best place to stay.

Flipping through the channels on the satellite TV, he stared at the screen, his eyes unfocused while he furiously considered his options. He could stay here and try to ride the current turmoil out, or he could sell out and join his brother in America.

Selling his store and his apartment would be easy; real estate was very valuable in downtown Frankfurt. But there was this outstanding loan. Mustapha owed him at least $250,000. He still had access to Mustapha's Swiss accounts. Perhaps he should transfer those accounts into his own name. They didn't need it; they might not even survive this war. He knew it wasn't even their money to begin with.

Suddenly decisive, he abruptly put his coffee cup down on the desk. He did not need much; he could easily take what he needed with him. He would call an agent, have his house and shop put up for sale. Let the agent sell or keep his furniture.

He would go to America with a brief stop in Switzerland to convert Swiss Francs into American Dollars for all his accounts. He would secure his future, because there was no longer one here. He would tell no one; tomorrow he would go to America and get lost. With relief, he unplugged the coffee maker and put on his coat. Turning the sign in the door to "closed," he locked the door and walked towards the subway, never once turning back.

CHAPTER 13

Khenjan, Afghanistan

Ahmed Youseff couldn't help but wonder what was going on outside. Normally quiet, this little village buried in the mountains north of Kabul was a sudden beehive of activity. He followed the muted roar of a speeding truck and the shouts of guards. Outside in the dusty street, a small pickup skidded around the corner, a large machine gun mounted on the back. Ali Najad jumped out and ran up to him breathlessly, a crazed look in his eyes.

"Mudier Youseff, the Tribals have taken Taloqan," Najad said, spitting every word, breathless with excitement.

"Slow down Ali, catch your breath. Tell me again what has happened?" Youseff said reassuringly.

With an effort, the thin man tried to calm himself down, beginning again he said, "Mudier Youseff, there was bombing. Only a few bombs, but the tanks and the Taliban defenses just disappeared. The village was left, but after the storm was over Tribal warriors came riding through the dust like the Hordes of the Khan himself."

Suddenly anxious, Youseff grabbed his messenger by the shoulders, shaking him slightly he asked, "How far did they get? What happened to the tanks? Think clearly now, did the Tribals get into town? Did you see this with your own eyes?"

"No, Mudier, you do not understand. It is gone. They took the whole town. The Tribals rode into town and killed everyone who resisted," Najad answered, fear in his eyes. "I was there, I did not see the end with my own eyes. I was checking the roads just as you told me. The Northern Alliance rode through the trenches outside of town and Abdul and I decided we immediately must come and tell you the news."

Looking at his feet, Najad continued dejectedly, "Every tank and machine gun exploded in vast balls of fire and dust. Everyone; there was no chance. And there was nothing left to stop the horsemen, all the Taliban were in the trenches."

"It is good you came to tell me; this is a significant change. The Tribals have not been so aggressive and we may not have learned of this for a long time. Tell me, did the Tribals move beyond the town? Are they moving towards Kunduz?" Youseff asked.

He had left before the fall was complete and had no way of knowing what happened after he left. Nevertheless, Najad wanted to make Youseff feel better. "Abdul and I saw the Tribals stop to ransack Taloqan."

Stunned, Youseff reassured Najad, "Go and refuel your vehicle. You will be needed soon as a guide. Soon we will be moving more men to Kunduz to fight; we cannot let the Tribals remain in Taloqan. Go now and prepare."

"Hello, Hello, Faud? This is Ahmed," Youseff spoke into his cell phone.

"Yes, Ahmed how is your health today?" Faud Saleh answered slowly. Sitting in the sun in front of the communications cave, Saleh was enjoying the warmth of the late afternoon. He was now in charge of the communications men and equipment that Mohideen had sent to the Salang Pass.

Without thinking, Youseff spoke hurriedly, "Faud, there is no time. We are in big trouble in Taloqan, I have just received a report that it has fallen to the Northern Alliance."

"This is true?" Saleh replied guardedly, "Are you sure of this, with your own eyes? I have seen many reports that this or that has happened. They are not always true."

Annoyed, Youseff related the story hurriedly, "It was Najad himself who saw it. He fled before the final defeat. It can only have been Americans; they bombed the Taliban defenses, the tanks and machine guns. The Taliban were destroyed before the Tribals charged with their horses. Najad has just come here to tell me what happened."

His mind a hundred miles away, Saleh sat in his chair, staring into the distant valley, "This is indeed terrible. Do you think the American spies we have heard about are the reason for this?"

"Najad did not see them with his eyes. But even the Russians cannot destroy tanks and guns like this, it can only be the American," Youseff replied, knowingly.

"Then what shall we do? Is Taloqan even important enough for us to fight there?" Saleh inquired hopefully.

"You fool, of course Taloqan is important. Mullah Omar and Muqtar bin Laden had planned to drive a wedge through the Northern Alliance there. In just a few days, we were going to mount an attack. Now we must move up our plans and fight to regain Taloqan. We must start sending our men to Kunduz. Do you hear me Saleh? We must move them now. Use whatever trucks are available," Youseff ordered.

"We cannot. There are not enough trucks to carry that many men, even if we carry no equipment. It also will be night soon. We cannot travel at night," Saleh replied fatalistically, still unconvinced that they needed to move quickly, if at all.

"Saleh, you do not understand. It is of utmost importance that we move quickly. Begin moving as many men as you can, now! Send who you can, now! We can send more tomorrow. Najad believes the Tribals stopped in the town. If they did not stop, the Tribals could cutoff the entire force in Kunduz and maybe even Mazar-e Sharif," Youseff said forcefully.

Suddenly tired, Saleh gave into Youseff's demands, "I will do as you say. I did not think that Kunduz was in danger of falling as well. I still do not think the Tribals can readily defeat such a force as is already there," Saleh said.

"Do not pretend to understand, you waste time. They have no need to defeat us at Kunduz. The Tribals only need to cutoff our communications and supply lines to those people that are already there. Eventually, they will not be able to fight if they are starved," Youseff lectured into the phone. "But more than that we must defeat them as they come out of their mountains. They are easier targets and a greater threat. We must not let them succeed."

"I see, Mudier Youseff. It will be as you say. I will send as many men as I can, perhaps within the hour," Saleh promised. "It will take, perhaps, an hour or so after that to reach you."

"Send them down the valley as soon as you can, Najad will be waiting at the Andarab Bridge. He knows the way and will lead them to Kunduz. Do so quickly. Lose no time." Abruptly, Youseff took the phone from his ear with one hand and pushed the end call button with his thumb.

Seconds after talking with Saleh, Youseff's cell phone began ringing. Surprised, he answered it, "Salaam a Likum, Muqtar. Pardon me, but if I may be so bold, I must tell you the news."

"Go ahead, but I do not like interruptions. I have just come from talking with the Mullah Omar and I am tired of bad news. What have you to tell me, now?" bin Laden asked.

"Muqtar, one of my men has just arrived with the report that Taloqan has fallen. He saw it with his own eyes and came here to tell me," Youseff interjected.

For a moment, there was only silence on the other end of the line. "This is bad news indeed. The Taliban are becoming afraid and weak and their leaders are worried more about their own skins. They no longer know how to defeat the infidel. Have they forgotten that Allah provides us substance and guidance, all they must do is his will. Tell me now of Taloqan. Have the Tribals taken the whole town or part of it? How were they attacked? Are there any defenders left?" bin Laden asked with a disgusted tone.

"Ali Najad was there because I sent him north to check out the roads to Kunduz and Taloqan. As you wished, we were preparing to move men to add to the strength of the Taliban," Youseff began.

Bin Laden interrupted testily, "Yes, Yes. It is little matter to me why he was there. What did he see? Did he see any Americans?"

"No he did not see Americans. The attack happened after all Taliban tanks and machine guns had been destroyed from the air. Tremendous explosions and then the Northern Alliance rode into town on horses. Najad said they are sacked the town," Youseff answered.

"Have you sent our fighters to Kunduz as I ordered?" bin Laden asked.

"Muqtar, we are doing this. We do not have enough trucks to move them all at once. It is impossible to travel by night. At night, if you are on the roads, the next thing you know you are dead. We can only move in daylight. As many as we can fit into the trucks we have will be in Kunduz before nightfall," Youseff related.

"We must stop the Tribal advance. But it is good they are coming out of the mountains. It will be easier to kill them in the open rather than pry them from their rocks. Make sure you send as many men as you can. I will call Mustapha and Mohideen and see if we can get you more trucks, and move them faster," bin Laden said. "Time is important, tomorrow or the day after will be too late, you must move now!"

"Yes, Muqtar, the first group of fighters will be there in hours. As soon as we get the trucks back, we will send more men to Kunduz. Do not worry; we will stop them in their tracks. They are weak and lack to courage of our brave fighters. Allah shall burn them in hell."

"Yes, Yes. But Youseff, there is something else we must do. We must capture some of these American devils. They were there and they are responsible for the false courage of the Tribals at Taloqan. If we can capture them and show who they are and reveal their fear on TV we can easily defeat them. We must capture them; once their weakness is shown the bombing will stop. I believe they are coming to you, I have arranged it. You must meet them and bring them to me bound hand and foot. Send the fighters to Kunduz to defeat the Tribals, but your special task is to capture Americans," bin Laden ordered.

Youseff listened with excitement burning in his eyes. "Yes, Muqtar. I will capture them. I will do as you say. We will defeat the infidel on the plains before Kunduz!"

Youseff turned off the phone and put it in his pocket. His eyes sparkled as he walked back inside the dark house. Deep in thought, he went to his room and began stuffing his meager belongings in a Nike duffel bag. Almost finished, he felt someone at the door looking at him. He spun around to face the door, suddenly angry.

With relief, Youseff said, "Ah, it is you, Ali. You surprised me. I did not hear you come in."

Embarrassed, Najad said with uncertainty, "Yes, Mudier. It is Ali. I am ready to go back to Kunduz."

Suddenly feeling talkative, Youseff wanted to tell Najad everything that had happened. "This is good, I have talked with Saleh and the first group will meet you at the Andarab Bridge. I expect them in an hour or two."

Still uncomfortable at Youseff's reaction, Najad wanted to leave quickly, nodding he said, "I will leave right away. What do you want me to do after I have led them to Kunduz?"

"You must come back early in the morning, as soon as you can move on the roads. There will be another group. Saleh will have more fighters that need to be led to Kunduz. You will be their guide and we will need another one. Tomorrow there will be more trucks arriving and we must have at least two groups taking our fighters to Kunduz."

"Abdul Saleem is with me, Mudier. He can guide the next group when they are ready tomorrow. He was with me and knows the way," Najad said.

"Good. Send him back to the communications cave and have him tell Saleh what he is supposed to do. The two of you can alternate trips. Do this quickly, we must leave soon."

"Yes, Mudier. Will you stay here or go back to the Salang Pass? You could take Saleem with you?" Najad asked.

"No, my place is with the fighters. I will go with you; we must retake Taloqan and stop the infidel. Mudier bin Laden has ordered me to catch the American spies. It is obvious they are there."

"As you wish, Mudier. I will send Saleem to Saleh. Then I will wait outside for you." Najad said abruptly leaving the doorway.

Bannu Cap, 35,000', Bannu, Pakistan

Lieutenant McKay leaned back in her seat, stretching her arms above and behind her head. Her flight suit bunched up around her neck and shoulders. Yawning, she tensed all of the muscles in her back and arms. These long missions were starting to wear. There weren't enough JSTAR's crews in theater for 24/7 Ops; they had to fly rotating shifts with less than twelve hours off between sorties. She had started on the night shift, now she was on an afternoon shift. She was so tired she didn't remember anything else.

Sitting forward, she leaned her forearms on the console in front of her. She wasn't sure what the problem was, but it was hard to get fighters reassigned to attack moving targets. She had found quite a few with the JSTAR's radar. Every now and again, the target was big enough for AWACS to give them support, but not often. And the big bombers were pre-assigned to targets or Forward Air Controllers. Today was a slow day, with only a little traffic worth noting.

From their current orbit, she could see the entire valley between Kandahar and Kabul; even parts north up to the Salang Pass area. The mountains of the Panjsher Range reached over 15,000' in the pass area creating a radar shadow that reached beyond Baghlan to the north. This new orbit allowed better coverage over the majority of the country, but to her mind, they were still blind over a lot of critical territory.

McKay yawned once more and deliberately blinked her eyes to stay awake. There was more traffic during the day, but less action. Yawning again, out of the corner of her eye, she caught the Moving Target Indicator revealing a group of three or more vehicles making their way north out of Kabul.

Sitting up, she stared at the screen; it was nice to have a little activity. In seconds, she saw another GMTI hit on targets north of Charikar. A few moments later she saw yet another GMTI moving on the road alongside the Panjsher River, east of Kabul.

Damn, she thought, *this was a lot of traffic, all at the same time.* "Hum, looks like they're up to something. Better call Buffalo over and have him take a look."

Thumbing the intercom button for the Mission Commander, she leaned forward to speak into the microphone on her console, "Colonel Horde, I've got three popup hits moving basically north out of the Kabul area."

"Is that right? Have you had any other hits there today?"

"No, sir. This is the first and they all started at once."

"Okay, Lisa. I'll be there in a second," Buffalo Horde replied. Putting his coffee cup down, he got up out of his swivel chair to go see her screen. Thinking he'd rather face-to-face, instead of calling up her screen on his computer. It's a lot better trying to understand what she's looking at that way.

"What'cha got?" he asked as he leaned over, resting his hand on her shoulder.

With her left hand, Lisa pointed to the GMTI indicators and scrolled the trackball with her right. Tapping a mouse button, she reoriented the screen so that Kabul was at the bottom of the display. "I've got three targets and the gate is set to show three or more vehicles moving 30 klicks or better. So, I've got nine plus trucks moving towards Salang Pass."

Reaching over her, he traced the lightly shaded crosshatch pattern that represented the radar shadow. "Yep, they're all headed towards that Pass. This is sorta like the convoy you saw a couple of days ago, the same area. Isn't it?"

"Yes sir, but nothing ever came out of that," she acknowledged.

"Well, I don't think we attacked that target, so we'll never know. But we did move to this orbit so we can get a better view of the valley and up to the Pass. You won that one at least." Horde replied, smiling down at her.

McKay steeled herself to complain one more time. "But sir, I still can't see the whole pass area. We've got to get in-country, we've got to be closer, to see past those mountain shadows."

Taking a breath, she looked at her screen again and gasped. Pointing she said, "Look, there are three more GMTIs coming from the shadow. These new guys are another group. See, the old ones have refreshed and are still enroute." With her freehand she colored the new GMTI hits yellow, to distinguish them from the previous group. "Look, there's another GMTI hit on the J-bad road. Do you think AWAC's will believe this new group is a worthy target?"

"It's unlikely that it's your old convoy, it has been a couple of days at least. It might be related, though. Keep a close watch on both targets and I'll call Horse. I'll check if there are any shooters available for us."

"Yes, sir. And while you're at it, could you ask permission to move the cap. We really need to see into that shadow!" McKay called to Horde's back as he walked back to his console.

Buffalo plugged in his headset as he sat down. Adjusting the mic against his lips, he thumbed the transmit button. "Horse, Cadillac Alpha, in the green, how copy?"

"Cadillac, Horse, loud and clear, copy green," the AWAC's Mission Commander replied.

"Roger Horse, Cadillac has ID'd three good target groups. Do you have any shooters for us?"

"Negative shooters, we assigned the last ones in the hold about forty minutes ago. We won't have anything for another hour or two," the controller replied.

To himself, Buffalo thought, *Shit, this always happens. We're always on the bottom of the stack, every time we find something.*

Trying again he transmitted, "Horse, Cadillac these are fleeting, time sensitive targets. We lost a similar, larger, target in this area just a couple of days ago. Haven't you got anything? Maybe you could reassign something."

"Sorry, Cadillac. Honestly, if I had anything I'd send it your way. If I did reassign anything, they'd probably be out of ordinance," the MC replied.

Buffalo replied, deflated, "No, I don't want anybody about to go Winchester, that wouldn't do us any good. This target is 12-30 trucks on the move. Is the Maddog available?"

The current JFAC airborne commander, codenamed 'Maddog', Lieutenant Colonel BC Lawrence, an F-16 Viper driver, had been listening to the radio traffic. He broke into the conversation with Cadillac, "Cadillac, this is Maddog on freq, go ahead."

"Maddog, Cadillac. We've got good hits on three fast moving groups. Two headed towards the Salang Pass and one headed north out of it. We understand there is no air available," Buffalo said.

"Cadillac, Maddog, that is correct. No air available at this time. Continue tracking your groups and as soon as we can get air, we'll send it your way. I wish we had a different answer for you, but that's just the way it is right now."

Buffalo saw his chance and asked, "Cadillac copies. Then we request permission to move to a cap north of Gardez. If we don't displace the orbit, we'll lose the groups in the radar shadow. How copy?"

"Stand by, Cadillac." BC transmitted, pulling a map of Afghanistan off the pile of papers on his console. Tracing the area around Gardez, he shook his head. Thumbing the mic he replied, "Negative, Cadillac, I can't let you get that far in country. You've got to stay where you are for the time being. Keep tabs on your targets from the Bunnu Cap."

"Cadillac copies. If we stay in Bunnu, we will lose the groups as they enter the pass. Is there anyway you can get eyes on the target area? Anyway at all?" Buffalo asked.

"Cadillac, the peaks are up to 11,000 feet in the Gardez area. I just can't let you get that close. As for shadowing your target, I don't have anyone to spare right now. How many vehicles are in each groups?"

"Twenty plus vehicles overall. Twelve plus in the southern group and eight plus in the northern group," Buffalo replied.

"Maddog copies. We do have some folks on the ground in that area. I'll see if we can get they're eyes on target. Meanwhile, keep up the good work. Maddog out," BC concluded.

Taloqan, Afghanistan

"Sir, I think you'd better hear this. We've got an incoming radio call from a Maddog. He's calling you personally," Brandon said, holding the microphone near his chest.

Dave, Mark and Woody were sitting in a circle on the ground, discussing what to do after Taloqan. Woody got up and walked a little unsteadily over to Brandon to pick up the radio. "What the frig are you talking about, a personal call? We're just flunkies out in the dirt, what's a big shot like that calling us for?"

"Well, sir. This Maddog guy is calling for you. He wants to speak to you, not me," Brandon said, thrusting out the handset towards his captain.

"You mean he asked for me by name?"

"No, sir, by callsign. Uhh, If you'd just take the radio," Brandon repeated, still holding out the handset.

"Maddog, Mako 51A here, go ahead," Woody said as he put the handset to his ear.

"Mako 51A, this is Maddog. Are you the Mako team leader?" Lieutenant Colonel Lawrence asked.

"Roger, Maddog, this is 51A. You are correct. Go ahead," Woody replied, trying to keep the "who the fuck are you" attitude out of his voice.

"Mako 51A, Maddog copies. I have a Priority One mission for you, it takes precedence over all other missions you have. Are you ready to copy?" BC transmitted.

Pausing, Woody looked at Dave and Mark still discussing operations with Fahim. Suddenly awake, he put the mic back to his ear, "Mako 51A is ready to copy. But I've got to tell you that I don't work for you. I am attached to support the Northern Alliance and we have an ongoing mission here."

"Mako, I fully understand your mission. And it may surprise you, but you do work for me. I am the JFACC rep airborne. I own all Air Force assets, and that

256

includes you. I've got a job for you that IS number one priority. I'll make sure you get confirmation orders through other channels, but I need you to move right now. Are you ready to copy?" BC said tersely.

Woody crooked his head and held the mic between his ear and his shoulder. Reaching down, he pulled a small spiral notebook out of his cargo pocket. "Mako is ready to copy."

"Mako, Maddog I need you to proceed immediately to the Salang Pass area. We have reports of large movements in that area and no assets to put eyes on target. We need you there ASAP to report. A massing of troops in that area will negate any advances we make in the north. We need to know what is going on there, how copy?"

Woody switched the mic to his other ear pinching it with his shoulder. Writing furiously, he did not have another hand to acknowledge the transmission. Dropping his shoulder, he also dropped the mic and fumbled it for a second as he picked it up. "Mako, copies. That area is over one hundred miles from here. We have no transportation and it will take several days to get there by our transportation."

"Mako. Don't worry about that. Some of the guys you are working with have lift available, I've already asked them to pick you up, and it's on the way. It's about an hour out. Report back to me, personally, as soon as you're on site."

"Mako copies. Understand Pave Low for the lift?" Woody said.

"Negative, it's a Hip. And it's about an hour out. Questions?" BC said.

"No questions. Mako will call as soon as we've arrived." Woody didn't notice the blinking red light as he put the mic down on top of the radio; Brandon had not encrypted the radio transmission.

Holding his notepad, Woody walked back to the brainstorming session they had been having on the dirt floor. "Hey, guys you won't believe who was on the radio and what he wanted."

Mark grinned, squinting up at Woody he said mischievously, "What, was that a MARS call from your mom? Was she worried about you brushing your teeth?"

Smiling slightly, Woody looked at them. "Well, you could say it was Mom on the radio. It was my Air Force Mom; well really, it was The Man. And he gave me a tasking. Ya'll want to hear what it is or do you just want to keep joking?"

"Okay, okay. I'm sorry you don't have a sense of humor. Go ahead with your story, you have our complete attention," Mark said, sitting back with his arms outstretched, ready to be entertained.

Woody sat down and crossed his legs, stretching the moment out. "Like I was saying, it was The Man on the phone and he wants me to pack up and go to the Salang Pass area. There is some sort of special activity because they can't get eyes on the area."

"Man, that sounds like a Wild Goose chase to me. Doesn't he know we've just started working with these Tribals? That we just had our first success?" Dave asked.

Rubbing his three-day growth of beard, Woody replied, "Yeah, I told him. He said he understood what my mission was. I told him I didn't work for him and he jerked me up short. But I figure this has got to be a big deal to somebody, he said someone is sending lift to take me to the area ASAP."

SFC Gary Wilkerson joined the small group, he leaned close to Mark's ear and whispered, "Captain we just got a message from group on the LST-5 that we are to support a road recce of the Salang Pass area. They want us to send an Observation Team and the USAF should be sending some folks on the team as well. The word is that Intel has tracked his movements and believes bin Laden may be there."

Mark shrugged his shoulders, "Woody, not many folks can get my chain jumping through hoops like that. It looks like your radio voice was indeed The Man. I guess I'm in on your party. The good thing is he's even sending in a chopper for us, it's a long way to walk."

Gary cleared his throat, "Uh, sir. Group also wanted us to leave an operational team here to continue working with Fahim. They like the progress so far and said they want more of it."

Woody nodded, "Well, this is a big enough deal that I think I should go. But Brandon can stay here and work targets with your guys and Fahim. He can keep our spotting scope and I'll just take one of the radios and a couple of batteries. It doesn't sound like we'll be running any air, so no big deal."

Mark was silent for a minute, slowly he looked up at Gary. "Okay, you stay here and work with Brandon. I'll take Mike and Luke with me, tell them to saddle up for a short trip armed for bear."

Up until this moment, Dave had been sitting quietly, but now he couldn't keep quiet, "Man, you guys aren't going to leave me out of the fun. No way. I'm going with. Besides, Fahim won't want to do anything for a few days now that they've had a big success. He'll want to secure the area and tighten up his lines back toward Bazan. Shoot, I'm just gonna get bored here."

Mark interrupted, "But Dave, if you go what about translation? Who's going to translate for our guys?"

"Well, Gary speaks Arabic. Fahim has a few folks that speak Arabic as well. And besides Fahim speaks a little English anyway," Dave said dismissively.

"The hell you say. Fahim understands English? Why didn't he let on?" Mark said with disgust.

Dave chuckled, "I guess it's a power thing, he knows something you don't. Or maybe he just doesn't think he can speak it very well. Anyway, don't worry about it. They'll get along."

"Then it's a done deal. When does our chariot arrive?" Mark began to get up.

"Maddog said within an hour. It's not one of ours. It's a Hip. Does the Northern Alliance have any Russian choppers?" Woody asked, curiously.

Brushing his pants off as he stood up Dave said, "Naw, that's one of ours. As a matter of fact, I think they were re-supplying Bazan while we're out here."

Brandon turned to look east over the ridge where they had started the morning. Shielding his eyes he said, "Speaking of timing, I think there's a chopper coming over that ridge. Is it one of yours Dave?"

Picking up binoculars, Dave put them to his eyes, after a moment, he said, "I think so. It's a Hip for sure. Don't see any pods, so he probably won't shoot us."

"Yeah, the trick is for the Tribals not to shoot him," Woody said.

Waving his hand in a dismissive gesture, Dave replied, "They know this chopper, you guys worry too much." In the distance the chopper flew towards the smoke that was tapering off from the tanks attacked earlier that day, suddenly it changed direction. "See, those guys are pointing him in this direction. They know where we are."

"Gary, get Mike and Luke up here. We need to go soon," Mark said hurriedly.

Thinking ahead to the logistics of the move, Gary asked, "Yes, sir. You know we've only got one LST with us. The other is back in Bazan. How are we going to stay in touch?"

"Shoot. You'd better keep the sat radio. Woody is taking one of the PRC-117s. We'll just stay in touch with that. We'll have to relay through Horse if we need to communicate to each other. Shoot, have we got enough spare crypto?" Mark said.

"Yeah, we've got two sets. But we'd better take a few extra sets of 5590 batteries. If we're going to run the radio more we'll run out of my supply quick," Woody replied.

"Okay, Gary, send back for some more batteries for the radio from Bazan. If you need UHF, use one of the freqs on the LST-5," Mark directed.

"Way ahead of you, sir. Already got a resupply setup. You guys go ahead and take a few extra batteries and some food as well." Gary left to round up Mike and Luke and get them ready to go on the new mission.

Kafar Jar Ghar Mountains, Afghanistan

Three four wheel drive vehicles bounced down the dusty road on the west side of the Kafar Jar Ghar Mountain Range. Two technical vehicles, Toyota pickups with machine guns mounted in the beds, and one Land Cruiser were headed northeast towards Ghanzi Province. Usama bin Laden, sitting serenely in the back seat of the Land Cruiser, watched the passing terrain without expression. A cell phone rang urgently on the seat beside him. Answering it, he did not divert his gaze.

"Hello, Hello," he said flatly.

"Muqtar, we just heard a radio transmission from the AWACS to someone on the ground."

Usama shifted the phone to his left ear; suddenly interested, he looked back into the car. "Was the transmission in the clear? Did you make out what was said?"

"Yes, Muqtar. We heard the American Devils telling someone to go to the Salang Pass area. They have done as you predicted."

"Is there anything else? Did you hear anything they said?" Usama asked.

'No Muqtar. That is all. The person on the ground is to go there as soon as he can, something about getting his eyes on the ground."

"This is indeed good news. Keep listening," Usama said, closing the phone, he laid it back on the seat beside him and looked back out the window. If one had been watching closely, they might have seen a slight smile play across his face.

His mind raced, *Americans are so predictable they act as if they are in a script from Hollywood. They follow like monkeys just where I lead them. They cannot see beyond their noses, they are worse than children. Soon we'll have prisoners to put on TV around the world, we will catch these cowardly devils, just as I predicted. All I need is one, the rest we can kill, maybe we'll even show that on television.* Usama's face split into a wide smile.

Hearing a grunt from the rear seat, the driver glanced in the rear-view mirror. He saw the Muqtar staring out the side window, a vacant look in his eyes and a broad smile on his face. Looking back to the road, he thought about the weighty decisions that concerned the chosen one.

White House Situation Room, Washington, DC

Leaning forward at the table, the Chief of Staff stressed his point in an even voice, "Sir, with respect to the last of the BDA photos, we can't upload the video of an AC-130 strike against a Taliban Headquarters on the videophone. It occurred last night and vividly shows the CIA Predator teams working with the gunships. If you have time we'll look at it right now, I'll put it in your email so you can look at it more closely when you get a chance."

"That will be fine, just send it to me. What else do you have for me this morning? The First Lady has Sunday Brunch waiting here at Camp David," the President said, his lips pursed in a tight smile.

"I understand, sir. We're almost done. CIA has a report for you from in country."

"Mr. President, We've had some success tracking al-Qaeda leaders. It seems that Air Force strikes on Taliban infrastructure as well as al-Qaeda communications sites has severely affected their communications capabilities. Hard telephone lines have been broken all over Afghanistan. The radio traffic we've monitored in the past is way down. But more importantly, the cell phone traffic is way up."

Instantly understanding the possibilities, the President interrupted excitedly, "Excuse me, but have you been able to track specific individuals and pin point where they are?"

"No, sir. Not exactly, at least not yet. I was saying their use of cell phones is way up, which makes our job of interception much easier. Between USAF ELINT capability in theater as well as long duration UAV's, we've begun charting the traffic and we believe that within a few days we will be able to identify specific, often used locations and possibly individuals."

"The good news is that their cell phones are not encrypted. We believe this will allow us to identify individuals as well as the thrust of their conversations. The bad news is that with the volume of traffic, there is an extraordinary amount of data to sift through. We are searching for as many Arabic speakers as we can find to put on the project."

Disappointed, the President had started taking notes on his notepad. At the CIA Director's last comment, he cleared his throat and abruptly looked up. "At that point you will be able to nail down the location of a particular individual? Yes?"

Shifting in his seat nervously, the Director continued, "Well, sir. Yes and no. Once we have charted the cell usage pattern, we should be able to identify the users. The trouble is that, as you know, cell phones are highly mobile. In general, the intelligence that we'll be able to glean from these interceptions will be historical. They will provide trend information. Possibly, future plans, although that remains to be seen."

"So, at some point, you might be able to identify a specific individual at a specific point?" the president interrupted again.

"Yes, sir. After building a database, we should be able to identify a particular individual in near real-time. The location in real-time is a completely different matter, cell phone usage as a marker, and is by its nature a random occurrence, which makes it a much harder task," the director said.

Waiving his hand, the President tried to take the pressure off the director, "Okay, okay George. I don't want to put you on the spot. I just want to know where this capability may be going and maybe how we might use it." Turning slightly, he looked into the video camera, approximating the direction of the Chief of Staff, "Andy, that's all for now. I've got a brunch and some thinking to do. I'll call you later. Everybody else, I want to thank ya'll for getting out this early on Sunday. Talk to you soon." The screen went blank as the president terminated the videophone connection.

Pushing his chair back from the conference table, the president looked at the woman sitting next to him, "Amy, this cell phone thing could be big. I want you to stay close to Defense and CIA on this. If we are able to do as the Director suggests it'll be big."

"Sir, I'm not quite sure I follow you. How do you propose we exploit that kind of intelligence?" Amy Bonham, the Nation Security Advisor, a close confidant of the president, asked.

The President stood up and headed out of the room, gesturing for her to follow him. Leaving the conference building, he turned towards the residence, walking briskly. "Well, I see it like this. If we can identify a particular cell phone user, in real time, then we know whom we've got. Right?"

"Yes, sir," the Advisor replied circumspectly.

The President went on, "Okay, so we know who a particular guy is. If we can also know where he is then what's he's really doing is waving a flag that says I'm here, right here, right now."

"Yes, sir. CIA said it would be hard, but he left it a possibility. Would it be more important to know where a person was or what he was saying and planning?" the advisor asked.

"Well, that's good stuff, but not exactly what I'm driving at. If we know the who, where and when of a particular call then we can hit the guy. He's no longer able to hide from us anywhere. They've got to communicate, and if they do, then we can get close to them and kill him. You follow me?" the President said matter-of-factly.

"Yes, sir. I think I do."

"It's plain that these guys are military targets. As far as I can see, they've set themselves up as legitimate players in the game. If we can take them off the board, we will be closer to winning the war, plain and simple. Didn't the Chairman of the Joint Chiefs say the other day that the key to winning any conflict, is being able to shoot accurately, move quickly and communicate better than your enemy?"

"Right now we're doing a damn good job of taking away their ability to shoot and move, by day and night. If this cell phone thing allows us to exploit their need to communicate, we can remove the decision makers. It's simple."

Stopping at the front of the residence, his hand on the doorknob, he turned slightly to the advisor, "You follow me? I want to find those guys and send them to meet their maker."

"Yes, sir. I think I understand. I'll stay on top of how this cell phone capability shapes up. If we can do as you suggest, I will make sure it gets done!"

"Good. We're gonna win this war. One way or the other, the terrorists will see that we mean business." Stepping in the door, he looked back over his shoulder before going inside. "Go relax. I'll see you later this afternoon on Marine One. It's Sunday."

CHAPTER 14

Mashhad River Valley, Eastern Afghanistan

A cold wind whipped forcefully through the open door of the helicopter reinforcing the stunningly beautiful rugged mountain valley they were flying through. Cupping his mouth with one hand, Woody leaned close to Dave, yelling in his ear, "Why are we going east? The Salang is south."

Dave tilted his head toward Woody. "The pilots feel they should stay over Northern Alliance territory. That way they won't get shot at. They'll turn south soon. You should relax and check out at the scenery."

"Say again last," Woody shouted back.

"I said enjoy the scenery, we'll turn south soon!" Dave said.

Woody settled back into the sling seat attached to the wall staring out of the open door on the right side of the helicopter. Yeah, sure, I guess it makes sense, at least I don't have to walk, he thought. Watching the starkly beautiful terrain, he slumped even further into his seat, becoming numbed to the rhythmic bumping of the helicopter.

Awakened from his reverie by a tap on his shoulder, he looked up to see Dave's face next to his. "Look out the door, that's Koh-I-Bandakor, it's the second highest mountain in Afghanistan. There are at least 10 peaks over 18,000 feet within 40 miles of right here. That's why we have to follow the valleys, and east is where this valley goes."

"How tall is it?" Woody asked, pointing at the huge mountain.

"Bandakor is over 22,000 feet, the tallest is nearly 25,000 feet," Dave replied.

"Man, they sure do grow 'em tall here," Woody whistled.

Flying down the narrow Panjsher Valley, they followed the river at the floor of the valley, with mountains rising to 16,000 feet on either side. Woody looked anxiously out the door scanning the terrain. Thinking it would take weeks to walk anywhere in this terrain, he leaned close to Dave and shouted, "Dave, how close will the pilot set us down to the Salang Pass? Are we going to have to walk it?"

"Good point. I'll ask him to get us as close as possible," Dave replied. With a nod, he got up and made his unsteady way to the flight deck.

Holding to the sidewall to keep his balance, Dave leaned into the cockpit to talk with the co-pilot. After a few moments, he turned and started back towards his seat, picking his way past various bits of cargo and people strewn all over the floor. To keep his balance inside the lurching helicopter he grabbed onto straps, or other people as he made his way down the isle.

Dropping abruptly in his seat, Dave told Woody, "He said he's going to set us down as near the pass as he can get. The mountains are 14-15,000 feet east of it. We hold the east side of the pass, so maybe you can see the pass and the tunnel."

"Great, thanks," Woody replied and settled back into his troop seat.

Thirty minutes later, the Hip settled onto a rocky slope, engines still running, blades churning the air furiously. Dave gathered his stuff and jumped out, followed closely by Mark, Woody and Mike. Luke was the last one out of the helicopter, lugging his gear and the heavy sniper rifle he had insisted on bringing. Luke had barely cleared the doorway when the pilot pulled pitch. The Hip took off in the center of a gale storm, peppering them with small rocks and covering them in dust.

"Hey, guys, I could use a bit of help here. This Barret weighs over 25 pound. Could anyone carry some of this ammo?" Luke asked.

Mark turned back to him and took two boxes of 50 rounds each. "Woody, come here man I've got something you need. You need a little character, timeshare this ammo for Luke. I'll carry one you carry the other."

"I gotta tell you I hate walking, it's not normally something I do. Now you're making it worse!" Woody said while Mark strapped one of the boxes on his pack. "This friggin' pack weighs almost as much as I do and you want to hike up this 14,000 foot peak."

"Woody, it's not like we're going all the way up ya know," Mark shot back, shaking the pack to make sure everything was tight.

"High enough, Pal. High enough," Woody replied. "You're such a comedian."

The five of them began walking single file west towards the pass overlook. After an hour and a half of sweating and struggling to put one foot in front of the other, Woody could only concentrate on the path in front of him. The heavy load dominated his every thought. Numb, he suddenly realized those in front of him had stopped for a rest. Gratefully, he sat on a rock and leaned his pack against the rough granite without taking it off. He fumbled for his canteen, taking a long pull. Woody dropped his hand and wiped his mouth with his other sleeve. Feeling more human now, he looked down the trail they had been climbing. He could easily see the bottom and the town of Golbahar. Nearly 8,000 feet below them, it lay just east of the main road out of Kabul. He reached over with his foot and lightly kicked Mark who was lying against the rock with his eyes closed.

"Hey, light weight how ya holding up?" Mark asked, without moving or opening his eyes.

"I'm great. Feel just great. I could out walk you any day of the week," Woody replied.

"Yeah, right. An Air Force guy that likes to walk with 90 pounds on his back, that'll be the day. Check it out, down the valley." Mark, his eyes still closed, pointed roughly downhill. "There are two irregulars coming up the trail and they've got a bunch of horses with 'em. It looks like your wish has come true."

Wiping his forehead, he laid his head back down and said, "Hey, Dave. Is this the work of your buds down in Golbahar?"

Down the trail, two Northern Alliance irregulars rode easily up the same steep mountain trail on which they had just been struggling. Leading eight mountain ponies, they were a welcome sight. After packing their gear on the horses, they resumed their climb up the trail. Moving quickly, they approached the pass within an hour.

In a cleft below the ridge, they left the Afghanis holding the horses. The rest of the team crawled up to the ridge. Lying on their stomachs, they observed the movement around the pass with binoculars. Woody began thinking it was about time to check in with Maddog. In six hours they had gotten here, traveling by helicopter, horseback and foot, he had never thought they could get here so quickly.

"I don't see anything out there, much less a convoy. And where do you suppose they've got a commo site setup?" Woody asked, the binoculars still pinned to his face.

"Shoot man, I don't know. I'll go ask the Afghanis what they know," Dave said. Turning, he slid down from the top of the ridgeline. Hidden from the other side, he stood up to walk back and talk to the two Northern Alliance irregulars. They were busy eating, sitting cross-legged on the ground.

Woody and Mark were still scanning the pass and the tunnel entrance, searching for movement and the convoy when Dave plopped down next to them. "I just talked with those guys. One of them is a Pathan. He's from the east, around Jalalabad. Says he's been here for several days watching the pass. He said they saw a bunch of trucks come by awhile back. I can't make out his sense of time, so I don't know if it was yesterday or maybe last month. But he says many trucks have come through the pass recently. The other one is from this area and he said there was a lot of activity this morning on the far side of the valley."

"Woody, maybe that's your commo site?" Mark suggested.

"Could be. The footprint on something that would get the ELINT snoopers excited would have to be fairly large, at least the antenna array would stick out. The commo gear and power supply could be hidden, but you can't hide the antennas. Did he see anything like that?"

"Well, he did say the Taliban had set up a lot of sticks near a cave on the far side of the ridge, that weren't there before. He was curious about that." Dave nodded. "He probably doesn't know what an antenna is."

"How did he get over to the other side of the ridge, I thought that was bad guy land?" Mark interjected.

"I dunno, remember he lives around here. Maybe the lines aren't so well defined after all." Dave shrugged.

Woody rolled over onto his back and slid down a few feet, leaning his head against the rocky ground he gazed into the electric blue sky. "Sticks. Yeah, I suppose tall antennas could look like sticks. That sounds like it could be our point. What was this about a cave? Maybe that's where they have the power supply and the radios," Woody asked.

Still gazing at the pass with his binoculars, Mark reflected, "You know, caves are almost a natural housing project for folks around here. Especially Pathan's. They've lived in caves for hundreds of years. Even this far north of J-bad, I expect there are caves all over the place. I'd bet the Taliban are using a cave for an operations center, that's what this commo place is. Makes sense."

"Yeah, could be. But there's sure not much going on right here. I guess I'd better check in with Maddog." Woody got up and headed for the horses to find the radio.

As Woody made his way down the ridge, Mark asked Dave, "So, what else did our guide say? Anything useful?"

"Well, sorta. He did say there was a lot of activity on the far side of the ridge this morning. He said there were many dust plumes headed north," Dave replied.

"It sounds like that's where the activity is. Does he know of any better place to observe? Maybe a place where we might be able to see over that ridge?" Mark asked.

Sitting up, Dave shrugged his shoulders and said, "I dunno, I'll ask him."

Turning off the radio, Woody stuffed it back into his backpack, leaving the stubby antenna sticking out. He walked uphill towards the ridge, passing Dave on his way back down. He plopped down next to Mark and gazed out over the valley to the southern side of the Salang Pass, a blue haze coloring the air.

Without looking at Mark he said, "Well, I talked with the Man. I told him that all was quiet on the western front. He told me that Rivet Joint still has a lot of traffic coming from this area and they are painting truck traffic as well. He wants us to check it out. Got any ideas?"

"Yeah, I guess. Our guide said they saw dust plumes on the other side of the far ridge this morning. Dave is asking him, right now, where we might be able to get a better look. I'm betting we'll probably have to move north. We might even have to go across the valley to the other side. We'll be out by ourselves, will your Maddog guy give us air if we need it?"

"I'll make a point of it next time I talk with him, before we go over there!" Woody agreed.

Andarab Bridge, Highway A76, Afghanistan

Youseff paced furiously across the rough pavement, talking to himself, "They are late. Doesn't Saleh know how important this is? Did he not listen to me?" Two hours he'd been waiting north of the bridge, waiting for a convoy of al-Qaeda fighters to escort to Kunduz. "Doesn't the fool realize that Taloqan has fallen? Does he not listen? I will have his head."

Turning to Ali Najad he said, "Tell me again Ali. Tell me about Taloqan. What is it you saw before the bombs fell?" Youseff had stopped next to the Land Cruiser with his driver.

"Mudier, I was in the village and did not see the first attack. When the first bomb fell, I ran outside. I saw the plume of smoke and dust. Some Taliban near me pointed out a large gathering of men and horses on the ridge. They were northeast of town several miles," Najad replied.

Leaning against the windowsill, Youseff urged him, "Go on. Go on. Tell me every detail. I may see something that you have missed. What were they doing?"

"I had glasses with me and I could see many Tribal soldiers around their horses. There was also a smaller group closer to the village. Some of them were sitting around what may have been equipment. I do not know what equipment it was, but it was not a weapon."

"Yes, but what were they doing? What did they look like? Were any of them different?" Youseff pressed impatiently.

Casting a furtive glance at Youseff, Najad continued nervously, "They were just looking at the village. I could not see them doing anything. They were just looking. There were a few that were dressed differently. Several of them were sitting and they were wearing light colored clothes, not like the Tribals at all." Anxiously he wiped his hands on his pants.

Nodding, Youseff half turned out of the window. "I see. Those must have been the American spies. They were dressed in light colored clothes. That must be their uniforms. What were they doing sitting?" Youseff said softly, almost to himself.

Najad didn't answer. He thought it was a dangerous thing to talk with his master, especially right now. Youseff often expressed his anger violently and Najad thought it best to avoid talking with him as much as possible. In an attempt to change the subject, he started scanning the road in the distance, maybe the convoy would show up soon.

Hearing a truck downshifting, Najad pointed south. "I hear trucks coming up the road."

Brought out of his reverie, Youseff followed Najad's outstretched arm, seeing, first, one and then suddenly a dozen trucks rounded the corner. He quickly strode out into the road to meet them. Changing his mind, he half ran back to the Toyota. Jumping in the passenger door, he shouted at Najad, "It is time, we must go."

Several hours later, they were jostling through the town of Baghlan. Youseff stared absently out the dirty window of the truck thinking how he might capture these American spies. Najad saw him shake his head deep in thought; Youseff did not notice the deserted streets much less his driver's glance.

His thoughts were focused on how he might capture Americans. *If they stayed close to Tribal horsemen, it would be hard to get close to them. I must find a way to separate them from the main body. If they were split up, as they were for the attack on Taloqan, we could overwhelm a small group of Americans easily. All he needed was one or two, alive. It would be better if the rest were dead.*

The Toyota lurched into a deep pothole, bouncing Youseff's head against the side window. Snapping to the left, he looked at Najad angrily. Najad, looked quickly at him once and then back to the road, an anguished look on his face. Youseff continued to glare at him; Najad quickly looked again, "I am sorry Mudier. This road is not in good shape. I am trying to avoid holes in the road."

Without comment, Youseff slowly looked out the front of the car, lost with his dilemma again. How to split them up? *First we must know where they are, they must have a target.* With a target, they will be seen. They seem to like watching from high ground, they must need to be within sight of their targets. When the Tribals attack, they will probably be alone, or with a small guard. That is the time we shall attack. The Tribals will be consumed with blood lust and will not see the danger their Americans will be in. *Then, I will capture the spies and bring them to the Muqtar.*

But what to use for a target? What would they be interested in after sacking the town of Taloqan? Bouncing through another pothole he looked at Najad through the corner of his eye. Something caught his attention, looking out the rear window. Following him were thirteen trucks with over 500 al-Qaeda fighters. With a satisfied gleam in his eye, he twisted back to the front. The target, of course, it would be these men trying to retake Taloqan. The Americans could not avoid a fight like that. *If I just attack from the front, they will not leave town and the comfort of the Tribal horsemen.* But the horsemen will not likely leave the town quickly, especially if they think the American bombs will save them. What would draw the Americans out of the town?

Struggling with that thought, he vaguely became aware of the ringing of his cell phone. He was surprised that there was coverage this far north. Picking it up he answered, "Hello, hello."

"Youseff, I have called to see whether you have sent men to Kunduz? It has been a long time since I gave you my orders, have you disobeyed them? Have you not sent our fighters? Kunduz and Mazar-e Sharif are very important. We must keep the infidel out of those northern plains areas. Tell me now, what have you done?" bin Laden asked angrily over the phone.

"Muqtar, I have sent 500 fighters to Kunduz. They are on the way and will be there by nightfall. More will go as we get trucks," Youseff replied.

"Send as many as you can, quickly. We must re-take Taloqan and drive a wedge through the mountains and into the heart of the Northern Alliance. They must be bottled up in their hills. Anything else is failure and I do not tolerate failure. Do you understand me?"

"Yes, Muqtar. Several thousand more will be there tomorrow. We will succeed. We will drive the infidels, crying before us, into the mountains," Youseff said with enthusiasm and fear. He did not know anyone who had survived bin Laden's anger.

"I know you will not fail. These are not men, worry only about success. Only Allah will judge," bin Laden assured him.

"Yes, Muqtar. It will be so," Youseff replied. "I will see to it."

"No, I will see to it," barked bin Laden.

A long silent pause sued while bin Laden struggled to control his emotions. Suddenly he said flatly, "There is another thing. We must capture these American spies. There are a few on their way to visit you; I have made sure it is so. You will capture them and bring them to me. I need only a few of them, any others you may kill."

"Yes, Muqtar. I am making plans now to capture them. I will bring them to you as soon as I…" Youseff tried to reply; before he could finish, the line went dead as bin Laden severed the connection.

Disturbed by bin Laden's call, Youseff struggled to resume his train of thought. Twisting around, he pulled a ragged map out of a stack of papers on the back seat. Looking at the map, he traced the road into Taloqan from Kunduz with his finger. Talking aloud to himself, he said, "It is obvious they like to look over their targets from above. There is a high ridge northwest of Taloqan; it looks down on the next village. This would be a perfect place for them; it is large and very rugged. A small group would not have enough men to see the other side. A nice big target would bring them out of their nest. Perhaps if we showed them we were coming to attack Taloqan from the south and west?"

Beginning to enjoy his deception, he thought, *If they think we had moved from the ridge while bringing in a strong force from the south, they would climb the ridge to be able to see our movement. If we made a show of moving off the ridge, they would follow so they could see the valley, and who would attack the defenders of Taloqan. If they saw tanks in the valley, they would come like fish to the bait.* Excited he rubbed his hands. "Yes, they would fall for this trap and then they would meet the spider."

Satisfied, he sat back in his seat; with a smile he closed his eyes. Tomorrow would be a busy day.

Taloqan, Afghanistan

Standing, SFC Gary Wilkerson stuck his foot out, lightly tapping the bottom of SSgt Brandon Ray's boot. Snoring, Ray was flat on his back, his feet crossed at the ankle, his fingers folded together over his stomach and his boonie hat covering his face.

Gary tapped Brandon's foot again. "Hey, wake up man. We need to go see Fahim. He wants to talk."

Stirring slowly, Brandon groggily pulled the boonie hat from his face. "What the hell do you want? Can't you see I'm getting some beauty sleep here? I'm just an operator, not a negotiator."

"Sorry, bud. I hate to be the one to break the news. Since sleep isn't doing much good, maybe you can do a little work. That's what we need to talk to Fahim about, we need to do some good." Gary said, squatting next to Brandon.

Still lying on his back, Brandon stretched. "So, what good can we do? It was my impression that Fahim didn't want to do a thing for a long while. Heck, they're still celebrating their first big victory in years. I say let 'em have their fun."

"Yeah, it's a real party. But the thing is, we can't stay in this town. Remember, we're in the middle of bad guy land. These buildings aren't much protection and the longer we stay here, the closer the Taliban are to attacking us," Gary said.

"You gotta be shitting me! We just beat those turkeys. We gotta stick with Fahim, which means we can't go far. So, where do you want to go anyways?" Brandon asked, looking at Gary curiously.

Gary absently fiddled with his watch. "Well, personally I'd rather be out in the open. Even if you can be seen a long ways off, at least you can see just as far. More time, more safety. But that's just me."

Putting his arms under his head, Brandon stretched again. "Me, I prefer a nice roof. Heat would be good too. Every now and again a shower would be better."

"Maybe so. But that's just comfort shit; I'm talking about the mission and survival. We need to have the high ground. We've got to have someone out to see what's going on. These guys aren't doing shit and we're not practicing good field craft, stuff like that gets you killed. So, you and I need to go talk to Fahim about setting up Ops around these hills. So, I invite you to get your ass up and come with me."

Sitting up, Brandon put the boonie hat on his head. "I suppose you're not going to leave me alone until I go with you, huh?"

"Hell no. There'll be plenty of time for sleeping later. We can fuck-off when it's over."

"Okay, okay. I'm coming. Keep your pants on." Getting to his feet, Brandon pulled down his utility shirt and followed him out of the room.

Together, Gary and Brandon walked across the bare dirt of the town plaza, passing Tribal soldiers and townspeople still talking and gesturing excitedly. The remains of the building used by the Taliban as their headquarters lay smoking on one side of the square as a mute reminder of the sudden change in events. It would be awhile before life returned to its daily grind.

"Do you think he'll talk to you? I remember you saying that Dave had to be the translator," Brandon asked.

"We'll see. But Dave said Fahim understood Russian anyway. So I'll give it a shot."

They stopped at a large mud walled building, pocked with shell holes. At the door were two of Fahim's personal bodyguards. Silently, the Americans nodded at them and the guards dropped the muzzles of their weapons. Gary stepped inside first, Brandon followed, only to bump into Gary in the dim light of the room.

Their eyes adjusting rapidly to the gloomy light, they continued toward the back where they found Fahim surrounded by a large number of very happy, very loud and boisterous men. The entire group was celebrating the nearly bloodless victory over the Taliban that morning. Approaching the ecstatic throng of men crowded around their leader, they were quickly pushed to the inside of the cheering group.

Gary leaned down to Fahim's ear; he spoke loudly in Russian, trying to be heard over all the noise. "General Fahim, we would like to talk to you about taking the high ground around the town."

Fahim looked back at them with a smile on his face, for a moment he didn't say anything, "A few moments. I will be a few moments. Meet me in that room over there," he said, gesturing to a dark doorway off to the side.

Gary tapped Brandon's arm and purposely threaded his way through the crowd towards the side room.

Waiting for several minutes, Brandon had just begun looking out of the single window in the room when Fahim and three of his sub-commanders brushed inside. Feeling as if he had nothing to add, he decided to join Gary and the small group around Fahim. He stopped short, standing politely to the side.

"General, I would like to congratulate you and your men on your stunning victory in taking Taloqan. Your men made short work of the Taliban defending the town. They performed excellently. Very well done," Gary began.

Fahim smiled a sparkle in his eye, "Thank you, Sergeant Wilkerson You and I both know this victory is not all mine. You and the American Air Force had a very great deal to do with it. For this we are grateful. I know I was skeptical at first, but these airstrikes are very powerful. But what has happened to Captain Mark and Captain Woody, they are not here with you?"

"Thank you, sir. We are happy to do whatever we can to make your fight here a success. The Captains were called away to the southern side of your area. That is one of the reasons I came to speak to you."

Before Gary could go on, Fahim interrupted him, holding his hand up. "Is your Captain Mark off to worry over the Salang Pass again? I expect he will find nothing of importance; he will miss a great party. No matter, my men have achieved a great victory, the first of this size in many years. I will not let Captains

Mark's fretting over that pass dampen their spirits."

"Uhh, yes, sir. Captain Mark did go to the Salang Pass area. One of the chief Air Force controllers directed them to go there at once. Apparently there is a lot of activity in that area and they cannot get anyone to eyeball what's going on," Gary explained.

"I see, will they be back soon? Do you know this?" Fahim said, speaking in halting Arabic.

Brandon shifted from one foot to another; bored he listened politely, not understanding a word they said. His thoughts drifted to Germany. He and Woody Campbell were stationed there. They had been drafted for this mission in a hurry. He missed his family and thought about their skiing vacation in Bavaria scheduled over Thanksgiving.

Trying to cover for the missing officers, Gary continued, "Sir, I do not know exactly when they will be coming back. I expect they will be back in a day or two at the most. I can contact them by radio if you wish."

"I see. No, do not worry them, let them waste their time in the pass. I shall consolidate our hold on Taloqan," Fahim replied with a toothy smile.

"Yes, sir. If you please, that is just the thing I would like to talk to you about," Gary began, happy to change the subject.

Laughing, Fahim slapped Gary on the back. "What is your ambition now? Do you want to move down the valley as well? Perhaps take Kunduz itself?"

Squaring his shoulders, Gary said, "Sir, I am not sure if it is time to move on Kunduz, it might be a good idea to pursue the Taliban so they cannot regroup. My immediate concern is with security in our present positions. I only suggest that we need to gain the high ground around Taloqan. We need to have outposts observing what the Taliban are doing, before they can surprise us."

"But we know where the Taliban lines are, we will get warnings before the Taliban move. Is this what you are worried about?" Fahim asked. "Do not fret, I know where the Taliban are."

"It is our custom, sir. It is good to do reconnaissance to find the Taliban lines. But what I believe is important here is that we have observation posts placed on the high ground. That ridgeline to the northwest is over six thousand feet and any Taliban on it can see just about anything that we are doing here in town. If they put artillery on the ridge they could shoot at us here and we could do very little about it," Gary explained.

"Could you not call in your Air Force to take care of them?" Fahim asked. "Like you did before we attacked this town."

Glancing at Brandon, daydreaming at the edge of the circle, Gary continued,

"Perhaps, but it is much harder to look up rather than down. It would be safer to have outposts there."

"Perhaps that is true. But it is already not an option. We did not take that ridge during the battle for Taloqan and there are still Taliban there. My men report many of the Taliban that were not caught or killed in Taloqan fled to that mountain. So, you see, they already have the high ground. What you are suggesting is that we fight to remove them." Shaking his head Fahim, lectured Gary like a benevolent father, "My men need rest before we fight the Taliban on that ridge. There will be a time when it is important. But not now."

Disappointed, Gary could see that this conversation was going nowhere. "I see. I didn't know they were still on the ridge. I thought the Taliban had fled down the valley towards Kunduz."

Nodding his head and clucking, Fahim spoke in a softer voice, "So, you see, do not worry. All in good time, we will move them off the ridge. But tonight, tonight, we will have a celebration. Tonight we will have goat and chicken, you will be my guest, I look forward to seeing you at dinner." With a slight wave, he left the room with his commanders in close trail.

"So, what did he say?" Brandon asked Gary, still standing silently where he had been.

"Yeah, he said that the Taliban were still on that ridge. And that he wasn't prepared to move and take the high ground. He said that it is not time yet to do anything," Gary replied.

"Yeah, I get it. Inshallah. God willing. I guess God hasn't given them a sign. What does God tell them to do?" Brandon asked.

"Have a party. We're invited. It's a special one, goat tonight, and chicken," Gary said as he started out of the room.

Brandon followed him out of the room. "Shit, we're knee deep in a war and he thinks it's time to celebrate. With goat! So, what do we do?"

"We do what we can. We gotta leave an out. If Fahim isn't going to worry about security, then we've got to keep a hip pocket option for ourselves. You'd better think of what you might have to do if we had to run. If these guys are partying, they won't be able to do much defending if the Taliban attack."

"Do you really think the Taliban could launch an attack? Is there anyway they could rally after getting beat like they did earlier today?" Brandon asked.

"Well, maybe I'm paranoid. It's plain that if the Taliban were any kind of real soldier, they would mount an attack very soon. You've got to re-attack and with your opponent partying, there would be no better time. I just feel like we're sticking our heads in a noose here and we don't have many options to run."

Uncertain, Brandon asked, "Yeah, I guess you're right. I've got to admit that since we landed the other day, I've felt a little naked. I'm used to having a bunch of armor around to keep watch. We're really out on the edge here, aren't we?"

"I'm not worried about being alone, this is the way we operate all the time. It's being with all these guys, that's the problem. The number one thing to remember is that to survive, you have to leave yourself a way out." Pausing, Gary stopped short and looked into Brandon's eyes. "And, you've got to pay attention to what the fuck is going on around you, all the time."

Listening to Gary, Brandon stopped suddenly, noticing several different smells. The tinge of burned flesh meshed with burning wood, diesel and cordite from the bombs, all overwhelmed by the odor of urine and cow dung. When Gary stopped talking, Brandon looked at the ridge rising from the valley floor less than a mile away. "Yeah, I guess I'd better get some pre-plans on that ridge. Just in case."

CHAPTER 15

37,000' over Safed Mountain Range, Pakistan

Captain Kelly Stromberg sat at the Radio Monitoring console, listening to an HF transmission emanating from the Afghani Mountains north of Kabul; she closed her eyes as she concentrated on the Arabic conversation, where she realized someone was trying to get her attention. She turned her head to the right where there was a man leaning over her shoulder, pulling her headset down she leaned towards him. The Collection Supervisor aboard the RC-135 Rivet Joint was desperately trying to whisper in her ear. Having trouble hearing him she said, "What? What did you say?"

"I said that Maddog called, he's got a priority mission and has directed us to look at this new area, and the valley just west of it." Stabbing a 1:500 map with his finger, the supervisor pointed to the Salang Pass area of Afghanistan. "He wants us to check for traffic here."

"Okay, I can do that easy. I'm already working on tasking; I'll be done in awhile. What's the time frame on this request?" Captain Stromberg asked.

"It's not a request, it's an immediate, or should I say a directive," the supervisor gushed nervously.

"Okay, okay, who is this guy and how can he re-task us airborne?" Kelly asked.

Slightly flustered, the supervisor hadn't quite understood the question. He had never received a call direct from the JFACC before and was in a rush to expedite the order. Replying to Kelly's question derisively he said, "He's the JFACC rep airborne. Who do you think runs the show from the AWACs right now? If he wants us to hop, I figure we'd better hop."

"Okay, so we've established that he can re-task us. So now the question is just what does he want us to look for? I can't scan everything you know," Kelly said.

Caught short, the supervisor stuttered, "Well, uhh, he didn't really say. Maybe we should look at the standard voice frequency ranges. Say, VHF FM and AM, UHF and HF."

Taking the map, Kelly looked at the target area terrain. With her finger she traced the ridge southwest of the pass, looking up she said, "Sure, I can do this. But you'll have to get the MC together with the pilot to extend the orbit to the west. Oh, say about 100 miles. I need baseline to locate any transmissions I find there. Plus these mountains are over 15,000 feet tall. I'll need some look angle to see in those valleys, especially the one to the west. They're all in shadow right now."

She twisted back to her console and wrote down the coordinates of both valleys on the pad in front of her. She pushed the map back towards the supervisor, still fretting at her shoulder. In response to his worried look, she just smiled wanly.

As he turned to walk away she called to his back, "Don't forget to extend the orbit west. If you don't I can't pin point anything! Oh, and I might need another linguist, I only speak Arabic."

Settling back in her seat, Kelly noticed the Search Radar operator in the console across from hers trying to catch her eye. Rolling his eyes he said, "Man, what's that all about? Was he hitting on you or something?"

"No, he's just new to the business, and probably a bit nervous I guess. We just got some new tasking, high priority stuff. I need to look for voice traffic in a certain place." In an attempt to end the conversation, she smiled, raised her eyebrows slightly and hunched over her display. Concentrating on her work, she rolled her trackball over the new coordinates and she tapped a key to slew the system onto the new location. Typing in the frequency ranges, she wanted she adjusted the headset over her ears again and settled down to listen to the scanner hop through the pre-set frequencies.

Nothing but static, Kelly lost track of time when she noticed a sharp pain in her shoulder. Reaching back, she massaged the muscle in her neck slowly. She hadn't heard a thing since she started and was beginning to wonder if the CS had told the pilot to extend the orbit. She'd been flying in this airplane so long that she automatically tuned out all but the big abrupt movements of the airplane. Thinking about it, she didn't remember noticing any turns. Working up the resolve to ask again about that extension, she began looking around the cabin of the airplane for the CS, when she noticed the Vu needle on her console peg to the right. Stunned, she said aloud, "Wow, that's a hell of a spike."

She focused intently on her display. Usually the scan rate was so fast that the needle only bounced. She thumbed the record button for all frequencies and called the supervisor on the intercom. "Hey, Danny. We've hit pay dirt. I've got lots of strong signal traffic on FM and HF. You oughta come over here, and bring another linguist will ya, there's too much for me to listen to."

"Watcha got?" Danny, the Collection Supervisor asked, leaning awkwardly over Kelly's shoulder. All large Air Force airplanes involved in surveillance or control were configured with operator consoles in groups spread along the inside of the fuselage. Displays and communications are arranged for the operator's convenience, but moving around inside the cabin was like being in a low crowded tube.

"Plug in! I've got heavy traffic on FM and HF. I'm not sure why we haven't picked up the HF traffic before. But the FM was hidden by the ridgeline. It looks like there are 10-15 active FM freqs and probably double that on HF," Kelly replied, intent on her screen, she scrolled the trackball over the yellow diamond on her display.

"Have you got a location for me yet? Do you know where these transmissions are coming from?" Danny asked excitedly.

"I'm just resolving that now. The system is working through the triangulation. I told you we needed a longer baseline; it give us more lines-of-position to fix the transmitter," Kelly replied.

As she spoke, the yellow diamond on her screen, representing the fix began oscillating left and right. She had put her cursors over the last stable fix and then tried to follow the swings of the diamond. As the swings became wilder, she put the cursors back near the spot where the diamond had been most stable. Taking her hand off the trackball she said, "See the way the diamond is swinging? It looks like we're losing signal strength. I'd bet anything it's the narrow valley and ridge line."

Worried, Danny asked her, "Did you get a good coordinate for the transmitter? With all that traffic I'd bet it was a headquarters or something."

The yellow diamond disappeared altogether, Kelly looked up. "No, I didn't get a good fix before it disappeared. I only got an approximate coordinate. We might be able to refine it when we head back to the east, but I doubt it. I'm thinking to do any better we'd have to get a much better look angle to see into that valley. That valley is so narrow, we've simply got to get closer."

"Well, I'll tell Maddog about what we found. I know he'll be interested in the traffic spike. Did you catch what they were saying?"

"No, I did hear a few snatches of Arabic, some Farsi, but most of it was a dialect that I didn't recognize. I only hear a bit on each frequency as the scanner hops through it, I was looking for bandwidth not specific transmissions. But I did record everything, though. Do you want me to datalink it to the exploitation folks?" Kelly asked as she looked up at the CS.

"Yeah, that's a good idea. Let me take the approximate coordinate as well. At least it's a start," Danny answered. "Hey, did you do any of the surveillance before the war started?"

"Yeah, I was here, I did the Gulf War as well. When we first got here, we were originally looking at Tora Bora, Kabul and Kandahar. I think there was a camp northeast of Kandahar as well. Why?" Kelly said, twisting in her seat to see Danny better, she took off her headset.

"Nothing, I was just wondering how this spike compared to the traffic at Kandahar and Kabul before the war?"

"Well, I didn't get to listen very long, with the signal cutoff and all. But I'd say there was every bit as much traffic as say Kabul or Tora Bora." She paused trying to remember traffic from a few months ago. "Yeah, I'd stick by that, same traffic level as Kabul and TB. Do you think that this is a C2 facility?"

"Could be, it's what I was thinking anyway. Are you sure these were bad guys?"

"No, I can't be sure of that. Everyone here speaks the same language; it'll take a bigger decoder ring than I have to sort that out. All I stick by is the traffic spike, I find 'em and the exploitation folks figure out what they were saying," Kelly said, turning back to her console, she was anxious to restart her first tasking.

"Thanks, good job by the way." Danny patted her shoulder in congratulations.

Sitting down at his own console, Danny held his headset to one ear, "Maddog, Racer 21, uniform how copy?"

"Racer 21, Maddog copies, go ahead, I'm showing in the green," BC replied immediately.

"Maddog, Racer also shows green. We have some info for you on your tasking."

BC pulled his note pad close and lifted his pencil out of his left sleeve pocket, "Racer, Maddog is ready to copy. Go ahead."

"Roger Maddog. The terrain is very rugged in the target area. This prevented a long look, but we were able to detect a large spike in traffic. Mostly FM and HF in that area. We were able to get a rough coordinate for you," Danny said slowly.

"Maddog copies. Were you able to listen in to any of the traffic?"

"No, too much traffic and not enough speakers on board. We datalinked it to the exploitation folks, if you need transcripts they should be able to provide," Danny answered.

"Copy, anything else to add?" BC asked.

"Roger, we think the traffic spike was consistent with a possible C2 site, similar to that observed in Kabul and Tora Bora. To get a better coordinate or a longer look at this area we need to move our orbit closer. Do you want us to do that?"

"Copy, possible C2 site. And negative on moving orbit. You guys are already partly in Afghanistan right now. I can't afford having you get any closer," BC replied.

"Racer copies. Is there anything else you would like us to do?" Danny asked imploringly.

"Racer, Maddog would like you to continue observing site and collect any Intel you can. If something changes then call me back ASAP."

"Racer copies, we'll probably be able to collect more of the voice. If something changes, I'll call you. Out." Danny answered.

The AWAC's Mission Commander sitting next to BC was listening in on the conversation, "Well, what do you think? Think we ought send some iron that way?"

"No, I'm not to sure about that. I'm not convinced that these aren't our paid good guys. You know how things are on the battlefield, mass confusion everywhere. I wouldn't be surprised if it wasn't one of Fahim's boys or maybe even Dostum jockeying for position and land for after the war. I just don't know enough to drop any bombs on their heads."

"So, what are you going to do? It'll be tomorrow before we can get our Predators up that way. The last I heard they haven't finished setting up in Pakistan yet. Doesn't the CIA have a Predator in Golbahar, maybe you can use that?" the Mission Commander said.

"The U2s and the overhead stuff can't quite get the resolution I need here. Plus, none of that will tell me who these guys are. As things develop here, they get more complicated. It's not so easy to tell friend from foe and I just can't afford a mistake. No, I need eyes on target more than anything else."

The AWAC's Mission Commander leaned forward, "So, do you want to send a jet in there for a look see?"

"No, they'd move too fast. I've already got an ALO going in on the ground to look at the Salang Pass. He should be reporting in anytime now, we'll see what he has to say," BC said as he adjusted his seat to lean way back. "Right now, though, I need some good coffee."

East side of the Salang Pass, Afghanistan

The handset speaker of the PRC-117 radio crackled, "Say again? You did not observe any vehicle traffic through the pass, correct?" BC asked Woody.

"No sir, no activity. We did get a report from a *Muj* irregular that there had been a lot of activity earlier in the day. In particular, on the far side of the west ridge of the pass," Woody said, holding the handset to his ear.

"Copy. Understand the valley west of the Pass. Have any of the locals observed evidence of commo activity? We've had reports of spikes in HF and FM that valley," BC asked.

"Sir, one of them described to us something that could have been an antenna near the top of that valley. But, without a better observation I don't feel that it's a definitive report," Woody said, releasing the transmit switch.

"Understand. I've got an approximate coordinate, are you ready to copy?"

Woody pulled a notepad out of his pocket and balanced it on his knee, "Yes, sir. Ready to copy."

"Hey Mark. You wouldn't believe what this guy wants us to do now," Woody said as he walked back to where Mark was still lying on his stomach watching the pass.

"Don't tell me, let me guess. He wants us to come over for a steak dinner with baked potatoes, right?" Mark joked.

"Yeah, and he wants us to bring some local wine!" Woody shot back. "He wants us to go have a look see at this coordinate. He thinks there might be a C2 operation going on at this commo site. They recorded a big spike in radio traffic from there and he wants us to take a close look. What do you think?"

"Well, I'd sure love to go for a walk around the mountains of Afghanistan, it's not like the natives hate us, or, anything. It's really pretty around here, and you know we just don't have anything else to do right now. Sure, let's do it," Mark said with a laugh. "We've got to wait for Dave, he went down to the airfield to scrounge from his buddy's down there."

Sitting down heavily, Woody sighed. "You're the tourist, I was just looking forward to chilling out for awhile. This running around in the bush tires you out. When is Dave due back?"

"Oh, I wouldn't expect him until late this evening. It's a couple of miles down the valley even on horseback. Hey, did you ask Maddog if we get priority on air if we go over there?" Mark asked.

"Yeah, I asked him. It sounded a bit more like a maybe to me. Do you think we can really do this? Will it be too dangerous to go over there by ourselves?" Woody asked nervously.

Mark replied flippantly, "Of course, I think it's doable. This is the stuff I do all the time, you're just used to riding around in an airplane. This is where the real war is. Shoot, we even have a guide to help us out. What do you think Luke? Does a little trip over to the far side sound like fun to you?"

Luke was cleaning his weapons, he looked up with a toothy grin, "You bet! I've been dying to try out my new Barret and this sounds like a perfect expedition to me. Lots better than just sitting around staring at a road. When do we go?"

"Not until Dave gets back. Just relax for awhile." Looking at Woody, Mark smiled and waved his arm towards Luke. "See? Piece of cake."

"Okay, okay. This sneaky peaky stuff just isn't my bag," Woody replied, unconvinced.

"No worries. You just keep the air on call. We'll find this place and drop something big on it."

Golbahar Airfield, Afghanistan

His arms deep inside the guts of the airplane, John fiddled inside the engine compartment at the rear of the Predator. Half to himself he said, "Can't quite get to this damn fuel control. The engine oughta be running rock steady, but it's not. I'd bet trash in the controller is causing it to surge. I'm afraid some of the fuel we put in it wasn't strained well enough."

Dave sat cross-legged on the ground, watching him work on the UAV. "Yeah, it's not easy to keep anything clean here in the mountains is it?"

"No, primitive doesn't quite explain this place. Plus my helpers don't have a clue about what I need, I'm not sure if they even know what a wrench is for. To make matters worse is that we're so thin. It's only Craig and me here; everyone else is back at the tactical HQ. There's just not enough folks out in the field. But enough of me, how you been doin'?" John asked, wiping his forehead with his sleeve.

"Yeah, we're fine. Dirty, but fine. It took forever, but we finally got Fahim to move. We got the Air Force to drop on some key Taliban positions and then Fahim took the town. I think we'll make some real progress. We got thrown a wrench when my Army and Air Force compatriots got a high priority tasking to come and look at the pass. It seems nobody else can get any visual Intel on the area," Dave said, idly peeling the leaves off of a weed stalk.

"I guess you mean me, huh? We did some good work the other night and pounded a Taliban Op Center. Besides, I'm trying to rush this thing, but if I do it wrong and we lose it, I'll be out of a job. I gotta be careful, this is hard enough for an old fat man like me and I don't want to be running around the boonies like you," John said with a dirty grin.

Embarrassed, Dave tried to mollify his friend, "Heck, I didn't mean anything on you. But now that you mention it, I guess that your baby here is the only thing that could get eyes on target."

"Forget it. No big deal. Have you gotten any Intel briefs for awhile?" John asked, wiping his hands on a rag.

"No, I've been living with Fahim and eating barely cooked chicken and rice for weeks. What have you heard?" Dave asked.

"Since Craig got datalink set up we've been able to tap into the Sippr Net. We've been reading the summaries and checking out what's going on. You know, stuff like status of investigations on the hi-jackers and searches for AQ around the world."

Dave perked up. "Yeah, got anything I can read?"

"No, Craig keeps it all on the computer, that way he doesn't have to worry about security, or burning the secrets. Sorry. But I'll tell you about one of the reports I read this morning. It seems that the collection agency's are picking up a lot of chatter from folks all over the world. Some of that chatter is coming from here, in country. They think that there is a C2 node here that is coordinating the next attack in the US, possibly a few more around the world. It seems that they think bin Laden himself may even be there," John said, tilting his head significantly.

Dave whispered under his breath, "No shit. Have they narrowed down a location?"

"Not in the analysis I was reading. But they felt pretty strong about its existence and his use of it."

Dave threw away the stalk he had been playing with, "Do you think it might have something to do with this Salang Pass deal. I mean no one really knew anything about this pass until recently. And all of a sudden there is all this traffic."

"Don't know, man. Could be. I'll tell you though if you found it, it could be a treasure trove of Intel and it couldn't look bad for you either," John said. "All kinds of good stuff, probably names of AQ all over the world. Maybe even the man himself."

"Yeah, could be," Dave said, deep in thought. Suddenly he looked at his watch. "Damn, hey John I almost forgot—do you mind if I take some of your food? We sure could use a break from MREs or fried goat."

"Sure, go ahead, take my only New York Strip for tonight's grill. Seriously, I've got some stuff in the back of the truck. It ain't much, but we get regular supply runs from the tactical HQ. So go ahead, take what you need."

Distracted, Dave got up. "Thanks a lot, man. And thanks for that info tidbit. I gotta go. Good luck."

"No big deal, man. Sorry I couldn't just shoot the shit with you, but I've got to get this UAV running again. I'm just praying it doesn't need an engine change," John said.

With a wave, Dave headed for the back of John's truck.

Kunduz, Afghanistan

Youseff entered the fortress like Mosque at the center of town; he had come to meet the Taliban leader of Kunduz. Expectantly, he walked into the darkened main hall, seeing a light shining through one of the doors near the back. Stepping inside he found a group of men sitting on the floor chatting. They were gathered around one man, Youseff assumed that was the local Mullah. When they all looked at him, he addressed the religious leader, "Mullah Bazanni, I am Ahmed Youseff. I have come to help you fight Fahim of the Northern Alliance. I have heard that Taloqan has fallen to their attack. I bring many fighters and more are coming tomorrow."

"Ah, yes. You are one of Muqtar bin Laden's men. I have heard of you." Standing up the Mullah moved closer, he gripped Youseff by the shoulders and held him close. "It is good to have you here with your men. I know they are very good fighters, it is very good to have them."

"I have heard this of Taloqan also. A few men that were in Taloqan have come back and told me of this. I'm sure it is true, but it is no matter. These things happen with the Northern Alliance. This is how we fight them. We win. They win. We win again. Eventually we push them back further into the mountains. It has been the way of our war with these Tajik interlopers for many years," Bazanni went on.

Looking for a chance to speak, it quickly became obvious to Youseff that the Mullah was out of touch with events; perhaps he did not know what had happened in the world in the last few months. When Bazanni paused for breath he interjected, "Mullah, perhaps this was the way of your wars in the past. But now this is different, this time the Americans are helping Fahim. This time they are using their bombs to help defeat you."

"I have heard of the attacks in Kabul and even in Kandahar. I remember when we all fought the Russians. When they left, we fought each other. If the Americans come here then we will fight them too. They will pass and we will endure. It is just a matter of time. But come, I do not wish to speak of philosophy, perhaps you would join me and have some *chai*?" Waving his hand towards his visitor, Bazanni called to his servant to bring out tea for everyone.

Sipping his tea, Youseff had not expected this reception. Bazanni was obviously living in a fantasy world, comfortable here he obviously didn't want to deal with the outside world. Distracted and determinedly out of touch, it would be difficult to convince Bazanni to fight the Tribes that had taken Taloqan. Barely listening to the Mullah drone on, Youseff tried to come up with a way to motivate him to fight the Northern Alliance. Perhaps, he thought, it would be best if he relieved Bazanni of the bother of thinking about it. Perhaps, he might be able to use the Mullah's men to join him in the attack. "If the Mullah wishes, I will take my fighters to Taloqan and retake the village. I would report back to you when the job is complete."

Sitting quietly, it was not apparent at first whether Bazanni had heard Youseff's offer. For several minutes, Bazanni remained as he had been, rocking slowly back and forth, stopping occasionally to take a puff from the pipe on the floor next to him. Youseff was about to repeat his offer, when Bazanni finally spoke, "If you wish to fight, then you are welcome to do so. You may report to me as you wish. I am busy here with my people, otherwise I would join you."

"Shukran, Mullah Bazanni. Then with your permission I will depart." Youseff bowed his head slightly in deference as he stood up. "Mullah, before I leave, I will need to take several tanks from around the town, they are required for the assault on the village."

Mullah Bazanni sat as before, without looking up he waved towards the door and said, "Inshallah, take what you need and may god protect you."

Youseff left Bazanni, walking out the door into the sunlight; he paused to smell the fresh air. Relieved to be in the land of the living again he went looking for his driver.

Youseff began talking even before he reached the truck. "Najad, before we send the trucks back, we need to move our men closer to Taloqan. Have the sawag drive them through Khanabad to Bangi. There we will gather for the attack tomorrow on Taloqan."

"Go, yourself, and when you get there have word sent all around the mountain, to all the fighters northwest of Taloqan to join you in the village. It is urgent, they must do this tonight and have them make as much noise as they can."

"Yes, Mudier. I will do this immediately. Where shall I find you after I have done this?" Najad asked.

"I will come to Bangi. I will meet you there; first, I must gather several tanks from the defenses here at Kunduz. We must have tanks for this assault tomorrow."

Reaching for the ignition key, Najad paused. "That is good, I will look for you in Bangi. The Mullah's tanks were at the airport south of town when I was here last. Perhaps you will find them there."

"Then that is where I will go. I will take the Land Cruiser. You take the trucks, move quickly, and get there before nightfall," Youseff ordered.

Najad twisted the key and the engine roared to life. "Mudier, I have asked the locals whether there have been any attacks in this region at night. They did not know of any like those in Kabul. The Northern Alliance Tribal leaders have also made no move outside of Taloqan."

"Shuglak, that is good news." Youseff slapped him on the back, silent for a moment Youseff said, "Go now and once you have reached Bangi get word to those outside of Taloqan. You must send the trucks back to Baghlan, from there they can easily drive to meet Saleh in the dawn." With a small waive Youseff walked towards the Land Cruiser.

Several hours later, an orange dusk lit the darkening sky. Youseff drove slowly into the village of Bangi, the noise of one dilapidated tank following him drowning any thought. He was sure others would follow, but tonight only one was ready to follow him. They had only come 15 miles from Kunduz, yet it had taken over two hours of stops and starts. Youseff stayed with the tank for fear that its drivers might decide to spend the night somewhere other than where he wanted them. Getting the tank into position was important to his plan, it would be the bait proffered to the American rats in the morning.

Seeing his boss arrive, Najad rushed out to meet him, pumping his hand he said enthusiastically, "Mudier, it is good to see you, I have done as you asked. The first wave has arrived and the drivers have gone back with their vehicles to Baghlan. I talked with Saleh; tomorrow he will be able to send 2,000 fighters with their weapons. He has found more trucks and there is much excitement about fighting. The faithful are looking to avenge the fall of Taloqan."

Najad had indeed accomplished a lot, Youseff was pleased, in a friendly voice he asked, "Najad, you are doing very well. It is time you do something besides drive. You need to be something other than a sawag. Have the men that fled to the slopes west of Taloqan come to meet us here in the village as I asked?"

Brimming with pride, Najad answered, "Yes, Mudier. All of the Taliban remaining outside of the town have come into the village. At first, they were very confused; it has been awhile since they have lost any battles. They didn't know what to do and were happy to get orders to Bangi. As you directed, they also made a lot of noise leaving the mountain. Indeed, now they are very happy to be near the cook fires of Bangi."

Youseff, beamed, clapping Najad around the shoulder he confided, "Good, excellent work. Then I have one more task for you tonight. Pick three hundred of the bravest fighters that we brought with us. Have them wait quietly for me outside of town to the north. When it is dark, I will lead them back to that mountain you made so much noise leaving today."

Worried that he had misunderstood his orders, Najad frowned. "I will do as you ask. But why will you lead men back to the mountain after I brought them off of it?"

Gripping his shoulder tightly, Youseff spoke quietly in Najad's ear. "Because there are Americans in Taloqan and I plan to capture them. I need fighters I can trust, not those that shaken by losing a battle and it will take both of us. Come walk with me."

Taking Najad's hand in his own, Youseff began walking towards the edge of town. "I will explain the plan to you. Tomorrow you will lead the Taliban here in the village to attack the Taloqan. It is important that you once again make a lot of noise in your preparations for the attack and I want it to begin in late morning. You can use the tank that I brought with me tonight. You will command over 1,000 Taliban fighters from this area and 200 of our best men. Move slowly and follow along the south side of the river. The Northern Alliance will have no choice but to ride out and meet you. With tanks, machine guns and fierce Taliban warriors, the horse riders will have no chance. Naturally, you will defeat them."

Stunned, Najad acknowledged his orders. "It will be as you say, I am very happy that you have shown such faith in me. To be sure, I have not had such an honor before. I shall not fail your trust, but why will you not lead this great battle yourself. Surely, you could do this better than I."

Silently, they reached the edge of town. Taloqan shimmered in the distance, the faint sounds of celebratory gunfire echoed down the valley from the liberated town. In the busy village behind them, the dirt streets were thronged with fighters. Turning to face Najad at close range, Youseff looked into his eyes with fondness. "I have great confidence that you will succeed brilliantly. It is the Muqtar's wish that we capture one, or two, of these Americans. I cannot do both tasks at once, I will capture the Americans and I will need your help."

Youseff held Najad's eyes in his own, "You have done very well, executing part of the plan, brilliantly. Earlier today, the Taliban on the mountain above Taloqan left their positions. The noise they made when they did this told the Americans that they were leaving. I am sure they will try to climb the mountain so that they can watch your attack from afar and I will be waiting for them. They will not know that we have returned."

With an evil grin he balled his right hand into a fist and hit the open palm of his other hand with a resonate smack. "And then I've got them. There cannot be more than ten or twelve of them and I will have three hundred. All I need is one or two alive. After I have destroyed the Americans, I will attack from the mountain. They will not be expecting attacks from the valley and the mountain. Later tomorrow, there will be four more tanks and two to three thousand fighters swarming down upon them. We will annihilate them."

Caught up in the moment, Najad looked at his boss, his eyes bright with pride. "And then we will drive the rest far into their mountains. Never to bother us again."

White House lawn, Washington, DC

Amy Bonham waited patiently, one of the last to get off Marine One. She had been sitting near the back of the Helicopter, near the dry toilet, and the President always sat near the front. Deep in thought, she had watched the arrival scene through one of the windows. The President had carried the couple's Golden Retriever puppy down the stairs, he waited at the bottom of the stairs and when the First Lady joined him, they powered by the press corps with a brief nod and a wave. That was several minutes ago and the press was just starting to break up. Looking up from the window she saw the Helicopter Crew Chief was standing politely by the door, studiously ignoring her presence. But, obviously waiting on her.

"I'm sorry, Chief, I guess I was day dreaming there. Thanks for the ride," she said, gathering her briefcase and papers, she ducked out the door and started down the steps.

"No problem, ma'am. Have a good evening," the Crew Chief said as he pulled the stairs up behind her and closed the hatch.

Amy strode quickly across the White House lawn. She was tall and her long legs covered the ground quickly. In high school, she had been a basketball player, a forward. She had used her undergraduate athletic scholarship as a springboard from poverty to graduate school, a Doctorate and a distinguished career in Foreign Relations and Policy Analysis. Twenty years later she never thought she would be in Washington, much less at the very center of power defending her country after a horrific terrorist attack on its very foundations. *A big responsibility for a poor jock from Southside of San Antonio, I hope I'm up to this*, she thought.

Walking quickly through the hallways of the West Wing, she headed towards her office. She planned to check her messages, look at tomorrow's schedule and then go home to her apartment and a nice hot bath. Moving around her desk, she spun the chair to sit down. Reaching for the mouse she wiggled it to bring the sign-in screen up, typed her password and double clicked the email icon.

Glancing through the 167 messages since yesterday morning, she absently picked up the phone. With her other hand, she reached behind her head and pulled out the scrunchy holding her hair up. Without her secretary working the office she was unused to answering the phone herself, it had been ringing persistently for several seconds.

"Hello, Amy, this is George," the CIA Director, George Armbruster intoned. "I'm glad I caught you in. Wasn't sure when you'd be getting back from Camp David."

"Oh, hello, George. We just got back a few minutes ago; I was just checking my email. What's up?"

"Well, I've got some hot news for you. Remember the cell phone issue I briefed this morning? Well, we've had a breakthrough."

Suddenly attentive, she moved the phone to the other side. "I'm all ears, what happened." Hurriedly, she pushed papers away from the center of her desk so she could take notes on a legal pad.

Armbruster went on, "Like I said, we were working on filtering the Arabic versus the Pashto speakers, as well as trying to identify the particular phone footprints. The good news is that we've done it."

Scribbling furiously, Amy tried to flesh out her notes. "So, you've figured out who's using the phones and where they are?"

"Yes, we've been able to identify several users and particular phones. We've even got a location on a couple," George said excitedly.

"This is fantastic! It's just what the President wanted. Tell me more," Amy said.

"Just a few hours ago we monitored a call from who we believe is bin Laden himself. The caller and bin Laden were discussing the results of a meeting, from the gist of it with a Taliban leader. We've also been able to identify a few of the major players. One by the name of Ahmed Youseff looks to be running the show in the north and Ahmed Mustapha is running Kabul."

"Wait, wait a second. Go back to the bin Laden stuff. What do you have on him? Where you able to pin point his location?" Amy asked breathlessly.

"Yeah, we were able to confirm that it was bin Laden, a perfect voice match. We also got the location, but I'll be honest, it was way after the fact. The phone call was very short, but we can say that he was on a surface road in the Tarin River valley. We're absolutely sure of that."

A little disappointed Amy said, "Go on. I'm listening."

"The good news is that the cell phone he's using is analog, and most analog phones have a unique signature depending on the manufacturer. In fact, that's why we think we've got Youseff and Mustapha, same deal with their cell phones. If we can keep getting hits from them, we can build up a pattern of movement. After we build up a database, we can cut down our positional uncertainty, if they stay within a certain area."

Writing furiously, she paused, flipped the pages of her notes back and forth. "Okay, let me be clear on this. One—you've been able to link a particular cell phone to bin Laden and a few of the top leaders. Two—positional information is still not real time, but with a historical database, it might be possible to detect movement patterns. Is that correct?" Amy asked.

"Correct. We're also trying to identify more of the Taliban and al-Qaeda leadership as we go. We're feeling very confident in that regard, the trouble is that we have to correlate voice exploitation with our Intel analysts. That takes time."

Flipping open a new page, Amy asked another question, "Explain this analog versus digital thing."

"Humm, were should I start?" Armbruster paused, thinking for a moment he explained, "Well, Afghanistan's infrastructure is weak, the only hardwired telephone lines are inside the cities and there are only a few of these. Plus they haven't been updated in decades. They've skipped modernizing their phone lines and went straight to cell phones. There are analog cell towers all over the country. They actually get good coverage with repeaters on the mountain ridges. Analog is good for that; it's a lot like radio. The best part for us is that analog is easier exploit, it is also good for longer distances, were digital is more short range and easier to encrypt."

Trying to listen and forecast what the president would want to know, Amy held the phone with her shoulder and doodled with her pen. "Okay, I think I've got it now. Any idea when you think you might be able to pin down a location, say within a few miles? And any idea on best case to worst case on how long it will take to have an ID?"

Armbruster knew she would try to pin him with a promise, trying to avoid the question he said, "Amy, you know I can't make a promise I might not be able keep. What I can do is assure you that I'll call you first with the news. Just as soon as I know, you'll know. Is that a deal?"

"I understand, I understand. Just asking. I know the President will be asking for a time frame, that's all. At some point, he'll press pretty hard for some reliable time forecast. Thanks for the call; I'll update the President in the morning brief. I know he'll be excited to her your news."

"Uh, Amy, there's one more thing. This one isn't quite as clear-cut," Armbruster said nervously, now that he was on less solid ground.

Taking the handset in her left hand, she switched it to her right ear, she leaned forward with her elbows on the desk, "Yeah, what is it? If you think it's important I want to hear it."

"Well, it's one of those calls we monitored. They discussed the status of some rabbits, we haven't figured out what those rabbits are, specifically. But the thing is that al-Qaeda always talks in some sort of simple code. They never refer to anything in the clear; it's always some everyday reference or something like that."

"Anyway, we are pretty sure that it's a reference to a planned attack on the US. Something that is close to happening, something that they are worried about getting off soon," Armbruster finished.

Amy stopped writing. They had gotten thousands of threats and clues of possible attacks and targets since 9/11, but the CIA Director had never acted so nervous about one before, "Hmm, Any ideas what it might be? Where or when?"

"No, no clues as to what or where," Armbruster replied. "I wish I knew."

"Then what's different about this threat? What's different about this time? Why does it shake you?" Amy asked.

"What's different is that it was bin Laden himself who talked about it. The vast majority of the traffic we listen to is just chatter. Mostly it's from non-players, functionaries that are not leaders. Some of it is chaff, some of it is real. But this came from the horses mouth so to speak."

"So, are you going to brief it to the President in the morning?"

"No, I've got no confirmation, no alternate source, no real idea of what the target is. The bottom line is that I don't want to go public with a hunch. We're working on it, but it'll take awhile to sort out. Amy, I know it's not as concrete as you'd like, but I'm worried about this one. And Amy, I want you to tell the President yourself. I'd like you to tell him tonight."

In the silence that followed, Armbruster waited patiently for Amy to reply. When she didn't, he went on, "Amy, some of our analysts feel pretty strongly about this. They feel that he's referring to a rocket attack. Bin Laden used the term "seeds of hell" and our analysts feel that is the code word for a missile. They feel the likely target is an airliner. If an airliner gets shot down it may mean the end of that industry, it could be the domino that sends the whole economy crashing down. I don't have to tell you how serious that might be."

"Yeah, I see your point." Taking a moment, Amy considered the implications. On one hand, they couldn't raise the alarm over shaky intelligence, crying wolf wouldn't solve anything and it might make many things worse. But on the other hand, they couldn't afford to let something important slip through their fingers, the risk was just too great. "Okay, I'll tell the president, right away. Meanwhile, get that confirmation. Find another source. Track this thing down. It is imperative that we know, and soon!"

"I understand. Amy, I'll be on this personally. I'll call you as soon as I know anything," Armbruster said. "Thanks for taking the call—I knew you'd understand. Have a good night."

"Sure I just love getting calls like these just before bed. Happens all the time, good night, George." Hanging up the phone, she sat in the yellow pool of light outlining her desk, trying to figure out how to tell the President what is essentially a rumor, a deadly rumor.

East side of the Slang Pass, Afghanistan

Riding his horse up the steep trail from Golbahar, Dave was getting comfortable in the saddle, beginning to feel like he was a horseman. Above him a misty white-orange pastel haze covered the ridges he could see, soon it would be dark with a new moon rising over the purple mountains. His horse was going slowly, a simple misstep could mean a long, quick trip back down the mountain. Dave looked at the new guide he had picked up in the village, one that had claimed to be familiar with the mountains. He was almost too eager to lead the small group to the other side, but he was also the only one who would go.

His mind raced with the possibilities. Instead of just tagging along, he was keyed up with the idea that he might be able get his hands on some real Intel. To do something besides just hold someone else's hands, he hoped that the others would go along with him; it was much safer to go as a group in this environment.

Suddenly dark on the ridge, two horsemen loomed on the trail, softly backlit by the now yellow-blue black of the evening sky. Mark called softly from below the trail. "Dave is that you?"

Not surprised to be met this far from where he had left everyone, Dave answered in a low voice, "Yeah, Mark it's me. We're good. I brought a new guide with me."

Standing, Mark let his weapon fall against the shoulder strap. "Dude, we were starting to wonder if you were going to make it back tonight at all. Like maybe, you found a party or something. Any luck?"

"Well, I got some Turkey T-Rats from one of my buds down there. It's probably too late to start a fire to warm it up. Not much in the way of fixins, but it'll beat an MRE any day. I've also got some news," Dave said, as he easily dismounted from his horse. Sliding to the ground next to Mark, he grinned in the dark.

Mark began rummaging through the stuff on the packhorse Dave had brought with him. "Luke, Dave brought us dinner, come on over and help unload this stuff."

A few minutes later Dave sat down on a rock, using his fork he cut up the Turkey and gravy scooped from the T-ration. Designed to feed 10 men, the six of them would have plenty to eat. After weeks of the bland tasting MREs, or the standard chicken and rice dinners, even cold turkey was a feast in these bleak mountains.

Mark, sitting cross-legged on a small boulder, swallowed a mouthful of turkey. "Oooh, that's good, I was beginning to think my taste buds had atrophied altogether. I hope you thanked your buds down the hill for dinner. So, what's this news anyway?"

Still chewing, Dave took a minute to reply, "Yeah, I told him we owed him big time. What would you guys think about poking around the pass area?"

"Well the word I got was that Group thinks bin Laden might be at this place. They think he's hiding out in remote areas and the possibility of this being a central commo sight has them real interested. I don't have a problem poking around," Mark replied.

"Well, John, my bud over at the airstrip, told me that analysis of the traffic is pointing to a C2 site somewhere around here, probably on the far side of the pass. They've seen a huge spike in commo traffic. It's probably not coincidental that Woody's high traffic area is near the same place. I'm all for taking a look," Dave mused.

Woody, quiet up until now, took a long pull from his canteen wiping his mouth on his sleeve, he said, "While you were gone, I talked with Maddog again. The USAF feeling is that they are positive there is a C2 node on the other side of the ridge. He even gave me a rough coordinate,"

Vaguely pointing north, his right hand out stretched. "It's about 12 miles northwest of us. So, if you want to go have a look see, I figure I'll go with you."

"Great, that settles that," Dave said he took the canteen Woody offered him and took a long drink.

Mark swallowed a mouthful, pausing with his fork on the plate he looked at Dave with a slight grin. "Okay, Dave. You're gonna have to fess up. I've seen you operate; it's obvious that you're not a civilian. What did you do before? If we're going to go on the dark side I'd kinda like to know what your deal is."

"It's no big secret. You know the drill, keep your mouth shut and don't say shit except what you need to. Besides, if you work for the OGA, it fits the culture. Secrets mean power. But as I said, it's no big secret. I was a Marine in a former life. I did the grunt thing, spent a little time in Force Recon. I've got a tendency to shoot my mouth off so I figured staying for a career probably wasn't in the cards. I'm an adrenaline junkie just like you. What about you, what's your deal?"

"Me, shit I told you already. My dad was an Air Force Fighter Pilot, the whole drill. He was an Air Commando in Vietnam, a couple hundred combat missions or something. He flew Spads and some other stuff, spent like three years over there and just never forgot it. We just grew up around the Military, I guess it's just our way of life."

Dave chuckled, "So, you've got the lifer mentality, huh? I don't see the coffee cup crock in your finger though."

"Well if you mean that I'm out to be a general or something. No, I like what I'm doing; I like SF even better than being a Ranger. The regular Army isn't for me, too much bullshit and not enough fun," Mark replied.

"Sorry, I didn't mean to touch a nerve. There are some lifer types in the suck, that's all. Who's this "we" stuff anyway?" Dave asked.

"My sister. I didn't want to fly, but my sister is all ate up over it. She's almost three years younger than I am; she and my dad have been tight, they've been flying together ever since she was about 10. She soloed in a Stearman on her sixteenth birthday; no shit."

Sensing jealousy, Dave decided to probe a little, "So, you didn't like to fly. Did you get sick or something?"

Mark shrugged his shoulders, "No, it wasn't like that. I've done a lot of flying and jumping out of airplanes. Just never had the interest, that's all. Besides, that

Stearman of my dad's is just a two seater. Not much room for three."

"Oh, I see. What's your sister like, are you close to her these days?"

"Yeah, we're close. She's in the Air Force, flying fighters somewhere. Come to think of it, we probably haven't spoken since she graduated from flight school. We're just both pretty busy these days. Neither of us have any kids, right now that's a good thing, because I spend most of my time deployed. I'm sure she's the same. I guess you could say we're both driven." He grinned. "But it's better than being bored!"

"What about you, Dave? Got any kids?" Mark asked.

"Yep, I've got two girls and a great wife. I met her in the Marines, so she knows what the life is all about. But the rest of my life is boring, just an average guy."

With a far away look, Mark nodded his head slightly, "Yeah, boring and an adrenaline junkie at the same time."

Woody, who had been quiet, spoke up, "I don't know about you guys, but I don't feel like confessing anything. Don't we have a job to do?"

Throwing a rock down the trail Mark said, "Shit yeah, that's enough soul baring for about a year. Let's saddle up."

Crouched in a slight depression near the bottom of the valley north of the Slang Pass, three Americans could see the road faintly glowing in the starlight. Holding the reigns of his horse, Dave could barely make out his companions. "Our *Muj* guide says this is the best place to cross. The road is narrow here and the watchers on the ridge can't see very well down this far, especially at night. We'll be fine, just move slowly and be quiet."

"Okay, Luke and Mike are on overwatch. I'll go across first, find a hide spot and then come back for the horse. When I give the signal come over one at a time. Move, slowly. Keep those horses quiet, hold their muzzles with one hand," Mark said and before anyone could reply, he slipped silently across the road.

Nearly and hour later, Mike, laying on top of a large rock adjacent to the road, was watching as Mark disappeared across the road. He was impressed with how quickly he lost him; even wearing NOGs he lost his movements quickly. He caught sight of him again just as he was about to cross the road right in front of them. Moving silently, in short bursts he was moving relatively rapidly, taking advantage of the terrain.

Gathering the men around him Mark began quietly, "Okay, there is a good spot across the road, over that small rise. Just keep that line of rocks on the right, and the open spaces on the left. I'll be waiting for you, remember, one at a time.

Be quiet. Pay attention. Luke, you come last. Make sure to get rid of our tracks, especially the horses."

"Yes, sir. Mike is going to take my horse across. I'll trail and clean up."

Griping his arm Dave whispered urgently, "Mark, I think we should leave the horses with the guide. He can take them back up the pass and wait for us to return. He thinks it would be safer if we move on foot, less noise and a smaller profile."

His plan interrupted, Mark just stood there impatiently, weighing the pros and cons of going on foot.

After a few moments of anguish, Mark said, "Yeah, you're right. We really do need to go on foot. I was just thinking of speed and hauling all this gear we've got with us. Kinda got in the habit of riding. Mike, string the horses together so the guide can take them back. Dave, tell him to wait for us at the spot where we met for two days and after that go to Golbahar and see your friend John. Is that good?"

"Yeah, you're the boss. I just thought it was an important point," Dave added apologetically.

"No worries, Dave." Looking around at the four other men he added, "Okay, ready? Let's go!" Mark handed the reigns of his horse to Mike and silently drifted across the road towards the hide spot on the far side.

Everyone silently made it across the road, moon light just beginning to make the scene bright enough to see. Luke was the last to come across, cleaning up their tracks as he crossed the road. On the other side of the road, the guide led the horses away, somewhat nosily.

Dave whispered into Mark's ear, "The guide says there is a notch that we can follow right up this side of the valley. There's probably a good spot to Laager up for the night near the top. I'll lead for a while if you don't mind. You guys ready to go?"

"Yep, lead on, but make sure you're quiet. This is the most dangerous time, if the AQ find us now, we're really sticking our necks out," Mark whispered back.

CHAPTER 16

15 October, 2001
The West Side of Salang Pass

Stars sparkled in the night sky, brilliant pinpoints of light thrown across the clear darkness. No moon lit the night sky; the Milkyway was in vivid relief with its furious belt of stars. Early morning, the temperature dropping rapidly in the crystal clear night sky, nothing moved in the stark mountains except a small group of Americans working their way down the ridgeline. Stopping above a level space on the steep mountainside, Mark and Woody lay next to each other on a small outcropping of rock watching below for movement. Leaning close to Mark's ear, Woody whispered, "Man, are we going to stop and sleep sometime soon? I'm not used to this all night stuff."

"Sorry, bud. No sleep for the wicked. Maybe you can catch a wink or two later, but right now we've got to move as far as we can under cover of darkness," Mark whispered back. Slowly scanning the valley with night vision binoculars, he was looking for signs of activity, guards, anything that might reveal the presence of al-Qaeda. "We need to get as close as we can to your coordinate before daylight. Once the sun comes up, we won't be able to move very far. I think we're really close right now."

Raising his arm to his face, Woody checked his watch to see how far away they were from the suspected C2 node. His watch was a test version of a personal GPS that allowed you to navigate from one point to another, studs on the sides controlled the screens and modes the watch used. In the dim glow of the luminescent screen, he could see by the bearing and range screen that they were only a little over a half mile above and to the right of the point.

Mike, searching a little further up the valley, crawled next to Mark and whispered in Mark's ear, "Boss, good news, bad news. Good news is we're pretty close to the right place. Bad news is, I've got some movement on the road, estimate thirty or forty dismounts. They are headed down the road on foot, in our general direction."

"Copy, just stay put and keep tabs on 'em." Rolling on his side, he lowered his binoculars and whispered urgently, "Woody, there are AQ moving down the road in front of us, possibly forty on foot. Looks like we're staying here for awhile; go ahead and grab a few winks if you want."

"You expect me to sleep with bad guys only a few yards away, shit," Woody said, adrenaline beginning to course through his veins.

"Dude, it's no big deal. We can't do anything and they don't know we're here. Just one thing though. Call it a safety tip. Don't snore."

"Yeah, right. I couldn't sleep right now if I wanted to," Woody said disgustedly as he reached for Mark's night binoculars. "Let me see those."

Mark decided to rearrange his men; he turned to Mike, whispering he said, "Mike, you and Luke find a place to overwatch the valley and the ridge above us. Turn on your short range radios, stay on line and keep your eyes open."

Woody slowly scanned the road and the clearing before them, "What would an al-Qaeda or Taliban command and control center look like anyway? What do you think these guys are doing out there this early?"

"Heck, I don't know, I don't think they're using any buildings out here. Probably using caves for cover. Outside maybe some antennas, inside a bunch of radios and papers I guess. After seeing their operation in Taloqan, it's probably just a pile of shit. The best Intel we can get out of this place is to blow it all up, make 'em cut and run and keep 'em running."

Whispering back, Woody replied, "I'm with you, man, I could have dropped a JDAM on this from miles away and been happy."

Dave, a veteran of field operations, had taken advantage of the short pause and rested in a small depression. Curious to see what the two were whispering about, he crawled forward to join them, "Hey, what's goin' on up here? Don't you guys go and diss this place, you're not going to blow it up yet. I've got a good feeling about it, you know real Humint is hard to come by and getting into the enemies lair is even harder. My gut tells me there's going to be really good shit on AQ operations, just wait."

Suddenly turning serious, Mark added, "Sure, it'll be fun. Listen, when we go in, we'll have to kill everyone there. There are more of them than us; we just can't afford to take prisoners. Okay? This is pretty dangerous stuff, when we drop this place we're gonna have to run fast."

Dave, anxious not to lose a valuable Intel source asked, "Sure, I understand, but how about if we find one of them that wants to talk? What about interrogations?"

"Yeah, that would be nice, suppose we ask 'em all before we shoot them? Look, any of those guys left alive is a big hazard to our survival and time is not on our side. I'm not shitting you, maybe you guys haven't noticed that we are way out on a limb here, it's just our pink bodies and a little Kevlar."

"Dave, I'm with Mark on this one. Let's just do what we've got to, and get the hell out," Woody added.

"Okay, okay. I'll do whatever you say. I just like to have things first hand, you get a lot closer to the truth that way." Before Dave could finish, Mark reached up and put a hand over his mouth, turning, he looked down the hill.

"Something's changed, I can feel it in the air," Mark whispered, he switched on the mic and asked, "Mike, how's it going? Anything up?"

Mike answered immediately, "It's funny you asked boss. Those dismounts stopped about four to five hundred meters straight down hill from you. They've just been joined by a huge group, maybe as many as 200. This last group came out of no-where, like they crawled out of the ground."

"Are they making a move towards us? Any sign that they know we're here?" Mark asked urgently.

"Not so far, they are just milling around. I don't see any guards; they're all armed and excited. But I don't think they know they're being watched."

Mark touched Woody and Dave. "Check your weapons. There are between 200 to 300 AQ just down the hill. We don't think they've seen us, but we might have to fight our way out. Just be ready, make sure you can get to all your ammo."

Lying on his stomach, Woody checked his M-4 by touch. He pushed the clip in the receiver one more time. Firmly seated, he just wanted to make sure, and somehow it made him feel better. He thumbed off the safety and twisted the silencer screwed onto the muzzle. Then he felt the pouches on his web belt to make sure he had several more clips available, just in case. Feeling under his armed, he touched the cold steel of his M-9 in its shoulder holster with a full clip and a round in the chamber. His heart pounded in his ears, almost covering his shallow, fast breathing. Waiting in the dark, he regretted the fact that he had left his NVGs with Brandon.

For Woody time slowed down, lying on the cold rocky ground, hours seemed to pass by every minute. Without NVGs or night glasses he couldn't really watch the group of AQ below, to him they were a dark mass milling about like cold flies. Slowly, the gray light of the rising dawn began illuminate a broad shoulder below them on the mountainside. Gradually, the gray dawn turned yellow and they discovered they were on top of a rocky rise, above a large clearing emptying into a slightly larger valley. The valley widened as it sloped down to the right. On the left, the valley narrowed drastically as it went uphill into a slash between 15,000-foot peaks. Virtually nothing grew up here, they were well above the snow line and the terrain was a rugged monochrome. Woody looked east, the dawn was spectacular, light yellows fading into dark blues and an orange gold lit the bottom of clouds just above the horizon, it was going to be a beautiful day.

Woody could just make out the mass of men below. Surprised, he saw them pulling canvas covers off a group of nearly 40 trucks, all parked in the small clearing below. There were also two technical vehicles and a Toyota Land Cruiser. Most of the men gathered around the Land Cruiser, surrounding someone at the front of the truck. Gently touching Mark on the shoulder, Woody pointed at the group. Mark followed his arm; he saw the big group just as the first truck started in a cloud of black diesel smoke floating above the staccato clatter of the engine.

Woody tightened his grip on the rifle and looked expectantly at Mark, mouthing the words, "Do you think it's somebody big?"

"Not sure," Mark answered the same way. Slowly bringing the binoculars back to his eyes, he scanned the crowd.

In the space of a few minutes, all the trucks had their engines running, the valley filled with a continuous diesel rattle. A steady stream of men emerged from an unseen doorway almost directly below them. Suddenly, the three smaller vehicles sped down the hill. The large group of men milling about the trucks began sorting itself out. Without command, they started climbing into the trucks. Shouting accompanied the loading as a larger group appeared from down the road and joined the hustle of men scrambling aboard. In minutes, every truck was brimming with al-Qaeda fighters. Watching the scene, covered like a blanket in the noise, Mark watched. He thought these guys are packing up for a fight, where exactly isn't important as long as it wasn't here.

Woody stared intently at the group. He had forgotten the rocks poking him through his BDUs; he had forgotten the fact that they were outnumbered forty to one. He'd even forgotten the fact he was inside Danger Close criteria of this juicy target. Woody could only think of one thing and that this was a target he could not let get away. subconsciously, he began feeling the mic button on the PRC-117; the handset was attached to his top pocket, the radio strapped to his back. He toyed with the idea of calling AWACs for an airstrike, how loud would he have to speak to transmit on the radio. Thumbing the rubber cover on the switch he pressed down until he could feel the switch itself, intently focusing on the group below. Jarred back to reality, Mark bumped into him apparently squirming to make himself more comfortable. Looking at Mark and Dave, both staring downhill, the thought of survival popped into his head. He wiped his forehead with his hand; he could feel his pulse behind his eyes.

As if in a fog, he began thinking about the consequences of dropping on the enemy. He realized that proximity was the problem. The AQ were just to close, and too many. One bomb and this place would be an anthill, kicked over and swarming with al-Qaeda. Targets were one thing, survival another.

Dave spoke for him when he asked Mark, "So, what do we do now?"

"Simple, Jeeves. We wait. We wait until we know where all the other players are. Then maybe we'll go have a look at your cave. Better get comfortable."

The sun was high in the sky, it was not quite overhead and they had been lying, unmoving upon these rocks for over 10 hours. There had been no movement since the big group left in the early hours of the morning. In the bright sunlight, they noticed the antenna farm Mark had guessed about, situated above the clearing to their left, less than 200 meters away. Mark was satisfied that this was not only their target, but that there was only one guard at the entrance of the cave. Mark decided it was time to coordinate the assault. He pulled Dave's sleeve and tapped Woody's leg to attract their attention.

"Okay, boys. I think it's time we move. We can hit this place and scoot back over the ridge before nightfall. I see only one guard outside, and there are probably one or two inside the entrance to the cave. We wait until just after lunchtime; I'm betting the current guard should be replaced around then. I'll reposition and take care of the new guard when that happens. After I've done that, I want you both to join me, quietly. We'll look at both sides of the cave. I'll take one and Woody, you take the other. On my signal I want you to make a small noise, just enough to get the attention of whoever is inside that entrance. I need them to look away from me."

Impatient that he had not been included, Dave asked, "What about me?"

Mark held up his hand and went on, "If one guard comes out, I'll take care of him, if two come out, Woody you take the second one. More and it's a free for all; Dave, feel comfortable about joining in. If the coast is clear, we need to get as close to the entrance as possible, quietly, without being seen. On my signal, we'll rush the entrance from both sides. Put your weapon on full auto, but don't hold it down, just pull the trigger and release. Remember, pull and release, sweep the room about waist high. Just keep doing that until nothing is moving inside. Aim when you can but don't stop shooting."

Watching Woody closely, he paused while he digested his instructions.

Quickly looking at Dave, Mark went on, "Dave, here's where you come in. I need you to watch from the top of the cave. Look for people coming out of other nooks, if you see one, kill him. Make sure you use the silencer. I'll let you know when it's safe to join us. You've got to watch our back to keep us from being surprised and caught in the cave. Do you understand?"

"Sure," Dave answered flippantly, "I wait for your call and mow down the rats running from the hole. What happens if you guys get shot?"

With expressionless eyes Mark looked back at the two of them flatly, "If we aren't mobile, then we bit off more than we could chew. You and the boys ought to see if you can get out alive."

"The hell I will, I won't leave you guys here," Dave answered indignantly.

Mark looked back at him, a staunch grimness gripped his face. "At that point we'll either be dead or captured and you won't do us any good. I say get out and let someone know what happened."

Dave looked between the two of them. Suddenly speechless there was nothing to say.

"Okay any questions? Anything at all?" With a practiced eye Mark assessed the members of his team; this wasn't training and these guys weren't SF. Dave looked game, and Woody looked a little pale, but Mark thought he'd stand in the door when he needed him.

Rolling away from them, he looked downhill; he called Mike and Luke on the short range FM radio and briefed them on his plan. "And Luke, once we're inside, let us know what you see. If it's a vehicle, make sure you keep them from making it onto that plain in front of us, until we can get out. We're going in quiet; if we hear anything from you outside, we'll be out as soon as we can. If we are trapped or killed, take who you can and E and E your way out of here. Get back home; don't worry about us. Is that clear?"

Woody and Mark crawled slowly, threading their way through the rocks to the cave entrance. Dave made his way to the left of their old position and snaked through the radio antennas; he stopped where he could almost see the cave entrance below him and most of the clearing in front of them. Quietly, he pulled the rifle in front of him and stacked four 30 round clips within easy reach. Satisfied, he was determined to fire on anything that wasn't Mark or Woody. He settled down to watch.

The two Americans approached the cave mouth from opposite sides. As if on cue, they stopped to survey the situation. On Woody's side, a single, empty chair rested against the wall, with no guard in sight. Mark held up his fist in front of his face and then opened his fingers and with the palm down, he lowered his hand towards the ground.

Watching Mark's hand signal, Woody sank to his knees.

The sun was high in the pale blue sky, the air crisp, with a cold bite. But Woody didn't notice, his heart was thumping so loud he thought he could hear the echo from inside the cave. He reached up nervously; to wipe the sweat from his face with the back of his gloved hand.

Not for the last time, did he wonder why he wasn't flying jets instead of sweating dust in the Afghanistan Mountains. He realized day dreaming was slightly distracting and wondered how long his mind had been wandering; a sudden movement caught his eye, he looked towards his friend.

Mark was waving his hand, palm flat in front of his face. Woody nodded and Mark held up two fingers and pointed towards the cave mouth. Trying to avoid sudden movement, Woody turned slowly back towards the cave mouth.

Surprised, he saw two guards, one sitting on the chair and the other standing, chatting next to him. They were both less than 50 feet from him. In plain sight, he hadn't seen them come out of the cave. Shocked, he glanced quickly at Mark to see what he should do.

Mark was holding his rifle to his shoulder and aiming at the seated guard. Within seconds, he fired two shots; the guard slumped and fell sideways off the chair. Stunned, the second guard did not move before Mark put two rounds into his head. Pitching face first to the ground, blood and gore splattered the rock behind where the guard had stood. Before Woody could think, Mark was on his feet running towards the cave mouth.

In slow motion, the scene played out in front of his eyes, almost as if he wasn't in it. Woody stood up and tried to run, but he hadn't noticed how heavy his boots were. Struggling to put one foot in front of the other, it seemed like he was fighting a strong current as he followed Mark into the cave.

Determined not to be a target, Woody pressed against the wall as he entered the anteroom of the cave. It seemed like minutes before his eyes adjusted to the darkness in the large room, and then he realized there were electric lights, and four dead bodies. He put the butt of his rifle against his shoulder and started for the next doorway. Pausing, Woody was startled by a man rushing towards him; Mark appeared from his left and shot him twice. Spinning around towards the doorway, Woody shot the next man running through it.

Mark yelled to him, "Twice, shoot 'em twice. Don't let 'em get up." Woody aimed once more at the body he had dropped and squeezed the trigger again.

Suddenly, Mark rushed by him towards the next room, the muzzle of his rifle leading the way. As he passed him Mark hissed, "Come on, we've got to clear all the rooms. We can't let anyone raise the alarm. Follow me!"

Copying Mark, holding his rifle at the ready, Woody followed.

The next room was the back of the cave and roughly the size of a small garage. About twenty-five to thirty pallets were scattered on the floor with almost as many men in various stages of hurried reaction. Their rush carried Mark and Woody to the center of the room where they stopped and, shoulder to shoulder, began shooting as fast as they could. The sound of AK-47s firing wildly was deafening in the small space and totally masked the light crack of their silenced M-4s.

Several minutes passed, Woody stopped to change magazines and recognized that silence had replaced the bedlam. His ears still ringing with the sound of gunfire, he pressed the magazine eject button on his rifle with his right thumb. Pulling the clip out he looked down to see only a few rounds left. He felt the empty pouch at his waist for the extra clips he kept there. Finding it empty, his focus shifted to his feet; amongst the brass, casings were two clips. He had changed magazines and did even notice.

Unaffected by the carnage, Mark slung his rifle over his back and pulled out his pistol. He began securing the room, one by one examining each body. Each weapon he found he threw into a growing pile by the door. Seeing Woody just standing by the door in shock he said, "Woody, hey Woody. I need your help. Grab all the weapons; shoot anything that moves. Another round won't hurt any of these guys. Come on, stay with me now, we don't have much time."

Taloqan, Afghanistan

"Brandon." SFC Gary Wilkerson shook Brandon Ray lightly on the shoulder. "Brandon, hey, buddy wake up."

His eyes firmly closed, Brandon mumbled something unintelligible and rolled over, cracking on eye open he blurted, "What the fuck do you want? Can't you see I'm sleeping here?"

"Dude, wake up, I've got news for you," Gary said, shaking his shoulder again.

Rubbing his face roughly with one hand, Brandon replied impatiently, "What do you want, is the Queen dead or something?"

"No man, the *Muj* told me that the Taliban moved off of the ridge north of town last night. You wanted high ground right? Well it's open now. Isn't that what you wanted to hear?"

At last, Brandon opened his eyes wide. "Yeah, that ridge is perfect. It has been bugging me for days. Where did all the bad guys go?"

"The report is they all went to the town of Bangi. Apparently the T is building up significant reinforcements there."

The significant change in their tactical situation and coming danger dawned on him, sitting up quickly Brandon unzipped his sleeping bag, slipped his feet out and began putting on his boots. "How high did you say that ridge was? How many T are gathering in Bangi? Have you seen the town? What kind of terrain is it?"

"So, you are interested, huh? The ridge itself is just over 6,000 feet high, about 3,000 above the valley floor. Bangi is between the Kunduz road and the Taloqan River. And as far as I can tell, the terrain is sorta hilly to the north but slopes down to the river. How close we can get, we'll have to see. Let's go get breakfast and talk about what to do next."

"Right. I'll be with you in a second," Brandon said, jerking his laces tight.

Outside he found Gary had opened a map on a low wall in front of the building, taking a drink from his canteen he joined him.

With the grayish purple light of dawn growing behind them, they concentrated over the map. Gary grabbed a corner of the map, picked up in the freshening breeze. With his other hand he reached into a pouch on his belt, pulled out an M-4 magazine. Laying it down to hold the map.

Breaking the silence between them, Brandon said, "Anyway I look at it, we gotta talk Fahim into getting some folks on that ridge. It is *the* high terrain and it dominates this town. Any defense of this place will depend on that ridge."

Straightening up slightly, Brandon looked at Gary, "If there really is an attack shaping up in Bangi, we've got to get to high ground to get some air on 'em. Or we're in trouble."

Nodding silently, Gary returned his gaze without comment.

"So, you agree? We gotta get something up there, and the sooner the better."

Clearing his throat, Gary shrugged, "Yeah, if we don't have terrain and air available we won't know if they are coming up the road or from the other side of the river, or both. Yeah, I agree that we've got to have an observation team up there. If we don't know where they're coming from it might be too late to reposition Fahim's forces. The river is shallow here, but it would be stupid to cross it under fire."

"So, maybe we can talk Fahim into moving on the ridge? I figure the T moving out is the sign he was looking for. Maybe that's his sign from God," Brandon said, looking back at the map distractedly.

"Maybe. What if he doesn't? Would you go up there with a few guys? A few of us?" Gary asked.

"You mean go up there without the *Muj*? Won't we be pretty exposed?"

"Yeah, just us. But, dude, that's what we do. Anyway, we've got to have someone on that high terrain. You said yourself it's a critical situation. Besides, if we have to, we can run real fast with just a few guys!"

A long moment passed as Bandon considered a combat situation alien to any he had ever encountered. His whole professional life had been spent with heavy mechanized infantry, out near the enemy with only his Kevlar body armor and a horse for protection was a big step. "Okay, I guess. I just ain't got any other ideas. How many T are in Bangi anyway?"

Ignoring the question, Gary folded the map and stood up. "Okay, then." Picking up a Shawl and a rug hat, he held them out for Brandon. "Take these. Let's go. I think we oughta head up there and work some air on those clowns in Bangi for breakfast."

"Gary, how many T are in that town?" Brandon asked again, insistently, taking the Afghan garb.

"I don't know. Call it a shit load. Dude, I just don't know."

Bannu Cap, Pakistan

Back from a break, Lieutenant Lisa McKay sat down at her JSTAR's console. On this crew, she was the operator most familiar with monitoring northern Afghanistan, and she personally wanted to keep a close eye on it. Scrolling the trackball over the display, she pulled up an overlay map of the Salang Pass area and parts north.

For the next half hour, nothing happened. Not a single ground moving target indicator hit anywhere on her screen. Funny, she figured that with the dawn, the Taliban would start moving on the roads again. In the last few days, this had become a regular counter-tactic of the Taliban. She stretched to see the other consoles around hers; everywhere else in Afghanistan there was quite a lot of traffic. But here, there was nothing. She felt the converted 707 aircraft begin a turn left, to take up a westerly heading. Absently, Lisa scrolled the trackball 30 miles north of the Salang area and re-centered her map.

Within seconds, she started getting multiple GMTI hits. Suddenly alert, she bolted upright in her seat. Again, she re-centered her screen with the latest hits at the bottom. When the new screen refreshed she had six, then ten, building quickly to 25 hits. She didn't notice her breathing, heavy and fast. With a dry mouth, she refreshed her screen one more time, counting just under 50 GMTI hits, all headed north out of Baghlan towards Kunduz.

Flipping her intercom to speak to the Mission Commander of her crew, Lieutenant Colonel Buffalo Horde, she spoke excitedly into her microphone.

"Colonel Horde, you won't believe it. Remember when I saw those bits and pieces of the convoy that started in TB a couple of days ago?" she asked.

"Yeah, Lisa, I remember. Have you seen anything else yet?"

"I'll say." Lisa snorted. "Yes, sir. This is a lot bigger than even the ones we saw going into Salang. I count 40 plus headed north towards Kunduz. Good strong hits, all moving 30 to 50 miles an hour and they are just leaving Baghlan right now. This is a big one!" she exclaimed, a gleam in her eyes.

"Thanks, Lisa. I'll call Maddog right away. Good job! Send me the bounding coordinates and I'll get 'em out."

"Maddog, Cadillac Alpha," Buffalo transmitted over the UHF radio. "Maddog, Cadillac Alpha."

After several minutes of silence Buffalo's headset crackled to life. "Cadillac Alpha, Maddog here what you got," the airborne commander called back.

"Maddog, We've got a large fast moving target for you, ready to copy?" Buffalo asked.

Lieutenant Colonel BC Lawrence, sliding his notepad over with his free hand, pulled out a pen. "Sure go ahead."

"Yes, sir. Cadillac Alpha has 40 plus large trucks moving 30 to 50 miles and hour on the A76, headed north out of Baghlan towards Kunduz."

"Copy that. Did you say 40 plus trucks moving fast?"

"Yes, sir. We think it's that large number of trucks that we tracked into the Salang area, all formed into a convoy over the last several days. It looks like they're moving towards Kunduz in a hurry. Perhaps they are reinforcements for Taloqan," Buffalo concluded.

"Could be, thanks for the heads-up. All I've got available are B-1s now; all of my fighters are tied up around Kandahar. Trouble is, I can't send Bones after a moving target, it's gotta be fighters. Keep a close eye on that convoy and call me back in a half hour, I'll try to scare something up."

"Yes, sir, we'll keep an eye on them. Any idea of the time frame you might have some fighters you could put on this target?"

"Well, it'll be an hour, or more, at least, before I can have assets. Just keep a close eye on their movements for me. Maddog out." Releasing the mic button on his comm cord, BC reached for the copy of the Frag lying on his console.

Buffalo flipped his commo switch to intercom, thumbing the transmit key he called McKay. "Lisa, I'm sorry, but I got the same answer as the last time. No assets. So keep your eyes on the target, call back if anything changes."

"Yes, sir! I'll keep a close watch on these guys; they're out in the open now. We got to get them this time!" Lisa replied. "It sure seems like Deja Vue all over again, or is it just me?"

Flipping back and forth through the Frag, BC decided to re-task an inbound two ship of fighters. *Time to get the ball rolling,* he thought. Switching his commo panel to the AWAC's frequency, he thumbed his mic switch. "Horse, Maddog on uniform."

The AWAC's Mission Commander responded immediately, "Maddog, Horse copies, go ahead."

Looking at his notes in front of him, BC began, "Roger, Horse. I've got a big target, a large fast moving convoy headed north on the A76."

"Horse copies. Maddog we aren't talking to any fighters right now. We're expecting some in the next block," the controller replied.

"Horse, Maddog is aware of that. There is a two ship of F-15E's on the ATO, Grumpy 31, due to report in an hour and ten, isn't that correct?"

"Ah, yes, sir. Let me look," the controller tapped a soft key on a second display setup at his console. The Air Tasking Order flashed on the screen and she paged down to the next time block due that day. "Okay, you want me to assign Grumpy on that target?" the controller queried.

"Affirmative, Horse, target Grumpy 31 on this convoy. Have him contact the JSTARS, Cadillac 55 on Tad 212 for further information. How copy?"

"Yes, sir. Just to confirm, that Horse will assign the convoy target to GRUMPY 31 and have him contact Cadillac 55 on Tad 212 for an update," the AWAC's controller read back precisely.

"If there are any questions, give me a call. Maddog out," BC said, releasing the mic switch on his commo cord.

Aboard the JSTAR's, Lisa refreshed her screen every few minutes, watching the northern progress of the convoy as it approached the little Afghani town of Aliabad. The road split into a Y at this intersection, one branch going to Kunduz and the other to Taloqan through Khanabad. She wanted to make sure she knew which fork they took or if any of them split off. Intent on watching this one convoy so closely, she began to wonder whether she was missing anything else in her sector. Scrolling the display to show Mazar-e Sharif she refreshed the screen yet again.

Speechless, she was surprised to see another convoy, as big as the first, appear on her screen. This one was heading east towards Kunduz.

Dispensing with formalities she punched Buffalo's intercom excitedly. "Buffalo, I've got another GMTI hit. It's every bit as big as the first and it's headed east towards the Kunduz area."

"Sheeiitt. That makes it around 80 plus trucks headed to Kunduz. That's the biggest movement we've seen in Afghanistan. Period dot. I haven't heard from Maddog, I think I'll press him again. I'll be back to you in a minute."

"Yes, sir. I'll stay on top of it."

"Maddog, Maddog, Cadillac Alpha on uniform how copy?" Buffalo transmitted.

BC had been listening to the coordination frequency and he answered immediately, "Maddog here, go ahead."

"Yes, sir. Update on our convoy status. Now we've got a second GMTI cluster headed out of Mazar towards Kunduz. That makes two large convoys. This is the largest target we've seen so far in the war. Any luck with assets?"

Shifting in his seat, BC swallowed hard and replied, "Negative on the assets at the moment. Keep your eyes peeled on both of these convoys, let me know of any changes immediately. I've already targeted an inbound flight of Strike Eagles, call sign Grumpy 31. They're due in a little over an hour and just as soon as they check in Horse will send them your way. You can target them on either target as you see fit. How copy?"

Buffalo wrote down the inbound call sign, "Roger, copy. Target Grumpy 31. Sir, we may need more ordinance than one flight can carry."

"Maddog copies, that's all I've got right now. I've got another flight of Strike Eagles due after them; we'll see what develops. Keep me posted, Maddog out."

Lisa, watching the western convoy closely, had neglected to update on the southern group. Realizing her mistake, she scrolled her cursor over the southern area and refreshed her screen. "Uh, Buffalo. I'm tracking both convoys and the southern group just took the eastern Y at Aliabad."

"Okay, so what does that mean?" Buffalo asked.

"That means that they aren't going to Kunduz. They are headed for Khanabad right now. That's the road to Taloqan."

"So, we were right! They are headed to reinforce the Taliban getting ready to attack the NA at Taloqan."

"Yes, sir. It looks that way. We've got Americans down there don't we?"

"Yeah, we've got SF guys with the NA troops. I hope Grumpy 31 shows up a little early today!"

On the ridge overlooking Taloqan and Bangi, Brandon un-strapped the tripod from the packhorse they had brought with them. Methodically, he took out the spotting scope, attached it to the tripod, and then began attaching the power supply. Concentrating on his work, he hadn't even looked down into the valley since they had arrived.

Gary sat cross-legged on a big rock; he steadied his Steiner binoculars on his knees as he focused on Bangi. He spoke loudly to Brandon, "Dude, Bangi is crawling with T. They are all over the place. There are enough of these guys to attack real soon now, are you setup yet?"

"Yeah, I'm almost ready. I sure am glad we got up here when we did. Here we can see what's going on. Plus it's better to get away from that shit down there. Damn, you know I hadn't thought about it but what if we get cut off from Fahim or he's routed by this counter-attack?" Brandon asked as he sat down behind the tripod, preparing to observe Bangi.

Dropping his binoculars, Gary twisted slightly to look at Brandon. "Yeah, I've been thinking about that as well. We still have Johar, so we've got a guide. I think we'd have to go at it alone. The shortest way back to the established lines is to head northeast, cross the north road coming out of Taloqan, skirt the town and head east for friendly lines."

"That's okay by me. But wouldn't that be running out on Fahim. Don't we need to warn him of an attack or something?"

"Brandon. I'll send a runner to tell Fahim that the T is preparing a big counter-attack in Bangi. I told him we were headed for this ridge so we could put airstrikes on the T. That's what he expects, if we have to run to survive, well we gotta run. That's it."

"Okay, you're the boss. I don't feel right about it, that's all."

Laughing, Gary said, "Sometimes running is the better part of valor. Remember there are only a half dozen of us against a shitload of them."

"Let's see if we can make sure that doesn't happen. It's about time we get to work here. Would you set up your LST-5 on 322.525 so I can talk to AWACs and get us some air?"

While Gary began setting up his radio, Brandon quickly surveyed the places where the Taliban were congregating inside the town of Bangi. Punching the laser at each point, he developed a short list of coordinates to use as target data.

Finished, he looked at Gary who nodded and handed him the microphone handset. Taking it from his hand, he transmitted, "Horse, Mako 52."

The controller on board the AWACs had been waiting for a radio call from one of the ground FACs who replied, "Mako 52, Horse, go ahead."

Pleased that Horse had been on frequency and had replied so quickly, Brandon got down to business, "Horse, Mako 52 with an immediate CAS request." Holding his notepad in his hand, he waited for the reply.

"Mako 52, go ahead."

Brandon read, "Mako 52 has massed troops in the open, coordinates to be relayed, target elevation 1910 feet. TOT soonest. Mako 52, Tad 227, point A69. Friendlies three miles northeast, weather VFR, threats small arms/AAA. How copy?"

"Horse copies. It will be a little while. The next fighters available are already targeted. Next available air is well over an hour out."

Brandon was shocked, just the day before they were able to get bombs on target five minutes after the request. Today things were thin; perhaps he should have gotten on the list earlier. "Mako copies. Is there anyway to get priority? If we don't get support soon, this will be a TIC situation and it could get bad."

"Mako, I'll see what I can do. But for now I can't even throw you a Bone. The current flight just left Winchester. Standby this frequency and I'll get back to you."

"Shit, Gary. We're on the waiting list. This must be a slack time for air availability and we're not high on the priority list."

"That's just great. I've been watching the town and there's a large dust cloud coming in from around the southwest, towards Khanabad. I'm betting that must be reinforcements. If that's the case, at least it buys us a little more time, they won't do anything until they all get in," Gary answered.

"That's all we need, a little time before they kick our ass. We need to get air here now!" Brandon said grumpily, as he punched in the tactical frequency.

Shouting over his shoulder Dave, the commo guy said, "Hey, Gary. I think you'd better check this out. I think we've been spotted."

Startled, Gary jumped up and ran over, to see the terrain to the west of them. Gary followed his outstretched hand and saw about 30 to 40 Taliban running in small groups down the ridge towards their location. Several of them dropped to their knees and began firing AK-47s towards them. The fire was inaccurate at this range, but a ricochet could kill someone as well as a well aimed round. One or two of the AQ began firing RPGs towards them, the rockets falling short and exploding on the rocks between them.

Trying to decide whether they should fight it out or run, his concentration was broken buy Mike tapping his shoulder. "Gary, over at that shallow draw north of us, there are another 100 or so AQ coming our way. Dude, it's gonna be deep here."

"Damn, they've got us in a Pincer. Plus they've got the high terrain and most of the surprise." Gary decided instantly, spinning around, he shouted, "Okay, let's get the fuck out of here. Everybody to the Horses, *now*! Let's *go!*"

Running back to Brandon he shouted, "Dude, we're gonna get hit. Let's go, right now!" Grabbing the spotting scope he disconnected the battery. "Dave get the power supply for this thing, Brandon you take the radio. Everybody get on your horses, now! Go, go, go!"

Carrying the tripod to his horse, they started taking fire from the Taliban to the north. A bullet hit the rock near him, spraying him with dust and rock chips. A few seconds later he felt something on his eyebrow, with one hand he wiped his brow and out of the corner of his eye saw it covered in red.

The AQ were getting better with their fire; in seconds, bullets started impacting chaotically all around them. One by one, they jumped on their startled horses. Brandon threw the radio over the horse, looping the strap over the wooden pommel. Fluidly, he jumped on the horse like an experienced rider. "Don't drop that scope," he shouted at Gary, climbing onto his horse.

Holding the reigns above the horse's neck, Gary dug his heels into its belly. "Thanks for worrying about me, but now let's get the fuck out of here!"

Bullets snapped all around them now. They had gone less than 100 meters and were just reaching their stride. Suddenly, Johar's horse stumbled and fell, pitching Johar forward onto the ground. The team was busy galloping eastward, Mike heard Johar's shout. Turning he saw his fall, he reigned his horse, spun around in a dust cloud and rode back into the Taliban rifle fire to reach Johar.

Standing up groggily, Johar shook his head and didn't notice the blood gushing from his forehead. Mike slowed the horse and Johar grabbed the pommel of Mike's horse and one smooth motion, swung himself easily up behind him. Putting his arms around Mike's waist Johar shouted, "Shokran."

Spinning around again, Mike spurred his horse furiously to follow the others. He galloped down the ridgeline, away from the surprise attack.

Bouncing headlong down the hill it was all Brandon could do to keep his grip on the horse. Desperately trying to hold, on he heard the radio squawking. His first impulse was to hold onto the horse, if he fell he might be caught or killed. Gripping the saddle with both hands he decided to worry about the radio later.

The third time he heard the voice on the radio he forced himself to reach for the mic with his right hand, with a fierce grip he held the saddle with his left hand. At that moment the horse took a sudden swerve to the right and he smashed the mic against his mouth. Oblivious to the pain he pressed the transmit key, shouting breathlessly into the radio, "Grumpy, Mako 52, we're under attack and are displacing to the northeast. You are cleared hot on any target in and around the town of Bangi. I say again, cleared hot all targets around Bangi. Gotta go now."

CHAPTER 17

Rock Knoll Cave, Salang Pass, Afghanistan

Mark surveyed the room, nodding to himself in satisfaction that there was no one left alive that posed a threat in the room. One of the dead al-Qaeda was a young boy, suddenly he was overcome with the impact of all the men he had killed in that frenzied few minutes; in the next moment he pushed the emotion away. *It was either kill or be killed,* he thought. This is a brutal business; reality and truth were simple, survival essential. With a grimace, he bent over the pile of AK-47s near the front door and methodically began removing the clips and stripping the ammunition. "Woody, get Dave. Next thing we need to do is exploit this place for Intel. Tell him that time is short and get the fuck down here quick; the AQ will know we've been here before too long. You stay outside and stand guard, tell Mike and Luke to displace to a closer overwatch position, closer to the cave mouth."

Woody stood rooted to the spot; he stared unseeing around the room, 43 men dead. He had no idea that combat was like this, he was filled with revulsion at having killed these men, and he was still on an adrenaline high from the battle. He was also exhilarated at being alive. Without a scratch, Woody was wondering about the conflict between killing and living when he heard Mark. Staring, he slowly saw Mark come into focus.

"Woody, are you alright? Did you hear me?"

Jolted back into time, Woody shook his head slightly and said, "You bet. I'll get them moving and then stay outside and help keep watch." Turning to leave, he became aware of the coppery smell of blood and released bowels of the dead al-Qaeda. A wave of nausea swept over him and he ran outside. Stopping in the sun, he breathed deep, relieved to be in the fresh air and out of the cloying embrace of the cave.

Dave was near the cave mouth. He approached Woody, curious about what had happened inside. "Woody, I was beginning to wonder about you guys. I heard a flurry of activity, a bunch of shots and then nothing. I was thinking of charging the cave to see if you guys were in trouble. What's this?" Dave grabbed Woody's arm, it was soaked in blood. "Are you okay?"

"Ah, I don't know." Shocked he felt his arm through the sleeve of his jacket; his hand came away, covered in blood. "I, I guess I got a scratch after all. But it doesn't hurt; I'll take care of it. Mark says you can go in. He wants you to hurry, there's not much time. The AQ will be here real soon." As Dave turned to go inside, Woody put a hand on his shoulder, holding him gently. "Dude, be careful, it's terrible in there. It's really bad."

Without a nod, Dave disappeared inside the cave. Woody stood there and breathed deeply. The revulsion seemed to leave him, feeling better in the desert air he remembered what he had to do next and began climbing the mountainside. In a few moments he caught sight of Mike and Luke, he waved to them to come down the mountain.

They immediately began picking their way down the mountainside. Woody sat down on a rock to wait. Deliberately taking his canteen out of its pouch, he raised it to his lips; it was the first he noticed that his hand was shaking, violently. Grabbing the canteen with both hands, he took a long pull. Lowering the canteen he dropped his head and shoulders, rolling his head around from one side to the other he tried to stretch the tense muscles. Splashing a little water on his hand, he wiped his face. Looking up the mountain to check on the two observers progress he decided to refill the clips for his M-4.

Woody looked at the two men standing silently next to him. "Mark wants you guys to set up an overwatch closer to the cave and road. He and Dave are going to go through the cave as quickly as possible. After that he wants to get the hell outta here."

"Okay, have you done anything with that arm?" Mike asked, when Woody just looked at it absently he said, "Luke, go ahead and setup, I'm going to dress this arm first."

Wordlessly, Luke nodded and turned back uphill. Picking a ledge with a good view of the valley, he began setting up the Barrett.

Mike finished bandaging Woody's arm. "Dude, it's like that for everyone the first time. You get over it, you won't forget it, but you get over it. You were lucky; that round only grazed you. A couple of inches left and it would have gone into your chest, missing your body armor altogether."

Shaking Woody's shoulder lightly, Mike looked into his eyes. "You with me? Keep watch on this side of the mountain. Look for any movement all the way up to the ridge. Luke will watch the road and I'll keep tabs down the other side of the valley."

Woody watched Mike join Luke in his well-concealed spot. He felt better to be back in business. He found a protected spot and concealed his position as much as possible. He set his radio and weapon close at hand, and then felt for his binoculars. Absently, he patted his chest looking for the glasses, not finding them around his neck he rummaged in his pack. With a shrug he figured that he'd left them in the cave, time enough to get them later. He put his sunglasses on instead and began searching the mountainside.

Mike moved silently to another rock, opposite the cave entrance. Shrugging his pack off, he sat down with his back against a large boulder. Taking out his binoculars, he began scanning up the valley and along the road.

Inside the entrance to the cave, Dave stopped and slung his rifle across his back. Reaching into the chest pocket of his tan Gore-Tex parka, he pulled out a small digital camera. Moving around the radios setup in the front room, he began taking pictures of the scene inside the cave.

Satisfied that he had recorded the gross detail of the room, he shoved the camera back inside his pocket. Ignoring Mark, he went straight for the radio tables.

Mark, seeing Dave reach for the radio tables said, "Dave just be careful of the equipment. I'm rigging thermite grenades to 'em."

Snorting, Dave said sarcastically, "Hey, man, thanks for the heads-up, you couldn't wait a few minutes to rig a booby trap? It don't matter, I'm not interested in the radios. I'm looking for books, notepads and stuff like that." Gesturing to several piles of paper on the floor, he asked, "Is this it?"

"Some of it. There's more stuff in the next room. Some spiral notebooks and other stuff."

Dave squatted and began rummaging around through the papers on the floor. Half to himself he said, "These are tables, something like contact lists, callsigns, frequencies, times and stuff like that. This is good shit; we can use this. One thing for sure, these guys aren't Taliban. These guys are al-Qaeda," he said excitedly, sorting the paper into piles.

Mark finished booby-trapping the radio equipment and went back to the pile of weapons by the door. Carefully arranging the loose ammunition into a large pile, he placed two thermite grenades and two frag grenades under the pile. He gently laid an AK-47 on top of the spoons and covered the grenades with a few more weapons. Almost satisfied with his creation, he called out, "Hey, Dave.

Give me a hand, will ya? I need your help to steady this pile."

Dave reluctantly got up and joined Mark at the large pile of weapons by the door, "What do you need?"

"Here hold this AK for me while I pull the pins on the grenades. Don't let the rifle move, okay?" Mark glanced up at Dave. "Not an inch, okay?"

Dave grasped the rifle with both hands and Mark cautiously reached under it and slowly, but firmly pulled the pins, one at a time. With all four pins lying on the ground at his feet, he said, "Okay, now let go slowly. But be real careful, those things can make a real mess."

With exaggerated slowness, Dave released his grip on the weapon, backing away he straightened up. "Okay, now it's your turn to help me. There's a lot of shit here and I don't have time to look at it all. You gotta help me look for as much Intel as we can while we're here. I found those contact lists, some of them have countries and stuff on 'em."

"Fine, I'm done. Where do you want me to start?"

Dave nodded. Gesturing with his hand for Mark to follow him, he headed into the back room.

Luke held the Barrett .50 caliber lightly in his shoulder; with his eye to the scope he scanned the valley and the road. He had developed a pattern and was beginning to reset when he heard Mike in his ear. Pulling his head back from the scope, Luke looked over at Mike's hide spot. Their eyes met and Luke saw Mike was silently pointing down the valley. Luke followed with his eyes and saw a single al-Qaeda terrorist walking up the valley in the middle of the road.

Shifting the rifle, Luke put his eye back to the scope and began tracking the terrorist, crosshairs planted firmly on his head. Mike whispered in the radio, "Way too loud. Even the M-4 is too loud. There's only one guy so far, it'll have to be quiet. I'll do it, you keep watch."

Moving slowly Mike crawled to where Woody was sitting, scanning up the hill. Whispering in his ear, he said, "Woody, there's one guy walking down the road. I'm going to have to take care of him quietly. Keep a sharp lookout. I don't want to be surprised."

Moving silently, Mike crawled slowly down the side of the mountain. Shifting loose rock out of his way as he moved, he stopped just before the cave mouth near a large boulder. Wedging himself where he could keep an eye on the entrance and the approaching terrorist, he settled down to wait.

No time to warn Mark and Dave inside, he would have to eliminate the man all by himself, quickly and silently. Slowly, he laid his M-4 next to the rock. With his right hand, he reached for his boot knife strapped to the outside of his calf. Putting his finger over the snap he lifted it up with his thumb and silently drew a black Gerber Mark I fighting knife from the sheath. His jaw muscles tensed rhythmically, he was hyper aware of everything around him. He crouched like a statue, a tightly wound spring, ready to spring.

The lone al-Qaeda stopped at the chair left by the guard killed in the first assault. He saw the backpack that Dave had dropped near the chair; it was obviously a Military issue item, not common for al-Qaeda to carry. He reached down to pick it up, straightening he turned towards the cave mouth. Coiled like a snake about to strike, Mike was less than ten feet away, waiting for his chance to come from behind. Concentrating on breathing out of his mouth in order to control the noise of his breath, he switched his grip on the knife. With the hilt in his fist with the point down, he was totally absorbed in the moment.

Mike silently exploded from behind his hiding place. A few seconds and he was across the clearing. With his left hand Mike reached around the man's head, grabbing his mouth and chin in his gloved hand. He violently snapped his head up and back, pulling him off balance against his own body. Mike pressed the point of the knife on one side of the terrified man's throat, nearly to his shoulder. In one fluid motion, he pulled the knife through his throat in a single swift, violent stroke. Mike pushed the lifeless body away from him like a useless rag doll; soundlessly it slumped on the ground.

"Mudier Saleh, Amer is missing. It is his turn to prepare lunch and he has disappeared again."

"Yes, Adel, I know that he has a habit of doing that, whenever it is his turn to do his part for the group. I also know he has a friend at the communications cave, Ibrahim Farouk; take the truck up there to look for him. When you find him leave the truck there, I need to leave a machine gun at that cave."

"As you wish, Mudier," Adel Zaidi said, as he backed out of Saleh's sight.

"Come Salwa, we go to drive to the communications cave. Saleh has ordered the machine gun to the cave and you must take me to the cave."

Salwa Latif grunted and started the engine of the Toyota pickup and put it in gear. He took his time, picking his way down the narrow track that led to the road at the bottom of the valley. Only a few miles to the communications cave, he was not in a hurry and he wanted to enjoy the drive, it was better than sitting on a rock.

Mike stood above the dead al-Qaeda; expressionless, he wiped his knife clean on the man's sleeve and slid it back in the sheath. Reaching down, he grabbed the man by the collar of his jacket and dragged him into the cave.

Mark saw Mike enter the cave, his cargo in tow. "Mike, watch out for that pile of AKs, I booby trapped 'em. What'cha got there?"

"A snooper. Don't know where he came from, but there'll probably be more soon. Boss, how 'bout we get outta here now?" Turning, he went back outside.

"Yep, you're right, we'll be just a few more minutes. Go back outside and keep watch. We'll be out in a second," Mark said as he turned to find Dave happily rummaging in the back room.

"Dave, we've been had. Pack up what you want and let's go!"

"Dude, just a minute. You know these spiral notebooks? They've got some sort of plans in them. This one here looks like notes on the World Trade Center. This other one, with the title 'raising rabbits' doesn't have anything to do with rabbits. It starts with a description of an SA-7, how's that for BS?"

"Take it with you, Dave. Come on, we're out of time. Let's go," Mark said forcefully.

Dave just stood there with notebooks in his hands. "Dude, this is a treasure trove of Intel. Do you realize this is hard evidence linking the al-Qaeda with the 9/11 attack? There's probably Intel on other attacks as well. We just can't leave it here."

A few seconds passed as the two men stood facing each other in the grim light of the cave interior. Before they could consider their options, a loud *KEERRRAACKK*, followed quickly be a second smaller report, reverberated menacingly in the cave walls.

Flinching, Dave broke the silence. "What the Fuck was that?"

"That, my friend, is the bell. It's time to run, *now*! If we stay any longer we're toast. Just pick something and go," Mark said, spinning on his foot he headed for the door.

"Do me a favor, Bud, grab that pile of contact lists on the way out for me!" Weighing his decision he finally decided to keep the WTC book and the book on rabbits, the rest he tossed on top of another labeled "Breath of God" and ran out of the room.

Woody ran up the hill to join Luke, flinging himself on the ground, he breathlessly said, "Something is coming up the valley. So you hear it?" Luke nodded silently, looking down the valley. Luke had heard the engine noise of a truck, swinging the scope of the Barrett to cover the road; he waited for what would come.

About 2500 meters Luke could see it plainly, pressing the throat mic he said, "Shit! Guy's it's a technical vehicle and they've got a 14.5mm machine gun. I can't let 'em get any closer with that thing, better watch your ears."

The truck straightened out on a stretch of road, taking careful aim Luke put the crosshairs on the drivers nose. Luke gently squeezed the trigger.

Surprised by the Barrett's recoil, Luke briefly lost sight of the target. Searching frantically he reacquired the truck and aimed at the engine. He concentrated hard; leading the truck with Kentucky windage he squeezed the trigger again. Seconds passed in eternity before the bullet hit, finally the truck turned sharply left and veer off the road. It climbed the mountain in slow motion, pausing it hung in the air for seconds. Teetering on two wheels, it fell and began to rollover and over back into the road.

Woody felt his chest, after Luke had fired the two shots he felt like someone had kicked him. He had been next to the muzzle of the gun when it went off and realized that the concussion of the two fifty caliber rounds had slapped him hard. Crawling backwards until he was behind Luke, he rolled over on his back. Gasping for breath he felt nauseous.

Luke used a Sound Tech sound suppressor on the .50 caliber sniper rifle. Five and a half inches long, weighing 2.7 pounds, it was screwed onto the end of the rifle. Calling it a silencer is a misnomer, what it really did was cut the noise of the muzzle blast below the sound of the bullet. It couldn't make the sonic wave disappear altogether.

Mike rushed out of the cave, his weapon in front of him, looking frantically around he called to Luke on the radio, "Where is the target? What's going on? Are we clear?"

Luke, scanning the scene with his Springfield scope, looked for survivors or any other activity. After clearing the scene he called down to Mike, "About two klicks down the road, technical vehicle. I had to take it out. Clear above; no other movement at the moment."

"Mudier, did you hear that? It sounded like a shot. I think there were two shots outside, very loud." Saleh's servant said as he rushed into the room. Slipping his sandals on, Saleh ran outside and looked around the mountain. He could easily see the truck, burning in the middle of the road less than a mile away.

"Where did the shot come from? Did anyone see or hear an airplane? Quickly, Abdul call the radio cave and warn them of an attack." Saleh went back inside the cave to pick up his rifle and pistol.

Solicitously, Saleh's servant said, "Mudier, the radio cave is not answering our calls. Our telephone line there has been cut. And no one has seen an airplane."

Like a rising tide, they were surrounded by over a hundred shouting al-Qaeda, waving their rifles excitedly.

Saleh faced the fighters, he shouted to the men, "First we must go to the aid of our brothers in the radio cave. Some of you follow me, the rest of you go and see what you can do for our brothers on the truck. If it is an airplane, hide in the rocks. Keep your eyes open and kill anything that is not Arab. Let's go."

He began running towards the radio cave followed by more than 50 of his fighters. Another group rushed down the hill towards the burning truck.

Mike decided to get Mark and Dave out of the cave, he ran towards the door. Just as he reached it, Mark ran out of the door, "What's going on, Mike?"

"Sir, Luke shot a Tech vehicle about two klicks down the road. Right now we think it's a singleton, but we don't know," Mike replied.

"Damn." Impatiently he spun around to call Dave to hurry up. Seeing him come out of the door, Mark just held out his fist, holding a wad of the contact lists that he had grabbed from the pile near the radios.

"Right behind you, Mark," Dave said as he bent over his backpack. Stuffing first the two notebooks, and then the contact lists, into his pack.

Looking up at the rock face Mark called to Luke on the radio, "Luke, what do you see now?"

"Sir, it was a Tech vehicle with a 14.5. I just couldn't let them get closer, so I shot the driver and the engine. The truck crashed and is burning in the middle of the road. No other movement so far," Luke replied.

"Fine, keep your eyes peeled." Turning back to Mike, Mark pointed at the man he had killed. "Where did this single guy come from?"

"We don't know he just appeared walking up the road," Mike replied nervously.

"Shit, he probably came from another cave complex on this side of the valley. I'd bet there are more that'll be coming soon," Mark said. Squatting down, he pulled out his map. If they couldn't go back the way they had come, he had to figure out a new exit route. "We've got to go west, the sooner the better."

Looking up Mark scanned the valley. "We gotta get some distance between us and this cave. We'll make for that knoll on the other side of the valley about a klick away. First rally point is that outcropping of rock on the other side of this clearing. Is everyone ready?" He looked into everyone's eyes, before he commanded, "Okay, it's about 350 to 400 meters away, let's move!"

Mike and Dave started running across the flat area for the rock outcropping. Mark quickly scanned around the cave mouth looking for anything they had left and then he too ran across the clearing. Picking up the 35 pound sniper rifle by the carrying handle Luke said, "Woody, do me a favor and take this bag of rounds for the Barrett, I can't carry it all like this."

Slinging his pack and the PRC-117 radio on his back, Woody answered, "Sure man." Picking up the ammo bag he said, "Damn this is heavy. How many rounds are in here?"

"Less than a hundred. But, they're big bullets! Let's go!"

Luke and Woody were the last to sprint across the small clearing in front of the communications cave. They ran towards the rally point. Reaching the relative shelter of the rocks, Woody tried to go around Luke to the left. He caught his foot on a stick or a rock and began to fall. Spinning to the left to keep the radio from hitting the rocks, he fell heavily on his injured arm. Luke stopped to help him up.

"Hold here a second," Mark said, he pulled his binoculars out to look down the valley at the burning truck. "There are nearly a hundred AQ around the truck." Shifting his gaze to the cave mouth he scanned up the hillside, "Shit, there are more coming down the hill towards the truck!" He spun around; with his back to the rock he slipped to the ground, letting the binoculars fall to his chest. The situation was deteriorating rapidly, furious, he tried to think of a way out.

Coming to a decision he threw his hand out in a chopping motion. "Guys, I don't have to tell you that we're in deep chim'chee, here. If we go across that valley floor now, they'll spot us for sure. I don't think they know we're here yet and I'd like to keep it that way as long as we can. We'll set up a hasty defense here."

Intently looking at each man in turn, he said, "Dave you take the west side, Mike you're on the north, Luke I want you on the southeast where you have a clear field of fire down the road and towards the cave, that's where our biggest threat is and that's where we need our biggest gun. Woody, I need you in the middle with your radio, get on the horn and call that silly son of a bitch air boss of yours and get some air in here. Fast! You gotta keep us alive!"

Mark finished his briefing, "If we're lucky they believe that there was an airstrike. Maybe we can keep up the charade and make it to nightfall. Woody, we need a few more airdrops to keep their heads down. Everybody, let's even out the ammo and don't shoot unless it's absolutely necessary. Any questions? No? Let's move!"

With silent purpose they quickly moved into positions amongst the rocks. Trying to make themselves small they huddled in the rocks, watching and waiting. The only noise was the occasional muffled explosion of ammunition cooking off in the burning truck and Woody's urgent radio calls whispered to Horse in the portable radio.

Above Bangi, Afghanistan

Grumpy, unsure of the radio transmission he had just heard, asked Pinto, his backseater, "What the fuck did he say?" They had been expecting a FAC brief before getting clearance to drop on any targets. Instead, all they had heard was a jumbled radio call from Mako 52.

Looking at his map, Pinto replied, "I think he said they were displacing and under fire. At the end he cleared us hot on any target in and around Bangi."

"So, it's up to us I guess. The AWAC's controller said there was a large convoy heading for Bangi. Maybe that's what we should hit. Get your Pod out and take a look see," Grumpy said.

"I'm on it, slewing it there now," Pinto said, gently pressing the TDC of the right hand controller with his thumb. He pulled aft once on the auto aqc switch to shift to wide field of view. "Dude we're about 12 miles out and I don't see anything through this soda straw. Do you see anything at all?" He was looking for some input, or direction, from Grumpy.

Peering out of the canopy into the distance, Grumpy replied, "I see a good sized dust plume leading into town. Hold on and I'll cue your pod." Gripping the stick, he pressed the castle switch down and flicked forward twice to take control of the pod. Pushing the nose over slightly until he was light in his seat, he put the diamond displayed in the HUD on the leading edge of the dust plume and at the same time pressed the throttle mounted TDC to designate a new target. "Done. You should be on the leading edge of the dust plume."

With a flick of a switch Pinto took control the pod, "I've got it. I see one, two, five, er, whew, there must over 35 trucks on that convoy."

Excited, Grumpy nearly shouted over the intercom, "Shit hot! Re-designate the lead truck as my target. I want to do a box pattern on that guy and drop two cans of CBU-87 in his face. Ha! He's gonna get a surprise!!" Rolling quickly, he made a sharp hard turn to the right to parallel the convoy's track. Over the back radio he said, "Marker Two, go trail. We're gonna target that convoy; visual box pattern at base altitude, straight ahead pull, two cans, I'll take the lead off the convoy, you take the tail, acknowledge."

"Roger, two has the trailer, CDIP pass with two cans."

"Pinto, how fast do you think that guy is going?"

"He's probably doing better than 30 miles an hour."

"Okay, I want you to keep designating him as a target, until we get about eight miles in front of him. That's when I'm going to turn base."

"Okay, Grumpy do you want me to lase him and go CDES?"

Looking left to gauge his offset from the rushing convoy, Grumpy said, "No, I don't want the distraction of the changing target diamond. I'll eyeball it at the end."

"Dude. If you do that you won't get accurate ranging and target elevation. If I track the truck and have the system update continuously, you'll have a good diamond on the guy. Just roll in a little long to compensate."

"Okay, go ahead. I'd forgotten about the ranging deal. But I'm doing this pass in CDIP." With his left hand, he reached to the Up Front Controller and punched the A/G button to switch the system into air-to-ground mode. "Don't forget to get the PACS setup for two cans per pass."

"Already done. And you've got a good track and CDES on the truck," Pinto said. "You've got about six miles spacing on the target now."

"Here's what I'm gonna do. I'm going to start at 15k above the ground and roll out level on the road in front of the lead truck. When the diamond gets to 15 degrees low I'm gonna roll-in. That way I think the bombs will come off around 25 to 30 degrees."

"I'm witcha buddy, your all green and I see a cross in the HUD."

Glancing at the Master Arm switch, the single switch that controlled the electrical current in the weapon release system, above his left knee, Grumpy replied, "Yeah, my master arm is on." Quickly looking back outside he decided that now was the time to turn. He rolled left, into an 80-degree bank and smoothly put five g's on the jet. As the jet passed 90 degrees of turn, he suddenly slacked off the pull and rolled out again on a base leg.

"Here comes the road," Grumpy said, repeating the previous turn to roll out on the road face to face with the convoy rushing headlong down the road. Concentrating on his altitude and airspeed he could plainly see the lead truck. "Good diamond, they're moving fast!"

It seemed like minutes before the diamond dropped down the pitch ladder to 15 degrees low. But at 540 knots it took less than three seconds. "One's in," Grumpy called over the back radio.

Rapidly rolling left, he stopped when the jet was upside down and quickly pulled about four g to bring the nose down to 40 degrees nose low. Rolling left again to move back to his planned dive bomb line, he stopped when the jet was upright. The CDIP pipper was bouncing around and he had trouble seeing the diamond. Thinking quickly, he thumbed aft on the autoacq to switch back to an auto delivery. The azimuth steering line appeared just touching the diamond, rolling in just a little bit of aileron, he pulled slightly to the right to get the auto pipper/velocity vector on the ASL. Settling on the line, he pushed the pickle button and pulled up the line to meet the release cue. Rewarded with two quick jolts as the bombs left the airplane, he immediately pulled five g to climb back up to altitude.

On the back radio he called, "One's off. Recommend an auto toss pass, terrain is too rugged for good ranging."

"Two," came the reply over the radio.

"Pinto, I almost screwed that one up. The CDIP pipper was all over the place and I couldn't see the truck for all the green shit in my face. I'm sure glad you had a good track and CDES going. You were right."

Checking the PACS weapons release parameters, Pinto said, "Yeah, you had about two seconds of track time. But look at it this way, with a steeper delivery angle the bomblet pattern is tighter. You got that going for ya!"

Pinto took control of the targeting pod and scanned the convoy before he punched off the video record button. "Good hit on the lead trucks. I think you got five or six on that pass. You'll have to go CDIP on the next one, there's too much smoke for us to track any of those heat sources very well. I'll get a good update and we can use the system for ranging, it should be good enough for what's left."

"Yeah, I think I'll do the same pattern, but give myself about four more miles so I can good and setup before the roll-in. I'd like a shallower angle for the next group."

Pinto, still watching the convoy, could see them starting to bunch up near the burning trucks at the front. He smiled inside his oxygen mask when two's bombs impacted. Little hot spots, the drivers and passengers of the remaining trucks, began running away from the burning vehicles like ants boiling out of an anthill.

"Marker, let's make one more pass. I'll take the leaders again, single can this time," Grumpy called on the radio.

"Marker Two copies."

"Grumpy, you've got a good designation. I've been looking around the town and there is a shit load of folks gathered in the middle of town. Do you suppose they are the targets Mako 52 wanted us to hit?" Pinto asked.

"Could be, but without Mako's eyes on target. I don't want to drop on anything we see, especially if it's in a town."

"Yeah, your right," Pinto replied. "I'll try and raise him on the radio while you make this next pass."

"Good idea," Grumpy replied, over the back radio. "One's base to drop one."

After his second pass, Grumpy stopped his pull at 20 degrees nose up, slowing his climb. He started a lazy, shallow turn to the left. Out of the canopy, he watched his wingman's as pass he continued to turn. When Marker Two had completed his safe escape maneuver, Grumpy called over the radio, "Marker, let's climb back to base plus eight. Stay in trail."

Marker Two's response was blocked by a call on the front radio, "Marker 31, Horse, I have emergency tasking for you."

Grumpy thumbed the mic switch forward and said, "Horse this is Marker 31. Ready to copy." To Pinto he added, "Quick, write this down."

"Marker 31, Horse. Proceed to the Salang Pass area ASAP. I've got an emergency troops in contact situation. Contact Mako 51 on Tad 277 for further instructions."

"Marker copies all. Horse, understand that we have been working targets already and we don't have a full load."

"Horse copies. You're the only fighters available. Good luck!"

"Roger, Marker copies."

"Grumpy, just turn south. Salang is north of Kabul and I'll have steering for you in a second," Pinto said.

"Pinto, before you change freqs let me check out with Mako 52," Grumpy said on the intercom, thumbing the front radio he said, "Mako 52, Mako 52, Marker 31 calling in the blind. We've been called off for another mission. Good luck."

Grumpy left the throttles in Mil power until the jet accelerated to .9 Mach. He knew that Two would be able to catch up once they got to the new target area. He pushed Marker south towards Kabul as fast as he could. When Pinto finished setting the new frequency in the radio Grumpy tried to raise Mako 51. "Mako 51, Mako 51, this is Marker 31, how copy?"

"Marker 31, Marker 31, this is Mako 51," came the weak reply. "Say posit."

Relieved to finally hear the beleaguered troops on the radio Grumpy replied, "Mako 51, Marker has you weak but readable. We are north of Bagram Airbase."

"Mako copies. Marker, you are too far south, Turn north now."

"Marker copies, in the turn. Do you have a GPS coordinate I can steer too?"

Woody realized that in the heat of the moment he was going about things the hard way. He did have a GPS and coordinates would make things a lot easier. With the microphone in his right hand, the earpiece pressed hard against his ear, he lifted his left hand to look at his GPS watch. The face was smashed, "Damn it, I must have fallen on it.'

"Negative, Mako 51's GPS has been smashed. I'll have to talk you onto the target the old-fashioned way," Woody transmitted in disgust.

"Marker copies, Mako can you authenticate with a 1551?"

"Marker, I can't do that either, we're kinda in a bind here. You'll have to trust us, our survival depends on you," Woody replied.

His heart in his throat, Grumpy was willing to give him the benefit of the doubt, "Okay, copy that Mako. I'm ready for your brief."

"Marker, Mako doesn't have a brief for you, either." Breathing hard, he worked the radio, oblivious to everything but the handset; he tried to put himself into the cockpit with the pilot. "The deal here is simple, the good guys are surrounded on a small knoll and the bad guys are all around us. We'll have to do this on the fly. Follow the road out of Kabul, past Bagram airbase. If you keep on that road it will run up to a mountain pass with a couple of villages on the right. The road will go into a tunnel at the top of the ridgeline- that is Salang Pass. From that, point hop over to the first valley to the west. About five miles further north, see the smoke from a burning truck. When you see that call me back."

"Roger Mako, we're headed north now, have the road in sight. Where are the friendlies? You know you're not giving us much to work with?" Grumpy replied testily.

"Sorry Marker, it's the best I've got right now. We're kind of in a crack." Woody was getting a little frustrated with the Flight Lead's attitude.

"Sorry Mako, if it wasn't for your accent I'd suspect you for your lack of procedure," Grumpy called.

"Well, Marker, if you'd rather speak with one of our hosts, you could just hang around a few minutes. It all happened real fast and we didn't have time to prepare anything. There are only five of us and several hundred of them, I expect they'll be little harder to understand."

Listening to their conversation, Mark patted Woody on the shoulder. "Take a breath, man, we need that guy."

Woody grimaced back at Mark, realizing that he was right. He decided to be a littler calmer on the radio.

Luke, squinting through his scope, said, "Boss, it looks like they are sending out a search party, they're looking for something. And they're headed our way."

Mark trained his binoculars on the group at the cave, there were about 10 T beginning to form and walk towards them. A few of them apparently were looking at the tracks made by the American boots. Mark watched their progress, when there was a sudden explosion from just inside the cave mouth. As a secondary blast filled the silence, the searchers dropped on the ground. Just in time, someone inside the cave had set off one of his booby traps.

Sensing an opportunity, Mark swung the binoculars to look down at the burning truck. "Luke, pick off a few of those T down at the truck. Sow a little confusion, they won't know where the shot is coming from."

"Glad to be of service," Luke replied. He spread his jacket below the muzzle of the gun in an attempt to suppress any dust blown up by the muzzle blast. Settling the butt of the Barrett firmly into his shoulder, he took his time and sighted on the Taliban around the truck.

"Mark, that cannon is going to tell the T right where we are. Let me get this air in first," Woody said.

Conspiratorially, Mark said, "Just watch, man. The shot will confuse the hell out of 'em. The silencer drops the noise of the muzzle blast below that of the bullet. They'll be 90 degrees or more out. Trust me, just watch."

Luke took three shots in succession, just as fast as the semi-automatic M82 reloaded. Four of the al-Qaeda around the truck suddenly exploded in a mist of red, showering those next to them. The rest of the Taliban, milling in confusion near the truck, ran for cover when they figured out their friends had been shot.

Some of the Taliban at the cave had begun to get to their feet when the first shot rang out. Before the last one had echoed down the valley they were all on the ground again and all of them were looking towards the truck.

Mark slapped Woody on the shoulder, with a smile on his face he said in a low voice, "The Finns in World War Two had a saying about snipers, they said that a silencer didn't make a sniper silent, it made him invisible. How's your buddy on the radio doing?"

Woody shook his head and put the microphone back to his ear, "Marker 31, Mako 51 how goes it?"

"Mako, Marker is at the pass now, we see the tunnel. We're coming down the first valley to the west," Grumpy transmitted. To Pinto he said, "When we get a good idea of where the target is and where they are, track it with your pod and get us a good coordinate of where they are."

Pinto, concentrating on the targeting pod video said, "Way ahead of you boss. I've got two separate fires in that valley, about two klicks apart."

On the front radio, Grumpy transmitted, "Mako, Marker has two fires, or hotspots, in the valley. The southern one is larger than the northern."

Relieved, Woody called back, "Copy that, there are two fires now. Use the two fires as the base of a triangle; we are the tip of that triangle to the southwest. Our location is a small outcropping of rock about 1,000 meters southwest of the northern fire on a small outcropping of rock. We are about 400 meters west across a clearing from the eastern fire?"

"Grumpy, I've got the fires easily. Give me a minute and I'll see if I can figure out this triangle and find that rock. The smoke appears to be blowing south and covering the area somewhat," Pinto said as he frantically scanned the area with the targeting pod, switching contrast and polarity in an attempt to breakout the knoll.

"Mako, I see the two fires but smoke has obscured the area somewhat. I'm going to set up an orbit, standby," Grumpy said.

"Grumpy, I'm in narrow and I see several small hot spots southwest of the northern fire. But I can't make out how many there are," Pinto said in frustration.

"Mako, this is Marker. We think we have you, but can't be sure. Is there anyway you can mark your position?"

"Marker, I'm sorry but no way. If we do anything like that we'll bring too much attention down on us, these guys are closer. What I need you to do is drop on both fires; there are large amounts of bad guys around those areas. What ordinance are you carrying?" Woody asked.

"Marker has CEM in wind corrected dispensers, two each. CBU-103," Grumpy replied.

Rolling on his side Woody looked at Mark with a scared look in his eyes. "Shit, they've got cluster bombs. That's great for the big crowd out there, but if they miss those guys at the cave, we're fucked."

Mark steadied his shoulder, "Dude, we don't have much in the way of choices here."

Nodding, Woody said, "Okay, have everybody hug their rocks tight. This might get bad." Putting the headset back to his ear he said, "Mako copies, I have you in sight, drop one can on the eastern fire, use a north-south line and a high angle. We're only 400 meters away, expect clearance on final."

"Roger, one can on a north-south line," Grumpy replied.

Watching the F-15 roll in on the northern fire, Woody waited until he was sure the nose of the fighter was headed away from their position. "Marker, cleared hot, repeat, cleared hot!"

"Marker One cleared hot," Grumpy repeated calmly and pressed the pickle button. As soon as he felt the jerk of the weapons departing he began a 5g pull to recover from his 45-degree dive. "One's off hot."

Woody covered his head with his arm, hugged his rock tightly and yelled as loud as he could yell, "Incoming!

Woody squirmed his head so that he could see the second fighter out of the corner of his Kevlar helmet. When he could see his nose was clear of their position he transmitted, "Marker Two, cleared hot, repeat, cleared hot!"

Breathing hard he could smell the rock inches from his face. He convinced himself that he could hear the whirr of the spinning canister, when the POP of the clamshell doors springing open surprised him. He knew the little bomblets were being flung out at high speed. Three or four of the bomblets hit each other and exploded in the air. Less than a second later the roar of the main group of bomblets struck the ground and enveloped them in a rolling thunder of dust and noise.

Stunned by the concussion, Woody waited until the noise had subsided before he peered over the rock. Raising the radio handset to his ear he said, "Marker, the smoke is a little heavy right now, but it looks like a good hit for both passes. Thanks a lot, you bought us a little more time!"

"Mako, no worries, glad to help. We'll orbit overhead until you need us. Be advised that we have one more pass each, and then we're Winchester," Grumpy called.

"Roger copy. I expect we'll have more trade for you just as soon as the smoke clears."

CHAPTER 18

Rock Knoll Cave, Afghanistan

The afternoon breeze slowly organized the smoke of the cluster bomb attack, pushing it up the valley away from the rock knoll where five Americans hid. The initial attack by the F-15E fighters, meant to drive off the group of al-Qaeda that threatened to surround them, served as a beacon call for the al-Qaeda fanatics in the area. Like ants they boiled out of other caves along the mountainside, in minutes several thousand men looking frantically for a target surrounded them. Woody slowly poked his head above his rock, looking for his next target. With two passes left, he had to be careful which target he chose.

Woody looked back towards the cave; the dust was just starting to clear when he felt a tap on his shoulder. Turning he saw Mark, a pair of binoculars in hand, pointing towards the ridge they had crossed in the night. Woody took the glasses, bringing them to his eyes he focused on the notch.

What he saw made his jaw drop, a dense group of AQ, several hundred, maybe more were coming over the ridge. One group was dragging something large and bulky across the rocky ground. "What do you think they're doing?" Mark whispered.

Watching the scene, Woody replied, "Shit! They're dragging a twin-barreled gun; I'd bet it's a ZU-23. It's an anti-aircraft gun."

Mark whistled quietly, "Yeah, an automatic weapon that big would tear the shit out of us."

"It's worse than that, they want to hit our fighters with it." Woody picked up the radio handset. "Marker, Mako, I've got another target for you."

"This is Marker, go ahead," Grumpy replied.

"Mako has a large group of Taliban dragging a wheeled AA gun. The target is east of the first strike. Near the top of the ridge, it's about four klicks away from us. Recommend one pass."

"Marker copies, looking," Grumpy replied. He shallowed his turn, flying a wider circle over the Salang Pass, to allow Pinto a longer look at the area with the target pod. He pushed the power to Mil to keep his energy up as he climbed slightly. Better to have a little altitude if that gun started shooting.

Pinto cued the pod to the first target and slewed it up the mountain. Toggling the polarity of the infrared pod back and forth, he tried to breakout the group of people. In black hot he saw a blob near the top of the ridgeline. It wasn't drastically different from the rest of the terrain, so he quickly switched to white hot. The airplane continued turning through the south towards the west, changing the contrast of the scene he was watching. Suddenly he saw people, and the gun, emerge out of the blob. Shouting, he said, "Yeah, baby, yeah. I've got it in white. They must have fired that thing recently. It's hotter than a Saturday night special. I wonder why I didn't see it before. Grumpy, I'll designate it so you can have steering."

Grumpy silently tightened his turn and rolled out with the diamond at the bottom of the HUD. With a flick of the stick he rolled the airplane over on its back and pulled the nose down about 15 degrees. Rolling upright, he looked intently through the HUD. Through the designation, he realized the target was winking at him, it was the muzzle flash of the gun, shooting at him! He slammed the stick over at 500 degrees per second, stopping somewhere near 45 degrees of bank he laid on five g to get out of the gun sights fast!

"Hell, yes, it's white hot, the fuckers are shooting at us right now!" Grumpy told Pinto as he climbed back up to altitude. Keying the radio he said, "Mako, I've got the target. I'll make a pass west east. Are you the only friendlies in the area?"

"Affirmative. Marker, you are cleared hot on that target," Woody replied. Sitting up, he had been following the progress of Grumpy's F-15E as it made its orbit overhead.

Woody lowered the microphone twisting to watch the plane. Suddenly, he couldn't breathe, searing pain filled his chest. Stunned, everything seemed to slow down, and all he could think of was being hit. Gasping for air, he looked down at his chest, searching for a bullet.

Mark grabbed a handful of Woody's shirt and jerked him down, yelling, "Get down, Woody, what the fuck do you think you're doing? You're a sitting duck up there." Seeing the distant worried look in his eyes he realized that he had been hit and began looking for an entry wound. Frantically searching Woody's Kevlar jacket, Mark's hand touched the still hot bullet. Burned, he flapped his hand to cool it off and then pulled out his boot knife. Working quickly, he pried the broken and ragged lead and copper bullet out of the jacket and dropped it on the ground. "That was a ricochet. They probably saw you hanging out up there like a hero or something. You're damn lucky you didn't get hit by the full force of that round."

Safely behind the rock, Woody looked at him uncomprehendingly, still in pain; Mark must have missed the real bullet. Unzipping the jacket, he frantically explored his chest in more detail. With pity Mark just repeated, "You're lucky you were wearing that flak jacket."

Their rock knoll had been an oasis in the cacophony of the battle, but suddenly a volley of incoming rounds struck the rocks around them in a rapid staccato fire. Mike announced, "Well, it looks like they know we're here for sure now. The north is clear."

"I think those incoming rounds came from the south," Luke said as he guarded the southern perimeter. Snuggling amongst the rocks, he shouldered the Barrett again and squinted into the scope.

The volley of machine gun fire on their position acted like a beacon to the surviving Taliban in the area. Soon the group began taking small arms fire all around their position. Not very accurate, it was heavy enough to make them keep their heads down.

Thinking the Taliban might be using it as cover, Luke fixed his gaze on the remains of the burning truck. Patiently he waited. As if on cue, another truck darted onto the road from behind a boulder, it stopped and fired a few wild rounds. Just as quickly, it pulled back behind shelter. Luke shouted, "Incoming!"

A fraction of a second later, the volley of fire from the technical vehicle's machine gun struck the rocks. Dust and rock chips covered them as the bullets ricocheted off the boulders protecting them. At the center of attention, they began taking heavier AK-47 fire from around the cave mouth.

"That machine gun is a marker for these other bozos. Luke have you seen it? You gotta take it out," Mark said, crouching behind a rock.

Without a word, Luke crawled out from behind his rock. Looking for a better shot, he was determined to nail him the next time the truck darted out into the open. He shouldered the Barrett again and quietly focused on where he had seen the truck emerge.

Rounds were cracking all around him as he calmly sighted into the scope. The truck darted out from behind the rock at an angle, its nose pointed slightly towards him. Luke tracked the front of the truck, when it stopped, he squeezed off two rounds in quick succession. The first .50 caliber round struck the truck in the radiator and penetrated into the engine where it broke into a thousand shards; the engine stopped running immediately, a tangled mess of broken metal. The second round hit the aluminum engine block just to the right of the first, barely slowing down it went right through. Missing connecting rods and pistons, it cut through the engine, through the passenger compartment into the back of the truck. Taking off the right foot of the gunner as it passed, the bullet continued on, finally hitting the rocks behind the truck.

Luke murmured, "That guy's toast." Twisting to his side, he cradled his rifle and began crawling back behind the rocks. A flurry of rounds impacted near him, kicking up rock chips in his face. He scurried faster across the ground like an ungainly crab, with the heavy sniper rifle slowing him down. Before he could make it to safety, more rounds impacted the rocks, abruptly spinning him around, falling with a loud *Choof.*

Mark saw Luke fall, immediately he scrambled towards him, reaching out from behind the rocks, he grabbed his feet and physically dragged him to safety. Mark pressed his fingers on Luke's carotid artery, checking for a pulse. Flushed and breathing hard, he shouted, "He's alive. Woody, get that rifle, you gotta save that rifle!"

Mark rolled him onto his side, Luke coughed harshly several times, but he didn't have any blood on his back. Mark gently rolled him on his back to check for a front entry wound. Mark found a small hole in the BDU jacket over the right breast; he poked his finger through it and wiggled it around. Unbuttoning the jacket he feared that he would find the entry hole, instead he burned his finger on the hot slug stuck in Luke's flak jacket.

"Luke, you're one lucky son-of-a-bitch. Your Kevlar saved your ass. That's two saves for Kevlar today!"

Trying to control a coughing fit, Luke just nodded, he put his hands behind his knees and pulled himself into a sitting position. Straightening his back, with his head held all the way back he took a deep breath. Bursting out in coughing fits between breaths, Luke tried to catch his breath and calm himself down.

"You'll be alright. Maybe your lung is partially collapsed. Breathing is the best thing, just don't breathe so deeply it hurts. Take it easy for awhile, you bought us some time," Mark encouraged him.

Woody crawled out near where the Barrett lay in the dirt. Afraid, he waited for a lull in the firing to grab the rifle. When the impacting rounds had slowed to a sporadic trickle, he lunged out and grabbed the rifle by its carrying handle. As quick as he could he pulled it and fell backwards. Rolling on his side he drug it with him as fast as he could go.

Making another pass overhead, Pinto watched the action below in the F-15E target pod. He could easily see white-hot rounds converging on the rock knoll. Clearing his throat he said, "Grumpy, are you watching this? Don't you think it's time we call for more air support. These guys are in deep, they'll need cover for a while and we've only got one pass left. We need to get ahead of the coordination game."

"Yeah, you're right. It's still over three hours till sunset and we just can't protect these guys that long. I'll stay on freq with Mako, you go ahead and call Horse," Grumpy replied.

Pinto briefly transmitted on the Aux radio that he would be off the frequency for a few minutes. Then he changed to the tactical Horse freq. "Horse, Marker, request."

"Go ahead with your request, Marker," the radar sector controller aboard the AWAC's replied.

"Horse, Marker requests a relief to work with Mako. These guys are in real trouble and we're a long way from done. Our flight is very close to Winchester," Pinto asked.

"Standby, Marker, I'll check," the controller replied, switching to intercom he thumbed the mic switch, "Hey Colonel BC, north sector, I've got Marker, flight of two F-15Es, working a Troops in Contact with Mako. They're requesting a relief; they're Winchester and it's time to RTB."

BC listened for a second, he had one set of fighters on the way in, but he'd already assigned them to work with Mako 52. The only thing he had left were JDAM droppers, he shook his head. "Tell him to stay on station as long as he can and then return to base. I've got a gunship headed their way after sunset."

"Marker, Horse here. Maddog says there is a gunship scheduled after dark, he says work with Mako a long as you can and then go home."

On his swing through the north—wide of the target area, Grumpy saw a disturbing sight. He immediately got on the radio, "Mako, Marker. I see a group of three vehicles coming south down the road from the other side of the ridge. They are headed your way."

Woody dropped his grip on the heavy rifle and grabbed the radio hand mic, "Roger, Mako doesn't have a visual on that target."

"Marker copies. Two tell me if you have the target?" Grumpy called. Pinto was still using the back radio, so he had to talk with his wingman on the 'public' frequency.

"Marker Two has the three vehicles. There are also many personnel on foot.

They are about four klicks north of friendlies."

"This is Mako, repeat, I do not have visual on that target. With a good ID on friendlies you are cleared hot on the target to the north." Grumpy couldn't make out Woody's last words, overridden by a dull *Karrruummp*.

"Marker copies cleared hot on the northern target." Woody ignored the radio call and hugged the rock in front of him. He was covered in dirt from the mortar round exploding less than 30 meters in front of him.

Woody heard Mark say, "They're ranging us with mortars. Anyone see where they are coming from?" Woody looked toward him in a fog; Mark was scanning the hillside above them with his binoculars. He was still talking. "Stay low, keep away from the frag. Save your rounds boys, we'll need 'em when they get close."

Luke coughing again said, "I'm okay. Give me my rifle back, maybe I can find those fuckers."

Woody pushed the rifle towards Luke with his foot, followed by the bag of extra rounds. Turning to Mark, his eyes burning blue, Woody asked, "Mark, what in the hell do you mean?"

Keeping his scan going Mark replied calmly, "Well our M-4s are great short range weapons, but they're lousy beyond 100 meters. It's simple, at some point they'll start to rush us. So, just pick your target and try not to waist any rounds."

With the Barrett firmly in hand, Luke crawled towards a spot overlooking the clearing to the east. Suddenly two mortar rounds landed just beyond the knoll, once again covering them in dirt.

"We need to know where those rounds are coming from, anyone see 'em?" Mark asked. Desperately, he looked to the right of the cave. Scanning up the hill, he hadn't seen the shot. Shifting the binoculars, he focused his scan to the left of the cave, watching for movement, or anything else, that might show him where the mortar might be.

Luke pulled out the clip and checked out his rifle. He wanted to make sure it wasn't damaged after its rough handling. He cleaned the dust off the lenses and calibrated the scope's alignment. Satisfied the weapon was in working order, he lay on his stomach and shouldered the rifle squinting through the scope at the mountainside above them.

Mark was trying to control himself, he let his eyes drift slightly from sharp focus, breathing shallowly, he scanned slowly along the mountainside. He was looking for movement, and didn't want his eyes to zero in on one particular thing. During a lull in the firing, he plainly heard a pop; at the same time he saw a slight movement downhill and slightly to the left. Shifting his glasses, he focused on the area, trying to pick out the shooters.

A voice behind him shouted, "Incoming!"

Mark stayed in position as everyone else hugged the rocks even harder; some were trying to get below ground level. Mark was determined not to lose sight of what might be the men firing the mortar. On cue, the incoming round exploded less than fifty yards to the right, showering them with dirt and rock chips.

"Luke, I think I have 'em. They are over two klicks away," Mark said.

Luke squinting through the scope, scanned the slope slowly. "I'm with you. Talk to me."

"Okay, look at the cave, then go one klick left, see the small draw going uphill slanting to the left. Follow that draw about 1500 meters up the hill, there's a small flat space. I see a couple of people there, but can't make out what they are doing," Mark said.

With the scope on the Barrett, Luke traced Mark's route, going slowly up the draw he thumbed the diopter of the scope to bring the rocks in focus. He saw a small pile of rock and suddenly, two men came into sharp focus. Standing, they were looking towards the knoll, gesturing wildly. "I think I've got them. There are two, no three of them. It looks like a mortar on bipods, say 60mm."

Settling in on one of the standing fighters, Luke steadied the cross hairs on his head. He took a breath, relaxed, trying to control the cross hairs as they wavered over the target. Forcing the movement into a pattern, he waited until the cross hairs began rising towards his target's head. Luke began squeezing the trigger slowly, putting tension on the trigger and the block holding the firing pin. Suddenly, surprised by the trigger release, Luke felt the weapon recoil into his shoulder. The recoil of the .50 caliber weapon was, in a word, moderate. He could fire it all day without hurting his shoulder. With the sound suppressor, the noise wasn't bad either, but after about 20 rounds he usually felt nauseous from the successive concussions. Trying to follow through on the shot he brought the cross hairs of the scope back to the target.

Counting silently to himself, Luke continued to watch his target, trying to gauge the flyout time of the bullet. Before he hit three seconds, the target's head just disappeared. For several seconds the body stood facing him, slowly it wobbled left and then right; finally crumpling over backwards. Luke quickly shifted his aim to one of the other men next to the mortar.

Crouching next to the tube, the man was holding something in one hand when Luke settled the cross hairs on the center of his back. Just over two thousand meters away he couldn't tell what it was, but he thought it was likely another round. Quickly settling back into the routine, he took a deep breath and tried to let the tension drain out of him. Steadying the weave of the cross hairs, he tried to make it as small as he could on his targets back. Slowly, he squeezed the trigger, the rifle fired just as the man dropped his arm.

In the two and a half seconds it took for the bullet to travel the distance between them, the man had twisted to the right, just enough for the bullet to miss its intended target. Instead, it grazed his shoulder and impacted the mortar. The frangible bullet knocked the weapon over, destroying one leg of the bipod. The round shattered into several hundred fragments. Shrapnel shredded the third man, carrying mortar ammunition; he was dead before he hit the ground.

Grumpy Westin watched his wingman begin his dive, rolling in from the west. Marker Two pulled his nose down to the vehicles north of Mako's position. Grumpy watched for his wingman to hit his numbers, a habit pattern any good flight lead would have on the range. More importantly, he was watching his back, looking for any large caliber triple A, or shoulder fired SAM's shot at him. Scanning the ground and seeing nothing larger than small arms fire, he went back to watching the wingman's flight path. He watched him pull his nose up in the safe escape maneuver and didn't see the munitions dispenser open, spinning the bomblets out to cover the valley floor, erupting in death and destruction.

Pinto looked out into the valley below, he saw Marker Two climbing back to altitude, he silently waited until Grumpy had begun making a turn to start another orbit. "Grumpy, Maddog said stay on station as long as we can, then head home. He said there was a Gunship headed out to help these guys at dark. But there aren't any fighters."

"That's bullshit. Doesn't he know these guys are in deep shit? They can't wait till dark. They need someone right now! There are just five of them and they're taking mortar fire. Man, we don't have shit left, they aren't gonna make it another three hours."

Pinto agreed, if there was a way to re-arm weapons, like they could refuel in the air, they could keep these guys alive. He ran through the options in his head and suddenly realized that there was another two ship scheduled behind them. "Hey, Grumpy! I think Jiggy's right behind us. Maybe, Maddog doesn't know about her."

Grumpy snorted, "Bullshit, I know that guy, he's a pencil neck if I ever knew one."

"Well, I'll just call him back and suggest that Jiggy's flight should be coming on station. He's got to understand the emergency nature of Mako's situation," Pinto said.

Grumpy's blood pressure was up. "Fuck that! You've got Jiggy's Aux freq, just call her directly."

"But what about Maddog. Don't we have to get permission first?" Pinto asked, confused.

"Look, I said I know the guy. I know he won't be able to make a decision to save his ass, fuck him! Mako, just doesn't have time for him to smell all the rules, cross all the Ts and dot the Is. This is a goddamn emergency, call her up!"

"Okay, okay. I'll call her," Pinto said as he punched in the Jiggy's interflight frequency into the Aux radio. He hadn't heard Grumpy get so mad about anything in the air before. This was Pinto's first time in combat, he was worried about the Americans on the ground, but he'd always followed the book. The book was usually right.

"Gumball 71, Gumball 71 from Marker 31," Pinto began.

Without a pause Jiggy answered Pinto's call. "Marker 31, Gumball on Aux go ahead."

"Gumball, are you in country yet?"

"Marker, Gumball is overhead Taloqan, we have been trying to raise Mako 52 for 15 minutes," Jiggy replied.

"Marker copies. We were working with Mako 52 a couple of hours ago, we hit a few targets and he went off the air. After that we got a call to work with Mako 51 for an emergency troops in contact."

Jiggy thought Pinto was just giving her background information. "Roger Marker, if we don't raise Mako 52 in the next few minutes I'm going back to Horse for further tasking."

"Gumball hold on a second. Mako 51 needs you right now. They are surrounded deep in Indian Country. We're Winchester and can't help 'em out anymore. Horse has a gunship scheduled at nightfall, but these guys won't make it that long."

Jiggy thought about it for a second. "I hear you, but I've got to talk to Horse for further tasking." Her first impulse was to help, but felt that as a new flight lead it was best for her to follow the rules. When you flew Fighters there was room for innovation, but to jump outside the box required a damn good reason. Besides, she had fought long and hard to get where she was.

"Here let me talk, Pinto," Grumpy said, taking over the Aux radio.

Thumbing the mic button aft, Grumpy dispensed with standard radio procedures. "Jiggy, Grumpy. There are about five guys down there, getting the shit shot out of 'em. We've covered them as long as we can, but we're Winchester. There's probably a thousand T down there and there is no way these guys will make it until dark. My flight simply can't do anything more for them, someone else has to cover their ass. No shit Jiggy, you're the only one around. It's time to do some of the Flight Lead shit, it's up to you."

Jiggy didn't respond right away. She had never considered that lives, outside of her flight, would hinge on one of her decisions. A new flight lead, she felt lucky that the Squadron Commander trusted her enough to lead during wartime. If she made a bad call here she could screw up her whole career, everything she had been working for.

She was going over her options when Hustler interrupted. "Jiggy, if it's any help, sometimes you gotta do what you gotta do. There's no raghead target out here that's worth one of our guys. I'm for it, besides Mako 52 is off the air."

Jiggy did not reply.

In the silence he added, "Jiggy, there's only one right thing to do here. We gotta try."

Jiggy considered Hustler's comments a fraction of a second longer before she thought of her brother in the Army. He was in Special Forces, her dad had told her he had deployed all of a sudden. He could be down there; she would want someone else to help him. In that moment, she realized that she had no choice, she had to take the risk; they were Americans and she could not just write them off.

"Marker, give me the freq and a steer point. Gumball is on the way," Jiggy said in the back radio.

Northwest of Taloqan, Afghanistan

Gary's team easily outdistanced the Taliban chasing them. They had crossed a wide clear area, devoid of rocks and other cover. The horses were making good time over this terrain. In another few miles, they would cross the river and be safe on the other side. He slowed his horse to a brisk jog.

Brandon was right behind, still holding on as tight to his horse as he could. He didn't see Gary slow down and closed the distance between them at nearly a full gallop. Brandon sensed something in front of him; he looked up at the last second and realized that he was about to hit Gary's horse. Brandon pulled the reigns right as hard as he could. The horse slowed slightly, trying to turn as best as he could. The horse's left front leg hit a patch of gravel, causing him to stumble. Falling forward, the horse pitched Brandon headlong onto the ground. Unprepared, Brandon skidded on his hands with the horse falling next to him.

Gary turned on his horse, looking back; he was just in time to see the pair stop tumbling, nearly at his feet. He immediately got off his horse. "Brandon, that was a hell of a fall. Man, are you okay?"

Brandon lay on the ground, stunned; he was just trying to breathe as deep as he could. Still coming up short of breath, he blurted, "Okay. I think. Horse tried to turn too fast. Probably my fault."

Holding the reigns in his hand, Gary's horse pranced around them. "Dude, if there's nothing broken, we should go. Are you hurt anywhere? We're not that far ahead of those guys chasing us. "

With a grimace, Brandon sat up and felt his legs. He looked up at Gary, standing tall above him, his horse snorting and prancing nervously. "I don't think anything's broken."

"Good, let's go." Gary climbed onto his horse.

Only then did Brandon look at his horse. He hadn't even given a thought about his horse. He covered the few feet between them; his horse was lying on its side. Thrashing frantically, Brandon could see his left foreleg sticking off at a ninety-degree angle. "Shit, my horse broke its leg."

Gary sized up the situation; at best they only had a few minutes lead. He had to make a decision quickly. "Shoot him, grab your shit and ride with me. Do it now!"

"Okay," Brandon replied, hesitating.

His reverie was punctuated by a sharp, liquid *craaack*. Startled, he looked up to see Our Dave, sitting on his horse next to them. He leaned forward on his horse, bent almost double he held his hand pressed against his leg. Brandon noticed a dark red stain growing from under his hand.

Gary, circling his horse, said, "Dave's been shot. Come on Brandon, let's go. Time's up."

"I'll ride with Dave! Let me get my stuff," Brandon shouted as he spun around, pointed his rifle and quickly put two shots into his horse's head. The horse shivered and flopped its head to the ground. As the horse fell over, Brandon could see that the radio was smashed nearly flat- totally useless. Leaving it behind, he bounded over to Dave's horse and swung up behind him.

Reaching around Dave, Brandon grabbed the reigns, and kicked the horse with his heels. He glanced over his shoulder to see a few Taliban less than 100 meters away. Spurring the horse, he started to put some distance between them. *I guess that's it for air today,* he thought to himself.

Rock Knoll Cave, Afghanistan

The last round launched by the mortar team was deadly accurate. Soundlessly, it flew over Luke's head and exploded in a deafening *Cruump*, a few feet away from Woody. The explosion picked Woody up and slammed him violently into the rock.

Before the smoke cleared, Mark low crawled over to check Woody out. He could see that the back of Woody's shirt was shredded; many fragments had hit his helmet as well. At that moment, Woody rolled over with a groan, his eyes wide open.

"Hey, Buddy, I thought you were a gonner. That mortar round hit just behind you."

"Yeah, my ears are ringing; I can't feel my legs." Woody gasped.

Mark quickly looked him over and could see no injuries. "Here, roll over again, let me check your back."

Mark gently held Woody's right arm and rolled him on his side, he quickly saw that blood was seeping from his back around his waist. Several pieces of shrapnel had entered Woody's lower back, just below the flak jacket.

"Woody, it looks like you took some of the frag in your back, just below the Kevlar. I can fix it up, just relax."

"Don't bullshit me Mark. Just bandage me up, stop the bleeding." Woody, through the pain, gasped for breath. "I guess it's lucky I was shielding the radio."

Mark pulled his pants down enough to clean the wound, working quickly he dressed the shrapnel wounds in Woody's back. Meanwhile, Woody put the microphone handset to his ear, with trouble he managed to say, "Marker, Mako. Say posit?"

"Mako, we're orbiting overhead. Marker is Winchester, but I've got another flight of Strike Eagles in bound. They'll be here within 10 minutes. I'll brief them and hand them over to you," Grumpy replied.

"Thanks Marker. We just took some pretty accurate mortar fire; most of us are wounded right now. We'll need you guys real soon," Woody said, grimacing.

Jiggy heard the exchange on the front radio and transmitted, "Marker and Mako, Gumball 71 is 15 miles out at Base plus 17, two Strike Eagles with eight GBU-12s"

Woody listened to the exchange between the two flight leads. He turned his head slightly and said, "Mark, we've got another flight of Strike Eagles inbound. This one has laser guided bombs. If I start drifting out you need to control this guy. I don't know how long I can stay coherent."

Mark finished dressing the wound, wiped his hands, "You'll be okay, man. I can stand in for you, but you're gonna be okay. Besides, we don't have any laser markers with us. We left them with the rest of the team."

"Doesn't matter, 15Es can't see a spot anyway? Pull me up so I can see,"

Woody said wearily. "Come on, prop me up so I can see what's going on."

As carefully as he could, Mark drug Woody to a boulder so he could see the clearing between them and the cave. He put the radio next to him and put the handset in his hand.

Five thousand feet above Marker, Jiggy's flight joined the circular orbit above the Rock Cave. Grumpy quickly briefed her on the location of the friendlies and the attacks that had taken place so far. Once she was satisfied, she took over control of the engagement and cleared Grumpy to depart for Ganci.

Hustler anchored their orbit on the smaller rock outcropping where Woody and the team were hidden. He scanned the area with the Targeting Pod. Jiggy occasionally watched the scope, but spent most of her time scanning the valley, occasionally she caught sight of her wingman circling in trail.

Jiggy was thinking about how they were going to be able to drop their LGBs in this tight pattern, coming to a decision she asked, "Hustler, what about flying a triangular orbit, with 12 mile legs? I think that'll be the best pattern for doing CAS with the Pod and LGBs?"

"Yeah, that makes my workload easier, we can drop and lase while we return to the cap. Good idea, I'll put in some offset points for you to steer to on the TSD." Working quickly, Hustler entered offset coordinates into the upfront controller and segmented triangles appeared on the moving map display.

In the back radio, Jiggy briefed her wingman on the new tactic. "Gumball, we're going to use a triangular cap for these LGBs. Let's use the cave as the target point and setup offsets with 12 miles legs. Put the friendlies location as an offset as well. When you are cleared to drop, turn in, drop and then join on the far side of the triangle while you lase in the bomb. Acknowledge."

"Gumball Two."

Ready to work Jiggy, transmitted on the front radio, "Mako, Gumball, we're overhead and have a good fix on your location. How can you guys work today? Visual or GPS?"

Woody reached up to the handset clipped to his collar, turning his head slightly he pressed the mic button. "Mako copies. We'll have to work visual today; we don't have GPS capability. That's about the best I can do. I can give you bearing and range to targets."

Before Jiggy could reply, Hustler quickly interjected over the intercom, "Jiggy, that'll work. I got a pretty good position from Marker and I can use his bearing and range to generate a new target point. That should be good enough to cue the pod."

Before replying to Woody's transmission, Jiggy considered Hustler's proposal. "Mako, bearing and range will work for us. We can cue our Pod with it and find your targets."

"Great. Let me know when you're ready to copy, Gumball, I've got five areas for you to hit right now," Woody said.

Saleh, and several of his troops, crouched behind the wreckage that had been the antenna farm for the communications cave, watched the Rock Knoll. One of the men beside him said, "Mudier Saleh, it is several hours before dark. We haven't killed them yet and our men have been struck from the air everywhere they have gathered. With nightfall, the Red Tongue of Death will come and we must hide. Either we attack them now or we will have no choice but to let them get away."

Saleh replied calmly, "We will attack before darkness, we will not let them get away. There cannot be more than ten or twelve of them. But we must get close, Americans in the air will not bomb us if we are close to those on the ground."

"But Mudier, what should we do? Every time we rush the clearing, the bombs fall. How can we do this?"

"We will setup a machine gun to the north and the south. Gather our men here, near the cave. Once the guns are firing we can rush the knoll from the east. It is simple, once we have taken the Americans we will not be bombed anymore."

Woody slumped against his rock, sweating. The shadows were growing and the temperature had begun dropping, but Woody was burning up. Mark moved closer to him, barely above a whisper he said, "It won't be long now, and it will be dark. Just hang in there a little longer and we'll get you out of here."

"Dude, I still can't feel my legs, but they feel warm. Why is that?"

"I don't know, buddy, but you're sweating like a pig. Maybe you are getting a little feeling after all," Mark replied.

Luke shouted from his perch, "They're setting up an MG to the south."

"Shoot the fucker before he can get it going!" Mark replied.

"I'd like to but I'm out of rounds for the Barrett, sorry boss."

There had been a firing lull since Gumball had dropped the last bomb almost an hour before. At that moment, a volley of AK-47 fire hit their rocks, falling off to a steady staccato, coming mostly from the east. The machine gun to the south began firing as well, joined within seconds by another from the north. With the heavy fire coming from three sides, Mark pulled Woody down to protect him from ricochets.

A sharp stab of pain coursed through his body, holding onto the microphone, Woody gasped, "Give me a bearing and range for those MGs."

Three minutes after Woody briefed Jiggy on the new targets, the first GBU-12 exploded on the southern machine gun. If anything, the pace of firing picked up, and then the second bomb obliterated the northern machine gun.

Mark watched the strikes. "Good hits, Woody, good hits."

Not hearing a response he glanced at his friend, and saw his head splayed back, mouth open. Mark reached up and felt Woody's carotid artery with his fingers. He was still alive, with a weak pulse. He took the mic handset from Woody's collar.

Pulling on the cord, Mark put the handset to his ear. "Gumball, this is the Team Six. Mako has been hit; he's taken a lot of shrapnel in the back and appears to be paralyzed. I'll have to be the one to talk with you now."

"Gumball copies, Standing by. Let me know what you need," Jiggy replied she could hear the weariness and pain in the new voice.

The AK-47 fire was not as heavy as before, enough to keep their heads down, Mark was worried that it was a precursor of an attack. He called to Mike and Dave to pull in closer together, shrinking the perimeter. Mike watched the approaches from the north and east, Dave the west and Luke the South. The small arms fire was augmented by the impact of RPGs fired across the clearing, aimed in the general direction of the knoll.

"There's a rush coming from the Northeast," Mike shouted.

"Add one from the southeast as well," Luke chimed in.

Mark shoved the handset to his ear. "Gumball, we're being attacked by troops on foot, two prongs from the northeast and southeast. RPGs and heavy small arms fire from both places. We don't have enough ammo to take all these guys on. Request you drop a bomb on the guys in the clearing. ASAP," Mark called.

"Mako, that's a danger close operation, are you sure you want to take the risk?" Jiggy asked.

"Gumball, it's either that or we're dead anyway. I'd rather go out with a bang, than out of ammo. Do it!" Mark retorted.

Jiggy bridled, but remembering the ordeal the groundpounder must be experiencing, she tried to reign in her emotions. "Get your head's down, bombs away in less than a minute."

Over the intercom, Jiggy said, "Hustler, let's drop our last bomb in the middle of that clearing. I'll roll-in from a north/south heading"

"Mark, here comes the rush!" Mike said.

Mark dropped the handset, he'd done all he could on the radio and now a hasty defensive plan was more important. "Luke shift to the right, I'll take the center. Dave collect ammo from Woody. Guys, we don't have a lot of ammo, so take your time and pick your targets. Gumball is going to drop in the next minute, very close."

"Mako, Gumball is bombs away, impact in 25 seconds," Jiggy called as she rolled the airplane into an 80 degree bank, pulled five g and checked sixty degrees to the right to get back to the cap.

The hail of RPGs dropped off as the mass of onrushing attackers reached the center of the clearing. Luke aimed and squeezed off each shot as quickly as he could, hitting several of the running al-Qaeda. Calling out he said, "Hey, you guys, it's taking two or three hits to bring a guy down. Double tap 'em, stay on your target until he's down!"

The onrushing attackers were less than 100 meters from their rocks when the 500 pound guided bomb exploded less than 300 meters away. Instantly engulfed in darkness and deafening noise, they were covered by debris.

"Luke, are you okay? You're bleeding from your ear," Mark shouted.

His ears ringing, Luke could barely hear him, "What, what did you say?"

Realizing that the blood was probably from a blown eardrum, Mark waived him off, pointed back to the clearing and shouted, "Nothing, never mind."

Mark could barely breath, he felt like he had asthma. His lungs felt full and he found he could only take shallow breaths. The air was heavy with the pungent smell of burnt cordite and fresh dirt. Peering through the smoke, he watched as it cleared, a fleeting silence encapsulated the moment. Before his eyes, over a hundred running men had disappeared. In their place were jumbled heaps of arms, legs and torsos, but no blood. Feeling a little sick at the sight, he was brought back to reality when AK-47 rounds began cracking around him again.

Dave scooted up next to him, in his hand a couple of full magazines. Without turning, Mark accepted the ammunition, "Thanks, man. By the way, remind me how in the hell you talked me into coming on this adventure of yours?"

"Hell, you get what you pay for, right? I don't remember anyone twisting your arm?" Dave retorted. Suddenly serious, he added, "Sorry, man. This isn't exactly the tour I had in mind."

"Me, neither!" Mark grinned lopsidedly, looking around at the other men on the perimeter he asked, "Everybody okay?"

Dave and Luke both nodded their heads. Mike, grazed by an AK round as the attack began nodded his head.

"Here they come again!" Mike grunted.

Picking up the radio handset, Mark spoke quickly. "Gumball, good hit on that last pass. They're raising their heads again, we need another pass before they start."

"Mako, I'm Winchester. We're trying to get something out here to replace us, but we're out of weapons right now."

"Gumball, we're down to a gunfight here. In a few minutes it'll be a knife fight. Every one of us has been hit. We need you guys now!"

"Mako, I'll make a low pass, dry, and we'll see how that goes." Jiggy said. Over the intercom she said, "Hustler I'll start off with a shallow pass, call me off at 4500 AGL. Are you with me? "

"I'm right behind you, Jiggy," Hustler replied.

Rolling in from the northwest she put the velocity vector on the clearing and let it settle around 15 degrees nose low. Approaching 4500' above the ground Hustler called out, "Read, Ready, Pull!"

Jiggy started the pull slowly and slammed the throttles into afterburner. The airplane bottomed out around 2500 feet above the clearing with a deafening roar.

"Gumball, that pass worked great. They ran back to the rocks. Have your number two standby to make a pass." Mark squinted through his binoculars, surprised to see the al-Qaeda turning around to rush them again. "Gumball, I need you again. They're massing again. Get the number two to make a pass."

Gumball Two rolled into a pass an exact duplicate of Jiggy's. This time the rushing mob dove to the ground in front of the screaming jet. With Gumball Two roaring overhead in his pull up they were up and running again, firing as they ran towards the rock knoll.

"Heads up guys. Here they come!" Mike shouted. "They figured it out, that pass didn't work at all."

"Gumball, dry passes aren't working, they figured it out. We've got about 150 crazies heading for us now. Have you got anything else in your bag of tricks?" Mark jested.

"Standby, Mako." Jiggy tried to think. The only weapon she had left was the Gatling gun embedded in the right wing root of her F-15E. Canted up two degrees, the gun was optimized for air-to-air engagements. To fire it at ground targets you had to point below the target and keep it there until after the shot. For Eagle pilots, strafing a ground target was a familiarization event; no one had to do it for score. Even in controlled conditions there was no margin for error. She had fired the gun at a target before, but the only thing she was sure of is that all of her bullets had hit the ground. Now there was no other choice; she only had one weapon. The decision made, she resolved to do the best she could and worry about it later.

"What are you thinkin'?" Hustler intoned, worriedly.

"We gotta strafe, there's no other way," Jiggy said matter-of-factly.

The danger of a strafing passed through Hustler's mind. He thought about objecting, but in his heart he knew it was the only way to save these guys. If there was anyone he trusted his life to, it was Jiggy. He reached for the MFD, "I'll setup the PACS."

Thumbing the mic button forward, Jiggy transmitted to Mark, "Mako, I'm going to strafe, get your heads down and keep them down."

"Copy that, now would be a good time," Mark said into the handset.

Jiggy didn't waste a movement. She was already turning out of the south towards the northern leg of her orbit; she left the bank in and kept the turn going as the nose dropped. Pointed east towards the clearing, she let the target area drift down the pitch ladder. She took command of the HUD, brought the gun pipper up on the display and checked the gun cross. Satisfied that the master arm was on and she had the HUD setup for her strafing pass, she waited.

When the clearing reached twelve degrees nose low she pushed the nose over, settling the pipper on the target area. With the velocity vector just below the target, it seemed that she had to push on the stick more the closer she got. Glancing quickly at the airspeed, she saw 450 knots and pulled the throttles back, standing them straight up. Holding the stick forward, she pointed her trigger finger away from the trigger; she didn't want to make a mistake now.

Jiggy watched the range bar on the pipper unwind past the range dot; she didn't want any rounds to fall short. Seeing the rock knoll disappear under the nose she squeezed the trigger. She wiggled the rudders with her feet slightly to spray the bullets around the clearing. subconsciously, she also released a little of the forward pressure on the stick and the airplane began climbing slightly. The result was that bullets sprayed all over the clearing and the cave mouth. She had dispersed the 20mm rounds across the clearing better than if she had planned it that way.

Holding the trigger down for just over four seconds, she let go and pulled back on the stick. At five g the rising terrain of the mountainside filled the windscreen in her face, she focused on the rocks. Suddenly scared, Jiggy slammed the throttles into full afterburner and pulled harder on the stick.

Hustler held the towel rack over the instrument panel in front of him with both hands, the G force dragging his head down. He watched the radar altimeter and airspeed indicators on the HUD repeater display. With nothing else to do, he decided to keep Jiggy aware of their energy. "Seven and a half g, 420 knots, 2,000 feet."

Wordlessly, Jiggy put more pressure on the throttles, as if she could eek a little more thrust out of the engines by bending them forward. She also pulled the stick all the way back to the seatpan.

"350 knots, 1,000 feet," Hustler intoned.

"300 knots, 500 feet."

"250 knots, 300 feet."

Tightening his grip on the M-4 rifle Mark watched the running, shouting al Qaeda fighters get closer. He took careful aim on the nearest one, thinking that this was probably the final rush. Suddenly, he was surprised by the thunder of dozens of sharp cracks as the supersonic rounds passed over his head. Following the rounds a deep-throated BRRRRrrrrr filled the air- the sound of the Gatling gun spinning up to the correct RPM. The clearing instantly was covered in a hailstorm of 20mm lead, over 500 hundred rounds viscously cutting everything down in their path.

Without pause, the searing roar of Jiggy's jet screaming overhead enveloped him. He looked up to see the white hot plumes of the afterburners reach for him as Jiggy bottomed out less than 100 feet above the clearing. He could feel the intense heat of the flames as the sixty-three foot long fighter filled the sky. Trying to avoid the flame, he threw his head down and covered it with his arm.

Inside Gumball 71, the nose of the jet rotated agonizingly towards the sky. The jet wallowed towards the rising terrain; Jiggy was beginning to consider how badly she had fucked up. She dropped her throttle hand to the ejection handle, fixed coldly by her side. Relaxing slightly on the back pressure on the stick to lesson the drag, she let the airplane accelerate. She looked left, out of the canopy, the mountainside in sharp relief. Rocks and people, a grizzly sight frozen in time, from her attack just seconds ago. For what seemed like an eternity, the jet seemed poised above the mountain. Ever so slowly, thrust began to overcome inertia, and the jet accelerated. Fluidly, it began to climb the mountain.

With a sigh of relief, Jiggy realized she had been holding her breath. The jet slowly accelerated past 300 knots, and Jiggy let it climb lazily past 15,000 feet.

"Wow, that was fun," she said into the silence of the cockpit. "I think we ran out of gun on that pass."

Jiggy could only hear Hustler breathing, after an eternity he dead-panned. "Yeah, at least we got that going for us. Better to be lucky than good."

Relieved, Jiggy began to think of what to do next. "Hustler let's switch over to Maddog's freq. We gotta get someone to replace us. It's still almost an hour until dark."

"Maddog, Gumball 71, on Uniform how copy?"

"Gumball 71 Maddog here, what'cha got?" BC replied.

"Maddog, Gumball has been working with Mako. Gumball is now Winchester and Mako is still in a serious TIC situation. They need a Med-Evac and air support ASAP."

"Maddog copies, I didn't know your FAC was in a TIC situation. What is the situation up there?"

"Maddog, Gumball was never able to raise Mako 52 on the radio, so we switched to support Mako 51. We've been working with them the whole time and the situation is critical."

"What are you talking about? I didn't give you permission to change tasking, what the heck are you doing down there?" BC growled.

Taking a deep breath Jiggy said, "Look Maddog, maybe you should have kept the air flowing to help these guys." Sensing her temper flaring, Jiggy went on more calmly, "but we can sort that out off-line. Right now there are Americans on the ground and they are in a critical situation. Everyone is wounded and I can't do anything else to keep them alive. Let's solve their problem now, okay?"

BC fumed, it was obvious to him that Marker had overstepped his bounds and contacted Gumball directly. He was the airboss, it was his job to run the air war, and not a bunch of fighter jocks running around making things up as they went along.

Jiggy waited as patiently as she knew how. "Maddog, how about that Med-Evac and air support for Mako?"

Gritting his teeth, he resolved to get to the bottom of this. "Gumball, confirm this is Mako 51 you are working with in the Salang Pass area?"

"Affirmative, the TACP has been hit badly and is paralyzed, he needs an immediate Med-Evac. Four other members of the team have been wounded as well. I've done everything I can to keep these guys from being overrun. We've strafed and dropped every bomb we brought. These guys need help now."

"Maddog copies, I'll scramble Deray, it'll be almost an hour before they can get to that area. I've already scheduled Spooky 33 to work with Mako after nightfall. He's inbound right now on Tad 321, give him a call and brief him on the situation."

With relief Jiggy replied, "Gumball copies. I'll need a top off for my flight on the way out. Until then I can hang around and work the SAR."

CHAPTER 19

Rolling into a turn, Jason Gorman easily handled Spooky 33 in the holding pattern. He liked hand flying the heavy aircraft, even wallowing slowly through the sky at 22,000 feet. It was a challenge and he liked making the big airplane do what he wanted, smoothly. The more he flew the better he got and he wanted to enjoy every minute. To Jason, the best thing about flying was that when you did it well you knew it, right away; the feedback is immediate and not dependent on someone else's mood or whim. Jason had done the takeoff nearly 30 minutes before and had flown the airplane to the hold. He wouldn't get to fly once the Aircraft Commander took over entering Afghani airspace and wanted to get as much stick time as he could. Looking at his watch, he could see that it was just less than hour before sunset. The rest of the crew were either sighting in their weapon systems or lounging before they started their nights work. For a while, he would be alone in the cockpit. Skeletor, the Aircraft Commander, was in the back stretching his legs; he'd probably go to the head and shoot the shit with the FCO before coming back to the cockpit.

Jason smiled. Casually he looked out of the multi-paned cockpit window and watched the shadows growing in the valley below. He counted on his fingers and realized that this was his fifth combat mission in less than a week. Before they got here, combat was a big unknown to him. He was scared that he might not be able to do his job, or maybe that he would freeze when things got critical. But so far, combat was pretty much like the training they had been doing since he started flying the AC-130. The only real difference was that the targets were more challenging and some of the terrain was higher; it was definitely more fun, but everything else was pretty much the same. Looking at the rugged terrain, he thought it was sure better to be flying than slogging it out on the ground.

"Spooky 33, Gumball 71."

Jason was startled at the radio call. This was a quiet time, he had already checked in with the AWAC's controller, Horse, when they had reported on station. They usually didn't get any more radio calls before they were due to go in country. Horse had even assigned a FAC for them to work with for at least part of the night which should be the next that call he would be concerned with. *As far as he knew, everything was routine. Who in the heck is Gumball 71 anyway, maybe they were calling someone else,* he thought.

"Spooky 33, Gumball 71."

There it was again, he hadn't imagined it. They were being called, but he didn't recognize the call sign. For a minute he thought the voice was vaguely familiar. It was a powerful radio, so it probably wasn't anyone on the ground. It had to be another airplane.

"Spooky 33, Gumball 71 on Uniform, TAD 321, how copy."

The third radio call jarred Jason out of his reverie, "Gumball 71, this is Spooky 33, go ahead."

Jiggy, orbiting overhead the besieged Special Forces Troopers at the Rock Knoll instantly recognized the voice. Even though she hadn't talked to him in over a year, there was no mistaking that voice. It was Jason, her ex-boyfriend. She didn't know if that meant trouble or if he would help her out. Remembering that he probably didn't know her tactical call sign she thought about whether she should use her real name. She quickly came to a decision to break radio procedure, transmitting in the clear she said, "Jason, it's me Jenn. Let's go green, we need to talk!"

Stunned, Jason suddenly knew why the voice sounded familiar. He had thought about Jenn almost every day of his life, he could see her face and feel her hair in his fingers. He couldn't figure out why that when he finally heard her voice, he didn't recognize it. Clumsily, he sat up straight and hurriedly punched 'secure' on the radio control head. Keying the mic once he heard the sync tone and released the transmit button. The radio was in secure mode.

"Spooky 33, this is Gumball 71, how copy green?"

"Spooky has you loud and clear, how me?"

"Loud and clear, Jason, it's sure good to hear your voice!"

"Jenn, I've been thinking of you, wondering where you were and if you were deployed or not." Jason plunged on excitedly, "I thought you might be back in Qatar with the other Strike Eagles, but you weren't there."

"It's a small world. Here I am, overhead Afghanistan. Listen, we've got tons to catch up on, but right now I'm working a critical troops in contact situation. I've got a flight of F-15Es and I'm working with Mako 51. I think you're tasked to support them at sunset right? I have to bring you up to speed on their situation, ready to copy?"

"That's correct, we are due to work with those guys at sunset," Jason replied. Reaching down with his free hand, he took a small notepad from his leg pocket, and laid it on his leg. Then he pulled his pencil out of the pocket on the left sleeve of his flight suit, he clicked on the autopilot. "I'm ready, go ahead."

"Okay, Jason here goes. I'm the second of two flights that have been working with Mako. We are just west of the Salang Pass about 60 miles north of Kabul; the target area is the first valley west of the Salang Pass. The valley runs north south and splits into a Y about halfway, the upper portion of the Y is on the north side. The western part of the Y, has a streambed in it, the eastern has a road. How copy?"

"Spooky copies, anything else?"

"The target area is two klicks south of the Y, where the road makes a curve to the west. Mako 51 is on a rock knoll to the east of that road bend."

Looking at the folded map on the console, Jason traced the valley west of the pass with his finger and followed it south. Seeing the bend in the road and the streambed, he felt sure that he knew the target area from her description. But to make sure he asked for a clarification, "Spooky copies all, understand this is the valley that starts with the 4800 meter peak, five miles west of the Salang Pass?"

Hustler, who had been flowing the brief, checked the map quickly and interjected on the intercom, "Jiggy, he's got the right peak."

"Affirmative," Jiggy replied and read him the coordinates they used for the offset target point where the Mako team lay on the ground. Patiently, she waited for Jason to get the details and location down, before she briefed him on Mako's actual situation.

"Jenn I think I can find the target area, what is Mako's situation?"

"Mako is in a critical 'troops in contact' situation. They are surrounded and over 20 miles from friendly lines. We've had two Strike Eagle flights supporting them for nearly seven hours. Frankly, they are a long way from being out of the woods and I don't think they'll make it to dark without being overrun. They've got at least one critically wounded man with most of the others wounded in one-way or another. I've got a SAR coming to evacuate them, ETA in just over one hour. I need two things from you," Jenn said.

Apprehensive, Jason gave his full attention to the radio. "Go ahead."

Jiggy began earnestly, "Jason, I am Winchester. We've got enough fuel to stay on station for a bit longer, but no weapons left. Jason, it is critically important that you provide protection for the choppers during the extraction."

And second, I need you to come right away to make sure these guys live that long."

Jason felt like his stomach rushed out of his feet. He knew immediately that he could not comply with her second request. It was a long-standing gunship policy to never fly over hostile terrain in daylight, in any daylight. They were sitting ducks if they did; in the first Gulf War, 14 guys had paid with their lives to learn that lesson. "Gumball, we can do the first easy, we'll be overhead after dark anyway. The second we can't do, we only operate after dark, we can't go into unfriendly territory in daylight."

Trying to keep the tension of the last few hours out of her voice Jiggy tried again. "Jason, you have to. It's a very simple equation, these guys won't live until dark; they just won't make it that long. I've dropped everything I have, they're almost out of ammunition, and there are still more of the bad guys. Right now I'm just an observer, without you, they're as good as dead. There isn't anyone else but you, if you don't do it all five of them will die, it's that simple. Listen, Jason, it's not training anymore, this is real. It's not about you and me, it's time to stand in the door."

"Jenn, Spooky's never do go into combat during the day, I just can't do it. There just has to be someone else. What about all the Bones and Buffs out there, or fighters, there have to be more fighters!" Jason pleaded.

"This has to be a visual operation, bombers can't do it and all the fighters are spread out. Believe me, I've asked! If there were another alternative, anyone else, I'd be asking them first. Jason, it's just you."

Jason slumped in his seat; it wasn't his job to make a decision. He was just a co-pilot. But here she was, accusing him, again. She thought he was selfish and didn't have the courage to stand in the door. He knew that he's just a survivor, and you don't survive by sticking your neck out. Whatever happened, he always lands on his feet, like a cat. It wasn't his decision, he had to ask Skeletor, and it's his choice.

Tactically, it was plain they just couldn't do it. Gunships went in at night, period. He put his fingers on the bridge of his nose and squeezed. Feeling no better, he rubbed his eyes, and then his temples. These were big decisions that weren't his to make.

In the silence, Jenn knew he was arguing with himself, weighing the odds just as he always had when they were in flight school. She decided to appeal to him one more time. "Jason. These guys need you, their families need you."

Frustrated, Jason blurted, "Jenn, what about Triple A? Any surface-to-air threats?"

Sensing the possibility of success, Jenn thought that maybe she could save these guys after all. "Jason, I can't say that we've taken them all out. But we've eliminated everything we've seen so far. I think it's clear."

Jason stared through the windshield, wrestling with his uncertainty. Suddenly he reached for the autopilot controller and turned the wafer switch to heading hold. Dialing in the GPS bearing to the target on the HSI heading bug, he turned the airplane to the new heading. "Okay, Gumball, Spooky is inbound, ETA in 35 minutes. We're 65 miles southeast of Kabul right now."

"Gumball copies, thank you Spooky!" Jenn replied. "You won't regret it!"

Skeletor was sitting behind the cockpit bulkhead, in the Electronic Warfare Operators seat, talking about food with the Fire Control Officer. Like an experienced seaman, he felt the aircraft rollout on a new heading. He sensed that they were no longer in orbit. "Excuse me, Donno, I gotta see what's going on."

In the darkened crew compartment, he made his way to the cockpit door, navigating by the small pools of light thrown off by the computer monitors lining the consoles. Opening the cockpit door, he saw the Flight Engineer busy at his console and Jason, the co-pilot, staring at a map. In a voice, pitched to carry over the loud thrum of the turboprop airplane he called to Jason, "Jason, man. What's up?"

Jason looked at him with a wan smile, unusual he thought, from such a serious young man. "Sorry boss, we got a call to support an emergency troops-in-contact situation with wounded and a SAR. It's the same FAC we are scheduled to work with and I figured you wouldn't mind getting started. I knew you would head this way once you felt the change in course."

Settling in his seat, Skeletor began strapping himself in. "Sure, tell me what's going on? It's a little early, but sunset'll be here soon. Who's in trouble?"

"It's Mako 51. You know, the FAC we were tasked to work with tonight. They are surrounded, about 20 miles behind the lines. They've got at least one critically wounded, and everyone on the team has been hit. Gumball 71 is a flight of Strike Eagles, they've been working with them, but they're Winchester. They'll hang out and run the SARCAP if we need them to." Jason held the map over the throttle quadrant, pointed to where he had marked the target area, and made notes on the situation. "This is where they are. We're about 30 minutes out right now."

"Shit hot. You do good work Jason; these guys hang their tails out all the time. If we can help them out, I'm willing to hang mine out every now and again," Skeletor replied, slapping Jason on the left shoulder. "You keep flying for awhile, let me tell the crew what's up."

Rock Knoll Cave, Afghanistan

Mark crawled west towards Dave's spot behind the rocks, when he got there; he tapped him on the foot. "Hey, bud. Is this enough adventure for ya?"

"Yeah, man, I got more than I bargained for. I didn't know you SF guys liked to play Cowboys and Indians so much."

"You know how it is, one man's meat is another man's poison. You gotta have your priorities. Besides, it'll be a good story in the bar," Mark said, with a tight smile, he wiped his face with the back of his hand, smearing the grime across his cheek.

Teasing, Dave said, "Yeah, man, I know how that is. I guess you never heard that a good story only needs to be ten percent true, you didn't need all this."

"Yeah, I've heard that. Don't know if there will be anyone around to tell this one."

Dave turned serious. "Mark, I was teasing. Enough with the negative waves, already. You're the man, you should be thinking of all the options. If you're not three or four steps ahead we're in deep shit."

Mark looked at him silently, his faced covered in dirt and grime, "Dude, you're the only one that's not wounded so far. Our fighter support is out of bombs, it's still almost an hour before dark and we've got maybe enough ammunition to handle one more charge. Maybe. Dude, one thing is sure, there will be no surrender."

Dave looked scared, "No shit. I know what they'd do to me if I surrendered. I'm CIA remember?"

Mark just nodded, "Look, Mike got shot in the arm and can't aim, I've bandaged him up, but I want to move him to your sector, it's quieter. I need you to go take his place?"

Nodding his head, Dave replied gravely, "Sure man, whatever you need."

Before he crawled off, keeping his head low, Mark held his shirt. "Oh, I need you to take the radio too. Gumball is the call sign of the fighters that have been helping us. I think they're out of ammunition, but you'll like talking anyway, it's a chick."

Dave grinned back, "I thought you said your sister was flying fighters, you trying to set me up or something?"

"No man, I figure she can handle herself. Besides, she's flying F-16s out of Lakenheath, England. Or something like that. These fighters are Eagles." Still holding onto his shirt he joked, "But Dave, I wouldn't set you up with my dog."

Dave crawled by Woody, stopping to check on him, his breathing was fast and shallow. Dave put his fingers to his neck and felt his pulse. "Fast as hell," he muttered. Grabbing the radio he began crawling towards Mike's position overlooking the north and east. To himself he thought, maybe Woody will be all right, if he doesn't bleed out. He needs to get med evac't soon.

Mark helped Mike settle into a new position where he could watch the eastern approaches across the small stream. With Mike's left arm bandaged against his side it took awhile to reach the spot. AK-47 bullets still spattered around them in an irregular disjointed pattern. The shooters, over 400 meters away, obviously had the range, but not the aim.

Settling in, Mike remarked, "I wish we had some of those AKs. We'd be able to keep their heads down for a change."

"Gumball, this is Mako, how copy?" Dave transmitted on the PRC-117 radio.

"Mako, this is Gumball. What happened to the previous speaker?"

Squinting through the binoculars, Dave studied the hillside. "Nearly everyone has been shot, I'm the last one with 20/20 vision. So I guess I'm the lucky one. I've got some trade for you, interested?"

"Mako, I'm sorry, but I don't have any weapons left."

"Mako copies that. The AQ are getting ready to make a run on us. If you can make another of those gun passes I think they'll go hide for awhile."

"Gumball copies. I can do a dry strafing pass. I just wanted you to know that I've got a Med-Evac chopper due in to pick you guys up in about 45 minutes or so. Also, I've got a gunship coming in to cover for you, ETA in 20 minutes."

"Mako copies. That's good news, the sooner the better."

Jiggy held a tight orbit above the western part of the valley, waiting until the al-Qaeda began their rush across the clearing. She immediately threw the jet into a dive to begin a dry strafing pass. "Mako, Gumball is in for a dry pass."

The yelling fighters ran across the field, gathering courage from each other, spurred on by Allah. A few heard the big jet aim at them again and almost as one, they turned and ran back to the relative protection of the rocks. Seeing them turn and run, Jiggy broke off her attack and climbed back to altitude.

"That was great Gumball, they're running for the hills. Keep up the show and maybe we'll make it till the cavalry arrives." Dave congratulated her.

Rolling on his side, he yelled at Mark, busy redressing Woody's shrapnel wounds. "I don't know what you were griping about, I'd date this chick in a heart beat. She's a great actor! Saved our butts again. She's also got a Med-Evac on the way to get us out of here."

"Great, you're doing a great job on that radio. You wouldn't have any smoke for the Med-Evac chopper would you?"

Dave's dirty face broke into a big grin, "No man, what are you thinking? I'm CIA, we live behind the smoke screen, we don't carry it around."

Without smiling, Mark nodded grimly and went back to Woody's dressing.

"I've got the plane," Skeletor said as he shook the control wheel. "Give these folks a call on the radio."

"You got it," Jason said, holding up both of his hands.

Adjusting the boom microphone against his lips, Jason transmitted, "Gumball, Spooky is about five minutes out."

"Gumball copies, I just finished a second dry strafing pass. You're just in time! I don't think the Q will believe another feint from me," Jiggy replied. Twisting in her seat, she looked down against the mountainside for the dark shape of the AC-130, it must be less than six miles away. Seeing the shadow skittering across the craggy terrain, she looked a little to the west and picked up the airplane. "Gumball has you in sight. I'll hold high, base plus five and above, you are cleared to the target. Situation is as I briefed it before, with enemy massing 400 meters west of Rock Knoll."

"Spooky copies," Jason replied.

Skeletor hand flew the AC-130 through the notch in the mountains. The road below followed the cut before plunging down into the valley. He banked smoothly towards the eastern side of the valley. Over the intercom he said, "FCO do you have the knoll yet."

"Yes, sir, I'm pretty sure. I've got the small Y shaped valley, the road in the eastern leg, the river in the western. Just south of the inner point I've got what appears to be a real hot spot. And I count one, two, three, no, five bodies there. Is that what we have, five friendlies?" the FCO replied.

Without replying to the FCO, Skeletor thumbed the radio button. "Gumball, confirm there are five friendlies at this location. Is that correct?"

"Affirmative, Spooky, five friendlies."

Dave, listening in to the chatter broke in, "This is Mako, look east of us about a half klick. Anything out there is bad, and you have my permission to help them find their way to paradise."

On the intercom, Skeletor suggested, "FCO, it looks like that is the friendly location. Look east about 400 meters for a larger group."

The FCO slewed the infrared sensor east, seeing two large hotspots, he exclaimed, "Whew, there look to be two groups, I'd guess over 80 plus in each group."

Watching his screen, a mirror of the FCOs, Skeletor threw the fire consent switch, "Roger, let's light them up. Target them with the 40 first."

Seconds later, in groups of four, the 40mm Bofors began rhythmically pumping out rounds. In the IR screen, it looked like white-hot blobs where flying towards the massing al-Qaeda. Seconds later, they were engulfed in even brighter mushrooms as the exploding rounds tore through them. Before the AC-130 had made its first pass, they had eliminated both groups of men threatening Mark's team on the Rock Knoll.

Skeletor wasn't surprised at the accurate shooting. He began thinking about the inbound choppers and decided to make a wider circle to clear the area for additional threats. Turning the aircraft through north, the FCO shouted over the intercom, "Hey, boss, check your screen. I've got about four or five vehicles coming up the road from the south, I'm thinking they're Tech vehicles?"

"Yeah, you're probably right. Take them with the 105, ASAP. We've got to clear the area or the choppers can't get in." He immediately steepened the bank for a few minutes and rolled out, heading directly towards the ridgeline. Turning to Jason he said, "Keep an eye on the rocks. There isn't enough time to setup another pass, we need to get those trucks right now and we need a little spacing for the gun."

"You bet." Jason nodded. Looking out the windshield he concentrated on the approaching ridge.

The gunner lined up the first vehicle, aimed a little short and squeezed off the first round. It impacted right in front of the trucks, like surprised birds they scattered to both sides of the road. With the trucks jammed down the valley from Mako, the FCO took his time, methodically picking off each one as fast as they could load and fire. "Score four, what next boss?"

The 40mm Bofors loader stood next to the gun, listening to the chatter over the intercom when a tinny, *smaacckk*, caught his attention. He looked down to see several holes open to the sky; bending forward he could see the ground and rocks through the holes. Without warning, he was knocked over by searing hot hydraulic fluid as the power line for the gun mount gave away. Screaming he fell to the deck. The 40mm gunner hopped onto the gun mount and drug the screaming loader into the center of the airplane.

In the cockpit, Jason felt the airplane lurch left, he quickly shot a glance at Skeletor. Skeletor was intently staring into the IR repeater, looking for more threats on the ground. Figuring the bump must have been nothing more than a little turbulence; he looked out the windscreen again. The approaching terrain was getting bigger fast and he was beginning to feel uncomfortable. "Skeletor, you'd better steepen the bank, the rocks are getting close."

Nodding absently Skeletor said, "Okay." Still concentrating on the IR repeater, he added a few degrees of bank. Suddenly, the airplane lurched violently left.

Out of the corner of his eye, Jason noticed the RPM gauge for the number one engine roll back. He looked intently at the gauges, surprised to see the number two RPM begin to increase dramatically, in seconds accelerating quickly beyond redline. He touched the number two-condition lever, without hesitation he snapped it to feather. The RPM wasn't affected and he felt the airplane vibrating violently. "Number two is a runaway. I've got to shut it down manually."

Reaching up, Jason flipped the guard off the Number Two Fire Handle, and pulled it, closing off all fuel to that engine. Glancing at the number one engine he saw that it had rolled back to a sub-idle.

Even with the engine shut down the vibrations were getting more violent. Thinking they might have to shut it off and restart it, he looked up at Skeletor to get his input.

Jason saw Skeletor staring at his leg, his eyes wide with fear. Skeletor held his left leg with both hands, a bright red stain rapidly growing on his tan flight suit, seeping through his fingers. The top of his thigh was misshapen and Jason couldn't make out what the problem was. It seemed like everything was happening in slow motion. Wind whistling through a gaping hole in Skeletor's side of the airplane caught his attention.

It finally dawned on Jason that Skeletor had been wounded. Like thunder, it occurred to him that maybe the engine problems were the result of ground fire. He just hadn't considered getting hit before. In slow motion, he looked out the front of the airplane toward the rocks. He reached for the yoke at the same time; only one thing was on his mind. He had to turn the airplane left and head back towards the valley. In seconds, the vibrations were so violent that he couldn't focus on anything in the cockpit. Turbulence or not, it was the worst vibration he'd ever experienced. Suddenly, everything smoothed out, or seemed to

Out of the corner of his eye he saw that the N_1 and N_2 instruments for both engines on the left side read zero, not knowing what had happened to the number one engine he decided that they had to try and fly on the good engines. He disconnected the autopilot and the airplane immediately began rolling into a steep left bank.

Remembering he only had power on the right wing, he pulled the throttles back. Rolling in right aileron and standing on the rudder he found that he could control the airplane a little better, but could not get it completely out of the bank. Out of the corner of his eye he saw the red light in the number four T-handle begin to glow. Glancing immediately at the temperature gauge he saw the needle rising steadily past the limit. Reaching up, he grasped the T-handle in his fingers.

The Flight Engineer yelled, "Pull the condition lever, not the fire handle! Sir, the condition lever!"

"Dude, the fire will kill us before the prop can feather, I gotta isolate that engine." He pulled the T-handle out sharply, shutting the engine down.

In that moment, for Jason, everything began to slow down. With Skeletor injured he was by himself and there wasn't anyone that could help him figure out how to survive. There wasn't anyone to suggest the right thing to do. His mind raced through the possibilities; they were in the widest part of the valley, about eight miles across, narrowing to less than a mile at the south end, with a 9,000 foot ridge at the far end. With three engines out and unknown damage to the airplane, he realized that he had severe problems controlling the airplane. He knew they were effectively in a box canyon. On only one engine he couldn't turn the airplane, and if he couldn't turn soon they were going to crash.

At their present weight, he knew they had no chance of climbing out of the valley. The unthinkable had happened; he had prepared for the possibility of crashing throughout his whole career, but had never thought it would actually happen to him. There was one thing for certain; they would crash somewhere in this valley, in the next few minutes. He decided to warn the crew. Thumbing the intercom button he tried to muster a calm voice. "Crew this is the co-pilot. We've taken severe damage and the airplane will not fly out of this valley. Brace for impact, we'll be on the ground in a few minutes. Repeat, brace for impact."

He looked at Skeletor, the question of whether he was doing the right thing, plain in his eyes. Skeletor nodded his head roughly in confirmation; with his free hand he painfully tightened his shoulder straps. Jason, with both hands on the control wheel, croaked, "Just hang in there, okay!"

Switching to the radio he transmitted, "Mayday, Mayday, Mayday, Spooky 33 has been hit and will attempt a crash landing on the road. Repeat, Spooky 33 is going down, Mayday, Mayday, Mayday."

Jiggy had been watching the AC-130 as she orbited overhead; suddenly it yawed sharply to the left, sending a chill through her spine. She froze when Jason made his emergency call. Her mind seemed to speed up. *Things are going horribly wrong, what should do I do first?* she thought. Suddenly it occurred to her, *the choppers!* Immediately she got on the radio. "Berry 21, Gumball 71. The AC-130 is making a crash landing. We need you here ASAP."

"Berry 21 copies, we are 20 to 25 minutes out, we'll be there as soon as we can."

Jason strained to look at the road through the left window. He pushed up the throttle on number three, his only remaining engine on the right wing. He tried to roll the airplane upright. He desperately wanted to get further down the valley, to have enough room to set the airplane down on the road. "Skeletor, there isn't enough road to make this turn smooth. I need to get down the valley as far as I can. When we get enough spacing, I'm going to try a skid turn to line up with that road. I can't get it totally out of this bank, so I might need your help to roll this thing out. I'll need you to stand on the right rudder, okay?"

Skeletor nodded and leaned his head back, enduring the pain. Gritting through his teeth he said, "It won't turn worth a shit on one engine, go to idle and put the nose down."

Afraid, Jason held the nose up as much as he dared; he felt a slight rumble as the airplane flew dangerously close to the stall. Approaching the road, Jason pulled the right throttle to idle and at the same time relaxed the rudder and the right bank. The airplane rolled sharply left and the nose began to yaw inside the turn. The rumble became more pronounced and Jason shoved the yoke forward, pushing the nose down. The airspeed rose slightly as the airplane tried to accelerate in the thin air.

What seemed like minutes, took only a few seconds, the nose had tracked nearly 100 degrees, but they were still 30 degrees shy of the dirt road. The airplane wasn't really turning. Jason pushed the throttle all the way up, rolling in aileron to the stop; he stood on the right rudder. "Skeletor, stand on the right rudder, I need you on the right rudder now!"

Jason felt the rudder move slightly as Skeletor joined him. The airplane lumbered out of the left bank, the yaw rate visibly slowing. He could not man-handle the airplane with the time he had left and the nose settled just to the right of the road. Realizing he had just this one shot at aligning with the road, he pushed the nose further down and took a little aileron out. The nose of the airplane continued left, but he could see that their ground track was lining up with the road. Less than 100 feet above the ground Jason reached up and pulled the Fire Handle on three, shutting it down before the crash landing.

The nose kept drifting left, even with all the aileron and rudder he could put in to stop it. About 20 feet above the ground, with both hands straining on the yolk, he brought it back as quickly as he could. The airplane slowed quickly, yawing even more to the left. It struck the ground first near the rear ramp, slamming the nose down, and settling quickly on the belly. Sliding across the rocky ground, sparks and dirt flying, pieces began breaking off the airplane

Bracing for impact, the flight engineer reached up and grabbed Skeletor by his shoulder harness, trying to hold him in the seat as best he could. The airplane slowed quickly, the fuselage still intact. Through the broken glass of the windshield Jason saw that they were climbing the side of the mountain. If they didn't turn over, maybe they would survive this landing after all.

The left wingtip touched the ground, and the fuselage spun further left as the wing dug in. The entire airplane spun slowly, almost gracefully, around, trailing a huge cloud of dust and smoke. The dust overtook the Gunship, and billowed into the cockpit blinding Jason. In seconds it had covered everything, making it impossible to see. By feel, he reached for the switches and turned off all the electrics and fuel.

At least the airplane wouldn't catch fire from a switch he had left on, as Jason stood up. He wanted to abandon the airplane as quickly as possible. Turning toward Skeletor, he could barely see the pilot, the dust was so thick. He unbuckled Skeletor's seatbelt and tapped the stunned Flight Engineer on the arm. "Help me get him out of here," he shouted. Together they pulled him out of the seat and down the stairs from the cockpit.

On the cabin floor, the Engineer said, "Jason, I've got him. I can handle it, you go get everyone else."

"Okay, meet you out the front of the airplane." Jason pointed towards the nose and repeated, "Remember, meet at the front of the airplane, count noses when you get there." He made his way deeper into the cabin, totally obscured by dust. He held the sleeve of his flight suit over his nose, trying to breath in the heavy air. The only light came from an emergency exit sign hanging over the door to his right.

Jason remembered that there was an emergency flashlight in a holder next to the door. He grabbed it, flipped it on and went into the cabin looking for survivors. Hearing moaning coming from the center of the airplane, he saw two men slumped on the floor. Without hesitation he leaned down, grabbing one he slung him over his shoulder in a fireman's carry. Seeing a gaping hole in the side of the airplane, he carried the crewman through it.

Dave shouted to Mark, "Mark, the Gunship is calling a Mayday. Something about a crash landing on the road."

Stunned, Mark jerked his head toward the big airplane. "Shit, those guys must have gotten hit. Keep your eye on 'em, we're gonna have to help them when they hit the ground," Mark said. The firing from the al-Qaeda had slacked off after the first Gunship barrage, risking a look around, he poked his head above the rocks. "Heads up, everybody. When that bird lands we're going to make a run for it. There is a chopper about twenty minutes out and they're going to head for the crash first. It'll be up to us to rescue any survivors and set up a perimeter. Get ready, there will be a lull right after the crash and we'll go then!"

Luke rolled on his side, "Mark, I'll carry Woody. Dave would you carry my Barrett?"

"Dude, you don't have any rounds left and there probably isn't another 50 caliber round within 500 miles of here. I say leave it, it served it's purpose," Mark answered. Turning to Dave he said, "Dave, call Gumball and tell them that we will displace to the wreck and have the choppers meet us there. Tell 'em it will be a hostile LZ." Mark called out.

Dave jammed the handset to his ear and relayed the information. Finished he called to Mark, "Gumball says that the choppers are about twenty minutes out."

Mark nodded and pointed down the valley. "You'd better watch this. It ain't pretty, but this kind of thing doesn't happen often."

They watched in awe as the big transport lined up on the road, with the nose pointing alarmingly low. For a minute, Mark thought the airplane was going to hit them. Slowly he noticed the nose began to pitch up, he could see the airplane continue to drift left and start to descend. In slow motion, it flared and touched the ground; even slower it began to rotate like a top. It had almost stopped when the left wing hit a large boulder and violently spun the airplane around. It settled with the tail almost facing them, the left wing broken off and huge holes in the left side of the airplane.

"Go, Go, Go!" Mark shouted. Standing up, he took the radio from Dave and began running towards the wreck. "Follow me!"

The others followed him in a ragged line, the rest of the valley seemingly stunned into silence.

Hustler tracked the wrecked Hercules with his target pod, watching for survivors. "Jiggy, I see four people running towards the wreck from the Rock Knoll. Mako says they are displacing to the wreck. At least that'll make it easier for the chopper to pick them up."

"Yep, you're right. I'll let Berry know. Watch for bandits, though. The Pave Low can handle a few of them but it'll go better if we know where they are."

Thumbing forward on the mic button Jiggy transmitted, "Berry, Gumball.

The team is displacing to the 130. The airplane is down and the fuselage is intact next to the north-south road."

"Gumball, Berry copies. Two questions. Have you seen a good place to land and where are the bad guys?" Major Tom Collins asked.

"The nose is facing to the south, tail north. The left side is adjacent to the road; there is a large clear area next to the left wingtip. Recommend you look at that area."

"Berry copies, we'll come up the valley from the south. 21 will land and recover the crew and the team. 22 will orbit and look for bad guys."

Captain Arnie Zimmerman, listening to Tom describe the plan on the radio, signaled his agreement before anyone else could reply. "Twoop."

"Gumball copies. We're looking for bad guys right now. At the moment, there don't appear to be any next to the airplane."

Mark ran up to the airplane, it was getting dark and he couldn't clearly see the wreck. He was beginning to pull his NVG's from his pocket when he heard voices on the radio handset. Looking behind him to see if the rest of his team had made it, he grabbed the handset from Dave and raised it to his ear. "Gumball, Mako has formed next to the crash site. All my team members are here and we are trying to locate survivors."

"Mako, Berry 21 copies that. There should be 13 guys on that plane. We're going to be your ride tonight, plan on a LZ off the left wing. Expect ETA in about ten minutes."

"Mako copies ten minutes, thanks," Mark said, as he hooked the handset to Dave's front pocket. "Luke, Mike, you guys help me. Dave stay with Woody, There are 13 guys on this plane, let's find them all! Be careful, the Q might start getting curious."

Picking up their weapons they headed out as if they were on a desert exercise back home, searching for survivors.

Sweeping up the valley, Captain Tully Broadshear flew the big helicopter using the Terrain Following radar and FLIR to pick his way through the deepening gloom. Tom Collins, the Aircraft Commander monitored their progress and ran the radio. "Tully, you should see the wreck on your side in a couple of minutes."

Tully took his hand off the collective; with his sleeve he wiped the sweat from his face and resumed hand flying the aircraft. "Two miles out," he announced.

"Two miles," Tom repeated on the radio. Captain Arnie Zimmerman, flying

Berry 22, slid wide to the right and climbed several hundred feet. Over the intercom he echoed Berry 21's radio call. "Two miles everyone. Keep your eyes open. Anything moving that's not next to the airplane is a bad guy, shoot it."

Tully slowed the helicopter when he saw the downed C-130. "Wreck in sight, Looks like a good LZ on the road. I'm going to set down there. The wreck will be on the left side of our aircraft," Tully said as he pitched the nose up and began to flare. The crewmen manning the guns leaned out further, trying to see through the dust and scan the area with their NVGs.

Mark pulled a chem stick from his pocket. Holding it in both hands, he broke it and shook it vigorously. He tossed it towards the helicopter. Two Para-rescue men, PJs, rushed from the side door towards the chem stick. Mark stood; his hands held out and up, he stopped them as they approached. "We've got one guy here that needs a stretcher, looks like four ambulatory. We're still searching for survivors."

"Copy sir, we'll get these guys in the chopper, do you need help searching for survivors?"

"Yeah, I've got two guys out right now, that's all I have," Mark said. He turned quickly towards the nose of the airplane. With his NVGs he noticed a flickering hot spot through a big tear in the fuselage. Concerned about explosion and fire he began running towards the front of the airplane, looking for the rest of the crew.

Seeing several people in front of him, he slowed down and yelled, "Luke, what's up?"

"Sir, we found the rest of the survivors. Seven total, four are hurt pretty bad."

"We'd better get moving. I saw a fire in the fuselage, there's still lots of ammo in there. It won't be long before this thing goes up in a big way," Mark said.

A dark figure in front of him stooped and picked up a wounded crewmember, "We can carry these guys with your help. One of you lead the way, let's go."

"Follow me!" Mark said and led the way, with the survivors faithfully following him into the cloud of dust blown up by the helicopter. Stopping at the door, he made a head count, two of his guys and seven of the crew. As he started up the ramp, thinking he was the last one on the ground he was surprised when a PJ came up behind him and slapped him on the back.

"Are you it sir?" the PJ asked.

"I think so. I was just doing a head count to make sure everyone is here," Mark replied.

"Sir, I counted eight before you got on board and with this group, ya'll make eighteen. Is that the number you are looking for?"

"I think so. How many crewmembers were on that C-130?" Mark asked, a little dazed.

"Thirteen, how many in your group?"

"Five, there were five of us," Mark answered.

"Well that's it, sir. Get on board, we gotta go," the PJ replied.

Mark tried to answer, but before he could speak the ear splitting roar of the mini-gun drowned all noise, as it began firing only a few feet from them. A tongue of fire arced from the rear ramp of the helicopter. The PJ unceremoniously shoved him in the small of the back, pushing him into the cabin of the helicopter. As soon as he was in, Tully pulled pitch. As the helicopter lifted, he spun it around.

"Berry 21 has all the survivors. Coming off to the right," Major Collins transmitted.

"Recommend left turn, around the C-130," Captain Zimmerman replied from the supporting helicopter, "We're engaging a group of Tech vehicles north bound on the road."

"Copy, Berry 21 is off left. Gumball, did you copy we've got all the survivors?"

"Gumball copies," Jiggy replied. Taking a deep breath she remarked to Hustler, "Damn, we were lucky today. Guess, I'd better face the music and tell Maddog what happened." On second thought she decided to enjoy the moment before she changed frequencies.

"Maddog copies. All players be advised there is a B-1 inbound to destroy the remains of the AC-130, ETA in 20 minutes. Maddog out."

"Dodged that bullet, didn't you?" Hustler asked over the intercom.

"I'm glad it didn't get so ugly on the radio, it's terrible to air your dirty laundry for everyone to hear." Jiggy sighed. "Let's go home."

Hustler tried to give her a pep talk. "I'm ready. Steering's in the INS. I wouldn't worry about that 130. Shit happens, it's combat. Besides, everyone's alive, that's what counts."

"Yeah. Do you still have any of those candy bars? All of a sudden I'm hungry."

"Sure, coming up on your right side." Holding a Butterfinger in his right hand, he slid it along the canopy rail towards the front seat. "What do you expect, we've been airborne for, what, nearly eight hours. It ain't a record, but hell, we only planned on a 2.5."

In the dark cabin of the helicopter Mark slowly made his way around, checking on his men and the survivors of the crash. Satisfied that everyone was okay for the moment, he plopped down next to Dave. Dave worked silently on an MRE, washing it down with water from the helicopter crew's canteens. The notebooks he had stashed in his backpack, piled next to him. When Mark settled down next to him, Dave offered him the MRE.

Mark waved it off, "I'll take a pull of that water though."

"Suit yourself. I'm hungry. So, what are you going to do now? Sell magazines and go to college?" Dave asked.

"No, I think I'll lay on a beach somewhere and bird dog some chicks. Actually, I need to get back to the team, no rest for the wicked. Aren't you coming?"

Dave gestured excitedly. "Yeah, eventually. First, I've got to turn this stuff in. I only just started looking at this notebook. It looks pretty amazing, some stuff in here about SAMs and airliners. I'm convinced that this is the plan for an attack. Probably real soon." Holding up the notebook with one hand, he pointed at some Arabic writing with a chocolate biscuit in the other, "See, this part. It talks about Chicago Midway. Dude, this is hot stuff. Maybe we can beat them, this time! We did good!"

"Great, I'm glad the trip was worth it. We owe that Gumball pilot for saving our asses and all those gunship guys too!"

"No shit!" Dave nodded. Then he concentrated on pulling the plastic foil from his brownie and went back to reading. Sensing that he had lost him, Mark got up and continued towards the front, bracing himself against the wall as the helicopter jostled back and forth. Finding the dark figure he had met on the ground, he sat down next to him. "I hear you're the pilot of the Gunship?"

"I was the co-pilot. The pilot was shot." Pointing to one of the men on a stretcher, laid out on the floor. "He's over there. I did the crash landing."

Sincerely, Mark said, "Dude, I just wanted to say thanks. You really saved our ass. If it wasn't for you we'd be dead about now. No shit. I know it's probably rough losing an airplane like that, but I just want all of you to know we owe you our lives."

"You're welcome. We're just lucky no one got killed. I'm surprised, to tell you the truth. When we got hit, we still had two engines running, and then I had to shut down number four because of a fire. I just couldn't control it, it kept wanting to turn left," Jason replied. The adrenaline was beginning to wear off and the enormity of the loss dominated his mind. He felt hollow inside and questioned whether he had made the right decision. With his mind racing, he said, "I was just lucky to get it on the road."

"Dude, everyone is alive. And that's thanks to you. The airplane is just a thing; you put your ass on the line and saved our lives. I just wanted to say thanks." Sticking out his hand, Mark said, "I'm sorry, I didn't introduce myself. I'm Mark Goode, Captain US Army." Jason just looked at him in stunned silence; Mark couldn't help the feeling that he knew this guy, from somewhere. He asked, "You look a little familiar, do we know each other?"

Jason looked at him and then at his hand, silently. After a long moment he took Mark's hand, and shook it firmly, "I'm Jason Gorman."

Mark shook his hand, the feeling that he knew him was leaving, "Thanks for saving our butts man, you don't know how much it means!"

Jason tried to control his voice. "You don't know me do you? We met at an Air Force UPT graduation. I'm Jenn's boyfriend, or I was."

Mark, not really impressed, wanted to be nice. "Yeah, that's right. Now I know why you seem so familiar. Imagine that, I guess it really is a small world."

Watching his expression Jason could see that he still didn't get it. "You still don't know do you?"

Mark hated playing guessing games and was getting a little annoyed. He didn't have a lot of patience for holding hands, his motto was, "Deal with it, get over it and move on." He just looked at Goode in questioning silence, a slight smile on his face.

"Dude, it was Jenn flying Gumball 71. Jenn was the flight lead on that flight," Jason said, incredulously.

Stunned, Mark sat back slowly, the slight smile still plastered on his face. He leaned his back against the sidewall of the helicopter, his eyes drifted out of focus. Wiping his face in disbelief, he said, "You gotta be shitting me. Dude, you mean that was my little sister in that jet. I can't believe it. I didn't even recognize her on the radio. Shit."

The coolness of the metal vibrating Mark's back didn't bring any relief. He thought about that strafing pass, where she almost killed herself. He was sure she had gone too low, just to save him. She probably didn't even know it was him. His little sister.

CHAPTER 20

Kabul, Afghanistan

The residential streets of the Taymani neighborhood were quiet and dark, very few lights shone on the abandoned streets. Stars shone like bright pinpricks in a dark blanket vaulting the mountainside town. Sagittarius hung motionless in the clear, cold sky. Faint engine sounds split the silence, background noise at first. Steadily, the sound grew louder, insistent. Suddenly, two Land Cruisers, followed by a technical vehicle, the rider in the back hanging onto the wildly swinging machine gun, stormed through the streets.

The convoy, scattering stones and dust, rushed to a stop in front of a walled compound. The driver and passenger leaped from the lead Land Cruiser, shouting at the gate. After a few minutes, a lone figure appeared and opened the gate deliberately. Obviously agitated, the two rushed back to their trucks, with engines racing, they disappeared behind the gate.

Ahmed Mustapha, Usama bin Laden's chief lieutenant for Kabul, got out of the rear seat of the first vehicle and approached the second. Resting his hand on the window he said, "My friend please, take the house on the right. As long as you wish to stay you are welcome, and anything you need will be provided."

"Ahmed, you are most kind. I think these are much better accommodations than I have become accustomed to in Tora Bora, thank you," Ahmed Mohideen replied. "Do you wish to have *chai?*"

"I am sorry, my old friend, I do not mean to be a bad host. It has been a very long day and I have several telephone calls to make before I sleep. I am very tired and I cannot do as much now as I could 20 years ago. But I must call our brave fighters in America." Turning left, towards one of the four houses arranged at the corners of the small courtyard, Mustapha walked away, calling as he went, "No need to rush, even in the morning. I will see you in the tomorrow. Good night."

"Inshallah," Mohideen replied, to himself. "Go with God my friend." Stiffly he got out of his vehicle, one of the caretakers appeared by his side and steered him towards the house.

Inside Mustapha sat on the floor. He pulled off his sandals and relaxed on a pillow. With everyday that passed, and all the bombing, the only place he was beginning to feel safe was here at home. Inside these walls, he could control what happened, things were familiar. Outside, things were, well, unsavory and dangerous. It was harder to hold onto his inner moral quality, his Taqwa. War made it very hard to uphold the Five Pillars of Islam. He was tired; he rubbed his feet on the thick Persian rug. He wondered how his wife and son were doing in Pakistan. Sent away when the Americans had attacked his building, he wanted them as far away as possible from the clutches of bin Laden. Someone had to live in this crazy time. For him, his fate was clear, his Taqwa compelled him to do God's bidding and guard against danger. Now it was time to strike back at the Americans. They had done enough damage, it was time to topple their government or destroy their economy. Whatever the result, it would be what they deserved. Without them, the world would be a safer place.

Mustapha pulled his cell phone out of his pocket. He scrolled through the memory until he found the number he was looking for, pressing the *Talk* button he held the phone to his ear.

Still hard of hearing from his near misses with American bombs, he virtually shouted into the phone when it was answered, "Tariq, Tariq?"

"Yes, yes. This is Tariq. Who is this?" Tariq Israni said, answering the phone call in his car. The voice was loud, but barely understandable, covered in static as if it was a poor radio connection.

"Tariq, it is Ahmed Mustapha. How is your health?"

"Ahmed, it is good to hear your voice. It has been too long. How are you my old friend?" Tariq said, his thick mustache curling in a smile.

"Tariq, the war goes very hard here. Twice American bombs have almost killed me. It is time you released the rabbits that you have been tending. The season demands you harvest them immediately!"

Suddenly serious, Tariq looked around nervously to see if anyone had heard the tiny voice in his ear. His windows were rolled down, but no one had noticed. "Yes, Mudier. I will do as you wish. We believe the crop will have results greater than we can hope."

"This is good. Waist no time, inform the others. Time is short and we must harvest the rabbits before it is too late."

Before Tariq could think to reply, he was listening to static. He realized that he must call New York and Chicago. God had finally called them and it was time to do his bidding. Dialing his roommate he too, shouted into the phone. "Abdul get the van ready immediately and call Ahmed Mohammed. It is time, we have received the call."

Without listening to Abdul's reply, he hung up the phone. His brow furrowed, he was trying to remember the telephone number of the cell in New York. He did not know any names and he didn't remember how to reach the Chicago cell, but he was sure those in New York would know. Pulling his cab over to the side of the road, he cradled his phone and tried to remember. Suddenly, the number came to him; dialing quickly he looked around nervously. Surely, someone had heard his conversation.

"Hello, Hello," Hazim Zakko answered with suspicion. For several days, he and Arif had been on the run. They had been moving from place to place, scared that they might be the next ones picked up in the FBI dragnet.

Tariq, without introducing himself began talking. "Now is the season to harvest the rabbit warren and you must tell Chicago to harvest theirs as well. Whatever you are doing you must harvest the rabbits in precisely three hours, from right now."

"Inshallah, I understand," Hazim answered. Staring at the floor, he hung up the phone. Clasping it in his hands he sat for several minutes. The time had come it was his turn.

Feeling the buzz of her cell phone Amy Martinez wondered who could be calling her, she unclipped it from the belt of her pantsuit. Sitting at a large table, she looked out across the crowd, all-waiting to be served lunch. Not wishing to disturb the formalities of the event she turned slightly, and quietly put the phone to her ear. "Yes."

"Amy, this is Armbruster. I've got that call you've been waiting for, you know, regarding Afghanistan."

"Great, hold that thought. I'm on a cell phone at a luncheon the President is giving at the White House. Let me move to a hard line. I'll call you back. You're in your office, right?"

"Right, I'll wait for your call. Don't take long, this is critical," Armbruster replied.

Less than a minute later, Amy was dialing a phone the White House Communications Agency had set up in the hallway outside the room. "Sorry, what do you have?"

"Two things really. Yesterday one of our SA guys was pulled out of an ambush with some Army guys, you might have heard of it?"

"Yeah, I saw the initial Intel report," Amy replied.

"Well, the SA guy had a treasure trove of Intel he pulled from an al-Qaeda cave. First, he found the goods on the 9/11 hijackers and even better he hit the gold mine on this rabbit harvesting thing we've been hearing about in traffic. Anyway, our analysts were right, it is a missile attack on airliners in the US. In fact they are targeted in Dallas, Chicago and New York."

"That's fantastic. It couldn't be better—hard evidence and Intel on future operations. That's great! By the way, the president is aware of your hunch a couple of days ago. Even if it wasn't a documented threat, he directed the FBI and Homeland Security to have response teams in all the major city/airport pairs."

"Great, thanks for that by the way. Thing is, that's not the best news. We were able to crack the code on cell phones, all the way. Less than a half hour ago we monitored a call from Kabul. It was to a cell phone in Dallas, we're sure it set off the timing for the rabbit attack. The actual time frame is unknown, but we think it will take place in the next three to twelve hours."

Turning slowly, wrapping the phone cord around her, Amy looked into the dining room. The President was grinning at the speaker's comments. "That's fantastic. The President will be happy to hear about the break. I can tell you that we must interdict this attack. There is no way we can afford to let even one team of these fanatics succeed. I'll tell him immediately, we need to get the wheels in motion for the response teams."

Sensing she was about to hang up, Armbruster rushed, "Wait, Amy, it gets better. We pinpointed the cell phone users. We positively ID'd three of the al Qaeda top leaders. This is real time stuff, they are in a compound in Kabul, right now."

"Have you passed that along to the Air Force? The President already authorized a strike on that type of Intel. The Air Force must get the strike going, ASAP!" Amy said breathlessly.

Tariq Israni, looked serenely at his roommate, rushing aimlessly around the house, "Abdul, calm down, all will be as Allah wills it. Think for a moment, is Ahmed Mohammed home at this hour. It would be best if he would help us."

In mid-stride Abdul looked at his watch, "No he is not home yet from school. It will be a little over an hour."

In a decisive voice Tariq ordered, "Then we will pick him up when he gets home from school. We will pick him up at his house. Go to the garage and make sure the van is ready to go. I will join you in a few minutes, together we will load the rabbits."

Mike Lambert, was deskbound at the Brooklyn FBI field office, catching up on paper work. His partner, Charles Bonner, was the first to answer the phone. Assigned to the Counter-Terrorist detail, they had gotten used to outside work in the last few weeks and had avoided filling out reports. No job was perfect, even good investigative work also involved lots of paper shuffling. "Brooklyn FBI, Bonner here."

Mike, seeing the surprised look on Bonner's face, sat up in a rush, knocking a stack of papers to the floor with a crash. Bonner slammed the phone down, jumped up and grabbed his coat. Pausing, he looked at his partner. Mike, a sheaf of papers still in one hand, stared at him, a questioning look in his eyes.

"Get off your ass, Bud. That was a flash, it seems like they just slapped a terrorist threat on three major airports and ours is one of them."

Before Charles could finish, Mike rushed past him blurting, "Well, what are you waiting for?"

"Wait up, I'm driving," Charles called after his partner.

Hustler, in the backseat of Gumball 71 the lead F-15E, could tell that Jiggy was getting antsy, he decided to get her mind off of the waiting. "Well, look at it this way, Jig. In an hour and a half we can go get another top-off, we've got that to look forward to. You know it's the Air Force way." Hustler added, "Do you want me to fly for awhile?"

Shaking the stick slightly fore and aft, Jiggy Goode said, "Yeah, I need to wiggle my fingers and toes for a bit. My neck is getting sore from looking at that damn tanker all the time."

Taking the stick, Hustler bobbled a little bit before he got the feel of the airplane. "After yesterday, this is a nice change. I'd say it's more relaxing, wouldn't you? A good nights sleep and a mission where I don't have to do any strafe. Now that's a good day."

Jiggy grasped the canopy handholds on each side and pushed her feet on the rudders. Tensing her muscles she stretched, hard. "I wouldn't call hanging around Oscar cap with a tanker at 32k relaxing. Boring maybe, but not relaxing."

"You'd better be careful, folks will think you're an adrenaline junkie. Stuff like this comes with the territory. You do something good and then they tend to call your name for a while. Then you do something bad, and they forget about you," Hustler said. "Hey, this deal tonight is better than not having them call your name."

"That's fucking brilliant. Did you think of that yourself?" Jiggy answered in frustration. As soon as she said it she felt terrible. "Sorry, I didn't mean that. It's just that I'm no different than before and now they think I'm great. I guess I should feel lucky that I didn't get reamed for not following the rules yesterday."

Running out of things to say, Hustler rested his right forearm on his leg, flying the airplane with his middle finger and thumb on the stick. He enjoyed flying smoothly and precisely. Gently walking the throttles with his left hand, he kept the airplane suspended on the wingtip of the KC-135R tanker, motionless in space.

The silence between them stretched into minutes, finally Jenn broke the ice again. "Yeah, that's good, right? Anyway, I didn't mean to bite your head off. I really had fun coming up with the attack plan this morning. Putting four GBU-24s into targets less than 1,000 meters apart isn't easy. And to do it all within five seconds of each other, now that's what I call a challenge. It was almost as fun as getting to do it for real!" Grabbing the right handhold in her left hand, she twisted around until she could look Hustler in the face. She still felt guilty for jumping on him, "The hard part is waiting, we could spend eight or ten hours up here and then go home." Not getting any reaction, she tried to be funny. "I came to dance, not go home."

Hustler forgave her. "Waiting builds character and you need all you can get. After getting frocked to a four ship Flight Lead in a combat zone, you gotta be careful about getting the big head. Pretty soon you'll be pinning on LC or something."

Ten Arlington police cars pushed their way through traffic on Highway 360, when cars slowed them down they took to the shoulder to bypass the *Commuter* traffic. Exiting on US 183 they dropped off one by one, spreading themselves out on the side of the freeway. Joined by six Fort Worth police cars, they blanketed the southern access of the DFW airport. On the north side of the airport, Grandprarie and Dallas Police cars spread out on the 121 and 114 Highways. Airliners roared into the sky, heading south over a horde of policemen protecting the departure end of the runways. Policemen also inundated the approach end on the north side of the DFW airport. SWAT teams were armed and ready on the airport itself, while patrolmen cleared the golf course immediately southwest of the airport. Within minutes the police were prepared to interrupt any terrorist activity.

Twelve miles away, Abdul Zadeh drove a dirty panel van down a sleepy tree lined street through a nice brick subdivision of North Dallas. Smoke curling from the exhaust, he stopped at a sprawling ranch house, a Blue Ford

Expedition in the driveway. The passenger, Tariq Israni got out, walking quickly he went to the door and rang the bell.

Howard Bowman answered the door. He was expecting the pest exterminator his mother had called and was surprised to see his friend from the mosque at the door. Stepping outside he pulled the door almost shut behind him. "Tariq, I didn't know you knew where I lived. Is there anything wrong?"

"Ahmed, it is time. We need your help now. You must come," Tariq said intently, grabbing his bicep in a vice like grip.

Trying to shake his grasp, Howard replied, "Right now? I just got home from school. And I have homework to do." Nervously brushing the hair from his face, Howard added, "I will be at the mosque at the usual time. Can it wait until then?"

Tariq tightened his grip and began pulling him towards the van. "No it cannot. This is your test of faith, as the Koran teaches, you must trust in God. Come with me now, it is time. God calls you."

Pacing nervously back and forth in front of the self-storage room, Hazim Zakko waited impatiently for his partner. "Arif, you should have put those new plates on yesterday as I told you. We should have been ready at all times, if we are late it is your fault."

"Hazim, do not worry. It will just take a few seconds to do this. People will get suspicious if we come to the storage room too often. Besides, I took these license plates this morning."

Obviously nervous, Hazim was not mollified. "It does not matter now. Just hurry and complete the job. We are running out of time."

Trying to sooth his friend, Arif replied, "Hazim you must relax. We are only fifteen minutes from LaGuardia. Even in this traffic, it will not be a problem to get there in time. As it is we have nearly 45 minutes, we must not be too early or that would be suspicious as well."

A dirty maroon Ford Econoline van bumped into the parking lot at Target on South Archer Avenue, shock absorbers barely working. A light drizzle filled the air heavily. Moving slowly in the parking lot, the van stopped near the curb, as far away from the store as it could. The driver remained in his seat keeping watch on the traffic around them. The passenger crawled silently into the back, using a small pry bar, he opened the wood box marked "muffler parts." The smell of mothballs permeated the enclosed van.

Slowly he removed an SA-7 from its packing material, Russian Cyrillic figures painted on the side. Someone had packed the weapon very carefully. Working quickly and silently, the man checked over the missile and attached the battery pack. Satisfied, he laid the missile down and began to prepare the second one, identical to the first.

The driver stayed in his seat; with vacant eyes he watched the comings and goings in the busy parking lot. He searched for the same cars he had already seen or anyone acting suspiciously. Nervously, his hands strayed from the steering wheel to scratch his scruffy dark beard and then back to the wheel to start a new cycle. Beside himself when someone parked next to them, he reached back and pulled a faded brown curtain behind the seats.

The passenger emerged from behind the curtain; he looked at his watch, and finished preparing both missiles. He sat down in his seat sideways and then spun slowly around to the front.

"You know Mike, I'd bet the target isn't JFK at all. I think it's LaGuardia," Charles said, bracing himself in the seat.

Throwing the Taraus around the traffic, Mike was driving briskly. Without taking his eyes off the road in front of him he said, "Oh, yeah, you've figured it out and both the command center and the CIA have it wrong. Why do you think it's LGA?"

"Look at it this way. The threat warning didn't actually say JFK, right? It said major city/airport pairs. Think about this, the approaches to JFK have a bunch of freeways around it. That makes it harder for anyone to stop and take a shot. They'd be sitting out in front of every nosy New Yorker around."

"Yeah and three of LGA's runways end in water. Explain that big boy," Mike interrupted derisively.

"Well, they could be going by boat. But I doubt that, the profile is most of them can't swim. But LGA has a lots of streets and back roads. Plus the airplanes get really close to the ground on approach, especially on 23rd Avenue. It just makes sense to do a hit and run there, at least to me. There's less security at a reliever like LaGuardia, JFK is one busy place."

Slowed down by traffic, Mike began to think, "Maybe you're right. Remember those two we picked up in a sweep a few days ago. You know the driver guy. They were only a few blocks from LGA. Maybe they were casing the joint."

"Mike, look I know it's a little thin, JFK isn't that far away either. But I just have a hunch that LGA is the target. Turn this thing around."

In a squeal of tires, Mike turned the car around. Bounding back onto the

Grand Central Parkway, they headed for the LGA terminal. "Shouldn't we tell the boss? I think we'll need back up?"

Charles looked at his partner, his lips drawn in a thin line. "Yeah, and do you think the boss will send us anybody on a wild goose chase like this?"

"Hazim, you must be calm and drive slowly. If you cannot, you should let me drive. You will attract attention driving crazy like this. Even if they do not know what we are about to do, the local police can still spoil our plans," Arif intoned.

"Shut up and keep watch. I know how to drive," Hazim spat. Going around the circle at 23rd Avenue, Airport Exit and Ditmars Boulevard, Hazim stepped on the gas a bit too hard and squealed the wheels. Pedestrians in the crosswalk turned their heads to see what was going on.

Resting his hand on his friends arm, Arif pleaded, "See, I told you. Hazim, you must drive slowly. No one must notice us."

"No one will suspect us. We are in New York! I will turn into the parking lot of the Courtyard Marriott Hotel. There we can wait the last few minutes and you can mount the batteries just before it is time," Hazim said. He was starting to feel calmer now that the time had almost arrived for them to shoot the missiles.

He carefully backed into a spot in the hotel parking lot. From his vantage point, he could keep watch on the road and the airport. He could easily see the approach path and airplanes whistling over the mechanic school 400 feet away. It was there, on the road just outside their fence that he intended to stop and shoot. They could launch their missiles and be back in heavy traffic within seconds.

Bracing himself against the door, with one hand on the dash and one on the seat beside him, Charles calmly looked at his partner. "So, Mario, were do you think we ought to watch from? Where do you think these guys will launch?"

"I don't know. But I'd bet they'd try to hit an airliner on final. It's the best time, close to the ground, with so little time to react. There's also less time for them to miss and no chance for the pilots to see the missile."

"Okay, well given the way the planes are landing today, let's go to the Courtyard Hotel parking lot. It's only a few hundred feet from the end of the runway, it's a great place to watch and we can get our bearings," Charles suggested.

"Good idea. I like it loud anyway."

Still driving too fast, Mike squealed into the parking lot.

Hazim saw the speeding car approaching, nervously he watched it pull into the parking lot. Inside were two serious men in suits, obviously cops. His blood pressure increased dramatically as the tires squealed entering the parking lot. Sitting straight up, Hazim reached for the ignition keys. Starting the van, he slammed it into gear and accelerated out of the parking lot in a cloud of blue tire smoke.

Charles saw the truck screeching out of the parking lot. "What the fuck is that? That looks like a guilty mother fucker to me!" Pointing towards the speeding truck, he added, "Hurry up! Follow that dude!"

Mike, who hadn't seen the truck, threw the Taurus back into gear; creating another cloud of blue smoke he exited the parking lot.

Sliding out of the parking lot, Hazim jammed the throttle to the floor and cranked the wheel to the left, fishtailing onto 90th Street southbound. Abdul, who had been standing in the back, was thrown to the floor as the van jerked sideways.

Charles, hanging on with one hand, reached into the backseat of the Taurus. Grabbing the beacon, he turned on the flashing light and attached it to the roof. Mike yelled, "Call for backup, Charlie, call for back up!"

The van careened around the traffic, waiting for a stop light at the intersection of 23rd Avenue. It slid sideways, jumping the curb; it bounced against the center median and jerked back onto the road as the driver turned the wheel too sharply. The vans front wheels dug in, jerking the van left and then lifting it gracefully on the two right wheels. Hanging, frozen in time like a movie, it finally tipped over and the top slid into a fire hydrant. The hydrant broke, sending a geyser of water into the air around the van.

Mike slammed the Ford to a stop and with guns drawn, they leaped from the car, approaching the van cautiously. Suddenly, one of the missiles inside the van ignited and crashed through the rear door. Barely missing them, it corkscrewed down the road, impacting against the wall of a store. Exploding, it sent a shower of bricks and debris onto the cars in the street.

Hustler enjoyed flying the Strike Eagle around the hold; stick time was hard to get these days. Point Oscar was 100 miles northwest of Kabul; they were less than 15 minutes from a go signal to impact. Jiggy took her water bottle from her g-suit pocket, she took a long drink and before she could swallow, the tanker called them on the boomer's frequency. "Gumball, Maddog wants you on TAD 533, ASAP."

Forcing her swallow, Jiggy replied, "Copy." Flipping through the mission flimsy on her knee she looked for the TAD 533 frequency. Punching in the new frequency, she called, "Maddog, Gumball 31 is up."

"Gumball 31, Maddog, your mission is a go. Understand your mission is a go. TOT is 13 minutes from right now. Copy?"

"Gumball copies, mission a go, TOT in 13 minutes."

Ahmed Mohammed rode in the passenger seat while Abdul drove the van. He carefully watched the traffic and the people along Marsh Lane as they headed south. Curious, he looked at Tariq in the back of the van. There were two large wooden boxes on the floor, each marked in English "muffler parts" as well as some German.

Abdul drove slowly with traffic, careful not to speed, he signaled every turn. Reaching down, he tuned the AM radio to 820 to listen to the local news radio station. If there were any problems with the others he knew that news radio would be broadcasting it first. It was his early warning network.

Ahmed ignored him; he was overcome with curiosity about what was in those boxes. With a small pry bar, Tariq finally got the top off the first one. Ahmed caught his breath when he saw the sinister, dirty white missile. Long and lean, it had the look of death on it. Shocked, Ahmed immediately turned to the front, staring out of the windshield. Abdul turned right at Northwest highway, a Southwest 737 thundered less than 200 hundred feet above his head. Ahmed watched it cross over Bachman Lake and touch down on Love Field's eastern runway. Overcome with a rush of nausea, he forgot all about crusading for Islam and he was Howard again; he knew what they were going to do.

Abdul calmly turned left into Bachman Lake Park on the west shore of the Lake. He backed into a slot with the rear of the truck facing the water and the runway. Methodically, he put the transmission in park and turned off the ignition, leaving the key in the ignition with the radio on. Calmly, Abdul looked at his watch, as if waiting for a special moment.

Howard, doubled over, pointed to the public restroom on the street side of the parking lot and said, "Abdul, I don't feel well. It must be something I had for lunch. I need to go to the bathroom, I will be right back."

Abdul nodded and said calmly, but forcefully, "Go ahead, be back soon. You have to drive. Five minutes and you must be back!"

Ahmed got out of the car and slowly made his way to the bathroom. Going around the corner he stopped at the door. Panting he pressed against the brick wall of the building. What should he do? If he ran from here, the public restroom would block Abdul's vision. Maybe he could make it all the way across

Northwest Highway, a four-lane road, before he would be noticed.

His heart pounding, he could barely think, this is not what he had imagined. He had to run, he couldn't be a part of killing innocent civilians. Americans. His neighbors. He couldn't possibly do this, it was horribly wrong. His head twitched from side to side in panic. He saw a police car at the Webb Chappell Road stoplight. His decision was made; he waited until the policeman was about to turn and then ran across the street in front of him.

In Chicago, the light drizzle had become a light rain, spattering little drops on the windshield. The driver of the maroon Econoline nervously looked at his watch. He started the engine and pulled out of the parking lot. Cruising slower than traffic on Cicero Avenue, the van passed the public terminal at Midway Airport. Bouncing over the ruts in the asphalt it turned right on 63rd Avenue and parked in a gas station parking lot on the corner. Checking his watch again, the driver got out of his seat and moved to the back of the van.

The passenger opened the rear doors slightly, as he poked his head out to look at an American Fokker F100 pass overhead on short final. As the airliner rolled out on the runway, its thrust reversers screaming, the man stepped back in the van. Sitting down on a wood box, he left the doors slightly open, propped with his foot. The driver held a missile in his hands, calmly watching the approach path of Runway 04. Checking his watch one last time, he saw an approaching Boeing 737. With a shout, they threw open the doors and jumped out, SA-7 missiles in their hands.

Running a little way into the road, they put the missiles on their shoulders, aiming towards the runway. Seconds later, the 737 thundered 100 feet overhead. They aimed at the engines mounted on each wing and pulled the triggers simultaneously.

For an eternity they stood still, like statues. Nothing happened, no smoke, no fire, and no rush of the missile towards the heavy airliner. Stunned, they pulled the triggers again, and again. The airliner had landed and motorists on the street had noticed them, their time had passed. One overweight man in a pickup truck, with the wheel wells rusted out, accelerated across traffic and rammed the two men as they stood in the road trying to figure out what had gone wrong.

Several other cars stopped around the scene. Huddling in the rain, several Chicago natives made sure the two men did not get up. Within seconds, sirens and police cars surrounded them. The two men did not get up, one obviously had a broken leg and the other's head was skewed at an unnatural angle. The broken missiles lay discarded on the wet street.

"Two minutes from the IP," Gumball 74 transmitted on the radio. Approaching the target in Kabul, the most complex part of their plan had been how to get the southern fighter in place without having to do an orbit. Timing was critical and it was critical to minimize the time before the bombs were in the air. Jiggy and Hustler had settled on having number four fly over the target, directly to his IP, passing it he would turn around and call the timing back to the Initial Point.

"Gumball One copies. Set TOT in four minutes, on my hack, acknowledge," Jiggy transmitted.

The wingman replied, one by one, "Twoop, Threep, Four."

Checking the clock on the UFC, Jiggy held the mic down. "Ready, Ready, Hack!" Releasing the button she said, "Okay, Hustler do your thing."

Hustler replied, "You've got a good designation. I'm going to the pod."

Jiggy concentrated on keeping the pipper on the ASL. With her speed set, she pressed the pickle button when the release cue appeared. She counted down the release. "Ten seconds TREL."

The release cue met the pipper and the airplane shook as the 2,000 pound laser guided bomb ejected from the bomb rack on the centerline of the jet. Jiggy thumbed the aft radio, "Bomb's away, one's coming right."

The others announcing their bomb releases immediately followed Jiggy's call. For the fourth time Hustler checked the laser code he had inserted into the target pod. He was nervous about making a monumental error, if he had someone else's code in and screwed up two bombs, it would be a disaster. Checking the time remaining before impact, he thumbed forward once to bring up narrow field-of-view. "Good track, laser on in ten seconds."

"Hustler, that looks like a good target," Jiggy assured him.

He was going to delay turning on the laser until very late in the terminal phase, they planned to use a mode of the bomb's guidance computer that would allow it to pitch over into a near vertical flight path. The bombs from each of the airplanes would be less likely to interfere with each other and the vertical flight path would allow for maximum penetration. The fuses had been set for a tenth of a second delay. They hoped to maximize destruction of the target and minimize collateral damage to surrounding houses.

"Hello, Hello," Mustapha said. This was his last phone call for the night and then he could have his secret nightcap and go to bed. "Hello, is this is Salman El-Bassri."

"It is the same. Who is this?"

Using a slightly disguised, deeper voice, Mustapha said, "It is no matter. I do not have much time, so I will be brief. I know you posses the 'Breath of God' and now it is the will of God that you release it according to plan. I will call again before the next phase to release the 'Seeds of Hell.' Wait for my call."

Stunned, El-Bassri stood still for a moment. He had prepared envelopes to deliver the deadly toxins months ago and kept them in a hermitically sealed box under his bed. He had devised an elaborate plan to maximize the fears of the infidel Americans, while playing to the stupid news media's ravenous desire for news. Even with all his bluster and hard work, he was not really prepared to actually release the Anthrax. He had never seriously thought that he would ever be asked to execute his plan; it was almost a game. He was relieved that the attacks of 9/11 had gone so well, and had come to believe that his time was past. Standing, with the phone in his hand, he had yet to reply when he heard a very loud thunderclap come from the phone earpiece. For a fraction of a second he thought he heard a scream; and then the phone went dead.

GLOSSARY

AB   Short for afterburner, also known as burner- raw fuel augmented thrust for a modern jet fighter. Vastly expands the thrust produced by the engine.

AFMSS   Air Force Mission Planning Support System, mobile planning system used to pre-load mission data to a DTM module.

AGL   Above Ground Level- a reference to height above the ground

AMRAAM   The most advanced radar/inertial guided air-to-air missile used by the US Air Force- the AIM-120

AOR   Area of Operations- typically the combat area with defined borders

ASL   Azimuth Steering Line- part of the F-15E air-to-ground system, the ASL gives steering information for the pilot to line up on the target. It is wind corrected.

ATO   Air Tasking Order- also known as the FRAG (for Fragmentary Order). This is the document that tasks subordinate units with specific missions and weapons. It is produced by the CAOC

Auto Acq   Auto-Acquisition switch, one of the HOTAS (hands-on-throttle-and-stick) controls on the F-15E.

AWACS   Airborne Warning and Control aircraft. E-3A Sentry, a Boeing 707 type fuselage with a very large radar. Their most important function is air traffic control and warning.

BDA Bomb Damage Assessment- Term used to describe the effectiveness of a particular air attack.

CAOC Combined Air Operations Center- a deployed command and control unit that plans, monitors and serves as the ultimate control for all air operations in a theater of battle.

CAP Combat Air Patrol- for example CAPs can be used for air-to-air purposes or search and rescue.

CAS Close Air Support- air support using bombs and direct fire weapons to support troops in contact with the enemy.

CEP Circular Error of Probability- a way of measuring the accuracy of a weapons guidance system.

Chopper A slang term for a helicopter.

CIA Central Intelligence Agency

Conex Container Export- a metal container used for shipping goods aboard ship. Commonly used for temporary secure, rain-proof storage.

CP Command Post- central area where commanders and staff exercise command and control over a unit or operation.

CSAR Combat Search and Rescue- Forces used to locate and rescue downed aircrew under combat conditions.

DTM Data Transfer Module, a device a little larger than a cigarette pack that is used to input waypoints, mission planning data and weapons information into the F-15E.

Danger Close A term used to describe CAS with friendly troops are within the danger area of an exploding weapon. Used when the enemy is very close to friendly troops.

ELINT Electronic Intelligence collection

ETAC Enlisted Terminal Attack Controller- a US Air Force enlisted member qualified to control CAS attacks and authorize live weapons drops.

FAC Forward Air Controller- a term used to describe personnel that control CAS air strikes in support of ground troops. The term could be used for ground FACs or Air FACs (airborne), normally a FAC is an officer.

FM Fox Mike- a Very High Frequency sideband used by ground troops for radio communications.

FM 31-27 US Army Field Manual- 31-27 was written by Special Forces Troopers to instruct others how to load a horse or pack mule with cargo.

GMTI Ground Moving Target Indicator- a symbol on an aircraft radar to depict a vehicle moving at a pre-determined speed.

Helo A slang term for a helicopter.

HF High Frequency radio- commonly used for long range, non-line of sight radio communications. Susceptible to atmospheric conditions.

HMMWV High Mobility Multi-Wheel Vehicle- the HumV, an excellent general purpose off-road vehicle.

IFR Instrument Flight Rules- a particular set of rules for separating aircraft. Does not necessarily mean that the aircraft is in the weather.

IMC Instrument Meteorological Conditions- actually in the clouds.

INS Inertial Navigation System- a machine that measures movement in three axis, this movement can be used to extrapolate position and speed.

JFACC Joint Force Air Component Commander- In the US Military a Theater Commander may preside over a land component, an air component and a sea component.

JSTARS A US Air Force reconnaissance aircraft whose sophisticated radar can detect moving vehicles.

LGB Laser Guided Bomb- a 500 to 2,000 pound bomb with a laser guidance package that guides on reflected laser energy from the intended target.

LZ Landing Zone- a designated area for a Helo insertion of extraction.

Master Arm A switch that arms the weapons release system in a combat aircraft.

MDA Minimum Descent Altitude- the lowest altitude an airplane should descend to on a non-precision approach to a runway.

MIFWIC Mother Fucker What's in Charge- a derogatory term used to describe those that are in charge of an operation.

Mil Power Military Power, or Mil- a term used to describe maximum power in a jet fighter without using afterburner.

MOPP 1-4 Mission Oriented Protection Posture 1, 2,3, or 4- a means of describing the stages of dress to combat chemical warfare in the US Military.

MRE Meals-Ready-to-Eat- a plastic bag containing an entire meal that can be eaten in the field with minimal utensils. Shelf-life is measured in years, each meal contains approximately 2400 calories. It is a matter of opinion whether the MRE is palatable.

MSL Mean Sea Level- A reference to altitude corrected for a standard barometer, or pressure setting. Used to deconflict air traffic.

NATO   North American Treaty Organization- a European based grouping of free nations originally formed to oppose Soviet Communist Block aggression.

NOTAM   Notices to Airmen- a means to disseminate information about the status of airfields and navigation aids.

OODA Loop   'Observe, orient, decide, act' a theory used to describe perception and action by units and commanders in combat.

OSS   Office of Strategic Services- an organization developed by the United States in World War II to plan and execute covert operations. The forerunner of today's CIA.

POPEYE   A term used by US Air Force pilots to describe being in the clouds and unable to see visually.

QSY   A term used by German Military air traffic controllers when they switch frequencies- short for 'Happy to Quit Speaking to You.'

RPG   Rocket Propelled Grenade- a light Russian hand-held anti-tank and anti-personnel weapon.

RTB   Return-to-Base- a term used by aircrews to refer to going home after a mission is complete.

RWR   Radar Warning Receiver- a device aboard US combat aircraft to warn them when a hostile radar has illuminated them.

SA –2/9/13   Russian Surface-to-Air missiles. Each one of these uses a different propellant, seeker and warhead. They compliment each other in capability.

SARCAP   Search and Rescue Combat Air Patrol

SATCOM   Satellite Communications- a reliable means of communicating across very long distances. Not usually susceptible to atmospheric conditions (although sun spots will interfere with communications).

SAW	Squad Automatic Weapon- a light machine gun carried by small units. The SAW uses the same ammunition the M-16/ M-4 uses.
Sippr Net	A secure network used by the US Military to disseminate intelligence and other data to deployed units.
SOF	Special Operations Forces.
Tad	A way of referring to a radio frequency without naming the actual frequency over the air.
Tally	A term used by pilots to denote that the pilot sees the subject in question- airplane, ground target or what-have-you.
TD Box	Target Designator Box- A symbol displayed in the F-15E Heads-Up display to denote a target that is locked by the on-board weapons system.
TDC	A HOTAS control on the F-15E throttle to slew the weapon system to designate a target for weapons delivery.
TDY	Temporary Detached Duty- A US Air Force term used to refer to deploying away from the home unit.
TOT	Time-on-Target- a term used to describe a particular hard time that weapons delivery is assigned or when a weapon actually detonated.
TWS	A mode in the F-15E radar where the radar track multiple aircraft.
UAV	Un-manned Air Vehicle- a remotely controlled aircraft. Used for reconnaissance and combat.
UHF	Ultra-high Frequency- the radio frequency band most used by Air Force aircraft to communicate.
UPT	Undergraduate Pilot Training- the course US Air Force pilots must attend to win their wings.

USAFE IG   United States Air Forces- Europe Inspector General. USAFE is the US Air Force command dedicated to support NATO operations. The Inspector General is an organization within the command that exists to investigate problems and maintain a check on the readiness of subordinate units.

VASI   Visual Approach Slope Indicator- a device used by pilots to help them approach a runway on a constant descent path.

VFR   Visual Flight Rules- more liberal rules for separation of aircraft, used primarily in good weather.

VHF   Very High Frequency- a radio band used for air-to-air and air-to-ground communications, most commonly for Air Traffic Control.

VORTAC   VOR is a ground based radio navigation aid used by pilots to navigate in the air. A TACAN is a Military specific equivalent. A VORTAC has both pieces of equipment co-located at one ground station.

Vul   A term used by USAF pilots to refer to a Vulnerability time, a time when they need to be on station and available for tasking.

Winchester   A term used by USAF crews to describe being out of weapons—all your weapons have been expended.

WSO   An Air Force Officer- a Weapon System Officer. The WSO is a rated Navigator, not a pilot, whose job is to operate complicated equipment aboard a two crew fighter aircraft.

ZSU 23-4   A Russian anti-aircraft gun. The ZSU 23-4 is a tracked vehicle mounting four 23mm rapid firing guns in a steerable turret.

ZU 23   A towed Russian anti-aircraft gun. Two 23mm guns mounted on a wheeled trailer that can be towed or pushed.

Printed in the United States
23149LVS00003B/40-204